WHITE WOLF

WHITE WOLF

AN EVAN RYDER NOVEL

ERIC VAN LUSTBADER

TOR PUBLISHING GROUP

NEW YORK

WHITE WOLF

A Forge Book
Published by Tom Doherty Associates / Tor Publishing Group
120 Broadway
New York, NY 10271

www.torpublishinggroup.com

Forge® is a registered trademark of Macmillan Publishing Group, LLC.

EU Representative: Macmillan Publishers Ireland Ltd, 1st Floor,
The Liffey Trust Centre, 117–126 Sheriff Street Upper, Dublin 1, DO1 YC43

The Library of Congress Cataloging-in-Publication Data is available upon request.

ISBN 978-1-250-34927-9 (hardcover)
ISBN 978-1-250-34928-6 (ebook)

Our books may be purchased in bulk for specialty retail/wholesale, literacy, corporate/premium, educational, and subscription box use. Please contact MacmillanSpecialMarkets@macmillan.com.

First Edition: 2025

Printed in the United States of America

10 9 8 7 6 5 4 3 2 1

For Mitch Hoffman,
more than an agent,
a consigliere

The graveyards are full of indispensable men.

—CHARLES DE GAULLE

WHITE WOLF

PROLOGUE

RADIK

Dawn cracked the sky open like an eggshell while Yuri Radik was starting on his third mug of steaming Russian Caravan tea. The sun, the very tip of a bloodred finger, slowly curled above the taiga of Oymyakon as if beckoning the unwary traveler on.

Radik poured a generous dollop of vodka into the tea, slurped it down. The burning of his tongue and throat woke him like nothing else. This was his ritual, the beginning of his morning in this desolate area of northeastern Siberia. Out of habit he checked the digital readout of the temperature: -34° F. Just about normal for this time of year. However, the wind was picking up, so he knew it would feel ten degrees colder.

As he stared out the window at the permafrost he thought of Tokyo, his one week in the city boiling with people, neon signs, sushi, pliant women, powerful men, an active underground, and fantastic tattoo artists. He ran his tongue across his teeth, making an unconscious sound: a sound like the rumbling of elephants far off across the African plains, a sound he felt—or thought he felt—late at night, as if the two molars were alive, whispering secrets to each other. He sighed. Nostalgic, always nostalgic for that week. But he had a job to do here. He'd received specific orders. He winced, a sudden pain erupting through his jawbone. Not the first time, but more severe this time. He rubbed his jaw knowing it would do no good.

Radik was an inordinately large man—well over six-five and built like a T-90M tank. His face at best looked crumpled, at worst bashed in. His eyes were small and muddy, yet nevertheless canny—trained to see and react to everything in his immediate environment. Once, he'd worn his hair shorn close like most GRU soldiers, but since arriving here he'd let it grow, thick and tangled as underbrush. A beard, full and wiry, was a necessity in the bitter cold. During the day, he occupied a room adjacent to Ilona Starkova's cell where he worked out for ninety minutes without fail. He loved working out—the pop of muscles, the quiver of veins and arteries closest to his sweat-slicked skin. He liked that he was visible to Ilona through a wall of inch-thick bulletproof glass. He particularly liked that she stared at him while he worked out, those uncanny opalescent irises, shot through with flecks of red. What he didn't care for at all was that she never seemed to blink. But that was impossible. Inhuman.

But then Ilona Starkova was considered by many in the GRU and SVR hierarchies to be something close to inhuman. Which was why this prison was built, why she was stashed here like a block of radium, so radioactive she could not be within a thousand miles of civilization.

With a sigh, Radik placed his glass in the sink. He was six months into this assignment and considering his progress chances were good he'd earn his bonus. He might never have taken the assignment if it hadn't been for his mounting gambling debts, necessitating him earning the extra money, the more the better since instead of paying down his debts he kept betting larger sums and, of course, losing. And this place—this assignment—was so dangerous, so important, he was being paid a barrelful of money—and in U.S. dollars, too. Not that any amount of money would tempt most officers in his branch of the GRU to willingly choose to guard Ilona Starkova. No one wanted anything to do with her—the farther away from her they were, they said, the safer they would be. This was neither rumor nor supposition blown up from wild stories. It was fact, pure and simple. Ilona Starkova worked for herself; she freelanced her services to the highest bidder—the Israelis, the Saudis, the Chechens, pretty much every warlord in Africa. Among her victims were key members of the SVR, the foreign clandestine service, the GRU, the military intelligence agency, even the Politburo, as well as African warlords, insurgent leaders. How she had penetrated the various lines of defenses to kill her targets was anyone's guess. She herself hadn't uttered so much as a word, despite the best efforts of two teams of interrogators—one physical, the other psychological. No matter what stresses and horrors they subjected her to she would not break. She never gave an inch. To Radik's knowledge she was the only subject who hadn't cracked and hadn't died.

Ilona Starkova was the most dangerous person inside Russia and, most likely, outside the Federation as well. Her list of assassinations, bombings, terrorist attacks leading to multiple deaths and strategic hostage-taking ran to twenty pages—and those were the offenses the GRU could definitely attribute to her. Many more outside Russia were ascribed to her.

The Russian clandestine services were terrified of Ilona Starkova, which is why their techs and their precious AI had devised and built the state-of-the-art escape-proof prison for her out here in the middle of the permafrost nowhere, with only the reindeer and the Indigenous Sakhas for company. Radik completely discounted the smattering of ethnic Russians and Ukrainians, too drunk or frost-bound to talk coherently about anything except their backbreaking work in the wells and mines, rich in oil, gas, gold, silver, and diamonds, as well as many other industrial metals. In fact, the Sakha region produced 99 percent of all Russian diamonds and over 25 percent of the diamonds mined in the world. All of that largesse belonged to the government, of course, closely guarded, impossible for him to get near, let alone partake of the spoils. Sticky fingers invariably got cut off. Case in point: Two days after he'd contacted the shady brothers to break into their illicit diamond trade, who turned him down for lack of capital, those same siblings fell—or, more likely, were pushed—out of their apartment windows, breaking their necks and backs on the icy pavement below. That was more than enough of a disincentive for Radik. So near and yet so far, he thought. And yet lucky not to be caught in the GRU net that had closed around them. He shuddered.

So no clandestine dealings with the Sakha, which, when he considered it in hindsight, was just as well. The Sakha were Asiatic mongrels, barely able to speak Russian without their atrociously guttural accent. They stank, looked at him through slitted animal eyes. No, he was stuck here. And because of the atrocious winter weather he'd been forced to buy a stinking reindeer from Sakha herders on which, like them, he rode across the icy snow-covered ground.

In the beginning of his remit he had experienced mornings filled with certain reluctance, like a rat beneath his bed, baring its teeth. An unwillingness to go to work, to confront her, to spend twelve stultifying yet agitating hours a day with her. It wasn't just that she was part of the boredom—she *was* the boredom. She was the source of both his boredom and his extreme unease. There was—not surprisingly—something about her that simply did not fit, that felt out of alignment. The truth was the nastiness of their conversations was about him, not her.

In the first weeks, he had wondered whether he'd be able to make this assignment a success. It was then that he had struck upon a solution. He had provided the Sakha who prepared her food with a supply of narcotic pills, instructing him to grind up two a day, feed them to her with breakfast. This dosage kept her docile, smoothed out her razor-sharp edges, made her more or less compliant. He had relaxed.

He huffed, turning away from those thoughts at the ring of his mobile phone. At once, he saw that the encrypted message from Moscow via the phone's satellite connection had arrived, and within it the jpg file he'd asked for ten days ago. It wasn't that the GRU was inefficient or overworked; it just had taken them this long to dig up the specific bit of intel he had asked for.

He hooked up his phone to the hi-def color printer on the counter, sent the file to the printer, which immediately sprang to life. Moments later he picked the photo out of the hopper, shaking off another burst of pain. He'd suffered worse, God knew.

He held in his hands an 8x10 photo of Rachan Dmitriyevich Starkov, Ilona's father. He scarcely looked at it; he wasn't in the least bit interested. In the photo itself, yes, he could use that, but not what the man looked like. Starkov could look like a goat and it wouldn't matter to him or to his remit. Unconsciously, his tongue again passed over the tops of his molars, a habit he'd formed ever since he returned from Tokyo.

He grunted with satisfaction, slipped the Starkov photo into a weatherproof envelope, stowed it within an inside pocket of his thick insulated coat. Bundled up, every square inch of skin covered, he stepped out into air that thrust tiny daggers into his nostrils, making his inhalations painful. It would have immediately glued a crust of ice onto his lashes had he not been goggled like a snorkeler. The unearthly bitter winter chill had a metallic tang he'd already grown accustomed to. At first, it had made him gag, the similarity to human blood inescapable. But that was weeks ago. Humans, he thought, were infinitely adaptable. Especially if they had an assignment that made them a small fortune.

He hurried across to where Viktor, his reindeer, waited patiently in his lean-to, kicking up shards of icy snow. He spoke softly to Viktor as he fed him. The Sakha mode of transportation was much more dependable than a vehicle, which because of the extreme cold required shelter in a heated space, the engine running even when it wasn't in use. Radik stroked Viktor's neck, fed him a handful of frozen moss and tree bark. He had named the beast after his son. A silly gesture perhaps, but it made him feel closer to the real Viktor.

"Good boy," he said, as Viktor munched away.

When the reindeer was finished, Radik climbed aboard. Slapping the reins, he headed for the prison.

Of course he hadn't yet included any of the progress he had made with Ilona Starkova in his thrice-weekly reports to his superiors back in

Moscow. No, not at all. He was waiting until he had gotten everything out of her she was prepared to give. Then the rush of reports, the accolades he was bound to receive. The hero who had broken Ilona Starkova, yes. Wiped the unnerving executioner's smile off her face, even when it was bloody and swollen. How great his victory would be! Thus fueled, Radik urged Viktor on.

He was almost upon the prison before he knew it—a metal brutalist box, all sharp angles. Back home in the GRU file system it had a numerical designation, but here in Oymyakon, where Radik was king, emperor of the north, of nothing, he dubbed it Nigde—Nowhere. Its high-tech skin reflected the flat, blinding whiteness of its surroundings. Others would pass it by without even knowing it was there. Squinting brought it into full focus, crouched low and wide. It was built of steel-enforced extruded concrete, especially manufactured to be used in subzero weather conditions. There was an alien air about the structure, something so out of place it might have been beamed in from another dimension. The result was an off-putting tension, sly, deliberate.

By design, the interior only exacerbated the feeling of deep unease. Nigde was AI-designed as a labyrinth; there was no direct line of sight from the entry to the rear where Ilona Starkova's cell was located, no throughput of more than fifteen feet at a time. Radik hung up his snow-covered outer coat, his headgear, toed off his thick-soled boots, drew the waterproof folder from the coat's pocket. He progressed from one section to another, gaining access by iris-reading devices set into plain white walls, the seams of the doors barely visible. There were four of these electronic gates to pass through before he arrived at the living area. The entire prison was run by a sophisticated AI, including the formidable security and defense systems. No one or nothing could get near the facility without the AI vetting them and, if need be, killing them.

There was no other human in attendance, unless you counted the cook who slept in the facility, an Indigenous Sakha in his late teens whose name Radik couldn't bother to remember; why would he want to? These things were little more than savages; they had nothing to impart to Radik. In fact, he resented the fact that he was obliged to interact with them from time to time for food to keep Ilona Starkova alive. He'd argued against a Sakha cook, but Moscow had insisted a Sakha was better than having another Russian inside the facility. The Sakha were too stupid, Moscow said, to know a secret when they saw one. Radik understood the logic of the directive. Still, he resented having one of them inside the facility, especially after he'd found it snooping around. He would have beaten it senseless had that not meant he himself would have had to prepare food for the prisoner, an ignominy he would not tolerate. He saw it now, this Sakha he sardonically called Ivan, which in colloquial Russian meant "Hey you."

"Ivan." He crooked a finger until the cook shuffled deferentially over, its head bowed. He was coming from serving Ilona her breakfast, the tray still in his hands. "You been anywhere you shouldn't be this morning?"

The Sakha shook its head. "No."

Radik's brows drew together. In anger or pain—perhaps both. "No *what*, Ivan?"

The Sakha stood, mute, in front of him.

Radik leaned in, slapped it across its face. "No, *sir*."

"No, sir."

He clamped the cook's cheeks in his hand. He felt good to take his pain out on this creature. "Learned your lesson, did you?"

"Yes . . . sir."

He hated these dullards, reeking of their animals and their own sweat. All they did was remind him of where he was, of the reason he was here and needed to stay here. Imprisoned like Ilona Starkova. The bitter irony was not lost on him. He knew his addiction but even here could not rid himself of gambling—and losing—every day. This . . . thing was a constant reminder of everything he hated about himself. "Don't forget again, Ivan, or I promise you there'll be more of the same, hear me." He took his hand away, the marks on its face turned from white to scarlet, and they were done.

Who else to take his ire out on than his Sakha?

"Bowl," he said. The Sakha stared at him dully. "Now!"

The bowl on the tray, filled with the scraps from Ilona Starkova's breakfast.

"Floor," Radik ordered, and as the cook bent over, placing the bowl before him, he said, "Why do you make me order you, when you know the drill? How stupid are you?"

The Sakha made no reply, kneeling in front of the bowl.

"Breakfast," Radik spat.

Lowering the head, the Sakha duly ate.

As he strode away toward Ilona's cell, Radik resisted the urge to wash his hands. Instead, he shook himself like a mud-soaked dog. He needed another shower.

ILONA STARKOVA

She rose out of the deep well of sleep into which she sank every night to the sound of crying. Was it her sister; her mother, even? She couldn't tell. She only knew it wasn't her; she never cried. But this was the first sound she heard every morning, while still wrapped in the tendrils of her dream. The same thing every night—at least every night since she had been incarcerated in this infernal puzzle box of a prison.

The dream still gripped her waking mind, and in it the crying voices faded while the sound of martial bootsteps grew loud. She heard her mother's groan of fear and despair as her father appeared at the head of his pack. Her sister mewled beside her, a frenzy of movement ensued, and then the inevitable.

Everything faded then except the sound of running feet, running, running desperately, which gradually resolved into the hyper beating of her heart. Fully awake now, she immediately went into *prana*, slowing her heartbeat, the rush of her blood through her arteries, until her pulse calmed, and inside her all was silence.

It was at this moment, right on time, that Nyurgun, whom she thought of as her private chef, delivered her tray of food.

"Good morning, Nyurgun," she said with the amused smile she reserved for him alone. She made it a point not to ask about his bruises at various stages of healing; she didn't have to, she knew where they came from.

He nodded, shyly returned her smile. She knew he liked that she called him by name, pronounced it correctly. He provided her with food twice a day: raw flesh, shaved from frozen fish for breakfast, frozen reindeer meat for dinner. Every Sunday, he prepared a special Sakha treat for her: ice cubes of horse blood with fried macaroni. He didn't have to; he wanted to. Ilona appreciated the gesture.

In the middle of the outer front wall of her cell was a security device that opened the cell door and could only be activated by an iris reader. Also within the wall, just below the device, was an oblong aperture that swung inward, serving as a platform for the tray containing the food Nyurgun prepared for her. This he opened now, as he had every morning since the start of her incarceration. He was a young, serious-looking teenager with a round face, wide-apart eyes, and a darkish complexion. He had been shy—verging on terror-stricken—when Radik had first introduced him to her. He called him Ivan. The slur seemed to have no outward effect on Nyurgun. Perhaps he didn't understand it as such.

Because there was no table in her cell she was obliged to eat her meals standing up at the platform. Nyurgun watched her with the gaze of the Sphinx. Sometimes he ate with her, as if they were companions. She liked that. During one of these times, he had told her the origin of his name: Nyurgun was the given name of a mythical figure in Sakha folklore, celebrated as a hero known for his wisdom, bravery, and his role in creating the world. From the moment she first spoke to him she could tell that he was proud of the name's meaning and lineage, though he was too shy to say so.

She looked down at the food, then back up at Nyurgun.

"Third day, no pills." Nyurgun whispered. He had begun flushing them down the drain in the kitchen. "How do you feel?" Nyurgun asked.

She smiled at him, a wolf gazing upon her cub learning to be an adult. "Like myself, Nyurgun. Like myself again."

When she was done eating, Nyurgun took the tray, closed the platform slot, and left.

Too soon after he was gone, Radik loomed up in front of her, his cheeks puffed and red, the mark of his goggles still surrounding his eyes like an invisible mask. "What shall we talk about today?" he said. There was no greeting from him, just the quotidian grinding of what he thought of as interrogation. "Your sister?"

"Again?" She produced a curdled smile. Save for her pale eyes her face was unremarkable. "I think not." They had shaved her head before flying her out here. She was neither tall nor short, heavy nor slim. And yet . . . there was about her an uncanny stillness, an economy of movement that marked her out as a professional—but what profession or professions? Both the GRU torturers and psych team had taken their best shots without achieving a scintilla of success. She was as much of an enigma to them as she had been the moment she was captured. And now, of course, behind her half-hooded eyes, was a mind glazed over by narcotics.

"So?"

She pursed her lips, nodded slowly. She did everything slowly now. "Your secret, your addiction."

Radik frowned, shook his head.

"Your gambling, Radik. It's out of control."

Radik stared at her.

"It will be the death of you." She chuckled, her eyes momentarily closed, sign of her drifting mind. "It's a rite of passage for Moscow men of your soldierly ilk." In an instant, her expression changed, hardened into obsidian. "Gambling, drinking, whoring." She clucked. "And so far away from home, from them. How can you stand it?" She cocked her head. "Or maybe you're the kind that doesn't care. Is that you, Radik?"

The right corner of Radik's lips quirked up into a sneer.

He lifted the waterproof envelope. "Speaking of . . ."

"Speaking of what?"

She watched him open the envelope, remove the contents—a single sheet of photo paper—gripping both sides tightly between his fingers.

"Speaking of secrets . . ." he said in what he no doubt thought was a neutral tone. He was trying to keep the jubilation out of his voice. "Here he is."

He released one hand just long enough to open the food slot, gripped the photo again, laid it on the platform, pushed it as far as he could toward her. "Rachan Starkov. Your father."

Her eyes flicked down at the photo, then back to him. "My father." Her laugh as harsh as a buzzsaw. "You want to know about my father?"

An odd flickering of the lights caused two vertical lines to appear above the bridge of his nose.

The signal, she thought with a quickening of all her senses.

She stared into his eyes, her mind clear now, sharp, honed. Skilled. She had never forgotten being thrown headfirst into the cell, the indignity of his kick to her kidneys when she didn't change clothes quickly enough for him, his avid eyes as he gaped at her breasts and thighs. He had made her turn around so he could run his rough fingers over her buttocks. He'd laughed then, his dominance over her absolute. Then while her back was turned he hit her so hard she had blacked out. She had regained consciousness to pain; the rawness of certain parts of her body made it clear what he had done.

She made sure her eyes remained hooded, her expression perfectly blank. "Here's my *father*." She grabbed him at the meat of his forearms, thumbs pressed into the nerve points in his inner elbows, and with the force of fury pulled him toward her and slammed his face against the glass above the food slot.

The lights flickered again, off longer this time.

Blood spurted. His head shook in spasm, but he was a big man— monstrously strong, which she knew intimately, having dissected every minute of his physical workouts; while his muscles were gleaming, his ego preening she was studying his every move, gaining a better assessment of his power with each workout. She knew what she was in for.

But she'd caught him by surprise. "You . . . you . . . How?"

She slammed his face again and again into the blood-smeared glass that would not break no matter how hard and with what means she attacked it.

Shoving her face close to his, she said, "You want to know about my father, Radik? All right, I'll tell you about my father. He came into our house after one of his long absences and took hold of my mother while his stony-eyed men watched. No sex, just violence and subjugation. You know something about that, Radik, don't you? Yes. I was eleven. My sister was eight. They began yelling at each other, then screaming. Such vitriol. I was in shock, had no idea what they were saying. Then he drew his sidearm and shot her through the heart. 'Run!' our mother cried as her eyes rolled up. 'Run!' And run we did."

Radik's nose bloomed a bloody pulp, his teeth tore into his lips, shredding them, and then one cheekbone cracked, splintering through fascia and skin until it seemed as if he had two sets of teeth, needle-sharp slivers everywhere, a weird mythological creature of her own design.

She shook Radik until his teeth rattled. "That answer your question, Radik?"

Her muscles bulged and rippled, popped and shivered. Blood and bone, yellow gristle and cartilage stained pink. She was in her element now. She could feel rage like a living thing, rising up around her, feeding her, so that, lips drawn back, she laughed—the screech of a banshee.

"How're you feeling, Radik?" she spat. "Not as good as when you got up today, I imagine."

He screamed as she pulled at him until his dazed and bloodied face was at the aperture's opening, and then she swiftly dug two fingers and her thumb into his eye socket, curled them around the orb, wrenched it out. It appeared with the optic nerve trailing behind it like a slug, slimy, glistening.

She thrust him away with all her strength, and he dropped away from her cell wall like a sack of cement. He lay curled into a ball as she reached out the slot's opening and manipulated his eyeball in front of the retinal scan just above it. It took her a moment or two to get the position right. The lock opening sounded like the north wind sweeping through an endless field of wheat.

Freedom.

But not quite yet. There were the AI defenses to defeat. But there was a plan for that. The lights going off was just the start.

She bent over Radik. "Ready for more?" Reaching down, she hauled him to his feet. He was a mess. His head lolled on his neck, his one eye rolled in its socket like a pinball in a tilted machine. His heavily muscled legs wobbled as if they had been turned into cooked spaghetti.

He hit her then. His fist, huge, rock-hard, came out of nowhere, struck the side of her head. Her hearing seemed to blank out on that side. Her vision collided with the wall of her skull. He delivered two more punishing blows before she could gather herself in the face of the pain his damage was causing, stuff it back into its black bottle. But by then he was blindly bull-rushing her. She held her ground, feet spread to shoulder width, dipped her right shoulder, wrapped her arm around his neck, swung to her right, using his own momentum to slam him into the floor.

He fell heavily, awkwardly but he was close enough to scissor his legs around her left ankle. As soon as she was down he was on top of her. He had no finesse. He had always relied on brute strength, the bulldozer of his torso, the weight against her chest and hips, clamping her to the floor.

He grinned through the blood and what must be terrible agony. He was a soldier, inured to pain and suffering.

Her upper body was pinned; she had no leverage, but she squirmed her left leg free of him, drove her knee into his groin. He groaned, shuddering, gifting her with just enough leverage to heave him off her.

This attack was meant to subdue him. She still had need of him, alive and at least semiconscious. He was hers now, truly and totally. She did not gloat or revel—she was too well-disciplined for that. And this was war. *Her* war; all the rules she had had drummed into her applied.

"Now look at you," she said, hauling him up by the back of his collar. "You couldn't bat away a butterfly."

Shoving him forward, she followed his inconstant shuffling gait down the corridor, paused when she saw Nguyen watching her.

"Come on," she said, and he did, joining her as she headed toward the first retinal scan gate. There was no problem, the reader released the lock as she held Radik's eyeball in front of it. But as his right knee started to give out and she had to hold him up, she saw the bloody trail he was leaving behind them. Now she had to wonder if—possibly when—the AI's sensors would pick that up, if it would switch to its Protect Mode. She had observed the AI in that mode when Nyurgun tried to fix the walk-in freezer where her food was stored. He'd stumbled upon a short corridor hidden behind the freezer. Curious, he explored it. The AI, immediately alerted, would have instantly incapacitated him had Radik not intervened in time. She very much did not want to run afoul of the system.

She arrived at the fourth gate, placed the eyeball in front of the reader. The gate did not open. Instead, the siren sounded, announcing the AI's Protect Mode.

"Behind me!"

Crouching down, Nyurgun did as she ordered. She turned, holding Radik in front of her like a shield. His thick body absorbed the first volley of bullets the defensive AI spat at her. Then he collapsed and she stood revealed, naked to the AI's weapon. More bullets but they were sprayed every which way, none coming close to her. No more bullets followed, only a metallic clatter and the groan as from a dying man. Then came a stuttering hiss. Smoke curled from the air vents. She caught the first whiff of the gas and held her breath. The gate remained locked. There was nowhere to run. And where would she go, anyway, back into the depths of the labyrinth? No. No. Never. The gas was catching up to her; she was already feeling disoriented. Nyurgun had begun to retch, his eyes streaming tears. She was so close she could taste her freedom. After all this time, all the watching, scrutinizing, she wasn't going to make it. She pressed her forehead against the wall of the gate, held the eyeball up again, this time at a different angle. The gate remained locked. Was something wrong with the gate? Or was it . . . ? She looked at the eyeball, saw bits of dried blood occluding it. Popping it into her mouth, she swished it around, rinsing it with her saliva. She swallowed the sweetish coppery taste of Radik's blood. Then nothing. How long? She must have lost consciousness for a second or two. Her body was now folded in on itself. With a start she stood up, spat out Radik's clean eyeball, held it up to the reader.

The gate opened.

She pulled Nyurgun through. On the other side, the air was clear and sweet. He remained crouched for a moment, regaining his strength. Behind them, the gas dissipated, lying low to the floor like ground fog. The air vents belched, a thin yellowish fluid dribbled out like snot from a nose.

Nyurgun's face darkened. "He's dead. Really dead."

She nodded. "He is."

"There was a lot of blood."

She nodded, frowning. "There was.

"Are you okay?" She moved toward Nyurgun. "I need to go back."

Nyurgun nodded.

"Stay put until I come get you."

She still had Radik's eye clutched in her fist. Turning, she held the eye up to the retinal scanner. The gate opened and she rushed in, opened the third gate. For what seemed a long time she squatted next to Radik's riddled corpse. Reaching out, she stuck a forefinger into a puddle of blood, brought it to her mouth, sucked the blood off.

"Ilona." Nyurgun's voice came to her as if from a great distance.

"Yes."

"We must leave. Now."

But the prison was dead quiet—no sirens, no bullets flying, no gas flowing. The defensive AI was done for. What had happened to it? Never mind.

She pried open Radik's mouth to a sea of blood. Without an instant's hesitation she dug her fingers in, ripping through disease-blackened gums, excavating Radik's two back molars side by side—the only ones remaining unbroken. Of course they were unbroken. God alone knew what they were made of. They were already loose in the diseased gums, gave her no problem as she liberated them.

"It's done," she said.

Outside, it was snowing. Ilona turned her head up, feeling the flakes on her skin, her eyelids fluttering in pleasure before her lashes became coated with hoarfrost. How delicious to feel the snow, the wind, the icy cold! She was clad in the outdoor clothes Radik had hung up to dry. Everything was of course too big for her but she had stuffed paper into the toes of his insulated boots, wrapped his coat close around her, settled his fur-trimmed hat onto her head.

Nyurgun brought Radik's reindeer over to her and she swung up, mounting it without difficulty. She had been proficient in riding ever since she was a child. Again, she threw her head back, filling her lungs with fresh air, reveling in the arctic chill.

Leaning down, she embraced the young man. "You get away from here, hear me?" she said into his ear. "As far away as you can."

He nodded. "I know. I have thought about it for some time. My cousin works in a mine. He'll take me in, no questions asked."

"Good." She rolled Radik's teeth around her palm. Held them up to the blue arctic light.

Nyurgun watched her as he would a magician. The teeth struck him as magic. They were both inscribed, incised with a sigil that when the two teeth were held side by side, as they were now, they created what appeared to be a caliper with the sun shining between the spread jaws. They made a toast with their fists, as one warrior to another, but Nyurgun didn't understand.

She smiled down at him as she slipped the teeth into a scarred leather saddlebag.

"In another life," she said.

"In another life." He reached up to wrap his arms around her. "Can I see it again?"

She nodded and he pushed the sleeve of her thick coat up, noted the ink on the inside of her right wrist—the sigil of the burning sun between the jaws of some instrument—he'd seen so many times before but hadn't worked up the nerve to ask about. But now . . .

"What is this?" he whispered, running his fingertip over the tattoo.

"It's a sigil," Ilona told him.

"And this?"

"It's a caliper. It's used in engineering drawings."

His eyes were wide. "Can I get this sigil?"

She laughed. "If I take you with me to Shibuya."

He frowned. "Where is . . . ?" He had trouble pronouncing Shibuya.

"It's a neighborhood in Tokyo." She eyed him. "Do you know where Tokyo is?"

"Japan," he said proudly.

"Indeed. Gold star, Nyurgun."

Ilona broke away, stood tall in her saddle. She nodded to him, almost a bow. She discovered she was reluctant to let him go. He had come to mean a great deal to her during her incarceration. But at length she did. She nodded. "Long life, Nyurgun."

He looked up at her through the snow. His eyes filled with tears, overwhelmed by the high emotion of the moment. He smiled, though there were tears burning his eyes, solidifying on the cliffs of his cheeks. "Goodbye, Ilona."

"Call me by my name, Nyurgun," she said with mock-sternness. "The name I have chosen."

He grinned, lifted his hand, palm toward her. "Long life, White Wolf."

BONE-TO-BONE

She's out.

Intact?

Of course.

So she has the package.

Those were your orders.

The package is safe with her.

Maybe yes, maybe no.

Meaning?

Meaning if she has even an inkling of its power she might attach herself to the package.

I'll know.

How could you possibly?

I'm surprised you ask. She and I will be instantly in touch. But I very much doubt that will happen. I know her through and through, believe me. She owes me a debt she can never repay.

I trust you're right.

I'm always right.

Pardon me for bringing this up but you were wrong about Yuri Radik.

Radik was ill. He never told anyone, including me. Was it a mistake? No. It's the cost of doing business.

And now?

Plan B.

Tell me.

It's already in place. I will trigger it if she heads to Tokyo.

I could have our people discreetly alert the GRU and the SVR as to her destination.

Please. She'll take them out without losing a breath.

But putting Tokyo in play may lead to unknown . . . complications.

Yes, it may.

We cannot have this. You've said this yourself.

No, we absolutely cannot.

But if worse comes to worst . . .

Finger on the trigger, my friend. Finger on the trigger.

PART ONE

THE IMPORTANCE OF BEING TIMUR

Time flies over us but leaves its shadow behind.

—unknown provenance

1

SUMATRA, NORTHEAST COAST
MARCH

They had spent themselves physically. Their entwining—sometimes violent, sometimes sensual, always desperate—had taken over four hours. Now they lay, still entwined, two lizards stunned into immobility, drenched in sweat, the sour-sweet odor of sex wafting off them like incense.

Wrapped in Marsden Tribe's strong arms, Evan Ryder allowed his warmth to sink into her. It was an altogether different heat from what she felt beneath the Sumatran sun or from any other sun, for that matter. The warmth exuded privacy and, she supposed, privilege, something in which she had no interest. But she did have interest in Tribe. He was a tech genius, a multibillionaire, the founder and owner of Parachute, the world's most advanced, privately owned quantum tech company.

He had fascinated Evan so deeply since she had met him nearly two years before, that she not only continued to work for him but now made love to him every month, his private jet always arriving when expected at the airstrip on the landside periphery of the enormous estate he owned. Here in the main villa, built atop a small headland with steps down to the beach, she had lived for a year. And over the course of that year, Tribe had signed long-term deals with the word-salad branches of the DOD, the Pentagon, NSA, a strategic portion of the Fortune 500 companies, as well as every tech company not named Google, Meta, Amazon, or Apple, all of which depended on Parachute's hyper-speed quantum computer clusters for everything from enhanced AI workflow to end-to-end cybersecurity. Publicly, Evan was just another member of Parachute's security division. In reality, she was its prime field agent, continuing the clandestine work she had done for Ben Butler's team under the DOD umbrella.

She began to roll over but Tribe's arms caught her. He stirred, rose out of sleep, and within moments their naked bodies entwined once more. He was an insatiable lover, perhaps because they were together only the one night each month. Inventive, too. She'd never been with a man who knew his way around the art of sex like Marsden Tribe.

Afterward, sweat-slicked, sated, he closed his eyes, asleep in seconds. She waited for her heart rate to return to normal, then unwound herself from him. Slipping out of bed, she shivered. Tribe insisted on keeping the air-conditioning on while he was in residence, whereas Evan preferred to be lulled to sleep by the night concerto of tree frogs, crickets, cicadas, moths. She crossed to the sliders, unlocked them, stepped out onto the expansive terrace. There were any number of exotic species of birds indigenous to the island but her favorite by far was the regal black-crowned night heron. Lucky for her the stream just yards away from where she stood was home to one. The water, reflecting the moon, wound from the interior, spilling into the sea. She saw the night heron by the light of the moon and the thick river of stars, tall, majestic, moving slowly or not at all, its head directed at the water through which it high-stepped. It saw her as she saw it—she was sure of it; sure, too, that it ducked its head in acknowledgment of being in the same place at the same time.

She leaned against the railing, watching the bird hunt in its singular fashion. She breathed the hot, humid air, heavily laden with night-blooming jasmine, frangipani, Melati. She still felt Tribe's sweat on her, his musk, and she grew wet between her thighs. As if her body became aware of him an instant before her mind, she felt his arm snake around her waist. She took his hand, ran a finger over the wide silver band circling his right wrist. He never took it off, at least not in her presence.

"Do you want to know how Timur is progressing?" she asked huskily.

For just a moment a cauldron of bats defaced the moon, then were swallowed up by the blackness.

"Are you happy here, Evan?"

"Why should I be happy here?"

"You've been here in my villa for over a year."

"And yet it feels like Lyudmila died yesterday."

"I'm sorry."

"Don't condescend, Marsden. You never cared a fig about her."

"But I care about you."

She took a breath, let it out slowly. She was not about to pull on that string. She tilted her head forward. "You see that bird in the stream?"

"The night heron, you mean."

She nodded, trying not to be surprised that he knew; but then he knew most everything. That was the scariest thing about him; it was also why she was drawn to him.

"The black-crowned night heron, yes. It took months, but we've developed a relationship, he and I."

"Should I be jealous?" He was half mocking.

"Seriously, we have a connection. Time and again, we're out here together, we recognize each other in the shadows and we communicate."

"And how do you communicate with a bird?"

"It's a secret," she whispered.

She could feel him moving beside her, a restlessness she had come to recognize as one of his trademarks. It was also a tell, if you knew him well enough. Very few did. To them it seemed like he was drifting, when really he was flowing, like mercury.

"Tonight this island, this sea, this night," he whispered into the shell of her ear, "was made for love."

She gave no response, stayed quite still as he stepped behind her, spread her legs. Soon enough all thoughts flew away like the night heron, having sated itself. Before dawn they too, were, at last, sated.

■ ■ ■

A week after Tribe's departure, the afternoon idled, glazed with a heavy light, heat and humidity combining to turn skin sweat-slicked, nut-brown. The intense blue, the white sand, green trees at their backs, here and there shadow-shot beneath the clattering canopies of palm trees.

Evan Ryder and Timur Shokov had just finished their daily ten-mile run. They had started months ago, running in the morning, just before sunrise, when the air was still cool, the humidity tolerable. But as Timur's stamina grew, multiplying swiftly, she had amped up their workout under the blazing tropical sun. Wordlessly, plunging into the surf, they cooled their bodies, then ran back up onto the beach.

Rehydrating with bottles of ice-cold water fetched from an insulated case, they stared at each other, their shared past scrolling through their minds, tremorous chords connecting them.

"Today," Timur said, "is my mother's birthday."

Evan dipped her head. "I've been feeling her."

"I know."

She looked up. "Really."

"I do." He drank more water. "I can always tell."

Evan frowned. She had thought she kept her sorrow separate from him, just as she kept Tribe's nighttime visits separate. "How?"

"You get this expression." He broke off, shook his head. "No, that's not right. Your eyes . . . they get, I don't know, dark, I guess you could say."

"I apologize. I didn't mean—"

"Don't," he said. "Apologize, I mean."

"Timur, I—"

"There's no need." He put the empty bottle neck down back in the ice. "I mean it. Really."

She smiled, knew it was a sad smile. "She's so close, sometimes, I swear I can hear her voice." *Her voice telling me to take care of you while she bled out in my arms.* Now she looked away so he wouldn't see the tears glittering, making her eyes huge, glossy.

Timur had grown, it seemed to her, past his actual age, both physically and intellectually. He soaked up ideas and equations like a sponge. He would be ten years old next month, but he looked and functioned as if he was thirteen. He was exceedingly handsome, his shoulders widening, his muscles coming into their own. The white-blond hair he sported when they had first met had darkened to the color of wheat, but his eyelashes were still white, and his large querulous eyes still as pale-blue as water in the shallows here between barnacle-encrusted rocks.

"So . . . ," he said now, his expression serious. "We promised each other one memory of Mom on her birthday." His gaze, when leveled, was already formidable. As dark and penetrating as his mother's. "A happy memory." He gestured. "You first."

"All right." Evan nodded. "Lyudmila was my best, my most loyal friend. There were times when we saved each other's life."

"Be specific, Aunt Evan. No cheating."

"Right." Evan sighed. Lately, it was getting more and more taxing to keep difficult and thorny truths away from this boy. In their time together here they had not talked about the past. Both understood that they needed a fresh start, a new life, unbound to the tragedy that had come before. Clearly this had changed. He'd already outgrown two tutors, smarter than they were in so many startling ways. Now he wanted to know about Lyudmila—needed to know his mother better.

"No cheating." She took a breath, stared past the froth of the breakers rolling in, rearing up as they struck the rocks along the shore, to the width of the wide section of the Malacca Strait, the body of water between Sumatra and Malaysia. There were the usual fishing boats and, beyond them, trawlers near the horizon. "Well, okay. I've already told you that my sister Bobbi and I were adopted as young children, raised by an American couple who told us our birth parents were dead." She paused, took a breath. Her chest felt tight. "One day when we were together in Odessa your mother told me that our parents—our birth parents—were still alive. She told me where to find them."

Timur leaned forward, his expression avid. "And did you go? Did you find them?"

"I did."

"So how was it?"

"Better than I had expected. Better by far. They were so happy to see me."

Timur grinned, pumped a fist. "Yes!"

She laughed. He could always make her laugh. "They're Russian, Timur. *I'm* Russian, just like you."

His eyes lit up. At his urging, they bumped fists. "And you told your sister, right?"

"Ah, well. As it happens I haven't seen Bobbi in almost ten years now."

"But you're in touch. You email, text. Maybe even call."

"No," she said firmly. "I don't know where she is or what she's doing." At least the first part was the truth. Bobbi had defected to the SVR. More than once, Evan had tried to find out something about her, but the name Bobbi Ryder no longer existed. But it happened that Lyudmila had known her, collaborated with her, but didn't trust her, would never allow her near either Evan or their birth parents. And it was from Lyudmila that Evan had ultimately learned that her sister had swiftly, ruthlessly risen in the FSB, was an assassin of the first rank, both feared and lauded until she turned against the previous regime, accused of being involved with the assassination of the previous Sovereign.

Timur's face clouded over and she more or less knew what was coming. "There's more, isn't there?"

"Lyudmila knew Bobbi. Somehow she knew my sister would be better off thinking our birth parents were dead." Evan reached out and smoothed his damp hair from his forehead. "But you will love my mom and dad. When we leave here, I'm going to take you to stay with them."

Timur frowned. "But I want to stay with you."

She sighed. "My work is dangerous, Timur. You know that better than most. I took a year off because . . . because of your mother's death and to be with you."

His eyes grew dark. "But you promised her." Sometimes she forgot that he was still a child.

"I promised I'd take care of you.," she said. "That's what I have been doing, what I will be doing. There are kids your age where I'm taking you."

"Uh-uh." His arms crossed over his chest. "No."

"How's this? Give them a chance. They're both doctors, scientists. You'll learn a lot, even maybe get some firsthand experience. You couldn't get that anywhere else." She registered the look on his face. "Give it a year."

"A whole year?"

She remained calm, steadfast in the face of his sudden volatility. "After that, if you're unhappy, I'll come get you and make other arrangements."

A crack appeared in his resistance. "Promise?"

"Promise." She crossed her heart with a forefinger, smiled. "Now it's your turn. A happy memory of your mother."

He cocked his head, eyes burning with curiosity, but he was too canny to push her into a place she clearly didn't want to go. He did the right thing—he acquiesced. "Okay, so you know I was taken from my mother at an early age. My father stashed me in his well-guarded dacha outside Moscow." He played with the screw top of another bottle of water, opening and closing it without taking it off. "I had a series of minders, then tutors. I hated all of them and made no bones about it. I was a little terror. They called me 'Master Timur.' Every time, I'd get a metallic taste in my mouth as if I'd bitten my tongue or the inside of my cheek." She placed a hand gently but firmly over his twisting fingers. They stopped immediately; he gave her a slightly embarrassed smile and she put her hand in her lap.

He took a ragged breath, let it out. It appeared this memory was as hard for him as hers had been for her. "Well, okay, one morning I was on my own. No tutor, just my father's stupid goons, who treated me like I was made of glass. I was bored out of my mind but, you know, I couldn't go anywhere. After lunch Marius arrived. You met him in the cottage on La Palma."

He took a swig from the bottle he'd been holding on to. "I had no idea what was going on until Marius, waiting until we were alone, leaned in to me, and whispered, 'Your mother says, "Be brave, Young Timur."'

"At that exact moment," he said, eyes shining, "I felt my mother's hand gripping my arm, pulling me forward. There it was, appearing out of nowhere. The first step in her plan—my escape from Moscow and my father."

• • •

Later, they plunged through the surf, diving into the oncoming waves, laughing, tasting seawater, licking salt off their lips. Out past the curling ridgeline of the incoming waves they played like dolphins, happy, care-free now that the ritual remembrances of Lyudmila Shokova were past.

Evan's head broke the surface and she shook the water out of her eyes. She was facing the shore, saw Mia, Timur's latest tutor, a lovely Malaysian woman, heading down the rock staircase from the villa to the beach. She was waving, calling to Timur that it was past time for his afternoon les-sons, but he was turned away from the shore, his gaze fixed elsewhere. Evan swam toward him, calling his name, but so intent was he on what had caught his attention that he didn't turn toward her. At last, when she was close enough for him to feel the wavelets her legs and arms made, he pointed. "Aunt Evan look, that fishing boat is close now. Maybe we could ask them if they could take us out with them tomorrow morning."

"Maybe another time," Evan said. "Mia is waiting for you on shore, she came all the way down to tell you—"

A soft whirr overhead, almost lost in the pull and suck of the water, the blinding glint of metal.

"Down!" She pushed Timur's head underwater.

A percussive whoosh, a blast of furnace heat. Mia, the staircase, the villa exploded in a flash. Grabbing Timur, Evan pulled them down under the water just before the blast wave surged across the water just over their heads. Turbulence knocked them sideways, then inverted them, helpless in the sudden riptide.

Evan knew better than to fight against it. So did Timur—she had taught him—but his panic made that knowledge temporarily inaccessi-ble. Tossed head over heels, in the grip of the churn, he no longer could tell up from down. Evan dove after him, even while she was aware that the water's extreme agitation was lasting far longer than it should have if it was just from the response to the explosion from the missile launched from the drone, the debris slamming into the surface of the Malacca Strait, knifing down like a fisherman's gaff.

She dove down, aware that Timur was being drawn into deeper water. The light was dim here but the chance of being struck by the wreckage of house, stairs, and human remains was lessened. Not that she had any time to consider this; her body was stretched to its limits. She caught Timur by the shoulder, felt her fingers slip off, propelled herself down. Arm wrapped around him, she kicked out, reversing course, dragging him up toward the surface.

Up and up she went, but something was wrong. Where sunlight should have been her guiding source there was only shadow. She only had a moment to register this anomaly when an actual fisherman's gaff found her. Remembering the fishing boat, she grabbed onto the gaff with her free hand, jerked it down to let the fishermen know the gaff had found its target. Immediately, she and Timur were drawn upward by strong arms. She breached the surface, hauled Timur into waiting arms before she allowed herself to be lifted into the air. Water streamed off her. Chilled in the shadow, warming where sunlight struck her, but she only had eyes for Timur. Pushing aside the fishermen crowded around him, she knelt down. They had laid him on the deck. Water sloshed beneath his shoulders, hips. The back of his head. Leaning over, she lifted one eyelid, then proceeded to administer CPR. Ten seconds later, he coughed. His eyes flew open as she turned him on his side. He vomited up seawater in two great heaves. She cradled his head, turned him back so that their eyes met.

"You're okay, Timur." Smiled down at him in reassurance. "You're safe now."

Hearing a harsh laugh behind her, she raised her head, got her first good look at their saviors. They were not fishermen, these six dark-skinned men, thin as electrical wire, with elongated heads, sunken cheeks. Hands filled with weapons—handguns, knives, submachine guns. Eyes filled with an insatiable hunger for things they didn't have and never would. Their sole possession was their anger and they wielded it with the inept brutality of the desperate. As thieves and terrorists they exhibited a mediocrity that made them more dangerous, not less. As thieves they were dangerous. As terrorists they weren't afraid to die.

2

The turquoise-and-silver branded corporate helicopter set down on the raised platform at the rear of the 440-foot superyacht. The boat's hull was striped turquoise and silver, the colors of Parachute, Marsden Tribe's company. At the stern two huge flags whipped in the wind: an American flag and one bearing the Parachute logo.

A slim, beautiful woman, hand held horizontally over her eyes against the swirling wind brought to life by the copter's rotors, waited to greet An Binh as, bent over to keep clear of the slowing rotors, An Binh descended the steps and hurried across the platform.

Alert as always, An Binh was aware of the momentary narrowing of the woman's eyes before a flat, professional smile overtook her face like mist rising at dawn. Short, honey-blond hair, topaz-eyed, wide-mouthed. She had that patented aura of the entitled, floating above the hordes of worker bees on their clouds of wealth and privilege.

"Miranda." She did not hold out her hand, as if she might be subject to contamination if she touched this outsider. "Mr. Tribe's personal assistant." She wore a pair of wide-leg trousers, a cap-sleeve silk top, both in warm sand tones. On her feet were what looked like ballet slippers. She wore a silver pin of the company's logo: three hands shaped like a parachute.

I'll just bet, An Binh thought, then gave Miranda her name and added, "A pleasure." But Miranda had already broken eye contact and turned on her heel, leading her to a spiral staircase that went down two decks.

"In case you didn't know, my name was created by William Shakespeare in the year 1611 for his play *The Tempest*. It derives from the Latin, *mirandus,* meaning someone to admire."

An Binh could not help herself; actually, she didn't want to. "Miranda is also a warning. In 1966, the Miranda Rights originated from the U.S. Supreme Court case *Miranda v. Arizona*, requiring the police to inform individuals of their rights prior to interrogation."

To this, Miranda said nothing. Whether she absorbed the barb or ignored it, An Binh had no idea.

They went along a narrow teak-lined corridor, laid with plush carpet. On one wall was stenciled Marsden's—and therefore Parachute's—motto: *In every moment, the present becomes the past.*

Through a thick teak door, Marsden awaited her. He was seated behind a large glass-and-steel desk. Arrayed before him were three open laptops. As soon as she was announced he lifted his head from the laptop screens. He studied her, gave no indication that he recognized her. *But why would he,* she thought. *I mean no more to him than his laptop or his desk.*

An Binh stepped into the room, which was filled with light and books in equal measure. The scents of cedar, oiled leather, and amber greeted her.

Tribe's welcoming smile was brief. "Good afternoon, An Binh. I trust your journey here was acceptable."

"First class all the way."

"Good, good." He made a sweeping gesture. "Take a pew."

She settled into one of the two leather chairs set in front of the desk, oversized, luscious. "I'm a bit confused as to why I'm here instead of Ben Butler."

"You've been in Sicily quarterbacking our intelligence team guarding the desalination plant we built outside Palermo and the quantum-guided drill we've established in the desertification area in and around Agrigento. The Sicilian Breadbasket has turned into uninhabitable desert. If our two initiatives don't work, seventy percent of Sicily will become desert."

"They're going to work, sir," An Binh said. "The desalinization plant is almost finished and our quantum computers are leading us to aquifers that were inaccessible before. Your billions of dollars are not going to waste." She was up-to-date, of course, as she received copies of the daily digests of the two projects sent to Tribe.

"I want to personally thank you for the excellent job you have done," he said. "You're part of the reason that the two projects are running so smoothly."

She dipped her head. "Thank you, sir."

"However, I cannot but think that you have felt yourself marginalized on what amounts to a babysitting remit." He lifted a hand, stopping her from protesting. "It's quite all right, An Binh. I would have become restless myself. But I do appreciate the work you have done."

"It was satisfying being a part of ecologically vital projects, sir."

"Come off it. No need to be formal with me. It doesn't suit you or how our relationship is going to evolve."

An Binh paused for a beat, trying to make sure he was serious and not laying some sort of trap for her. She mentally shrugged. It was all or nothing now. If she didn't trust him, why work for him? "Yes, the job was a bit of drone work, but I was being truthful about my support of our Sicilian initiatives. They're monumental—and desperately needed. The last four summers have seen no rain to speak of and temperatures in the mid-nineties."

A sly smile played around the corners of his mouth. "And how did you find ordering groups of male security guards around?"

"I was fine with it," she said. "But as for the men . . ."

He laughed. "Cracking heads must be one of your specialties."

"Sir, I—"

He waved away what surely was going to be her apology. "Save it. The outcome of your . . . shall we say 'discipline lessons' is one of the reasons I called for you today."

He tapped the desktop. "But before we move on to the main event it's necessary to catch you up. Butler has his hands full minding the store." Tribe meant the large limestone house in DC. "He took over when Isobel Lowe was called back to Israel, to the IDF. She allowed herself to be drawn into the war." He shrugged. "I suppose she felt she had a duty." He did not look happy. "I misjudged her, you see. She had money, she had class, she knew the right people in DC, but in going back to fight Palestinians she revealed her true colors. Everything she projected was a façade. A damn good one, admittedly. But underneath, what was she? Nothing more than common, a person who is content to roll in the blood and excrement of the street." He seemed to shudder. "Not someone I wish to be associated with." He threw his arms wide. "I have nothing but contempt for such people. Their world is so tiny, An Binh, so limited. They're ants on their hill, congratulating themselves on what they have built, when it's nothing. Nothing." His fists curled on the desktop. "Exceptionalism, that's all that matters. Either you understand that or you get run over."

An Binh had heard rumors, nothing more, and Ben had been tight-lipped on the subject. But, in fact, this confirmation of Isobel Lowe's activities came as a relief to An Binh. Isobel never fully accepted her and An Binh was appalled by Isobel's arrogance and blunt way of speaking, which went contrary to her ethos. And what about Tribe's "exceptionalism"? He had summoned her to him. He knew she was exceptional, otherwise he would have run her over.

"But even if Isobel was still running my intelligence show I wouldn't have called for Butler." Tribe spread his hands. "Don't get me wrong. You did a spectacular job rehabbing him. Frankly, I never thought he'd walk again after being shot. However, it's my opinion that his days as a field agent are over. He's strictly operations now, and I strongly suspect that he'll be as good if not better than Isobel. I bought her house when she left, so there's no reason to look for a new HQ. Plus, you were already in the vicinity and, as you will soon see, time is of the essence."

Tribe brushed his hands together. Isobel was now yesterday's news, which she knew was how he worked—eyes always fixed on the horizon, always six steps ahead of his competition. That ability was what made him so successful. Exceptional.

He rose, came around from behind the desk. He was dressed casually in dark-blue slacks, a plain white shirt, untucked, the sleeves rolled up revealing his muscular forearms, nicely toasted by sun and salt. A tall man, rangy and solid-looking. Thick, dark hair, worn long, an oval face with a prominent nose, a wide almost sensual mouth, strong jaw, and extraordinary violet eyes. There was a crackling of energy about him she had never before encountered. She could see why Evan might be drawn to him.

"It's time for you to break into the big league full time." He put his palms together as if in prayer. "An Binh, this company is at war, has been for some time, but three months ago we had a breakthrough. Using LLM—large language model learning—we've created a program that learns in real time. This is called Deep Learning, where the algorithm can make judgments and even extrapolate the near future from patterns occurring in the present."

"I read about this, of course, but I had no clue it was ready for prime time." An Binh shook her head. "How is that possible?"

"The program can compute up to twenty trillion facts, equations, you name it, per second."

"The applications?"

"Are endless," Tribe said with no small degree of pride. "Flight routes, shipping schedules, buying and selling stocks, derivatives, commodities, currencies, crypto, real estate—anything, really, that can be bought or sold, that involves moving masses of things—"

"Or people."

Tribe leveled a gaze at her, said nothing.

An Binh, intuiting he had gone as far as he was going to go on the subject, decided to tack out of the wind. "Who is our adversary?"

"Russia, Iran, China, North Korea, Kazakhstan. Any of the usual suspects." He gestured. "The apex predators of the bad actors. As yet unknown entities within those state-run security services have been trying relentlessly to burrow through our firewalls to get control of our quantum computer network, the generator of our new program.

"That was dangerous enough, but now . . ." He broke off, looked out the window. So far as An Binh could tell there was nothing to see except sea and sky. He seemed to be mulling a specific set of possibilities, branches leading away from this moment in time.

She knew nothing about him apart from what information was leaked to the public, though she had watched all of his TED Talks and was impressed both by his insights and his grasp of the increasingly breathless forward thrust of technology. She knew, of course, that he and Evan had been in the field together, that they were close, but didn't know whether she believed the rumors that they were having an affair.

When he turned back to her, he said, "I must know definitively whether you're prepared to go into the darkness, to put your life on the line, if need be."

"So." She rose, looked him straight in the eye. "I work for Parachute, for you. Set me on the board, I move forward."

He nodded. "All right, then." Reaching behind him, he took a small oval object off his desk. At the press of a button, blackout shades came down over the windows. At the same time a soft whirring presaged a screen scrolling down from the ceiling. "Up until just hours ago our war had been waged in cyberspace. But now, we've moved into a new, real-world phase . . ." In the darkness, he stood beside her, pressed another button. The screen bloomed with color: a villa nestled in what appeared to be the beginning of a palm grove. Blue sky, a few clouds, puffy and bright. Concrete steps led down to the narrow strip of beach visible at the bottom of the photo. Blues and greens: a serene setting. An Binh found herself wishing she were there.

"This is my villa in Sumatra," Tribe said. "One of many around the world." The photo changed to an overhead shot of the villa. "This one is where Evan Ryder has been living for the past year, along with a young boy named Timur."

"The late Russian Sovereign's son." This much, at least, An Binh knew.

But that was all, except that after a series of bloody skirmishes, ruthless political purges, dooming the reformist coup to failure, the new Sovereign took power. By all accounts, he was as bad as the previous one. Perhaps worse; he had stacked the Politburo and Duma with friends, relatives, toadies—all hard-liners.

"His father's irrelevant," Tribe stated emphatically.

Then who was? An Binh wondered. Since Tribe had chosen Evan to be his personal field agent, reporting to him, rather than to Ben or Isobel, she had all but disappeared to the other members of Parachute's clandestine investigative network, Ben included.

Tribe cleared his throat. "As I said, Evan and the boy have been living here at my villa." He paused, ran a forefinger down his cheek. "Or at least they had."

The screen lit up again, this time with what looked to be a real-time video feed from a drone. An Binh stifled a gasp. An overhead view of the villa revealed it completely destroyed down to the foundation. Three figures in sterile boiler suits, masks, and booties were carefully picking their way through the charcoaled debris and the remnants of toxic smoke.

"No one could survive that." An Binh's voice was a reedy whisper.

"No one did." Tribe's voice was deliberately flat, but beneath that she could sense a cauldron.

She felt as if she were free-falling. "What . . . what happened?"

Tribe looked away, a sign that he was agitated. Maybe even humiliated, An Binh thought. A man like him: big ego, bigger sense of his place in the world. An apex predator himself.

"A missile shot from a drone. Bits of the skeleton were thrown up onto the shore. Iranian."

"So . . ."

Tribe shook his head. "Not the Iranians. Malaysian pirates."

"With an Iranian-made drone missile?" An Binh shook her head. "Low odds." She turned her head so she could see his profile. He hadn't taken his gaze from the wreckage of his property. Sacred for an apex predator. "And Evan? The boy Timur?"

Tribe seemed to make a sound. A sigh or a growl, difficult to tell. "No sign of them. By that I mean no remnants, no teeth, no bones. Nothing."

"Could they have been incinerated?"

"Not from this size missile. No. Absolutely not." His voice had changed, grown deeper, sharp-edged. Menacing.

A chill crept down An Binh's spine. "Then they were abducted." She knew firsthand what torture was like—to receive and to give.

The image went dark, the screen retracted into its hidden niche in the ceiling. From out of the shadows, Tribe said, "That is the only logical conclusion."

The darkness seemed to close in on her, as if it were alive, malicious. "Perhaps Timur's paternity is relevant after all? And someone in Moscow wants Timur back. Very badly."

Out of the darkness, his voice: "Yes, perhaps." His words might have agreed with her conjecture, but his tone left no doubt that Timur's lineage, and perhaps even his life, remained irrelevant to him.

An Binh considered this. She had been wrong. It wasn't the villa that was sacred to him. It was Evan. He had gone to great lengths to hide this from her, but she knew now.

"Needle in a haystack," she offered.

Tribe turned to her as the blackout curtains rose and light flooded the cabin. "And there's your remit." He raised his hand, pointed at her. "And, as I assume you know, with abductions time is of the essence. The longer Evan remains missing the higher the percentage she is dead."

She waited until she had crossed the room, hand on the doorknob before she said, "One more thing."

"What?" He seemed surprised that she was still there.

"About the boy. The late Sovereign's son."

"What about him?"

"I'm to find him, bring him back as well, yes?"

Tribe's eyes narrowed and he took what An Binh interpreted as a threatening step toward her. "Your remit concerns Evan Ryder. The boy is collateral. Under no circumstances are you to endanger the success of your mission by going after him. Once you have ensured Evan's safety you may do as you wish, but not before."

Though Parachute's helicopter wheeled away and the superyacht grew distant, Tribe's charismatic presence did not fade from An Binh's mind. Nevertheless, she was able to identify the feeling of unease—or maybe it was anger—that had clogged her throat the moment she set foot on Marsden Tribe's yacht. Besides being intimidated by the German, as she thought of Miranda, her resentment of being ordered around by her had interfered with her normal calm. Then there came her first contact with the billionaire. She was ashamed that she arrived with a certain set of prejudices. People like him were the same as governments, who didn't see those below them as human beings, only pieces to move around a board. Privilege fostered entitlement, arrogance bred contempt. She had come into this position as field agent at Parachute's security division purely by accident, through Ben Butler. She was used to Ben, trusted him. He was her control. Until now. With Isobel gone, Ben moved into the leadership spot, and with Evan dead or abducted the entire structure of the security division was upended. Everything was moving at the speed of light. Rugs had been pulled from under her feet. She now reported only to Tribe; she had moved up the espionage ladder. She resolved to plant her feet firmly on the changed ground beneath her and take advantage to the fullest extent of the new world that had opened up to her.

3

MALACCA STRAIT

Not fishermen, no. Pirates. Malaysian. These observations floated to the top of Evan's mind as she returned to consciousness. She did not, however, open her eyes. She smelled them, a combination of male sweat and days old fish. She heard voices in the cabin with her, wanted only to hear what they said, thinking she was still out cold. At this perilous moment, playing possum was her best defense against them.

"We need more of those drone rockets."

"We need to do more favors for the Russians."

They were speaking Malay in a dialect that indicated they were from somewhere on the northwest coast.

A harsh laugh, explosive in a space Evan now knew was small, low ceilinged. She felt the pitch of the boat; she felt the visceral thrumming of the engine and heard its cycling noise. So they were still at sea. She could place herself in the world. This was vital. But what about Timur? Where was he? Had they hurt him? She felt the release of adrenaline, had to keep her body in check, continue to lie still, keep her breathing slow, even. They had to think she had not yet come around. She continued to listen while outside the wind shivered the sails.

"Time for the rendezvous."

"Past time."

"If I'm honest, I hate the Russians."

"Who doesn't?" A third voice, a bit deeper than the other two. Older? So there were at least three of them in the room with her.

That explosive laugh again. "They do business with Iranians but they hate us."

"All Muslims." The third voice.

"They're nothing if not practical."

"Fuck your grandmother. They're hypocrites."

A noise from above, a low whistle: high, low, high.

"They're here. Go. Face Mecca and on your knees pray."

"You don't trust them."

"When are Russians ever trustworthy? I just want the massive amount of money promised us and be rid of them."

"The Russians or the boy?"

"Both." The tromping of boots down the steep wooden ladder. "Now go."

Heart pounding, Evan kept herself together. The good news: Timur was still alive and well. The bad news: the Russians were behind this abduction.

New voices: two males, speaking rough, accented Russian. Sounds of a chair scraping along the floor.

"Get her up." A female Russian, one accustomed to being instantly obeyed.

Evan accepted a less-than-gentle kick to her midsection. Her eyes flew open as strong hands dragged her to her feet, slammed her down onto a chair—cheap plastic, chipped, scratched, stinking of fish and something human far more noxious. Her arms were jerked backward, wrists crossed behind her back, a plastic zip tie bit into her flesh.

Evan found herself facing a woman, younger than she would have imagined spearheading an SVR operation. Her eyes were like pale topaz gems, her face thin yet with prominent cheekbones. She had a wide forehead, rosebud lips. The hint of a sardonic smile informed her mouth. She was flanked on either side by two men. Evan studied them. They were not SVR or GRU; she'd had plenty of experience with both. Further, they almost certainly were not ethnic Russian. So who the hell were they, and who was this woman?

Ranged behind them were the three Malaysians she'd heard talking before the Russians arrived—two young, the third older, as she had suspected. He didn't seem to be in charge, one of the younger ones had the look of command, but he, too, was cowed by the Russian contingent. And why not? They held his reward money.

Amid the creaking of the ship, an uneasy silence held sway while the woman bent forward so her eyes were at the same level as Evan's and the two women stared at each other. The Russian woman's face was unusually seductive. In fact, she might even have been ripe for their Swallow program, Evan thought. Swallows were field agents specifically trained to lure targeted enemy assets into liaisons that would lead to them being turned or blackmailed for intelligence. None of the men dared to move. It seemed as if they scarcely breathed. The atmosphere grew thick with sweat and exhalations. The rank heat of too many bodies in an enclosed space.

"Where's my son?" Evan asked, ending the heavy silence. "Where's David?"

"He's not your son," the woman said without breaking eye contact. "His name is not David."

Evan made no response to this, neither did she break eye contact. The point here was to keep this woman talking; the more she talked the more she revealed about herself.

"Why don't you and I take this discussion private, go topside and work this out together."

The woman stood up straight, took one long deliberate step to stand directly in front of Evan. Then she slowly bent down again, took Evan's jaw between thumb and fingers, forced her head up. Her lips parted, pressed softly against Evan's ear. "Nice try," she whispered. "But I'm already spoken for."

Evan wanted to twist away, but she held herself still. "When did that stop anyone?" she said.

The woman pulled her head back, her words coming in short, sharp bursts. "My name is Alyosha. The boy's name is Timur, and I know who you are, Evan Ryder."

Evan felt the heat of Alyosha's breath against her cheek as if it were a branding iron. There was something about her, faint but familiar just beyond the reach of Evan's memory. Alyosha produced a switchblade, opened it an inch from Evan's face, and then Evan had it, clear as if her conversation with Lyudmila had happened yesterday instead of two years ago:

"Have you any more intel on this major who had been sent to find you and kill you?" Evan asked.

"I'll send what little Alyosha Ivanovna has been able to scrape together to the sandbox on your mobile."

This shard of memory was an icicle pressed against Evan's spine. *You know my sister; you're her strong right hand.* Bobbi Ryder, now known as Kata Romanovna Hemakova following her defection. *My sister is running this op.* What was her plan? She was currently in disgrace after her power grab failed. *She's in desperate need of a lifeline out of Russia,* Evan thought, *but how does that connect with abducting me and Timur?*

Patience, she told herself. She had confidence that soon enough all would be revealed.

Grinning, Alyosha jerked Evan to her feet, shoved her roughly into the grip of one of her musclemen, who pulled her back to the far side of the room.

"All right." Alyosha signaled to her other muscleman, who disappeared through an open doorway. The muscleman returned shortly thereafter with Timur in tow. Evan was relieved to see that he was bound as she was but otherwise unharmed.

Timur looked at her, lips beginning to part, but then quickly clamped shut in response to the infinitesimal shake of her head. He struggled in the arms of the big man, to no avail. Evan kept her eyes on Alyosha, who said now, "Here's the child."

"I'm not a child!" Timur shouted. That got a laugh out of everyone but Evan.

Alyosha faced him, gestured to him. "Who is this? You know her?"

"She's my mother."

Alyosha lifted an eyebrow. "Really?" She huffed. "And what's your name?"

"D-David." Evan had coached him for the possibility of a dangerous situation. But then, even in his short life, he'd been in more than one dangerous situation.

"'David.'" Alyosha shook her head. "Not Timur?"

He squinted at her. He knew never to show fear in the face of the enemy. Fear was weakness. "Who's Timur?"

"Enough of this." One of the pirates stepped forward. "We brought you what you wanted." He held out his hand palm up. "Give us our payment."

"Payment?" Alyosha whirled on him. "How's this for payment?" The blade of her knife flashed so quickly and with such force only Evan saw it slice through the inside of the pirate's wrist, slashing through veins down to the bone.

An unearthly howl erupted from his wide open mouth. Spittle flew from his lips. His good hand grasped the other until Alyosha's second strike hacked through the joint. The pirate sank to his knees, cradling his severed hand against his chest.

His two compatriots were in the process of swinging up their snub-nosed submachine guns when Alyosha's second muscleman kicked one of them in the chin, chopped down on the other's shoulder. Disarming them, he stooped, slit their throats.

At a silent signal from Alyosha, the muscleman cut the twist-tie binding Evan's wrists.

"Now," Alyosha said to Evan, "take this pathetic simulacrum of a man and put him in the chair."

"What is this?" Evan said. "No."

"No?" Alyosha cocked her head. "Fine." She stepped over to Timur, who could not help cringing away from her. She stuck the point of her bloody knife blade at the place where his carotid pulsed on the side of his neck. Her eyes burned as she stared at Evan. "Say 'no' again, bitch."

Evan took a breath, then another. The room was beginning to swim around her, but losing consciousness was no escape. She deepened her breaths, oxygenating her system. Even with the befouled air, her vision cleared.

"Now, Evan, obey me." She did not have to pronounce sentence on Timur. It hung in the air like the specter of death and destruction. Of the last person Evan held dear, her last and only lifeline to Lyudmila. She looked into his eyes, saw Lyudmila looking back at her.

Fuck it, she thought, went behind the injured pirate, lifted him by his armpits, slung him unceremoniously into the chair. "There," she said, wiping her hands down her naked thighs; she and Timur were still in their bathing suits. "Done."

But already Alyosha was shaking her head. "Not done." She took a step toward Evan. "Not even close."

Keeping the point of her knife against the skin of Timur's neck, she said, "Go ahead, Evan. Hit him." Her eyes glittered. "I know you want to. Anyone in your position would. Everyone would."

Still, Evan kept her gaze directly on the other woman. "What is it you want? Just tell me."

"I want you to beat the living shit out of this animal."

Evan's blood ran cold. This situation was already spinning out of control. Part of her mind was desperately trying to find a way out of this spiderweb, but the more she racked her brain the surer she became that Alyosha had thought of every possibility. If it had been just her, she would have taken a chance of breaking free, turning the tables, no matter how slim the odds, but she was hamstrung by Timur. She would do nothing to jeopardize his well-being. And judging by the smirk on Alyosha's face her opposite number knew it. She had known it the moment Timur had told her Evan was his mother. That had been a mistake. Hindsight was perfect, she knew, choices were not. By his answer he'd told Alyosha how close the two of them were. Now Alyosha knew Evan would do anything she asked in order to keep Timur from being harmed.

"Well?" The knife blade dug in just enough to draw blood, and now Evan saw it on Timur's face. The terror of dying. She couldn't blame him, knew he'd done his best to hold out as long as he could. He'd done better than many grown men, she knew. She was proud of him, gave him a private smile to let him know. Then, swinging from her hips, she punched the pirate flush on the jaw. His head snapped to the side. He spat out two teeth.

"Nice," Alyosha said in a conversational tone. "Again."

Sick at heart, Evan obeyed. The pirate's cheek split open, blood flew. He was making gargling sounds, like a pig being slaughtered.

"And again."

After that, Evan no longer waited for her command. What was the point? Her body worked on its own; she detached her mind from what she was doing. That was someone else, working away in some other room, on a pirate who deserved everything he was getting, a pirate who had masterminded their abduction, brought them to this perilous pass. Through the blood and gore she kept her mind firmly on Timur, on their sun-splashed days, nights awash with moonlight, the whir of bats, the calls of macaques. Those sounds mingled and then overtaken by the sounds of semiautomatic fire, the heat and stink of the lava crawling down the volcano. And she, with Lyudmila's head in her lap, Lyudmila breathing her last. A fire sparked in Evan's belly, a terrible rage at what was taken from her, and it was this blackness that overwhelmed her now, the beating she was administering taken to a new, dreadful level as partial retribution for Lyudmila's death.

And at last she heard Alyosha's voice addressing her, calling a halt to the merciless beating she had inflicted. She staggered back, her chest heaving, her muscles still coiled, adrenaline still in spate. And it was at this moment that she realized her life had changed. There was the time when Lyudmila was alive and now, when she was dead. She would never be the Evan that was. That Evan had died on the shuddering volcano with Lyudmila.

"Good girl." Alyosha wrinkled her nose, turned to Timur. "Has your mother taught you how to tell if someone is dead?"

Timur looked at her but his eyes were glassy. Evan knew he had drawn deep inside himself.

"Come, come," Alyosha urged. "Don't pretend to be stupid—or ignorant."

"Tap the carotid artery, put a mirror under the nose." It was no more than a dry, raspy whisper.

Alyosha chuckled. "For those you'd have to touch the body. But actually, as you can already tell, you won't want to get that close. At death, the sphincter muscle collapses. The corpse shits itself."

Catching the boy's eyes filled with tears she smiled, her work done, and turned back to Evan. "It smells like an abattoir in here. The murder you committed has granted your wish. We're going topside." She tossed her head. "And bring the child. He's white as a sail. He can vomit over the side."

Which is precisely what Timur did the moment they set foot on the upper deck. Evan's heart broke to see him heaving, his body shaking with the intense distress of seeing the killings below. Worse, seeing what violence his beloved Aunt Evan was capable of. Overhead, gulls were circling the three pirate bodies as two more of Alyosha's crew—not SVR, not GRU, not ethnic Russian—tossed them overboard. The deck was awash with blood.

Timur stood, chest against the rail. He was shivering, shaking, even. Evan took a step toward him, but an iron grip on her shoulder stopped her. She called out to him but he wouldn't look at her. All she wanted to do was hold him tight, but by his body language she knew he wouldn't let her even if she was set free.

"Timur, talk to me."

He shook his head, remained with his back to her. He still couldn't look at her. He lifted his shoulder, turned his head to rub the tears and snot off his face. The eye she glimpsed for just a moment was red, swollen with more tears.

A memory triggered, arose in a sulfurous mass.

Alyosha faced him, gestured to him. "Who is this? You know her?"

"She's my mother."

Evan had spent years hardening the carapace she wore in the shadows, the armor to protect her. But with that simple, seemingly innocuous exchange Alyosha had cleverly found the one chink in Evan's armor: *Mother.* Inserted the tip of her knife, drove it in, twisted it to inflict the most damage.

Now, too late, she understood why Alyosha had forced her to batter the Malaysian pirate. She had broken Evan and Timur's unspoken bond of trust. He had been forced to watch her systematically take another human being apart with her bare hands. He would never forget it. Alyosha had coldly, calculatedly done this to them. Her grievous transgression was something Evan would never forgive—or forget.

Alyosha swung her gaze away from Evan, said to one of her men, "Take him down to the launch. Get him into some dry clothes. The last thing we need is for him to get pneumonia."

Evan made one last try. "I'll go with him." And saw him flinch away, press himself against the railing. As if eager to go with them, to get as far away from her as possible.

Alyosha's Medusa gaze swung back to her, the smirk back on her face. "He doesn't even want to be near you, and who can blame him." The smirk vanished as quickly as it had appeared. "The point is moot, since you're not going anywhere. Not until you're ready."

A venomous serpent seemed to be uncoiling in the pit of Evan's stomach. "Ready for what?"

"Why we came for you," Alyosha said almost kindly, as if they were long-lost friends reuniting after years apart. She could work her face and voice like a ventriloquist or someone with multiple-personality disorder.

Timur was gone now, helped over the side and down a rope ladder that had appeared from nowhere.

She felt a hollowness inside her, as if a part of her had been ripped away. She found it difficult to breathe, and she had another presentiment: *This child, Lyudmila's son, who I've sworn to protect, will be the death of me.* "Where are you taking him?"

"Somewhere safe," Alyosha said. "Where no one can get to him, Evan. Even you." She took a step toward Evan, reached out with a forefinger, ran it along the raised scar across Evan's throat. "What have we here?"

Evan looked her in the eyes. "Someone tried to garrote me."

Alyosha pursed her lips. "Shame."

Did she mean she was sorry that Evan had been disfigured or that the attempt had failed?

"She's dead," Evan clarified.

"So I would imagine." Alyosha nodded. "Again, the boy is perfectly safe. Not a hair on his head will be mussed. He will remain with us until such time as you fulfill the task I am about to assign you."

Evan's eyes narrowed. "What kind of task?"

"One you are eminently qualified for, one you have become proficient in—preeminent in your field, if even half the stories about you are true."

Alyosha removed a photo from her breast pocket. She flipped it back and forth, snapping it with her thumb. "You are a death-dealer, Evan."

"The SVR has more than its fair share of death-dealers."

Alyosha nodded. "True, as far as it goes. But this target is beyond their realm."

"For instance?"

"She's worked for the Iranians, the Saudis, the North Koreans, Malaysian pirates, Hamas, African warlords, Houthis, when they can afford her."

"The current Axis of Evil."

Alyosha studied her a moment. "Is that what you Americans call it?"

"If you have a better name, tell me."

"We call them *Chlenososy*—cocksuckers. But, frankly I like your term better." Alyosha took a step back as if she'd suddenly realized she'd inadvertently ventured out onto a patch of thin ice, could hear the distant crack of a thaw.

Alyosha's brows drew together. "Time after time, our people thought they had found her. Instead, she led them into a trap. Deliberately baited us, mocked us." *Snap, snap, snap* went her thumb against the corner of the photo. "It pains me to tell you that none of our death-dealers had success against this target."

"Hard to believe."

"Five of them are dead." Alyosha's voice was thin, as if the words were being forced out of her. "The sixth is so disfigured her own sister didn't recognize her. She'll never walk again or even want to. Her will to live was taken from her, drained as if it were blood from her veins."

"Now you're overdramatizing. This part sounds like a midnight horror story of a boogeyman meant to frighten children."

"Think so? Well, I'm about to disabuse you of that notion."

Alyosha thumbed open her sat phone, scrolled with one hand, came to the selected photo, held the screen up in front of Evan's face. The thing in the ICU bed was scarcely human. Evan's stomach churned, the muscles in her neck and shoulders seized up at the sight of what had been done to the poor creature. After the moment of shock that froze her, Evan turned her head away. The heavy hand of Alyosha's man on her shoulder tightened its grip, holding her in place.

"This is Alisa, my sister," Alyosha said in a voice that seemed to be all strangled emotion.

"*Is* that your sister, Alyosha?" It was important to use her name, to try to claw back even a tiny bit of the ground she had lost. She kept her gaze fastened to the other woman, seeking to pick up micro-expressions. "Do you even have a sister?"

Alyosha struck her an openhanded blow across her cheek, the flesh turning from white to bright pink. "I have a sister," she pushed out through gritted teeth. "Her name is Alisa. You said this sounded like the story of a boogeyman. More like a demon out of hell."

Evan studied Alyosha's face, found nothing untoward there. If she was handing Evan disinformation she was the most expert liar Evan had ever met. Barring Lyudmila. She took a breath, two. Gathered herself. "Show me," she said in a voice made hoarse by emotion. "Show me who did this to her."

Alyosha handed over the photo. It was a head shot—the face very striking, almost preternaturally, in some magical way made more so by the cuts, bruises, and swelling on forehead, cheeks, neck.

Evan glanced up into Alyosha's face. "This demon from hell is a woman."

"Perfect prey for you, no?" It was not a question.

Alyosha handed Evan a second sat phone. "For you. It contains all the intel we have on Ilona Starkova."

Evan took it. "No patronymic?"

"Oh, she has one. Rachanovna."

"Is Ilona Starkova her name at all?" Evan was more than familiar with pseudonyms, not only for field agents but in this day and age for anyone with a laptop or a cell phone.

Alyosha shrugged. "It's the name she's known by. Ilona Starkova. For whatever reason she has dropped her patronymic. Maybe she hates her father, maybe it's for another reason. Either way, it's irrelevant to your re-mit. She's your target. Kill her. Bring me proof of her death and Timur will be set free. You have my word." Her face darkened. "But if you don't . . ." She shrugged. "Well, you won't be coming back for him anyway."

She looked off for a moment, as if she had spied something on the unchanging horizon only she could see. "Whatever her true name may be, she does have a name we can all agree upon: she calls herself White Wolf."

"A flair for the dramatic, your Ilona." This op—Kata's op—was at the behest of someone who had promised to set her up somewhere outside the Federation. Ilona Starkova's death in return for a new life in a new land. Only someone extremely powerful could arrange Kata's exfiltration from Russia. Another piece of the puzzle fell into place. But where were

Kata—and Alyosha—headed? Where might their new base of operations be where they could be safe—or relatively safe—from all the arms of the Russian clandestine services?

"Not really. She has lived up to that name many times. You'll see when you read her dossier. It's all on the phone."

Evan, staring at the face in the photo, took a moment to digest this new information. "She must have taken quite a beating . . . like one of your prisoners."

"Out of date." Alyosha snatched back the photo. "She was incarcerated in a prison specifically designed to be escape-proof."

"And yet she escaped."

"Now you know something vital about her." Alyosha sighed. "It's been three months. Three months of murder and mayhem. She's still very much at large and we're down six highly skilled field agents."

"Not highly skilled enough," Evan observed.

"Which is why we've turned to you."

Evan could not help herself, she laughed. "Alyosha, you're the enemy. This woman is killing your best field agents. Where do I sign up to help her?"

Alyosha frowned. "Are you saying no?"

"I'm saying go fuck yourself."

All at once Alyosha was in her face. Evan tensed and she felt the grip on her shoulder dig painfully into its meat. "Here's what I say, and you'd better listen carefully because I'm only going to say this once. If you deny me, if you reject this remit, consider what you and I did to that Malaysian animal down below. That precise fate, cut by cut, blow by blow is what will befall Timur." They were almost nose to nose now. "He will take a long time dying. Days, weeks, months even." She shrugged. "You know him best, Evan. How strong is he? How long d'you think he can hold on before his heart, his lungs, his kidneys fail?"

With a forceful lift of her arm, Evan shrugged away from the Russian agent behind her. She saw Alyosha give a "Stay" hand signal, as if he were nothing more than a dog. She crossed to the rail, leaned on it with her elbows. The cutter with Timur in it was long gone, God only knew where. A terrible presentiment gripped her. Alyosha was telling her the truth. Wherever they stashed him she'd never find him. She'd never get off this boat alive, either. Unless she agreed to take on this mission. She shuddered at the thought. Timur was Lyudmila's child but he was hers now and there was a fierceness inside her she had never felt before. The year she had spent with him on Sumatra had changed her. Her kinship with Timur made her vulnerable. This should have saddened her for in the life she had chosen no vulnerabilities were allowed lest they allow an enemy to destroy you, either by death or by turning you. And yet . . . Timur's mother had been murdered as had his father. He had no blood family. *I am the gatekeeper,* she thought, *between him and the world,* and she knew now that without question she would protect him with her life. She would do whatever was required of her to keep him from peril.

Evan cocked her head. "Just who are your people? SVR? GRU?"

Alyosha produced a smile as enigmatic as the Mona Lisa's. "Ask me again when we know each other better."

A feisty bitch with a wicked sense of humor, Evan thought. *Every bit of what she reveals no matter how small or seemingly irrelevant is important, as opposed to the intel she's showing me which is, by definition, suspect. Knowing my enemy is the surest path to getting me and Timur out of this alive.* "Any intel on where she's going, what she wants?" she asked.

Alyosha squinted into the distance. "That's what you have to find out." Her gaze swung back to Evan. "You have five days. That's all the time you'll need to carry out your remit."

"And if I need more?"

"Don't," was all Alyosha said.

So they were against the clock, Alyosha and Kata.

"Five days of life is all Timur has left. Unless . . . well, that's entirely up to you."

So I'm up against the clock, too, Evan thought. *But why? Why five days and then* finis, *it's over?* With a terrible foreboding she would never reveal, she nodded her acquiescence. *What is she not telling me? Everything. Everything that will make their position weaker and mine stronger.*

An instant later, she saw a black speck in the sky. As it approached, she could hear the *thwop-thwop-thwop* of its rotors, softly at first under the swells lapping against the boat's hull, then louder until it overrode everything else.

Alyosha stepped up beside her. "Your ride."

The copter loomed large now, blocking out the sun at its zenith. It hovered over their heads, turning the waves nearest the ship to froth. A door slid open, a rope ladder was tossed down. It dangled within Evan's reach.

"Everything you might need is up there." Alyosha pointed. "If there is anything we haven't thought of my direct line is inputted into your phone—which, by the way, is encrypted. Also, you cannot call out to any number that's not already in the phone." She placed her hands on her hips. "Well, that's it."

"Where am I going?"

Alyosha visibly relaxed. "That depends on you. To the prison she broke out of? The place where she destroyed my sister? You're the death-dealer. You're on your own now."

Evan reached up.

"Oh, and one more thing."

Evan turned. There was always one more thing. She waited while a slow, sly smile spread across Alyosha's lips, baring a tiny bit of her teeth.

"Ilona Starkova is in possession of something you must bring back to me."

"No doubt I will have to kill her to obtain it."

"Exactly."

"And what is this item? A card reader? A finger drive? Plans for the Death Star?"

Alyosha barked a laugh. "It's a pair of teeth."

"Say what?"

"Molars, to be precise."

"Is this a joke?"

Alyosha drew her sidearm, pressed the muzzle against Evan's temple. "What do you think?"

"Right, then." Reaching up. Evan began to climb into the sky. The stretch felt good, her over-tense muscles relaxing as she ascended. She had been long out of the field, and now her body told her she was back.

Halfway up, Alyosha called to her, shouting over the copter's racket. She paused, swung around so she was holding on with one hand. She looked down to where Alyosha was shading her eyes against the wind.

"Do us both a favor, Evan," she shouted over the clatter of the rotors. "Don't fucking die."

Not until you're done with me, Evan thought.

4

"So," Miranda said, as she stepped into Tribe's office. "You decided not to tell her."

She had seen An Binh off the yacht, watching the refueled helicopter lift off, waving to An Binh as the craft turned and sped away.

"Need to know," Tribe said.

Miranda huffed. "It's more than that, isn't it?"

Tribe went and sat behind his desk, steepled his fingers as he rested his elbows on the desktop. His gaze was enigmatic.

"What if she asked you the question?"

"I would have stopped her." Tribe's tone was entirely neutral.

"Marsden, what if she asked you, 'What good is an AI program no matter how smart or fast if it can be hacked?'"

"This was the problem we encountered recently."

Miranda's eyebrows rose. "But our quantum servers weren't really hacked."

"Not for lack of trying," Tribe said.

"Not by any of the 'usual suspects' you enumerated for An Binh."

"Of course not. No." He sighed. "Any of them would be less dangerous than our enemy."

"And yet you got Ilona out."

He laughed. "QuintonBTB hacked the prison's security net as soon as it came online—a supposedly unhackable system." He cocked his head. "Çelik was responsible for her arrest and incarceration. He's sure I don't know this."

"You and Çelik are partners—friends, even—"

"I have no friends," he cut in. "Except von Kleist."

"Your third partner," she said with a sardonic smile. She was stung by what he'd said. That Bernhard-Otto von Kleist was his only friend. After all these years with him she was still in one sense naïve. She shouldered her hurt aside. "So now you and Çelik are enemies?"

"I might have given him a pass on Ilona—he said it was a mistake."

"But you suspect it wasn't?"

"I didn't then, but when he abducted Evan I understood he knew precisely what he was doing. Once he discovered Ilona was free he was forced to make a countermove."

"He wanted to take Evan off the board."

"Worse," Tribe said, "Much worse. Evan developed a kind of maternal attachment to the kid. I saw it myself when I visited them. And why not? He's the son of her best friend, who died in her arms." He crossed to a sideboard, took two bottles of tonic water out of the half fridge, poured the contents into two old-fashioned glasses, added a squeeze of fresh lime to both, handed one to Miranda. He sipped meditatively, his eyes never leaving her face. "So what did that fucker do? He's used the child, coerced Evan into going after Ilona, stopping her, killing her."

Miranda had no need to ask Tribe how he knew all this. She had long ago ceased to contemplate the width and depth of his knowledge of the global network of people who worked for him, in which countries they resided, in which organizations, cadres, families they were embedded.

Asking questions of Tribe was often counterproductive, but there was one that continued to eat at her. "Marsden, why is Ilona so important?"

He set his glass down. "A discussion for another day."

Miranda knew when she was dismissed.

After she left, Tribe added gin to his tonic, inhaled the botanicals, then took a gulp. He never drank liquor when any of his people were around. They knew he was completely sober, but there were many things about him they thought they knew but didn't.

He went down the corridor to the lounge, sat on a sofa, switched on the flat-screen, watched the latest war footage of Russian troops and Ukrainian troops killing each other. War disgusted him. As far as he was concerned war was the instrument of the myopic, one tribe of ants trying to set fire to their neighbor's anthill.

He sat back, crossed one leg over the other, savored his gin and tonic, closed his eyes against the explosions, the rocket fire, thought instead of his mentor. He had just turned eighteen when met Nikki Fischer. She was then thirty. He assumed she was an escort. She was in fact a genius; she had no need to sell her body. She kept to the background, the shadows. From this perch she sold her consulting services, which made her clients tons of money. She had an uncanny ability to maneuver through and manipulate the pitfall-rich topography of high finance. She never made a mistake. Never. Her IQ was MENSA level. Her genius had accelerated her education to the point where she had graduated Harvard Business School at the age of nineteen.

She took Tribe's younger self under her wing, taught him all the tricks—the weaknesses, tells, hubris of men, how to use these faults against them. "Mental aikido," she called it, and naturally she was right. The basic principle of aikido was with an unexpected turn to use your opponent's momentum against them.

He was with Nikki when the embolism hit. For the thirteenth time they were watching the director's cut of *Apocalypse Now*, a favorite of theirs. They had reached the scene where Captain Willard says, "Charging a man with murder in this place was like handing out speeding tickets in the Indy 500."

Of course the younger Tribe laughed. They were both supposed to laugh, but all Nikki did was cough. Her tongue appeared between her lips, her mouth hung open, a spider-silk thread of saliva extending down, down.

Tribe called her name, grabbed her, shook her. Her cheeks were deathly pale. There was a line of sweat beading her hairline. Looking into her eyes was like staring into glassy eternity.

"No, no, no, no," he cried. "No, no, no, no," calling 911. "No, no, no. no," he cried as the EMTs pronounced Nikki dead, draped a sheet over her face, rolled her away, away.

Tribe's eyes popped open. He needed to control his breathing, which was coming hard and fast. He swiped sweat off his upper lip. He sat up, stared out the window at the seemingly endless sea. He felt safe here, aboard his floating city, these days safer than he did in his triplex high above Manhattan's Billionaire's Row on Fifty-Seventh Street between Sixth and Seventh Avenues, overlooking Central Park, all the way north into rehabbing Harlem. Safer than when he was in his sprawling estate in the Hollywood Hills, safer even than when watching his impenetrable "survival home" being completed in New Zealand. Always moving, his floating city, in one place or another only long enough to reprovision. Safe. And yet still haunted by Nikki.

Here's what Nikki said to him while they watched the opening of *Apocalypse Now*, while Martin Sheen's Captain Willard was freaking out in his hotel room in Saigon: *"Never tell anyone the complete plan. Each one involved gets a piece, and only a piece. Now you're invulnerable."*

Neither Kurt Çelik nor Bernhard-Otto von Kleist knew how much those two molars torn from Radik's mouth meant to him. They were the prototypes, the first ones his quantum computer designed. To Tribe they were priceless, symbol of his greatest achievement, the creation of the Daedalus Project. *I got Ilona out of prison without Çelik knowing, an achievement in itself,* he thought. *But until Ilona brings them back to me I won't rest.*

He switched channels from the war in Ukraine to the war in the Middle East, the same thing, over and over, death, destruction, agony, sadism on a grand scale. Anthills being set on fire.

He rose, crossed to a mirror, stood with his nose touching the glass, opened his mouth wide. There they were, the two molars, the two halves of the sigil rising side by side from his gum line. The tooth farther back was the transmitter, the one in front of it the receiver. Totally sealed end to end. No one, nothing could eavesdrop on the conversations using this ingenious device. Why? Because his quantum AI agent, or agentic, Quinton, delivered instructions, whether between humans or between human and agentic—bone to bone, directly, no matter the distance between users.

Like Evan, who took the time to get to know her night heron, Tribe took his time in getting to know the qubits in his quantum computers, the long and at times painful process of testing. First he had to deal with the qubits—quantum bits—the basic building blocks of the quantum universe. Qubits were both fascinating and vexing.

He discovered two things: qubits were happier, much happier while inhabiting incredibly cold temperatures. He also found out that qubits were ADHD poster boys for the subatomic world. They worked so fast, could be in more than one place at a time, that they grew quickly bored—hence the mistakes. It turned out that the mistakes were deliberate—a form of communication to let whoever was directing them know they weren't happy.

Thus, Tribe's quantum computer array existed in the ocean's Abyssopelagic Zone, between 13,000 and 20,000 feet below the surface. The array was encased in a watertight, corrosion-free housing. The temperature in the deep was such that Tribe needed much less power to get the qubits to a temperature that, while not optimal, proved acceptable to them. The engineering problems plus the expense was astronomical, but Tribe, true to his nature, found neither a hindrance—at least not for long. Actually embedding his quantum array in the deep was his Plan B. Plan A was to bury the array outside of Oymyakon, in the Sakha Republic of Siberia, the coldest accessible place on earth—hence recruiting

Yuri Radik, a dissatisfied member of the GRU, to be his point man. But Radik had run afoul of his own people—the GRU—who were crawling all over the area, due to its diamond, gold, and silver mines. Instantly, he became useless—worse, he was a liability. Tribe needed to find a way to eradicate him plus get the Daedalus teeth out of his mouth before a GRU forensic team started crawling over the corpse. In the end, he turned to Ilona Starkova, a homicidal employee who would actually enjoy murdering Radik.

He stared down at the inside of his right wrist, at the Daedalus tattoo of the sun between the jaws of a caliper, signifier of his game-changing communication network. He'd never allowed Evan to see it, wearing a silver naga bracelet handmade for him by John Hardy. He crossed to the window, stared out at the restless sea, thinking of the Greeks, Romans, Phoenicians, Arabs whose ships had plied these waters centuries ago—adventurers, conquerors, far-sighted planners just like him. His thoughts raced forward.

Before his experimentation made it possible to create Quinton, the Daedalus Project had hit a series of speed bumps among his subjects: bleeding gums, infections, new tooth root tips shifting, making the molars unstable. And then there was the issue of subjects going mad or killing themselves. Seventeen percent of the first cadre of test subjects. Gradually dropping but remaining unacceptably high. The Syrian refugees he'd saved in Istanbul three years ago had proved perfect fodder for the trials. But those early days were long gone. As soon as purpose-built Quinton, his quantum agentic—agent AI program—had come online it had solved all the physical problems in what amounted to a matter of minutes. Now fitting the new teeth was a snap, and the incidences of psychological catastrophe had fallen to zero.

He wished he could share this coming triumph with Nikki. How proud of him she would be, how in awe. He had taken the principles she had instilled in him to another level. A quantum level. She had not lived to see his quantum triumphs—a single computer solving whatever was thrown at it far faster than any array of computers, no matter how fast the chips. His quantum baby was the key to how the Daedalus communication worked. The advent of Quinton opened up dimensions previously unimaginable. Agent AI was the next step up from generative AI. And it was a massive one. Even the best generative AI programs were just genies in a bottle—absorbing massive amounts of data that allowed them to perform complex tasks. However, their progress was totally dependent on how much data they ingested. But that was a huge disadvantage; no matter how much data they absorbed they still had no knowledge of the outside world.

Quinton, on the other hand, was designed to act autonomously, making decisions, turning those decisions into actionable tasks. The agentic on its own identified specific goals. In other words, Tribe's Quinton functioned as an independent agent. As such it perceived the outside world, could reason and adapt to achieve its objectives in the most efficacious manner possible. All in a matter of nanoseconds.

Tribe had let the genie out of the bottle. As such, it was never going back inside.

Back in front of the mirror he stared intently at himself, smiled at the thought of those Silicon Valley titans competing with each other for social media eyeballs, digital ad dollars. He had need of neither. He was so far ahead of them they would never catch up, preoccupied as they were with gouging each other, delivering body punch after body punch. And in the meantime, he was left alone to create his marvels, his historic breakthroughs that would change society as they knew it.

When combined with Daedalus, his breakthrough communication system, Quinton would be able to direct a cadre of human agents worldwide to manipulate anything that could be bought and sold—stocks, bonds, derivatives, cryptocurrencies, blockchain networks, precious metals, uranium, rare earth metals, agriculture prices, all futures markets, even the movement of armies, big and small—without fear of being hacked. Which was why Mike Harrison, Parachute's ambitious vice president of communications, who never met a power grab he didn't covet, was anxious to receive the first mass shipment of Daedalus. The system named after the father of Icarus, the famed genius who invented the wings his son misused, flying too near the sun. Daedalus also designed the labyrinth of Crete to hold the Minotaur. Harrison was immediately dazzled by a future built on riches—riches amassed in a way no one else could even imagine, let alone try for. Harrison's hubris was just what Tribe required. Should anything go wrong Harrison would be hung out to dry, leaving Tribe blameless.

He closed his mouth, turned away from the mirror. He did not return to the sofa. He turned off the constant death on the flat-screen.

He picked up his gin and tonic, left the lounge to return to his office.

On the way he ran his fingertip over the molars. The program residing within them was nothing short of revolutionary. He knew without his array of quantum computers he never would have been able to solve the puzzle of bone-to-bone communication over distances. *Quinton will control the ebb and flow of finances around the world,* he thought. *Nothing can stop Quinton. Nothing at all.*

PART TWO

THE DARK LABYRINTH

If there were no monster, there would be no labyrinth.

—unattributed quote

5

Ilona Starkova, shotgun seat–sitting beside a burly, bearded driver in the sooty, drafty cabin of his long-haul truck, closed her eyes against the present. As snow was ground to crystals beneath the truck's enormous tires, Ilona rested her head against the icy window pane for a short while. She welcomed the cold of the glass against her temple, it calmed her ever-overheated mind.

The hours rolled on, the driver expertly guiding his rig through islets of ice cracked off from the mounds of snow lining the side of the highway. A different passenger might have slept, but not Ilona. Instead, she talked. At length. She talked to the driver about her past.

"The memories take the form of a waking dream," she said. "My past looms up before me, an admonishing finger, reminding me of what happened, why my mission is vital to my mental health.

"Inside my waking dream, a prison, a labyrinth within which I am trapped. I'm eleven years old, my sister is nine, and we are happily spinning around the family ballroom, hands clasped in our mother's long, delicate fingers, her skirts ballooning out, making us giggle. Our mother swings us so powerfully we're launched off our feet. This is entirely appropriate since we are dancing to Modest Mussorgsky's *Night on Bald Mountain*."

She turned to the driver. "Do you know it? *Night on Bald Mountain*? No? Pity." She shrugged.

"The music is so loud that none of us hears the banging on the front door nor, rude moments later, the wood splintering as a small cohort of GRU in black leather coats storm in from the streets of St. Petersburg. Outside, the sun is shining, the wind caressing the leaves on the plane trees, but no traffic moves on the street outside our house; the GRU officers have seen to that.

"There are six of them. Five award an almost religious obeisance to the tall, muscular lieutenant who is clearly their leader. I remember him with a supernatural clarity that the intervening years have not dimmed even one iota. He was well over six feet tall. His thick hair was pure white, his piercing eyes a shade of gray so pale as to be almost clear. Just like mine. His bloodless lips were vampiric in aspect. His men were clearly terrified of him. Belyy Volk, they called him. White Wolf.

"My father.

"It was from him that I learned her family's history, that Tatiana, my mother, a former prima ballerina at the Marinsky Ballet, was descended from an immensely wealthy White Russian family. The patriarch, seeing the thundering writing on the wall for the Tsar and the aristocracy. The Cossacks confiscated all his assets, then slaughtered him and most of his family.

"In the rarefied atmosphere in which she had lived, protected by her husband who now had become her enemy, what could have prepared her for such treatment? To her, the GRU was a fever dream from a grubby world that had nothing to do with her. But now that world of grime and gore collided with her pristine ivory tower so powerfully it brought it, all of us, to ruins in less than an hour.

"My father crosses the ballroom, runs his fingernail across the record grooves, rendering Mother's treasured and very rare recording by the Leningrad Philharmonic Society unplayable. The others stand in a perfect semicircle, one of them gripping me and my sister while their boss stands in front of Mother, sat in a wood-framed silk-covered chair. Every time she tries to look away from him he clamps her jaws in a punishing grip, jerks her head up so that her eyes meet his.

"I try to break away, to get to Mother, to do . . . what? Protect her? A child's desperate wish, nothing more. But our captor keeps us close by his side, fingers digging into me so deeply a ring of bruises is already forming. I see Mother glance at me. I want to cry out, but a minute shake of her head causes the words to stick in my throat like thorns. I am completely overwhelmed, disoriented, helpless. I can scarcely believe what is happening, scarcely understand the words, but the deeds never leave my mind. *This is a nightmare*, I think. *I'll pinch myself and wake up.* But the nightmare continues and then Mother is mouthing words to me whenever she is sure she won't be discovered.

"'*Don't struggle.*'

"'*Wait.*'

"And then, '*Go! Go now!*'

"What? I can't. I remain rooted to the spot, too terrified to make sense of Mother's words. *Go! Go now!* My father removes his pistol from its holster and shoots her dead. *Go! Go now!* In the shocked aftermath, I wrench away from my captor, I grab my sister's hand. We run. Tears stream down my sister's deathly white, drawn face but I cannot afford tears, not yet, perhaps not ever. I am too busy working out how to save us from Mother's fate. Later, I will wonder why my father turned on my mother like that. To shoot her dead. I cannot fathom this."

Ilona paused, licked her lips, found that she was breathing hard, pulse loud in her ears. She took several breaths but she only inhaled the driver's sweat-stink.

"It was a large house," she said, as if words could dispel the human miasma of the cab. "I knew every room, door, hallway, staircase, every nook and cranny. But my knowledge went unneeded. I heard my father's deep, commanding voice ring out, 'No. The children mean nothing. I have punished her for her sin.'

"We fled the house through a secret passage we had discovered, eluding the officers that had cordoned off our block. But almost at once my sister and I were separated by the river of people on the English Embankment. I looked for her, more and more desperate. Crying, heartsick—she was my younger sister, I was meant to take care of her, but I couldn't. I didn't. Hours passed, then days. She was gone."

"And after that you never looked for her?"

Ilona shot him a glance. "I spent five years looking for my sister. Finally I realized there were only two possible outcomes: either she didn't want to be found or she was dead."

"That's some story," the driver grunted. "As good a fairy tale as I've ever heard. Except there was no knight riding in on a white horse to save you."

"I'm riding in," Ilona said. "On a white wolf."

His eyes narrowed and he shook his head. "Whatever that means."

"You know what it means."

He frowned, slowed the rig. "In any case, like all the best fairy tales it passed the time, didn't it? We're almost there."

Ilona stared straight ahead through the snowy windshield. "You know," she said in a conversational tone, "there are three types of people in my world. Those who avail themselves of my expertise; those who are eliminated by my assignments; and those who fear me, certain I'm the most dangerous human being in the world. The FSB fear me, as do the GRU."

Ilona drove the flat of her hand against the driver's ear. "Like you, you GRU pig." He gasped, his head recoiling. She reached over, broke his neck quickly and efficiently. The truck was already skidding toward the opposite side of the road. She did nothing to stop its erratic trajectory, rather, kicked open her door, sprang out, curling her body, so that she rolled across the highway, fetching up against an icy wall of cleared snow. Across the road, the truck and its dead driver careened into the snowbank, hitting it so hard it crushed the front end. The truck slewed around, flipped on the ice-covered highway, slammed onto its side, came to rest in the same snowbank in a hissing explosion of ice.

Picking herself up, Ilona started walking. Forty minutes later she arrived at the town. Gulls wheeled overhead and the oily bouquet of brine and fish was almost overpowering. She went straight to the port, sat in the darkest corner of the pub closest to the water, ate a plate of hot food, washed it down with a bowlful of steaming Russian Caravan tea into which she poured half a bottle of vodka.

She ate slowly, savoring each bite. She did not want to remember the last time she had eaten food that was cooked, and she didn't. Instead, she was briefly again immersed in her waking dream.

Sin. What sin could her mother have committed to turn her father into her implacable killer? Had she been having affairs while he was away? Had she stopped visiting the marital bed? What? What could it be, so awful it elicited a response that led to him shoot his wife dead?

No answers. Only her father had them.

Thirty-six hours later, she left Russia behind. Her Siberian incarceration was finally over. She had booked passage on a small merchant ship, its hold filled with sealskins and wolf pelts to be cured, worked into fashionable jackets and coats for wealthy Japanese women. The captain asked no questions of her, too entranced by the money she waved in front of his nose to care who she was or where she came from. It felt good to be free. It felt even better to be carrying the key to Marsden Tribe's new communication system. Safely alone now, she removed the teeth from the saddlebag she'd taken from her mount, held the two molars between her fingers. She had cleaned them of blood and shards of pink tissue. They gleamed now in the uncertain light of her cabin.

She hardly knew herself. No matter. She knew where she was going and what she had to do. Find her father. So far as she had been able to find out, some time ago he had been abruptly defenestrated from the

GRU—that was their term for made redundant. Something he had done had made him enemies—powerful enemies. He had either lain low for a while or left Russia directly. In either case, he was elsewhere now. Inside the Lubyanka she had been told where he might be found. Prison rumors were always sketchy but this one was the only lead she had.

6

SUMATRA, NORTHEAST COAST

Eighteen hours after she left Marsden Tribe's superyacht, An Binh was overflying the site of the villa disaster in a Parachute helicopter. The missile had done its work. Not a single wall still stood. There was nothing left but rubble.

As soon as the copter landed a man strode from the edge of the landing pad to stand beneath the rotors, grim-faced, lips pulled back from nicotine-stained teeth as if he were in pain. He scarcely allowed her egress, shouldering roughly past her. He swung a traveler's bag into the copter, climbed in after it, slammed the door shut. As soon as she was outside the radius of the blade, the copter took off, banked left, and quickly disappeared. Turning, she was greeted by another man, tall, with a big nose and bigger teeth. From the way he moved, the manner in which he greeted her, she instantly knew his type down to the bone. He was a human Malinois—loyal, smart, strong, lethal. Now, however, he was smiling with those big teeth, shaking her hand, welcoming her to the site.

"Cal Andrews." His hand grasped hers then let go. It was a big, square hand, with calloused fingers, dry and strong. He motioned with his shoulder. "Don't mind Philip. He used to be the head honcho out here. Just got canned over what happened. A major fuckup." He swept his arm out. "We're quite secure. Well, we were supposed to be airtight. The property is owned by a company unaffiliated in any way with Parachute or Mr. Tribe. The company's attorney made sure it has a monetary understanding with the police and local government officials."

"What about the sea side?"

"Ah, well, that's where ol' Phil fucked up. He thought he had it covered. He had one patrol boat. Boarded, four security guards killed, bilges opened, sunk shortly before the attack." They were picking their way through the periphery of the debris, heading toward the estate's entrance. "We've got three boats out there now, bristling with weaponry, I made sure of that first thing. We're covered on all quadrants."

"A little late for that," she said. Something about the diffidence of this man annoyed her. She didn't like him, had no qualms letting him know that. He might be top dog here now that the disgraced Philip had been sacked, but the moment she stepped foot on the villa's property he answered to her, in all and every thing. The sooner she made that clear to him the better.

"Do you want a tour of the grounds?" he asked deferentially. He'd gotten the message.

"I want to interview the guards—all of them, the ones who were on duty and those who weren't."

"I've got 'em all rounded up over this way," Andrews said as they circumnavigated the debris field, "but I already re-vetted them."

"I haven't." She glanced at him. "Any of them missing?"

He shook his head. "All accounted for."

"Any new ones brought on recently?"

"Nope. They've all been here for years."

"And what about provisions? Local vendors?"

Andrews shook his head. "Absolutely not. As long as Evan and the kid were here provisions were flown in from a trusted source once a month."

"Pilots?"

"Not employed by us anymore."

"So I can't interview them."

"I'm afraid not." A thin line of sweat had appeared along Andrews's hairline and he picked up his pace. The quicker to get out of the sun, she wondered, or to open up some space between them?

They reached one of the guard shacks at the entrance to the property. It wasn't much to look at—bare concrete blocks, thatched roof, an air of breathless waiting.

An Binh started asking questions of the men the moment she stepped across the threshold. Thirty minutes later she had satisfied herself, as Andrews had, that they were all innocent. None of them had had a clue of the attack. The ones who had been on duty were still in shock; she had to be particularly gentle with her questioning.

"Go on about your business of tagging and bagging," she told Andrews when they emerged into the brutal sunlight. "I'll let you know when you're needed." She parted ways with him, not looking back, not caring what he thought. There was no point in her poring over what they'd already tagged. She'd been to these kinds of sites before. There was nothing left at ground zero, never. But she also knew that they were required to go through the motions. It was pro forma.

She returned to the sea side. Picking her way down the embankment, she headed for the beach. The way was made treacherous by the ragged chunks of the concrete steps that had been blown in all directions. She required quiet, the solitude of the sea where it washed against the shore, the rhythm of life. After studying aerial footage of the villa and its surrounds for the entirety of her flight time, the last thing she wanted was to stand at ground zero, inside the destruction. What was required was for her to close her eyes, imagine the attack from outside the kill zone, to see the targets as their attackers saw it. Only then would she gain some knowledge of what had happened and why. An Binh's chronological age was somewhere around forty but in all respects she looked and felt a decade younger. Her body was a finely tuned engine. She did one hundred one-arm push-ups a day, fifty with each arm. She ran, boxed, spent at least an hour on her martial arts, cycling through them all each week. She meditated twice a day. In her mid-twenties she had taken eighteen months to travel to Nepal and Tibet, much of Indonesia, including Sumatra, gathering syncretic knowledge, medical and otherwise. She returned a changed person.

Now, having returned to Sumatra after nearly twenty years, on this remit from Tribe, she removed her rubber-soled shoes and socks and slowly lowered herself to the sand at the water's edge. With the sun beating down on her shoulders, the soft clack of the onshore breeze stirring the palm fronds, she almost reverentially closed her eyes. She struggled against the overwhelming emotions unearthed by her being back here where her younger self had lived, worked, loved, raged. She kept her breathing deep and even, tried to clear her mind of the dark memories swarming just beneath the surface of her mind, memories she had carefully packed away in the lightless recesses. Now that she had returned her mind fizzed, swirling with recollections of love and death. Tilting her head, she heard the cries of the shore birds just as Evan Ryder must have in the peaceful moments before the attack. As she imagined the attack itself—the whir of the drone, the scattering of the birds, the release of the missile passing like the briefest eclipse over Evan's head, followed by the percussive shock wave—her bare toes clutched reflexively, digging into the sand.

Finding something hard.

Perhaps a piece of sea glass, or the hollow claw of a crab long dead.

But, as she grabbed it between two of her toes, she thought not. A tiny shiver trickled down her spine as she lifted her leg, shaking the sand from a severed toe. Bending over, she took it into her palm for a closer look. The toe was from a young female adult, most probably the tutor Evan had hired for the child, but that was hardly the most interesting thing about it.

An Binh looked more closely at the ring encircling the toe between the top and middle knuckles and froze. Despite all her martial arts training her heart beat wildly in her chest, her extremities turned cold. She felt her gorge rise into her throat, burning it. She felt as if she was hallucinating, over-bright colors swirling at the periphery of her vision. In reflex she bent over, put her head between her legs. Her fingers trembled as she turned the severed toe. The flesh was blue-white, ghostly, but not yet bloated; the ring slipped off with minimal effort. Holding it up to the sun revealed the ring's shabby origin; but she already knew that. Sand and blood covered what she knew would be blackwood, silver, and malachite bands on the outside, and the gold color had already partially worn off the inside. She knew that, too. She knew everything about this ring; she had seen a thousand of these cheap imitation toe rings. She herself had been gifted with one of them once upon a time. And therein lay the truth, tamped down, shunted into a dark corner of her mind never to see the light of day. And yet here it was glinting brilliantly, in this sun-washed setting. She felt sick, overcome, diminished. The filth of betrayal upon her again.

She was sixteen, working for her father. He was a struggling trader in tea and Chinese herbs, always lacking the right contacts to whom he refused to kowtow. He was always in debt, on the edge of staving off poverty. He ran his business out of a shabby bamboo building behind the family living quarters in Yunnan province. Over two bridges and through the rosewood forest, a ninety-minute drive from the nearest town. Now, decades after she'd left, that town had become a sprawling city; there were no trees left, let alone a forest. Her ancestral home had been ruined by the greed and graft of developers.

She was just a file clerk then, learning the trade at her father's right elbow, but she was smart and quick, catching the occasional errors her father made. They were always skating on thin ice, in and out of profit, and what profits there were were minimal. Her mother, who was Vietnamese, had died of dysentery when she was four. Tears of sorrow but one less mouth to feed. Such practicalities were more than a way of life for them, they were a matter of survival.

On his blackest days, her father often talked about folding the business. She would drag him from behind his desk, take him walking through the acres of his beloved rosewood forest, breathing the pure air that was already lost in the town. He had turned down offers from loggers to sell his considerable acreage. Rosewood was increasingly in demand as the favored material for home furniture. After their meager dinner following their last walk through the forest, when her father brought up quitting again, she said to him, "But then there would be no income at all. We need to expand, not shrivel up and die." "To expand," he said, "we need money we don't have and never will." That was the end of that discussion and so things went along as they always had.

She knew the forest as well as he did. She had been seeing a young Malaysian man named Ramelan and in that forest at night they consummated their trysts. He was six years older than she was. Of course, she had kept their ongoing liaison secret. If he'd found out, she knew her father would send her away to her bitter aunt, who lived in the wild hills of Yunnan; as far as she was concerned, a fate worse than death. Whatever additional punishment he would find appropriate she had no idea. She didn't even want to contemplate it. And yet, she continued the affair.

To stoke her devotion Ramelan had given her a ring—a beautiful toe ring with precious materials on the outside, and real gold lining the inside, he had told her. He sported his signature wicked grin as he had slipped it over her toenail, settling it between the top and middle knuckles. She felt him there, a line of electricity from her foot to the place between her legs, where he doled out nightly pleasure that set her hips to rocking.

Not a month later Mr. Budi Khong, president of Far Eastern Distributors, appeared. A Malaysian businessman whose company was shrouded in mystery, he was obsessively desirous of the family's rosewood trees. Her father said no, as he had to all the other company representatives who had approached him. But Mr. Budi Khong was unlike any who had come before him; he refused to take "no" for an answer. Day after day, he returned to her father, offering gifts along with more and more money for the acreage, until the offer was so rich her father couldn't refuse it. "After all," her father said to her when she had asked him how he could sell his beloved trees, "with the money from Mr. Budi Khong we'll be able to expand, just as you suggested."

But Mr. Budi Khong was a venomous snake. The gold he paid turned out to be fake. Budi Khong's men, already on-site, had begun to saw down the best, most mature rosewood trees. And how did they know which ones to sever? She had told Ramelan during one of their trysts, when she was afloat in the afterglow of their lovemaking.

In the days to come, the scope of the disaster was made clear. The police and local authorities turned a deaf ear to her father's written objections, his strident vocal complaints. An Binh discovered that they had all been paid off by Mr. Budi Khong; that was the way of the world. She had known that but had never believed such corruption could exist in her own village. Stupid. Naïve. She berated herself endlessly. The rich ate the poor, took advantage of their helplessness, exploited them until they died of disease or exhaustion. She sought solace in Ramelan, poor like her, only to discover that he was a worse liar and betrayer even than Mr. Budi Khong.

On the morning of the day that he vanished into thin air as if he had never existed, she told him she was with child. Thinking this would cement their liaison into a more permanent arrangement, she had been grinning from ear to ear when she spoke the words that had set him in motion. He slapped her across the face, then punched her three times in the pit of her stomach. Eighteen hours later, with him vanished into the night, her father's deal gone bad, she had begun to bleed. Bad enough but then something no bigger than a clot of blood slithered out from between her legs, and she was done. She knew then the depths of his betrayal. He had never loved her, never cared about her, he had seduced her into telling him what his boss needed to know. The trees, the trees! And now they were being chopped down, one after the other.

Devastated beyond words, racked with guilt and agony, she crawled on all fours to her bed, passed out. Who had cleaned her? Who had changed her clothes? Who had tenderly tucked her under the bed covers, laid two blankets over her? She never asked, and no one ever said. For six days after the unspeakable event she was beset by cramps that doubled her over. On the seventh day they faded and she rested. In the weeks that followed, no one in the village would look at her. Every day her father visited her both before and after work, tending to her. She couldn't meet his eyes, let alone talk to him and, in any event, he was disinclined to speak to her, even to admonish her. Instead, she stared at the ceiling, the shadows drifting across the walls as morning dissolved into afternoon, dust motes dancing in the sunlight slanting in through the window—anywhere but his closed face.

Her humiliation was such that when at length her father summoned her she was so terrified of his wrath she vomited every last mouthful of her breakfast on the way from the family house to the company office across the compound. In the pit of her stomach pain like a fist—Ramelan's fist—doubled her over. She gasped for breath, scrabbled to hold on to a bamboo wall. Blood pulsed behind her eyes, momentarily blinded her. Moments later, with an extreme effort of will, she put one foot in front of the other, made her way to her father's office.

Whatever terrors she imagined waited for her did not, in fact, manifest to knock her flat on her face. Instead, her father, making no mention of her terrible sin, sent her to study with three renowned martial artist masters. Three years she spent with them, isolated when she failed, a single word when she achieved each of the goals they set for her. The training was rigorous, horrendously difficult, meant to either lift her up or break her spirit. She continued achieving until she was released, "graduated." By that time she had come to love her time with them, their esoteric teachings having sunk bone-deep, becoming the essence of her.

Upon her return, her father finally told her that he knew about Ramelan, knew how he had used her, betrayed her and him. Knew that he was working in secret for Budi Khong, the prospective buyer who had cost her father so much money.

At last, she understood her father's reason for sending her away. She was returned to him a sharply honed instrument of vengeance. Now, at the age of nineteen, he sent her across the water to northwest Malaysia, loosed her upon his enemy, Mr. Budi Khong. And what a job she did. She spent three days and nights closely surveilling the business and those who worked inside, discovered Far Eastern was distributing more than silks, herbs, rhino horns, and shark fins. The building was an opium warehouse. By muscle, garotte, knife, she swiftly and silently killed everyone inside, save two. How many? Once, perhaps she knew. Now it didn't seem to matter. Their deaths had become flashes, like a reel of film broken into pieces that no longer seemed to fit together. What did matter was Mr. Budi Khong and her former lover Ramelan.

At length she made her way to his office, the inner sanctum where Khong sat bloated and self-satisfied behind his vast, ornate desk, consummating another corrupt deal on his cell. Behind him crouched a large old-fashioned safe. Inside was FED's money, plus a treasure trove of valuables.

He tried to bribe her—of course he did. She shook her head, clapped one hand across his forehead, tipped his head back, placed the blade of her knife against his throat. He was a criminal, not a fighter. Thus induced, he knelt in front of the safe. He tried one last time to induce her to spare his life but he hurried to open it when the blade drew a line of blood across his throat. She directed him to clear out the safe, stuffing the stacks of bills, promissory notes, diamonds, and gold ingots into a thick plastic bag she unfurled from one of her pockets.

As for Ramelan, she had a special punishment in store for him. As he rushed into the office he skidded to a stop, so shocked was he to see her. Was it really her? She saw his confusion, eyes glassy, body paralyzed. She was upon him before he could aim his handgun. He wasn't much of a fighter, either, as it turned out. Minutes later, she had stuffed him inside the safe, closed and locked the door, but not before she had placed the toe ring he had given her on his tongue, clamped his jaws. She left with Mr. Budi Khong's throat slit and the building on fire.

Focusing her eyes, An Binh returned to the present, to the waves washing the shores, the palm fronds clattering, the sunlight making glittering diamonds of the sea's surface. The fake gold ring between her thumb and fingers. She held it up out of her own shadow into the sunlight. Using a fingernail, she scraped off the last of the sand and crusted blood. And there it was, unmistakable, the tri-banded exterior of blackwood, silver, and malachite.

Cal Andrews had told her that Tribe had gone to great lengths to keep this place a secret. And yet it had been infiltrated. And now she knew how.

Mia. The Malaysian tutor. She had been indiscreet. Someone had gotten to her. Just as Ramelan had gotten to An Binh.

A shadow fell over her. "Come to any conclusions?" Cal Andrews asked as he sat down beside her.

"Not a one," she said.

But the ring was warm inside her fist. She knew where this investigation was leading her.

7

For seventy-six days following his release from Ilona Starkova's terrifying prison, Nyurgun was as good as his promise to her. He was indeed taken in by his cousin, no questions asked, put to work in the nearby gold mine, owned by the vast conglomerate, Zavtryaz. For the first weeks he was terrified that the Russian soldiers would track him down and interrogate him about what he knew of White Wolf's escape, but as time wore on and no soldier even sniffed around, he felt he was home free.

Not that he'd been shown an easy path. His days were backbreaking, his treatment by his Russian overlords vicious. Case in point, he had come to the attention of Zig, one of the Russian overseers. How or why he would never know but it was clear from his first day of work at the mine that Zig despised him. Zig had the face of a hog and knew it. It was possible he despised himself more than he hated others, but someone had to pay for his unsightliness; it wasn't going to be him. Nyurgun was ripe for the position. As a Sakha he was considered less than a second-class citizen, a pack animal to work until his hands bled and his lungs were coated with metallic dust that would surely kill him within a decade or two.

Zig assigned Nyurgun to the worst part of the mine—the place where it was most unsafe, where just weeks before there had been a cave-in killing six Sakha workers, injuring a dozen others.

"You'll be cleaning out this debris," Zig told him. "All of it." He spat a yellow glob between Nyurgun's legs. "There's a rich vein of gold beyond it. We were almost there until you idiots caused the cave-in. Now you'll have to dig your way back." It didn't matter that Nyurgun hadn't been part of that detachment, Zig had chosen him as a scapegoat.

"By myself?" Nyurgun asked and knew that was a mistake as he took a hard backhand blow to his face from the Russian.

"You'll do as you're told." Zig struck him again, this time a fist to his midsection. Nyurgun doubled up, could not catch his breath. Stars sparkled at the edges of his vision.

"Shit," Nyurgun huffed, barely getting the expletive out.

"What was that, worm?" Zig's leg lashed out, his boot hooking around Nyurgun's ankle, sending him sprawling. "Who said you could speak to me, worm?" Zig stood over him, balled fists on his hips. "You look good there, worm. Dirt becomes you." With a booming laugh he spun on his heel, strode off, leaving Nyurgun with a splitting headache, pain in his stomach, blood trickling from the corner of his mouth. Moments later, he rose, using the heavy shovel as a brace, and got to work.

He couldn't afford to think about Zig now, let alone plot his revenge. In the wider scope of his life he was safe from those who were surely hunting White Wolf even after more than two months. How far could she have gotten in this endless ice-encrusted wilderness?

If the days were difficult and pain-filled, the nights were blessedly serene, filled with good food, lively conversation with his cousin, his boisterous wife, and two mischievous sons, shelter from the bone-freezing cold, and sound sleep.

In the deepest part of his slumber he dreamed of White Wolf, of her incandescent eyes, her scythe-like smile, her whispered words to him. Her touch against his skin like an electric shock. And why wouldn't he dream of her? It would have been strange if he didn't. But his dreams of White Wolf were not all erotic. In that sacred space of dreams he spoke to her. He asked her questions that vexed him and she answered them and everything became clear. The trouble was that when he awoke he knew they had spoken, remembered his questions, but her answers remained beyond his grasp no matter how hard he tried to retrieve them.

He missed her terribly. And with her in his mind he came to realize that he had exchanged one prison for another and there was nothing he could do about it. Was this to be his lot in life? That was one of the questions he asked White Wolf. She had answered—he knew she had. But her answer was torn from his memory by the chaotic gale of his waking life.

In this way, in dreary sorrow, the days bled into one another, the nights blurred into one long dreamscape, his one release from prison.

And then, as often happens with young men, a woman entered Nyurgun's life. Her name was Aya. He almost missed her. Had he not come up to the main level of the mine to give his lungs some temporary respite from the foul atmosphere lower down he surely would have, and his life would have plodded on as it had for so many days before.

She had traveled all the way from Oymyakon to the mine to give her father a spare pair of pants, the ones he had on having become thread-bare and borderline useless. As these things happen in fairy tales he saw her from afar and was immediately smitten. She was slender, tall—taller than he was—unusual for a Sakha, who tended to be short and wide. You could handle bone-chilling temperatures and the winds that swept the breath from your mouth far better if you were built low to the ground. She must have had a lot of Tatar blood in her, with her dark skin, and Asian, too, with her long, uptilted eyes, dark as a forest on a moonless night. And her movements! As if she were made of water. He was drawn to her like a moth to a flame. He crossed the filthy, crowded, stinking space between them. Nothing existed for him except her. When she spoke he heard temple bells chiming.

With an enormous effort he had gathered his courage to tell her his name. She told him hers: Aya. He was drowning in the pools of her eyes, but she looked at him as she did everyone else she spoke with: shyly, withdrawn, possibly (oh, how he hoped not!) disinterested.

"Do you want to leave Oymyakon as much as I do?" he blurted before he had a chance to second-guess himself.

There. Was that a spark in her eye? "I do," she said. "But no one else I know feels the same."

"Well, now you do," he said with a smile. His heart flip-flopped when she returned it.

"Will you be coming back here?" he asked her.

She wouldn't. Her mission to give her father a new pair of pants was a one-off.

"Will you be back in Oymyakon anytime soon?" she asked.

He did not know what to say, but three days later he was quits with this second prison; he set off for home. For Aya. He knew he was taking a chance. He knew White Wolf had told him to leave Oymyakon at once, to stay away. He knew she wanted to keep him safe. But he also knew that he would follow Aya to the ends of the earth if he had to. Luck-ily, he didn't; he only needed to follow her to Oymyakon. Her aura was such that he could not recall their conversation. What had she said to him? How did she answer his questions? It was just like his hallucinatory dreams of White Wolf—emotion swamping memory.

He felt cocooned with Aya, as he had with White Wolf in reality, as he did with her in his dreams. He would be safe; he knew he would. He was aware of the Russian soldiers, knew what to look for, knew how to keep out of their way. Also, it was now three months since White Wolf took him with her out of the prison. Surely the initial furor had by now dissipated.

In any event, he would be fine. And he'd be with Aya. That's all he cared about now. He had found his path.

At last, at last. He was free. Heading toward Oymyakon and Aya, clinging to the rear of a commuter bus with clawed fingers and toes, he began to understand the meaning of happiness. His heart leapt with joy.

8

A CONVERSATION AT 20,000 FEET

"Timur has been secured," Alyosha said into her encrypted sat phone.

"That's what you begin with? The boy?" Kata Hemakova said. "I don't care about Timur."

"No one does, apparently," Alyosha said dryly. "Except Evan Ryder."

"Is that so?"

"Joined at the hip." Alyosha stared out the airplane's oval Perspex window. They were still forty minutes out from Casablanca airport. Not that she would stay there for long; Morocco was just a way station on a much longer journey. "Well, they were. I put an end to that."

"You clever thing, you. You put Evan in her place."

"That's right." Alyosha unstrapped herself, stood up, and moved about the cabin. She was unused to taking public airlines but after their cabal's failed coup last year she and Kata Hemakova had been forced out of Moscow, out of the SVR, on the run for months, always looking over their shoulders. All the others were dead. She and Kata were marked. Agents had been assigned to find them and terminate them. How would it happen? she constantly wondered. A bullet to the back of the skull? Defenestration? Poisoned with Polonium 210? So many ways, so little time.

"Thoughts?"

Her lover's voice sounded hollow, harsh. She hated the encryption algorithms, which had a way of turning anything human into the inhuman. She closed her eyes, conjured up a mental image of Kata—who was not Kata Hemakova at all. She had defected from the United States as Bobbi Ryder, Evan's sister, but had quickly made a name for herself in the SVR. When she had murdered the real Kata, up until that moment the SVR's most feared assassin, she had taken Kata's name. Kata hated her sister for reasons Alyosha knew she would never pry out of her.

"Ways we'll die," she said.

"Unproductive. We're beyond the point of no return."

"You're right, of course." Alyosha glared at a flight attendant approaching her down the aisle. On these public flights you couldn't fuck with these people. But she had a work-around. She was unrecognizable as the woman who had confronted Evan Ryder hours ago. She wore her hair long, the wig the color of warm chestnut. Under her suit was a body-changing layer of padding, on her feet inexpensive men's brogues, suitably scuffed. Colored contacts turned her irises from pale blue to a dark gray.

"Alyosha?"

"A moment." She waited until the flight attendant was close enough to open her mouth preparatory to a scolding until she flashed her bogus air marshal ID, discreetly of course.

When she was alone again, she resumed the conversation. "Look where this life has led us."

"Kusnetsov was brought down by hubris," Kata said. "He climbed too far, too fast."

"And now all the remaining old guard—the wiliest ones—are back in place with even more power. The Sovereign's death meant nothing. The new Sovereign has made sure the political climate back home is worse than ever."

"I am used to this," Kata said. "Being an outcast, living in the shadows, on the fringes of society."

"But we have so few of our own people," Alyosha said softly. "And how much can we trust those new recruits?"

"But we have resources," Kata reminded her. "The Chechens are bankrolling us. You must learn to trust them."

But Alyosha's mind was elsewhere. "We must be so careful not to admit a mole into our ranks."

"You let me take care of that. My vetting process is foolproof."

"Nothing is foolproof, *moya lyubov',*" Alyosha said as gently as possible.

"Which is why we have mounted this operation. Evan Ryder will get us what we want, what we need."

"And if she does not?"

"That will mean the White Wolf has eaten her alive."

"And if Evan succeeds?"

"Then I kill her in front of Lyudmila Shokova's child."

"So either way she's on a suicide mission."

"Precisely," Kata said.

There was a short pause while Alyosha digested this news. Kata had not told her before she set out, of course she didn't. Like all missions in the field intel was divulged on a need-to-know basis. "She insisted on a daily proof-of-life," Alyosha said now. "She needs to know the boy is alive and well."

"I would expect nothing less. Make sure she gets what she needs." There was a hesitation that became an awkward silence. At length, the voice started a thread, tangential but, Alyosha suspected, vitally significant. "So tell me, how does she look, my sister?"

Alyosha licked her lips. She was dreading this moment. "Quite striking. In fact, the two of you look somewhat alike." The moment she said it, she knew she had made a mistake.

"We look nothing alike." Kata's voice snapped like the end of a whip and Alyosha winced. She knew better than anyone Kata's volatile nature, especially when it came to her sister. She could be cruel, heartless, even, but that was okay with Alyosha; Kata's particular volatility drew her like an insect to a globe of heat. Kata was strong—the strongest human being Alyosha had ever come across. She bathed in the halo of that strength, deepening the shadows that dwelled deep inside her.

"Still," Alyosha said carefully, "it would be best not to underestimate her."

"And yet you got the best of her."

"I did," Alyosha acknowledged. "But only because she has a weak spot now."

"The boy."

"Yes."

"The son of Lyudmila Shokova." There was bitterness in Kata's voice. "Will that fucking bitch never die? Even after her demise part of her lives on."

"A part that gives us the edge we need against Evan Ryder. We are incredibly lucky."

Kata huffed. "Luck had nothing to do with it. Planning. Meticulous planning." This was an attribute she had learned from Lyudmila Shokova, though she would bite off her own tongue rather than admit it to anyone, even Alyosha—especially Alyosha, who adored her, worshipped her as a kind of dark goddess without flaws, whose power and resources came solely from within herself. To reveal otherwise was to damage that shining image beyond repair.

9

Two years ago: Two women met in Istanbul, kissed in the European fashion, briefly stared into each other's eyes, touched foreheads in private celebration of their reunion.

"*How is your first year with Marsden Tribe?*" Lyudmila Shokova asked as Evan settled beside her.

"*You know how it went.*"

"*Ah, yes. But underneath. Where even angels like me are blind.*"

"*He likes me.*"

"*Ah.*"

"*Nothing has happened.*"

"*Yet. Watch out for him.*"

Evan nodded. "*You didn't call this meet to find out how Tribe and I are getting along.*"

Lyudmila's hand covered Evan's, squeezing it with some urgency. And Evan thought, she's vulnerable. For the first time since she disappeared from Moscow she's vulnerable. A quicksilver shiver of fear lanced through her.

"*We're friends,*" Lyudmila whispered, leaning close. "*More than friends. Sisters under the skin.*"

"*Of course we are.*"

Lyudmila lowered her voice. "*You're the only one I can trust, Evan. Everyone else . . . I've been walking a tightrope of lies for so long . . . There's no one else. Because I've never lied to you.*"

Evan felt another shiver of fear . . . fear for her friend.

Lyudmila's pale eyes glittered. "*The Sovereign assigned a certain GRU officer, once captain, now major, to track me down and kill me. As to why, it's a story old as time.*"

"*She's the Sovereign's mistress?*"

"*One of,*" Lyudmila said. "*Her name is Juliet Danilovna Korokova. But in any case it won't be easy. She's a very nasty piece of work.*"

"*You know her?*"

"By proxy only."

Evan considered for a moment. "So. Another thing I must know. How tightly is Korokova bound to the Sovereign?"

"She is Khadive," Lyudmila replied. "Velvet, directly translated. But not its meaning. In the parlance of the Ottomans she is his favorite." She seemed uncharacteristically unsettled. Maybe, Evan thought afterward, after it was over, Lyudmila had at that intimate moment caught a glimpse of her demise.

It was because of Korokova that Lyudmila was dead. Evan had not been able to get to Korokova in time. But she had meted out justice, retribution. Found it wasn't enough. Lyudmila was gone forever.

But her son, Timur, was alive—and out of Evan's reach. Only Evan could save him. And she would, she had promised herself that the moment he had been taken away from her by members of Alyosha Ivanovna's cadre aboard the Malaysian pirate vessel. She loved him. Though love came neither easily nor often to her there was no doubt Timur had settled firmly under her skin as, she supposed, her own child would have.

Her newfound vulnerability terrified her. The field was no place to spend your life when you loved someone so much—someone with all of their life ahead of them. She found herself clutching her seat arms so hard she could see the bones beneath the skin. White-knuckled though the plane ride was perfectly smooth.

■　　■　　■

By the time she landed she was all cried out.

When, bundled up in the cold-weather clothes that had been provided for her, she stepped off the old Soviet commuter plane into Yakutsk, the capitol of the Sakha Republic, the diamond-hard practical part of Evan's mind was done with grieving for Lyudmila. It was as if the sweet balm provided by her time in Sumatra with Timur had never happened. She had to get on with her mission. Timur's life and her sanity depended on her success; she could not bear to lose him. But she was also aware of a secret part of her, buried deep, that would never stop grieving. She and Lyudmila had killed for each other, protected each other, lied for each other without ever lying to each other. They had bled together, vowed eternal fealty, worked together for mutually agreed goals all the while pretending they were sworn enemies. Theirs was the quintessential platonic love affair. A unique broad-spectrum bond she knew could never be repeated, and so while she met the arctic chill with slitted eyes and ice-coated lashes she had no choice but to acknowledge the inner abyss opened inside her by Lyudmila's death. A tremulous space that would accompany her to the end of her days.

She spent several hours walking the town's streets. Once, she stepped into a hardware store, made some purchases, asked for directions to the nearest hunters' provisioner. There, she selected two items before she felt ready to continue her hunt.

On her twenty-hour journey along the Road of Bones to Oymyakon via a truck that looked more like a military-grade vehicle, she reviewed the new identity Alyosha had provided for her. According to the official documents she carried she was Sofiya Mikhailovna Rostova. Her profession was mine inspector, which according to the intel supplied her gave her the widest latitude for being wherever her investigations might take her. How Alyosha had had the passport made was a mystery best left for solving after the mission. In any event, after studying it meticulously, she discovered that the image of herself was AI generated, which explained how quickly the passport had been assembled.

Ice, snow, permafrost, low ugly cubist structures built strictly for practical purposes. Here and there the familiar onion domes surmounted by black cast-iron crosses marked the churches. There was nothing aesthetically pleasing about this industrial city, seemingly dominated by ethnic Russians. On the periphery, slender smokestacks streamed clouds of sooty smoke and noxious gasses, clouding the already dimming afternoon sky with swaths of oily gray. The air vibrated with a sharp metallic tang that clung to the back of her throat like a coat of varnish. She drank from a bottle of water to take the taste away, but it was no use. It stuck to her mouth with frightening tenacity.

Outside the environs, however, stands of Siberian dwarf pines marched majestically over hills and ranges, halted briefly on the high banks of rivers frozen solid, only to begin again on the opposite side. Eight Sakha, riding on reindeer, passed, heading in the direction she had just come from, perhaps bringing wares into the city to sell. Here and there, among clumps of arctic willow, she noted signs of arctic foxes, little pawprints delicate as ballerinas on pointe.

Her thoughts turned to White Wolf. How much of what Alyosha told Evan was a lie? Alyosha was an expert liar, that much Evan had gleaned from the occasional microaggressions that crossed the Russian's face faster than a heartbeat. Were she not trained, Evan would have seen only a stoic countenance, stony eye contact, giving away nothing.

Where was Ilona? Where had she gone when she had broken out of her state-of-the-art prison here? Where would she go? No one knew; no one knew her proclivities, her mind. Nothing. Scouring her previous hits and kills there wasn't a single thing that stood out or was repeated. She did not, so far as Evan could tell, have a defined MO.

Evan had pondered these questions long and hard during her seemingly endless, tortuous passage here. How had White Wolf gotten from the middle of nowhere to wherever she was now? Could she have managed it on her own? There was yet another possibility: what if White Wolf was still in the vicinity? What if she had gone to ground, waiting for members of the SVR or GRU who must be here to get tired of searching for her, to move on, leaving the field clear for her to make her escape complete?

Oymyakon at last, after mile after crunching mile, two brief pit stops, passing eight abandoned cars, looking like dead beetles, their front ends crushed into the ice along the side of the road. Long, looping skid marks punched into the icy roadbed. How long had they been there? The driver had no idea. No interest, either.

Oymyakon, the coldest town on earth. Population: five hundred frozen Sakha souls.

Following the GPS directions on the sat phone Alyosha gave her, she had the driver drop her in front of a house. Evening had come down with the absolute sharpness of a knife cut. Blue shadows in the street, the sheen of ice frosting the deep snow drifts. The village houses were built in the traditional Sakha style: one-to-three-story wooden structures, log walls laid horizontally, not unlike American log cabins, but with steeply pitched roofs of thatch or shingles held up by tall, slender richly carved pillars. There was a Sakha man wrapped in animal skins and furs waiting for her. She nodded to him but his browned face remained stoic. He was narrow-hipped, narrow-shouldered, thin as a stalk of wheat. He held out an outsized hand and she produced her fake passport. He opened it, looked at her, then at the official stamps, then back up at her. He held out the passport and she pocketed it.

"You know my name," she said in Russian. "I'd like to know yours."

He squinted at her. "You're Russian. What d'you care?"

"I'm Chechen, actually."

He grunted. "Chechen, huh?"

"That's right."

"And what brings you to our little patch of paradise?"

She laughed. "I'm here to enforce the many violations at the mines."

Now it was his turn to laugh. "And you a Chechen. And a woman. They'll eat you alive here."

She took a step toward him. "By 'they' who do you mean?"

"Elley," he said, when she grasped his outstretched hand. It was huge, square. It enveloped her hand.

"I'm delighted to meet you, Elley."

"Come in before you freeze to death." He indicated a nearby pillar. Like most, it was intricately carved, beautiful on all sides. She followed him through the thick wooden door, carved like the pillars inside. The insulated house was all wood inside; a gleaming staircase led to the second story. The rooms were large, ill-defined spaces, sparsely but comfortably furnished in a utilitarian manner. A fire was burning in a vast tile fireplace. They took off their outer garments, Evan hanging hers on wooden pegs next to Elley's.

She sat at a trestle table, clearly hand-hewn, while her host made tea and prepared a plate of frozen fish. The tea was strong and biting, the first sip burning down her throat.

"Slivovitz," Elley said, clearly amused. "One hundred twenty-five proof."

Evan, eyes watering, cleared her throat.

"Mother's milk to us." Elley gestured at the food. "Plus, it'll take the taste of the frozen fish right out of your mouth." He sipped at his laced tea, swept his arm out to take in the interior. "I'm a fastidious man, as you can see. A place for everything and everything in its place."

There ensued a small silence. The flames crackled as they ate the logs in the fireplace. The interior smelled of smoke and cedar. At that moment, the phone Alyosha had given Evan vibrated. Evan excused herself, crossed the room, thumbed on the call. She watched a short video of Timur. He spoke into the camera directly to her, saying he was being treated well. He sounded like himself. There appeared little sign of stress in his voice or facial expression. There was no warmth in his voice, either. Tears welled up in her eyes, burning her cheeks as they overflowed so that she had to wipe them away in order to see clearly the date of the newspaper he held up. The video cut out so abruptly it took her breath away. She was reminded in the most painful way how much she missed him. In the video he looked more like Lyudmila than ever before. Evan's heart ached, a pain in her chest as if a stone was lodged there, a weight that she knew would be with her until she found him and freed him from his captors.

She made sure her eyes were dry, the tracks of her tears scrubbed away before she rejoined Elley, who sat, waiting patiently.

"So," he said almost as soon as she sat back down, "you aren't really here for the mines."

When Evan made no reply, he went on. "I sincerely wish you were. Zavtryaz is bleeding us dry."

"Zavtryaz is the 'they' you referred to earlier."

Elley nodded. "The company owns all the mines in the area—gold, silver, diamonds. Zavtryaz is sacrosanct. No one can touch them."

"Oligarch owned."

"Possibly. Probably. But for certain wired into Moscow central. The GRU presence is here because of them. Their numbers doubled because of the prison that is not supposed to exist." He shrugged. "No one knows who the owner of Zavtryaz is. At least not around here. Whoever it is, is amassing a fortune."

He sipped at his alcohol-laced tea. He didn't touch the fish; neither did Evan. He put his cup down. "So then." Hands flat on the tabletop. "Why do you need the use of one of my reindeer?"

Evan blew across the top of her tea. "Were you not paid enough not to ask questions?" She did not need to see Elley's expression turn sour to know she'd made a mistake.

"If that's what you think . . ." He dug in his pocket, drew out a white envelope, thick with bills. His eyes grew small, hard as diamond. He pushed the envelope toward her, but she reached out, stopped him when the envelope was midway between them.

"I misspoke," she said softly. "Elley, listen to me—I misspoke. This is what I meant." She dug out a roll of American dollars, flattened them, placed them atop the envelope. "In my opinion, you weren't paid enough."

They both withdrew their hands and there the money lay—his and hers—a mountain between them. Or a river to be forded. Whether they could find a bridge or shallow water was up to him.

He rose, crossed the boards to a freezer, took out a bottle, frost twinkling like stars along its side. On the way over he gathered up two shot glasses. Sitting down opposite Evan he uncorked the bottle of Beluga Gold Line. Evan recognized it as an ultra-premium Siberian vodka. She'd shared many a bottle with Lyudmila over the years. It was a favorite of theirs.

Elley filled both shot glasses, held his up. Evan lifted hers.

"*Zdorov'ya,*" she said.

Elley echoed her and they drained their glasses. He immediately filled the glasses and they drank again. After the third shot, he set his glass down on the table, reached out for the envelope and the US dollars to him and pocketed it. A bridge, at least.

He looked her in the eye, said, "Now we understand each other, yes?"

By way of answer, she poured them more vodka and they drank. Elley rose, stepped over to the fireplace, stood with his back to her, hands clasped loosely behind his back.

"There's a reason I ask," he said after a time. Then he turned to face her. "For the last three months or so there has been quite a large step up in GRU activity in the area. Not that they're not always buzzing around, but more in the background. And there's more of them than I've ever seen."

He gave her a shrewd look as he came back to the table, sitting down opposite her. "Their activity wouldn't have anything to do with you, would it?"

"How could it?" Evan spread her hands. "As you could see by the stamp on my passport I just arrived today."

Elley leaned forward, elbows on the table, hands clasped in front of him. "But, see, the thing is I know where you're going—where you must be going, since you actually have no interest in the many violations at the Zavtryaz mines." He spread his hands. "There is only one place that could be of interest to you, Sofiya Rostova. Or whatever your real name is."

"My name is S—"

"Yes, yes. Name, rank, and serial number," he said dismissively. "That's what you tell to the enemy, no more." He cocked his head. "Why do you cling to your cover story when I can help you?"

"Can you?"

His eyes grew small and dark again. "I just said I could."

"Mm. I wonder."

"I'm not your enemy."

She felt herself step out onto the edge of an abyss. "I'm not Chechen."

"No surprise," Elley said. "I don't think you're Russian, either."

When Evan made no reply, he said, "All right. Let's leave that."

Evan set aside her glass. The fish, starting to thaw, was beginning to stink. "Why would you help me? Especially with the place crawling with GRU personnel."

"It's precisely because this place is crawling with these vermin that

I very much want to help you. I believe whatever you're up to will hurt them. I don't have the power or the wherewithal to hurt them, but I think you might."

"I'm flattered," she said.

"No reason for that," he growled.

"But, to be honest, I don't need your help. I have detailed instructions—"

"Without my help those instructions are sure to get you captured, beaten, and killed."

"You can't know that."

"Oh, but I do. The situation here has changed in just the last twenty-four hours. And I ask myself why. The only answer that makes sense is that the Russians know you're here."

"But it sounds like they've penetrated my alias," Evan said. In the field you were never safe, never completely protected from the enemy. They could obtain intel about your movements in any number of ways, especially these days. But here, now, if Elley was right, it would mean that Alyosha or someone in her group had sold her out to the GRU. This revelation brought home to her as nothing else that she was in the midst of the fog of espionage. She no longer knew who was on what side, if she ever had. Did Alyosha want her to accomplish her mission or did she want Evan captured, tortured, imprisoned for the rest of her life? Unanswerable questions. All she could do now was put one foot in front of the other, advance into the darkness that lay ahead.

"Whatever your instructions," Elley was saying now, "they're out of date. They won't protect you, of this I am certain."

"But you can."

"I have stated this."

Evan took a breath, let it out. "And if I agree?"

"Then I will take you to where you want to go. I will ensure you get inside."

"How could you know where I am headed?"

"There is only one place that would draw someone such as you here."

"Yes?"

"The prison. We all knew about the breakout three months ago. News like that travels at the speed of light here, despite the Russians' attempts to keep it secret."

Evan paused to assess the situation. In the last five minutes the rug had been pulled out from under her not once, but twice. She should have been better prepared. The year with Timur in Sumatra had sanded down all her sharp edges. Surely, she would be killed or captured unless she could hone those edges back.

She nodded, coming to a decision. "All right."

"Good." Elley lifted a thick forefinger. "There is one thing."

Of course there is, Evan thought. *What is a bargain without quid pro quo?* "Let's hear it."

"I have a niece, my brother's only child. She's as dear to me as if she were my own daughter." He heaved a sigh. "Somehow she became tangled up with a boy—someone, it seems, the Russians have been looking for."

"Why?" Evan asked. "What do they want with him?"

"He was involved in the prison break."

"What?" She was genuinely surprised. Did Alyosha know of this intel? If she did, she had neglected to pass it along to Evan. "How?"

Elley shrugged. "No one knows. Beyond his name—Nyurgun—no one knows a thing about him, other than he's an orphan."

"No other family?"

Again, Elley shrugged.

"How is that possible?"

"Given what he was into, I doubt anyone was too keen on learning anything that the GRU fucks could extract from them."

"And your niece—"

"Foolish girl, she fell in love with him. Now both of them are in the hands of GRU interrogators inside that fucking prison the Russians built."

"What's her name?" Evan asked.

"Tell me yours, first."

"It's Evan."

Elley nodded. "Aya. Her name is Aya."

10

"Frankly, I don't know what you see in her."

Marsden Tribe looked into gemlike topaz eyes, sighed. "Not for you to know, Miranda. I do not want you wondering about Evan Ryder. You have much more important matters to occupy you."

"She enticed you out into the field with her. You could have been hurt, even killed. Then what would we have done? Where would Parachute be? The war would instantly be lost."

"One matter especially," Tribe said, ignoring her.

They were in the superyacht's vast master suite, in the middle of its king-size bed, the silk sheets rucked around their bare legs. Each time either of them moved even a fraction the sheets whispered and slid like water off rocks. The curved mahogany walls, polished almost to a mirrorlike surface, peeped out between glass cases in which were housed Tribe's astonishing collection of artifacts from ancient civilizations. Apart from a vase from Carlo Scarpa glassworks and a pair of Qing Dynasty porcelain jars, the collection leaned heavily toward Roman and Etruscan armor and weaponry, all immobilized against the vicissitudes of the sea. Of course this was only a small fraction of Tribe's collection, housed in his many residences and offices. But all of them, in every space he called his own, were meticulously aligned, perfectly spaced one from the other. And symmetrical: the cases, the number of occupants, left wall the same as the right wall. Tribe loved symmetry, except when it came to war. Then it was asymmetry all the way.

"It's not just me." Miranda stroked his chest with her long, lacquered nails. She knew the precise amount of pressure to apply to stiffen him. "No one who has met her likes her."

Tribe grasped her wrist, pulled her hand, her insistent nails, away from him. "What they don't like, what *you* don't like, is her proximity to me. You think she crowds you out, that you've slipped down the totem pole."

Miranda shook her head. "She's managed to crawl inside your mind, Marsden. You have given her too much leeway. You give her far too much credit."

"I witnessed what she can do in the field. I saw with my own eyes—"

"That's where she seduced you. When she was with you in La Palma— the sun, the surf, the swaying palms. You playing at being James Bond. Who wouldn't be seduced? Even you—*especially* you."

"Explain yourself."

"You believe Evan Ryder is special."

His eyes blazed. "I know it."

"All right. She's one of a kind, a rarity in your world, wouldn't you say?"

"I would, yes." His voice had turned dark and silken, a prelude—but to what she didn't know. Nevertheless she plowed on.

"Take a look around you. Cases filled with precious artifacts from all over the world."

"I'm a collector."

"One of the world's premier collectors," she said. "Has it ever occurred to you that maybe your collector's mindset is what's underlying your . . . mm . . . what amounts to your obsession with Evan, that she's just another precious thing for you to possess. What you call her 'specialness' is simply another trophy—a specimen, one might say—for your collection."

He struck her then, an open hand across her cheek. Perhaps he hadn't meant to, perhaps it was a matter of if not instinct, then a sense of self-preservation—more accurately the preservation of his image, his exalted status. But this was also—he knew this deep in the recesses of his mind—because she was right. He wanted to possess Evan just as he wanted to possess Ilona, the White Wolf. They were both unique. He was drawn to them like Icarus to the sun. But unlike Icarus he did not have wings of wax.

Miranda's cheek went from white to bright pink. To her credit she made no move to touch the place where he struck her, to show any weakness whatsoever. Tribe despised weakness. Weakness led to distrust. Distrust led to, well, whatever it was she didn't know, didn't want to know.

Tribe glared at her. "Do you really want to continue your diatribe?"

"It was hardly a diatribe." Her voice was no more than a whisper. "It was another point of view for you to consider."

He laughed. "Now you're selling your jealousy as an actionable point of view? Really?"

She moved away from him, pillows supporting her back and neck, their coolness reassuring. "My reason, Marsden—my *only* reason—is to protect you."

"Not Evan supplanting you here in this bed."

"What you find so compelling about Evan Ryder is that she takes you away from a place you don't want to be."

He snorted. "What? You mean the here and now?"

"Because here and now there's a possibility you might fail."

"I don't fail at anything. Ever."

"And yet you failed with Evan. Unlike me, bound to you, she stepped into the web you spun for her, then stepped right out again. Your obsession is for an object you can't have. And you know why she eludes you, Marsden. Because she knows who she is. Unlike you, who only know what you aspire to be."

At that moment one of Tribe's twenty-seven cell phones buzzed. Sliding out of bed, he picked up the one vibrating, stepped out of the room, closing the door behind him.

■　　■　　■

In the bathroom down the corridor, he switched on the shower, making sure the dial was turned to cold water; he didn't want steam interfering with this call. He instructed Quinton to switch the call to the laptop he had brought with him, along with *Sun and Steel*, the Yukio Mishima book he was reading in the original Japanese.

He sat on the closed toilet lid. "Quinton," he said, "you're on."

"As you wish, Marsden," the agentic replied.

Quinton toggled on the receive button. "Hello, Mike," Quinton said in a perfect imitation of Tribe's voice. "How are you?"

"Busy," Parachute's vice president of communications said as he looked at a perfect facsimile of Marsden Tribe's face perfectly synced by Quinton to his part of the conversation. For all intents and purposes Harrison was speaking with Marsden Tribe. Only he wasn't. "Time is my most precious commodity."

"I hear you," Tribe replied, Quinton knowing instinctively what the call was about.

Harrison chuckled. "Except Daedalus, your astounding communication system, Marsden. The demo you gave me last week is still reverberating."

"That is inspiring, indeed, Mike."

"You're a stone-cold genius, Marsden. I'm happy as hell I'm in your inner circle." When Quinton made no reply, Harrison cleared his throat. "Now when can I expect that shipment? I'm all set up here, raring to put Daedalus into the field."

"You see how he uses 'I' instead of "'we.'" "I love your enthusiasm, Mike. I really do. The teeth have already been manufactured, tested, and packaged for shipment."

"So what's the holdup?"

"I am merely adhering to the guidelines of shipment."

"Well, the sooner Daedalus is deployed the better, Marsden, you know that."

"I've got to wrap this up," Quinton interpreted, *"before the convo gets away from me."* "Security must be absolute. You know that, Mike."

"Absolutely airtight, yes, of course. That's paramount. I don't want those goddamn Chinese hacking units to get wind of what we're doing. And God forbid the Russians get their hands on Daedalus."

"Exactly," Quinton said. "Therefore, the shipping method requires alternate routes utilizing anonymous forms of conveyance. Of necessity, such absolute security takes time. Please be assured the shipment will be on its way within twenty-four hours."

"Good. I'm sure you'll keep me informed so I can have my people ready and waiting."

"Every step of the way, Mike. You have my word."

During this conversation, Tribe was immersed in *Sun and Steel* while at the same time monitoring Quinton's side of the convo.

"Well, that went well," Tribe said when the video call ended.

"He's something of a schmuck," Quinton replied in the voice Tribe had given it, a combination of Winston Churchill and Alistair Cooke.

"Massive." Tribe snapped the book shut. "Better for us, eh?"

"I would say so, Marsden."

Time, Tribe thought, *to get back to dealing with Miranda.*

He was at the bathroom door when Quinton said. "I could bring her back, you know."

Tribe froze. "What are you talking about?"

"You could see her on that screen," Quinton said. "You could talk to her. It would be just like it was. Better, even, because I—"

"No, it wouldn't."

"But of course it would. I would ensure it. You'd never know—"

"Stop." Tribe was still staring at the door. There would be nothing to see. Just an unfathomably complex algorithm pretending to be something else, something more. "Don't ever mention her again."

"As you wish, Marsden."

He pushed on, away from Quinton. But you could never really be away from Quinton, could you? Not anymore.

∎   ∎   ∎

Miranda stopped playing Wordle the moment Tribe stepped back into the bedroom. By this time, she was used to Tribe's absences during their time together; he was an exceptionally busy man. He set the cell down precisely in its place amid its brethren. "I'd like to make something clear," she said, picking up where they'd left off. In the shadows her eyes took on a deeper hue. "I'm not jealous—well, okay, I am jealous, but not of her being in your bed. And if I am jealous it's because I'm concerned she's living rent-free inside your head."

Nikki once said to him, "*Never confuse strategy with tactics. This is where the smartest men go wrong. Strategy is your long-term plan. Tactics are the methods you use to achieve that plan.*" And she was right. As always. One of the things he loved about Evan Ryder was her brilliant use of tactics to secure her strategy. The other thing he loved about Evan was that she reminded him of Nikki so strongly it made his heart hurt when he was with her. No one knew this, not even Miranda—especially not Miranda. She was far too clever to be let in on even the most benign of his secrets, let alone his most intimate. It was unsettling enough how much Evan reminded him of Nikki. But perhaps even more so was that Quinton had sucked up all the video and audio of Nikki without his consent. But that was the downside. "*Everything has a downside,*" Nikki had told him. Even an agentic.

One of his many cell phones buzzed. He picked it up from the bedside table, read the text. Considered a moment, made a quick call. Then he turned to Miranda. "You're needed elsewhere. The copter is fueled and standing by. Pack lightly; you won't be staying long."

He showed her the text. She scanned it, raised her head. "Doesn't Phillipe handle this?"

"This shipment is different. It needs you to shepherd it. You'll be joining Lena."

She paused, trying to ascertain his state of mind. Failing, she continued more softly, though only a touch less forcefully. "So you trust me."

This response seemed to have wrong-footed him, she could see it in his eyes. It was as if they clouded over for just an instant. Then he was back to his normal full throttle. "I'm surprised you have to ask."

"And yet I *am* asking."

"Isn't my entrusting you with this assignment proof enough? Of course I trust you."

"And you trust Evan Ryder as well."

"I do."

She took a breath, let it out slowly, to give her some time to stoke her courage. "Well, I'm just saying there might come a time when you can trust only one of us."

She quit the bed. "And then what will you do?"

11

KAMPUNG PASIR PANJANG, MALAYSIA

Kampung Pasir Panjang was mostly a coastal community, spread along a wide scimitar swath of beach along the Malacca Strait, where swimming and fishing were the main activities. But less than a mile inland was the actual, modest, and rather unlovely town of Pasir Panjang. And there, the three-story headquarters of Far Eastern Distributors occupied a full square block. The bland, blocky building was not the company's original home, of course; An Binh had burned down the old one some twenty-plus years ago. And no one who ran and worked for the company was original either, of course; she had killed all the original ones, including the president, Mr. Budi Khong and the man who had betrayed her, Ramelan, whom she had consigned to Budi Khong's enormous safe.

Few people were in the lobby, all seated in chairs along one wall, presumably waiting for their names to be called for their appointments. The space was air-conditioned to tundra level. A shocking contrast to the thick tropical heat outside. An Binh made her way to the front desk. She wore lightweight black trousers, an old T-shirt of the same color, emblazoned with the words FLOWER POWER in psychedelic script across the chest. On her feet were what appeared to be ballet slippers, the difference being the toes and heels were steel-shod under the black leather covering.

The young, bland-faced man behind the desk looked up from his computer monitor. "Yes? How may we help?" He was tall, slender, androgynous, with the face of a jackrabbit.

"I'm looking to buy a toe ring," An Binh said.

"How many?"

"One."

The man scowled. "We are wholesalers, madam. Do you represent a company?"

Sure, she thought. *FuckYouSoMuch-dot-com.* What she said was the first thing that came into her head, "Wagyu Enterprises."

The man sighed. "Do you have a card?" He meant a company card she could hand him.

"I have me," she said. "That should be enough."

The man's gaze returned to his computer screen. "Good day, madam."

"Please allow me to finish," she said.

"I already allotted more time than you're worth." The man did not even look up at her.

"You don't understand." She produced the toe ring that had belonged to Timur's faithless tutor, placed it on the desktop. "I already have one, you see. I need another to match it."

The man's brows drew together. "So why come here?"

"Look on the inner surface, if you please."

The man gave her a passing glance. He looked more than ever like a jackrabbit. With a sigh, he drew out a jeweler's loupe, picked up the ring, looking first at the interior. "Pah! The gold is already worn off here, and here, and—" His voice faded out as he switched his scrutiny to the uniquely-banded exterior.

"That banding look familiar?" An Binh asked in her best little girl voice.

All the man's bodily movements had come to a complete stop. If An Binh's senses weren't so acute she might have thought he had ceased to breathe. He cleared his throat. "Where did you get this?" he asked, again without looking at her.

"I already allotted more time than you're worth," she said, echoing his own words. His head snapped up, his eyes small and piercing. He stood up. "Wait here."

But she snatched the ring out of his hand before he could stride off. "The ring stays with me," she said.

The man looked like he was going to snap at her, then for some reason changed his mind. He shrugged instead. "Your funeral." Then he was off, crossing the lobby, heading through a door on his left that needed a code to open.

For the moment, An Binh was left alone. Men came and went, some looking like legitimate businessmen, others, with their dark, glowering stares, not so much. Their degree of sketchiness would have been somewhat alarming had she not known Far Eastern Distributors' real business. Still, she could not help being impressed. By the physical plant alone it seemed a certainty that FED's business was booming. Whoever had taken over for Mr. Budi Khong was a shrewd businessman.

She had just enough time to note that she was the only female in the lobby, when the man she had spoken to returned, a sour look on his face.

He hooked a thumb over his shoulder. "That way," he said curtly, and sat down behind the desk before she could reply.

She looked toward the direction indicated, saw another man, larger, broader, standing in front of the door to the left. His bull neck, slightly spread stance, the way he held his hands at his sides, fingers just slightly curled caused the hair at the back of her neck to stand up. Crossing the lobby, she stood before the brute.—

"Arms up, legs apart," he said in a voice like a dead man—lusterless, without affect.

She complied, watching him closely as he patted her down for, she supposed, concealed weapons. He left the inside of her legs for last, his slab like hands rising up her inner thighs. When he reached her crotch, one hand curled around her belt, the other rubbed against her while he looked at her with a salacious smirk.

"You like that, do you?"

She wrapped her fingers around the wrist of his offending hand. "Off," she said softly.

He grinned. "Whatever you say." He curled his fingers, feeling her, then removed his hand.

Now that she was thoroughly humiliated he turned his back on her, unlocked the door, using his body to shield the entry code from her. Up close, she could see that the door was made of metal. She intuited, therefore, that it was more than likely bulletproof. In FED's line of work you could never be too careful.

Beyond the door, she stepped into a dimly lit corridor. The floor and walls were rough poured concrete. There were doors on either side, all open. No windows. It smelled of mouse droppings and an unpleasant alkaline odor that might have been animal urine. The corridor seemed to her more like a tunnel, the air heavy, damp. She could see the corridor's end a good way ahead. Cheap fluorescent tubes buzzed above her head. One of them flickered like the heartbeat of a dying bird.

During their walk along the entire length of the corridor she felt an unpleasant tingling at the nape of her neck, as if the blade of a guillotine were about to fall on her. The brute in front of her said not a word. In fact, he might have been entirely unaware of her presence. This she found even more disturbing than the physical oddity of the echoless corridor itself. She glanced into each doorway they passed, glimpsed large numbers of wooden crates. Some of them were open, high-end electronic components showing their shining faces. One room held what looked like an industrial walk-in freezer.

"The boss likes his food," the brute muttered as if to himself. "Maybe a little too much."

At length, they reached the end. Another metal door requiring a security code to open. The brute stood aside, waved An Binh through. In the dimness she could make out an enormous space—a warehouse filled with stacks of wooden crates in neat rows, at least a dozen to a row. Beyond, there seemed to be a horizontal line of lighted windows ten or twelve feet in the air bulging out from the rear wall. An overseer's office of some kind, she suspected.

"Well, go on," the brute commanded. "This is what you want, no?"

The threshold was the choke point, she knew, the place where if something were to happen it would. She entered mind-no mind, emptying herself of expectation, doubt, fear. Asserting the power of pure will, she went into *prana*, the slow, deep breathing required for instant response to physical attack.

As she crossed the threshold she could feel the brute's presence a step behind her, so close he might have been her shadow. She could scent the film of sweat on his forehead and cheeks, but she sensed no tremor of intent. That came from both sides, two more brutes to her right and left, one tall and heavy, the other short and heavy. They stepped toward her and she did nothing. Nothing at all. Still as a statue, she let them into the radius of her defense. Then from absolute stillness to blurred action. Her raised right forearm deflected a powerful blow from the guard on her right. Her right heel struck the instep of his leading foot, fracturing a welter of bones. Grabbing his head, she slammed it down on her rising knee.

Whirling, she grabbed the shirtfront of the guard on her left, wrenched his torso to the right, smashed her steel-shod heel into the side of his leading knee. It cracked, he went down, grabbing his knee, breath whistling through his clenched teeth. The toe of her shoe caught him in the throat and he was done.

She was jolted backward by the brute's hand at the back of her collar. His free arm came around, a knife slid crosswise toward her throat. But she had already lifted one of her arms, positioned it between the blade and her throat. Clutching his forearm, she pushed back against his superior strength. It was a losing battle. But that was all right; it was drawing him closer behind her in order to increase his leverage. That's what she wanted; the brute close as possible behind her for when she slammed her head back. The satisfying crunch of cartilage as his nose was crushed, the hot spurt of his blood out of his slitted nostrils. The strength went out of the hand gripping the knife. She wrested it away, turned and pushed him back with her forearm. Off-balance, he went down on one knee. A swipe of the knife blade to the back of his knee severed tendons. He keeled over, face a knot of pain.

She bent over him, grabbed his crotch, squeezing. "You like that, do you?" she hissed in his ear, echoes of humiliation. His mouth opened, teeth bared. Blood was everywhere.

She left him like that, heading into the warehouse, the rows of crates rising on either side of her as she stepped silently down the narrow aisle between them. She had with her the weapon the brute had used against her—a gravity knife with a wicked blade. She also had picked up from one of the guards a steel rod that with a flick of the wrist extended into a two-foot baton. From here on out stealth was her best friend so no guns, though she did relieve the guards of theirs, tossed them up onto the top of one of the stacks.

As she picked her way toward the row of lighted windows at the far end of the warehouse, she moved from aisle to aisle. There were six of them and she used them all. She encountered nothing but shadows, dust, the smell of motor oil drifting up from the forklift like mist at dusk. The forklift was parked in the far left-hand corner. She encountered no one. At the end of the aisle she found herself on the far right. In front of her, just to her left was an iron staircase up to what looked like a cabin bulging out from the rear wall like a cyst. A brief recon confirmed no one was about. She climbed the stairs, the unfurled baton held before her, the brute's knife tucked into her waistband.

The door had a wide wooden frame around a single glass panel. Through it, she could see a row of metal filing cabinets along the right-hand wall, two desks side by side to the left. A young man, bald, thickly bearded, sat at one desk. The other chair was unoccupied. No one else seemed to be in the office. Reaching out with her free hand she opened the door, stepped through. The bald man, his back to the room, appeared totally absorbed in whatever was on his computer monitor. She coughed softly

He raised his head, swiveled in his chair to look at her. "So you have arrived, after all," he said, in an unexpectedly deep voice. "The door at the far end of the filing cabinets." That was all he was going to say, apparently, as he went back to staring at his monitor in precisely the same position in which she had found him when she entered.

Moving carefully, An Binh passed behind him. Sure enough, where the cabinets ended she found a door. With her hand on the knob, she turned to look over her shoulder. The overseer—if that was what he was—seemed to have forgotten she was in the office. His attention was wholly on the monitor.

The knob turned. The door wasn't locked. It swung inward and she stepped into her past.

12

I've always thought there was something verstohlen *about him.*

Who? Çelik? If you thought he was furtive why did we go into business with him?

Kurt Çelik has the contacts—furtive, shifty, criminal—we require.

I thought you had all the contacts, Tribe.

Listen, von Kleist, my contacts are legion. They're also legit, or mostly so. I— and certainly Parachute—do not venture into those shadows. Far too risky. You and I understand the need for legality.

Absolutely.

Right. Kurt Çelik does not. Which would all be well and good if he wasn't pushing to get our communication devices out the door.

What's the rush?

Apparently, he has entered into a deal with the Russians. He provides our devices directly to the Federation troops temporarily stationed in Odessa. They have a cadre of dentists standing by to do the implants and away the troops go into Ukraine territory, directed, in communication without the enemy the wiser.

But neither you nor I authorized this deal.

Bingo!

We wouldn't. It's morally—

That shipment has been promised and paid for elsewhere.

I hadn't been notif—

Kurt Çelik has overstepped his remit, which was to open the lines of distribution and like the djinn who lights the way grease those lines.

So he's about to send the Russians product he has no business sending them.

I have no wish for the Russians to have my Daedalus communication tech.

Is this why Çelik isn't part of this conversation?

Çelik has neither the tattoo, nor the Daedalus teeth.

So he's a worker bee without knowing it.

That's the way I set it up. I never trusted him. I don't want him using the Daedalus himself.

So we're stymied, then. We need Çelik but he's about to fuck us.

He won't do it alone—he's too smart for that. Before that shipment is delivered to the Russians he's going to contact you—call a meeting of two.

He'll try to entice me over to Team Çelik.

He needs your high-level international business contacts. In his mind the two of you will be more than a match for me.

Foolhardy.

Fools are reckless—and worse, unpredictable; which makes them dangerous.

13

SAKHA REPUBLIC, SIBERIA

They set out under cover of the arctic night. Elley led the way, his lean torso straight as a military veteran astride his reindeer. He was armed with a ball-peen hammer, an X-Acto knife, a spade-head telescoping shovel from his well-appointed home workspace. Evan would have found those "weapons" amusing if it weren't her guide sporting them. In this too—his choice of implements—she had to trust him. As they emerged from the house, Elley had tossed a little bag of frozen nuggets to Evan. She paid him what she had been ordered to. Obviously considering the transaction complete, he handed her the reins of the reindeer.

As it turned out it wasn't that different from riding a horse. She spent some time with the animal until it got used to her. She let it look her in the eye, fed it a handful of the nuggets. They smelled bad but the reindeer gobbled them up as if they were candy. Maybe to the animal they were.

She mounted the reindeer as she would a horse, standing at its left side, grabbing its neck with her left hand while she swung her right leg up and over the blankets that served as a saddle. The reindeer settled almost immediately. Slapping the reins and using her knees against its flanks, she set off behind Elley. A three-quarter moon slivered the banks of snow, reflected in the sheets of ice, a trail of spectral streetlights.

"This much moonlight will put us in increased danger of being spotted," Evan said as she pulled her reindeer up alongside Elley's.

"I wouldn't worry," he said dismissively.

And sure enough within twenty minutes the moon was extinguished by vigorous clouds of snow, driven down from rolling cloud cover. Evan pulled the hood over her head, adjusted her goggles for a more comfortable fit. The way forward was now a gray shroud; it was next to impossible to discern whether they were even on the road down which they had been traveling. It was clear she was at Elley's complete mercy. Without him as guide she would have been completely lost, would have had to turn around, if she could even find the correct direction. Her phone was of no use even if it had GPS service installed, which it didn't. All she could do was receive her daily proof of life from Alyosha's people and answer calls from her of which there had been none so far. Otherwise it was useless. Still, the sight of Timur's face, the sound of his voice, brief though it was provided a tiny spark of comfort. He was alive and well. He wasn't being mistreated. Something to hold on to while she made her uncertain way through the darkness.

The world closed in on them, as if they were traveling down an endless tunnel. Sometimes, when the snow was at its heaviest, the tunnel contracted but it never grew wider. Once, the snowfall became so heavy she lost sight of Elley and his reindeer. She felt the icy whiplash of panic at the edges of her reasoning mind. Slapping the reins, she urged her mount to a faster pace and almost ran headlong into Elley's reindeer before she jerked the reins to come alongside Elley once again.

Not only did the snow obliterate any sense of movement it also affected time. Despite her best efforts Evan had little idea how long they had been traveling. Hours, surely. But how many? The only sense she had of the passing of time was the unearthly cold, its grip perfectly solid, slowly seeping through the seams of her thick coat and furred headgear. Her extremities felt near to freezing. She wondered how she could shiver and sweat at the same time, as if she were in the midst of a terrible flu.

"Tell me about what it's like in the mines," she said, her voice fracturing the windowless monolith of the storm.

"You would have to ask my brother that," Elley said. He seemed perfectly at home in this sopping hellscape.

"The way you spoke of Zavtryaz I thought you worked at the mine."

Elley shook his head, causing eddies of snow. "Most of my family, though. My brother has black lung disease. Our father asphyxiated in a cave-in when his crew was forbidden to dig through to save him. They had to call in GRU to make his buddies stand down. Then there was my uncle whose legs were crushed by a machine that had needed fixing for over six months. He killed himself shortly thereafter." He took a breath. "I owe my family everything. My father gave his life so I wouldn't have to follow in his footsteps. He forbade me ever to set foot in a mine of any kind. It was his savings that allowed me to buy into my construction company and to finally take it over. As for my brother, his family is now my family. I made an oath to take care of them, protect them. I have to bring Aya home safe and sound or die trying."

Evan leaned over. "I'll make sure that doesn't happen."

"I believe you are sincere otherwise I would never have agreed to take you." Elley sniffed. "And toward that end I feel comfortable letting you know that my company provided the bulk of the basic building materials for the prison."

Evan's heart began to race, thawing her insides. "So you know—"

"I know what I know," Elley said flatly. "You will see soon enough."

"You asked why I'm here," Evan said.

Elley grunted. "The prison, yes?"

"No." Evan took a deep breath, a mistake as ice seemed to pierce her lungs like tiny knives. She coughed, tried to catch her breath by slowing her breathing, in and out. Elley watched her with careful eyes but said nothing. "I don't care anything about the prison," she continued when her lungs had recovered sufficiently, "only as it pertains to the prisoner."

This caught Elley by surprise; his eyebrows raised. "You know the prisoner?"

"Her name is Ilona Starkova."

Elley shook his head; he'd never heard of her.

"She calls herself White Wolf."

"White Wolf I know of but . . ." Elley's frown was dark, almost oppressive. "White Wolf was a legend."

"Was?"

Elley nodded. "As the story goes, during its last years the turbulence within the KGB produced an officer so ruthless he rose through the ranks like a hot knife through butter. According to the legend this officer went by the name White Wolf. Apparently, he was cruel to excess, reveled in the pain and misery he and his cadre caused."

"A sadist of the first rank. What was his real name?"

Elley shrugged. "No one knows."

"Well *someone* had to know—several people, actually. His superiors."

"Sure, sure." Elley nodded. "But recall this is a legend. One of many told about those last years before the KGB was reorganized into the FSB." He shrugged. "Did White Wolf actually exist? Your guess is as good as mine." He looked ahead. The curtains of snow had been transformed into veils as the storm began to blow itself out in the permafrost wilderness beyond where Ilona Starkova's prison supposedly lay.

"As to this Ilona Starkova," Elley went on. "No one around here knew a thing about her. If they somehow did you can bet they're buried somewhere out there." He nodded ahead.

"There's the teenager who prepared her meals. A local boy. Ah, of course, this is the boy your Aya got herself involved with. The one she's now imprisoned with."

"Nyurgun, yes. So you're here for him." Elley eyed Evan. "You think maybe he has a clue as to where Starkova is, yes?"

Instead of answering directly, Evan took a parallel track. "Elley, there is another boy being held prisoner. The only way to free him is by finding White Wolf, either killing her or bringing her back to my son's captors."

"So." Elley let go a breath. "You have a son. A family."

"Timur. He is my family. He is my child; his birth mother, my best friend, is dead. Before she died she charged me with his welfare, his happiness. His life." She reached out, grasping her companion's forearm. "Elley, in all likelihood I will never give birth. Timur is my son in every way except blood."

Elley nodded gravely. "So we are bound, you and I, by sacred oaths. The immediate imperatives of our lives, yes?"

Evan nodded. "Yes."

From this point forward, they rode in silence, connected by that silence, by the thoughts each of them carried in their minds, in their hearts. Slowly, the snowfall, nearly exhausted, drifted softly without purpose. Shortly thereafter, Elley called a halt.

"From here," he said, "we must go on foot."

Evan tried to peer through the curtains of snow. "So we're here."

"Nearly, my friend." Elley dismounted. "Nearly."

They tied up their mounts to the trunk of an ice-crusted pine, gnarled and twisted by the weather's violent extremes. Evan turned, about to set off when Elley took her arm, held her back. He stood very close to her, spoke into her ear to ensure his voice would not carry.

"This prison. It's a labyrinth inside. People say. Myself, I don't know, never having been inside. I don't know anyone who has. My niece is in there, being held like the Minotaur.

"You know the myth of Theseus and the Minotaur?"

Evan nodded. "The Minotaur is at the heart of a clever labyrinth on ancient Crete."

"But Aya is not the Minotaur. She's more like Ariadne, let's hope, laying down a thread that will lead us through to her.

"But you have your own labyrinth waiting for you, Evan. At the heart of it is a woman with the head of a wolf, yes?" He didn't wait for an answer; he wasn't expecting one. "But unlike Theseus, you won't have an Ariadne with her string of glittering jewels to help you escape. I can only go as far as the prison; I can get you inside. Hopefully, I can help us get to Aya and Nyurgun. Beyond that, your future is unknowable." The wind shifted. He squinted through a sudden snowfall from the top branches of the pine. "Tell me, does this White Wolf know you are pursuing her?"

"I don't see how," Evan said.

"That is not an answer, my friend." He squeezed her arm. "You see what I mean. From this moment on you must be very careful." His thick forefinger tapped Evan behind her ear. "Eyes in back of your head, yes?"

She clapped him on his snow-covered shoulder. "Always."

"Then let's get on with it."

They began their trek through the new snowfall, high as their calves. "You won't see the prison even when it's in sight," Elley said. "We sheathed it in Mylar-wrapped titanium over foot-thick reinforced concrete. Quite a job getting the specs right."

"Where in the world did you get a wrapping like that?"

"Imported from BriteBar Metallwerks in Germany. I have no idea how the Mylar was bonded to the titanium, but I can tell you it won't ever peel off, not even in these harsh conditions. Never seen its like before. It's kind of a miracle, if you ask me."

The snow had finally moved on, leaving in its wake a curious fog, dense, damp, as if summer had abruptly arrived out of season. Evan, listening intently for GRU soldiers, heard nothing, then gradually something came to her, a soft almost rhythmic exhalation, as if the fog or something within it was alive, was trying to speak to her. A shiver crept down her spine like a trickle of sweat. She opened her mouth to ask Elley if he heard what she did but in that moment it was gone. Absolute silence had returned. Elley, apparently unaware, led them forward until Evan spied two red eyes burning through the fog. They waxed and waned, as if the creature was blinking at them. Then as they crept closer she realized the red "eyes" were the ends of cigarettes. Emerging out of the mist, two guards stood side by side smoking, chatting. Their voices, muffled by the fog, were indistinguishable both in tone and in words.

Elley silently signaled this was the front of the prison, though, as he had warned, Evan could not distinguish it from its surroundings. Again Elley signaled, they headed left, around the side of the prison. Here, as they passed the corner's edge, it was possible to make out at least partially the outside of the structure.

Moving closer, she removed her glove, put her hand out, swiped it against the metallic skin. To her surprise, it felt neither hot not cold. When she glanced at Elley, he shrugged, whispered, "As I said, a miracle, yes?"

Evan blew on her cupped fingers before slipping the glove back on. Whoever was running BriteBar Metallwerks were way ahead of their competitors. It also surprised her that a German company was doing business with the Russian GRU, but of course there would be a legitimate business fronting for the army intelligence service.

They moved silently along the left side of the building. Evan kept one gloved hand on the surface, testing for any sign of a door, but she didn't come across so much as a join. Improbably, the entire side seemed to be one continuous sheet of mysteriously treated metal.

At what point Evan became aware that Elley was counting his footsteps she could not say, but shortly thereafter he stopped. Pulling out the spade-bladed shovel, he telescoped the handle, began to dig at the base of the wall. Without being asked, Evan got down on her knees, scooped the loose snow away from the hole Elley was making. He dug down to precisely the depth of the new snowfall, then joined her in scooping the snow away from the wall. At length, a metal square revealed itself. A thick metal ring was set into one side. Reaching down, Elley pulled the ring and the square hinged upward,

"This was how the food was delivered to Nyurgun inside the prison," Elley whispered. "This way, whoever brought the daily requisition never was allowed inside. Nyurgun never even caught a glimpse of them."

"Ingenious," Evan replied.

Elley nodded, pointed to the opening. "It's a chute. We need to go in headfirst to ensure we don't get stuck."

"What are our chances?"

"The dimensions were made for boxes, not humans. But this is the only way in without being assaulted and shot by GRU guards."

Elley went first. Evan watched as he divested himself of his furred skins, held them in front of him as he slithered headfirst down the chute, then she followed him, bundling her thick coat in her hands. The chute was round rather than square, the better to ensure box corners wouldn't get hung up. Evan drew her shoulders in, legs tightly together, arms outstretched as if she were about to dive into a pool. Using her elbows to propel herself, she inched down the metal tube. Her progress continued unimpeded until she came to a curve. The chute arced to the left, precipitously downward, probably to accommodate a quirk in the prison's infrastructure. But what was perfectly fine for the food cartons wasn't for the human body. Evan was obliged to turn on her side, bending her torso to accommodate the curve. With her arms and head through and angled sharply down, her knitted sweater stuck at the shoulder on the top of the chute where a seam was poorly joined. With her arms in front of her she could not get to the sweater. She tried pulling her shoulder in toward her chest, almost dislocating her scapula in the process. She tried shrugging off the sweater but she was still holding her coat and there was no room. She cursed herself for not thinking to take off the sweater before she entered the chute. But they had been so eager, in such a rush not to be caught outside the prison. She looked ahead. No sign of Elley. She returned her concentration on herself but no matter how she turned or twisted she could make no progress, nor could she back out. She was stuck. She stopped wriggling, calmed her body, calmed her mind. Still stuck.

"Elley," she whispered.

Nothing. No answer. Had he abandoned her? Was his entire story a lie? Was he undercover with the GRU? No. No, impossible. She was sure of it. But why did he not answer?

She was about to call again, louder this time, when she felt her coat and gloves being pulled away from her. Moments later, rough fingers entwining with hers. Then he had hold of both hands.

"Relax," he whispered. "Relax . . ."

Slowly but surely he drew on her arms, pulling ever so gently. Her body, relaxing, elongated. That was enough. The sweater ripped free. She rounded the curve, slid agonizingly slowly down the chute.

A brightness ahead assured her that she was nearing the end of the chute. And then she was out, tumbling head over heels. Only to come up on her knees. Elley faced her, also on his knees, stripped of his outer garments. His hands clasped behind his head, an expression of pain and humiliation on his face. Standing over them were a pair of GRU soldiers, their big, bulky automatic pistols aimed at them. They were Udavs, noted the part of her brain trained to absorb every detail of her immediate surroundings, the newest model using heavy cartridges.

"Hands over your head!" one of them shouted to Evan.

She obeyed.

14

KAMPUNG PASIR PANJANG, MALAYSIA

Incredibly, An Binh found herself back in Mr. Budi Khong's office—or at least an astonishingly accurate reproduction, down to the large black safe. The safe crouched in a corner behind Budi Khong's desk. She looked at it more closely and realized it was not a reproduction. It was the original. The fire she had set that raged through the original building had left its mark on the safe in black shadows of the flames that had once consumed it. The fire had burned so hot that it fused the door shut, but all these years later it looked ragged, forlorn, something kept for what it represented, not because it was useful or lovely. No one had ever opened it and seen what she had put inside. Clearly, no one had an inkling what had happened to Ramelan.

She stood stock-still, her gaze cemented to the safe, while inside her head a whirlwind of memories and emotions arose. She felt again the betrayal of the man still curled inside, the pain, terror, and humiliation— the horrific *aloneness*—of her miscarriage. The horror of seeing that red thing slither out from between her thighs. Tears facing a blank wall, trying and failing not to think of what had befallen her. Ignorance, stupidity, naïveté—her burden to carry. Until she had mastered the rage ravaging her psyche. Until she learned to master every muscle in her body. Until she learned the secrets of mind-no mind, taught her by the martial arts masters her father sent her to.

Now, in this moment of extremis, her own personal tsunami rose up in front of her. She was almost undone by the sight of the safe in which she had entombed Ramelan forever. Seconds seemed like minutes, minutes like hours as she was hurtled back into her dark past. But then, her training reasserted itself, stronger than any memory, stronger than any emotion.

Strangely, she saw the figures last. There were two of them—a man and a younger woman. The man sat behind the uncanny replica of Mr. Budi Khong's oversized desk. His hair was black, long, and straight, gleaming with pomade. Since he was facing away from her that was all she could discern. The woman, sunk into a rattan chair far too big for her, was an altogether different story. She sat with her legs drawn up under her. In her left hand was a book, which it appeared she had been reading before An Binh's entrance. The cover and title was in plain view: *Heart of Darkness* by Joseph Conrad, one of An Binh's favorite Western authors. In fact, she had read *Heart of Darkness* so many times she could quote from it as if she were a nun with her catechism. Without taking her eyes off the two figures, she kicked the door closed, reached behind her, locked it. She would tolerate no more guards coming at her with batons and knives.

"The Director of Companies was our captain and our host," she said, quoting the beginning of the novel's third paragraph. *"We four affectionately watched his back as he stood in the bows looking to seaward. On the whole river there was nothing that looked half so nautical. He resembled a pilot, which to a seaman is trustworthiness personified. It was difficult to realize his work was not out there in the luminous estuary, but behind him, within the brooding gloom."*

The woman rewarded her with a faint smile while, to her right, the chair behind the desk creaked as its occupant swiveled around to regard her with suspicious eyes beneath a wide brow that resembled nothing so much as Budi Khong's. *His son, then?* Ah Binh asked herself.

Leaning forward, elbows on the desk, his hands spread palms down in front of him, he said in a voice like nails dragged over cement, "There's nothing I like less than a girl educated beyond her station."

The statement fell upon An Binh like a whiplash, as it was meant to. She decided not to mention the woman reading Conrad. Why get her involved when this was between her and Budi Khong's son? There was a time for retaliation but only after you had caught the measure of your opponent.

"My name is Budiharta Khong, An Binh," the big man said. His arm swept out. "And this is Diti, my sister."

"You know my name."

Budiharta nodded. "Indeed. Your actions were crucial to my sitting where I am now."

Her muscles tensed.

"Oh, yes. You murdered my father and all my brothers. Diti and I were lucky we were out fishing during the time of your assault." A smile spread across his face like marmalade on toast. "Imagine the shocked expression on our faces when we returned home to find the business engulfed in flames."

"No one left alive," Diti said in a voice as soft, as sensuous as satin. She was small, thin, well-muscled. Dark-skinned, with pale eyes, high cheekbones, a wide mouth with full lips. She had a way of forming those lips into a moue that reminded An Binh of Lo, the main character in Nabokov's novel. *Lolita*. Her hair and clothes added to that image: hair parted down the middle, braids on either side, lightweight cotton shorts, a T-shirt with an incomprehensible logo emblazoned on the front. "Bar-bequed," she said and, to An Binh's surprise, meant it. She wondered whatever happened to family allegiance.

"I was not the eldest son nor was I the most business savvy," Budi-harta said. "My older brothers were designated to take my father's place at the head of the business table. You changed all that in a matter of min-utes. I salute you."

"And yet," An Binh said, "you grew your father's business even fur-ther, into this sprawling enterprise."

"Are you here to claim your piece of my pie?" Beneath the layer of bantering tone there was a clear vein of menace. "Well, you can forget that. We have deep pockets. We are everywhere. We have partnered with Sybirsk Associates. A canny deal I negotiated myself."

"I couldn't care less about your pie," An Binh said. "I'm here about the ring."

"Ah, yes, the ring. Perhaps you would put away your weapon?" He nodded toward the metal baton. It was still in her left hand, its bludgeon-ing end lifted higher than its hilt, which she gripped tightly.

"Perhaps you will be good enough to show yourself fully," An Binh responded.

"But of course." Budiharta rose, came around from behind the desk. He was big—bigger than his father. His face was like a blob of suet, cur-rents for eyes. Tiny ears, flat to his skull. He bore no resemblance to his sister. He held his hands open, palms outward to show his benign intent. His fingers were like sausages about to burst.

An Binh shot Diti a glance. Acutely aware that she hadn't moved, she stowed the baton at the small of her back, sliding it into the waistband of her pants. She had not yet shown them the gravity knife and didn't intend to until or if its use became a necessity.

"Now." Budiharta clapped his hands together. "To business, eh?" He smiled with all the warmth of a python. "You have one of our toe rings." He held out his hand. An Binh had no other option; she dropped it into his palm.

"Mm," he exhaled, holding it up to eye level. "Yes, it is ours, no question." The ring vanished into his fist. He eyed An Binh. "But you don't want another, do you?"

When she made no reply, he went on. "I want to know where you got this. A friend of yours, maybe, hmmm?"

"She's dead," An Binh said. "I took this off her toe." A squeak from Diti as she stirred in her chair, her legs visible now. They were long; they would provide her stature. "It was the only thing left of her."

"That's a pity," Budiharta said without an iota of human emotion. His eyes narrowed. "You knew her, this girl?"

"Not a girl. A young woman. And no, not at all," An Binh said. "I never met her."

"And yet here you are handing me her ring." He opened his fingers, bringing the ring back into the light. "A ring—especially one such as this, a toe ring—is an intimate piece of jewelry."

"Mia would never have taken it off," Diti blurted. "You must have killed her."

An Binh's eyes cut to Diti; that's where she intuited the soft spot to be at least as far as the dead woman was concerned. "She was killed, Diti."

Diti started at the use of her name—the intimacy of it. Making An Binh's words personal—a eulogy, of sorts, rather than a dry report. She was off her chair now, her eyes wide and staring. Standing, it was surprising how much of a presence her slim body projected.

"Murdered," An Binh went on. "Blown to pieces, to put a fine point on it." She saw what she was looking for in Diti's face. "That toe, blue and bloodless, skin partially flayed off by the force of the explosion." The girl was close to breaking. "Scarcely identifiable as human, Diti."

Her eyes sparked as she whirled on her brother.

"Hatti!"

"Lies. All lies!" Budiharta said, though like a burr caught on a sleeve An Binh could hear the note of doubt in his voice. "This is nothing but—"

"You know I'm not lying, Diti," An Binh said softly. She sensed a potential ally in Diti, though she could not be sure. Nevertheless, she took a step farther into the dark. "You knew her, didn't you?"

Diti opened her mouth to answer. Budiharta glared at her and she subsided. *Deflated is more like it*, An Binh thought, intensely interested. She had yet to get a grip on the siblings' interpersonal relationship.

The young woman turned away, facing the wall.

Her brother took a step toward An Binh. "My sister isn't part of this. I don't know what you're up to, trying to drag her into it."

"She's here, isn't she?" An Binh said. "She's made herself a part of it."

Budiharta glared at her. "Why have you come here? What do you really want?"

"I had a ring just like the one you're holding, the one worn by the murdered girl."

"Yeah?" He shrugged meaty shoulders. "So?"

"So it was given to me by Ramelan. Remember him?"

A shutter came down behind Budiharta's eyes and stayed there. "You knew—" He stopped himself abruptly, began again on a slightly different tack. "Why would Ramelan give you one of these?" He opened his fist again to show the toe ring. He had been gripping it so tightly its imprint left a red circle on his flesh.

She turned to Diti. "Why do you think?"

Diti seemed to shudder. She still had her back to An Binh. When she spoke it was merely the ghost of a whisper. "Why?"

An Binh leveled her gaze at her. "He also gave me a baby."

The bombshell hit the siblings equally. Diti whirled around, eyes wide and staring. Budiharta's mouth quirked in a kind of unconscious spasm of pain.

"Ramelan," he said. "I haven't thought of him since—"

"The baby." Diti interrupted him. She faced An Binh fully. "What happened to the baby?"

An Binh felt rather than saw the danger, moving her hand to where the knife was hidden. *Not yet*, she told herself. *The threat is not yet imminent.* Once again she had no intention of giving away her advantage unless it became absolutely necessary.

"I misspoke," An Binh was careful to keep her voice without inflection. "The baby Ramelan *almost* gave me." She kept her attention on Diti. "It slipped out of me unformed."

"Ah," Diti sighed. "Ah."

"So there were no . . ." Budiharta cleared his throat. "No consequences."

"No consequences?" An Binh kept her eyes on Diti. "No consequences to me?"

This brought Diti a step closer, a murderous look in her eyes. An Binh's muscles tightened. "And Mia? Did you kill her?"

"I told you," she said softly. "She was killed, in a drone strike."

Diti's eyes narrowed but she said nothing.

"The curious thing," An Binh went on, "is that the Malaysian pirates launching the attack used an Iranian-made drone. A very expensive drone." She turned to Budiharta. "You wouldn't know anything about that, would you?"

He spread his hands, a form of ritual gesture, An Binh noticed. "Why would—?"

But Diti interrupted him. "You told me Mia was simply on a reconnaissance mission. You swore to me she would be safe."

"I protected her as long as she was here." Her brother's tone was sanctimonious. "But once she left for Sumatra . . ." He shook his head. "In any event, her family has been well compensated."

"Tell me," An Binh said, "what is your going rate on a human life?"

"A question best left to accountants and bookkeepers," Budiharta said. "But tell me, An Binh, why have you come here?" He tossed the ring up in the air, caught it, tossed it again, higher this time. An Binh noticed Diti's eyes following the vertical path of the ring. She never seemed to take her eyes off it. "It's surely not to buy another ring like this one."

"Why would I?" she said. "I am not your company spy."

The big man's brow furrowed. "What do you mean, 'spy'? Make your meaning clear or leave. I have important matters that require my attention."

"There's nothing more important than this," An Binh said. "My ring came from Ramelan. He was a spy sent by your father, Mr. Budi Khong, to gain knowledge of my own father's struggling business, to assess how willing he might ultimately be to selling his precious rosewood trees."

"I know nothing of this," Budiharta said in a strained tone that undercut his words.

An Binh ignored this lie. "Mia was sent to Sumatra—to where two guests were staying in Marsden Tribe's villa. She was sent by your company specifically to infiltrate the villa."

"Mia wasn't supposed to be injured!" Diti cried. "Hatti, you promised she would not be put in harm's way."

Her brother sneered. "This again? I already told you—"

An Binh forged ahead. "Mia was deliberately put in harm's way. She had served her purpose. She sent intel on the villa and its guests back to your brother and he passed it on to the Malaysian pirates who destroyed the villa and everyone in it."

One thing that had been nagging at her: Mia knew the daily routine Evan had set for herself and the boy. She knew it down to the minute, which meant that the mission was definitely kidnapping, not killing Evan. Chances were good now that Evan, and perhaps the boy, were still alive. But she had to remind herself that Marsden Tribe made it abundantly clear he didn't care whether the boy was alive or dead. In any event, her immediate objective here was to find out who hired Budiharta to destroy the villa. Only trouble was, Budiharta was never going to tell her. But the way things were shaking out there might be another way. Time, she thought, to poke the pig.

"Listen, Khong, I'm already halfway there," she said. "I know your client is Russian." She didn't, of course, but it was a good guess and if she sold it correctly Budiharta would never know how she came upon this bit of intel. "Now all I need is to know which Russian hired you."

Now, as was almost always the case with poking the pig, everything seemed to happen at once. Diti opened her mouth, got out one word: "There's—" before her brother shouted her down.

"Keep your mouth shut, idiot girl," he spat. "Open it when I tell you, not before."

The movement An Binh knew was a possibility the moment she stepped into the room came in a blur. She had her knife out and at the ready when Diti's arm extended and the small dagger she had been hiding flew through the air in an underhand flick. In a slice of a second it was buried to the hilt in Budiharta's throat.

His hands came up to pull it out but he was already choking on his own blood. He gasped, a bloody bubble formed between his lips, growing larger as he coughed thickly and fell to his knees. His eyes bulged out, bloody-veined. He pointed at Diti, silently mouthing the same word over and over: *You, you.*

Diti strode over to him, her face flushed. "Fuck you, you fat fuck!" Diti spat in his face. Her saliva quickly turning pink, then red as it was absorbed by his blood.

She struck his hands away from her dagger, grasped the hilt, pulled it free. Blood gushed. She stepped nimbly back, giving An Binh the impression she had done this before, maybe several times.

Then she wheeled on An Binh, raised her dagger. Blood dripped from the blade, pooling at her feet.

15

They inhabited a small square space into which the chute gave out, a room no bigger than a prison cell, one door, one burning bulb encased in a metal cage, no windows, bare concrete walls, floor, ceiling, a metal table against one wall where once upon a time she guessed Nyurgun opened the food parcels. Smelling of nothing but stale sweat.

Closer to her, the ball-peen hammer, X-Acto knife, telescoping shovel: Elley's implements of destruction displayed in a neat line between them. The GRU officer who had ordered Evan to her knees strode toward her. His dark-blue eyes held hers several beats longer than necessary. He was tall, hard, with the kind of face that must have had women running after him when he was in Moscow. Whose wife had he taken as a mistress to get him sent out here? It was curious what popped into one's head in moments of extremis, Evan thought, slightly amused with herself.

It was his uniform that surprised her. She had expected that Nyurgun and Aya would be interrogated by *spetsnaz*, Eighth Directorate's special forces. But Mr. Blue Eyes was an officer of Ninth Directorate, military technology. This was no ordinary prison or even a black site. It was something of a much higher—and more secretive—order. No wonder GRU wanted to interrogate Nyurgun, the person who had escaped with White Wolf.

She felt Blue Eyes' presence like a pressure, as if she were back in the chute's curve that had almost been the end of her. He stopped directly in front of her. She on her knees, he standing over her, enjoying his position of dominance. Without warning, he leaned in, grabbed the front of her shirt.

"What have we here?" He was no longer looking at her face.

Silence. Stillness. She watched Elley's gaze turn away from her, toward the blankness of a wall.

What was coming?

Suddenly, she felt his hand in her hair, fingers curled, grasping tight.

He jerked her head back so hard she barely suppressed a gasp. Now she was looking straight up into his face.

"I know just what I have here." His head descended until his lips were mere inches from her own. "What is someone like you doing crawling around in my domain?" She made no sound; she wasn't expected to. "What could you possibly be looking for in this partially decommissioned facility?" He pulled harder, fire along her scalp. "Ferreting out secrets, possibly?" His lips came down over hers, the tip of his tongue hard against her clenched teeth. Denied entrance, he bit her lower lip, drawing blood. "You are *shpion*, surely." He pulled on her hair so hard, Evan heard her neck vertebrae protest.

"Enough!" As if she had been speaking, not him, as if she had been assaulting him, not the other way around. He let go of her, pivoted to stand between her and Elley. "Divest yourself of weapons."

Mind no-mind. "I need to stand to do that," she said.

Eyes gleaming, he watched the blood make its way to her chin, liked what he saw. "Rise," he said like a regent to a recalcitrant subject.

Once again, she obeyed, rising slowly from her knees. Then, in one fluid, lightning-fast motion, she took a step forward, stamped her left foot on the end of the hammer's handle, levering it up, bent down, grasped it, and buried the ball-peen in Blue Eyes' forehead. His eyes rolled up, he staggered back as skull and brains exploded like a flower opening to the sun.

Then she was on the move, slamming Elley prone as the second GRU soldier, stunned and rattled, started spraying bullets in every direction, the kickback from the Udav so powerful it was near impossible to aim correctly when firing multiple shots. Reaching out, Elley grabbed his X-Acto knife, sliced the tendons at the back of the soldier's right knee, bringing him down. Blood gushed as Elley's blade opened the soldier's throat.

Silence then—silence of an altogether different nature, punctuated only by the drip of blood. Like wind rising through trees its meaning outstripped the tiny sound it made. Evan ached all over from her ordeal in the chute. She wiped her lower lip free of her blood and Blue Eyes' saliva.

Elley's gaze flitted about as he regained his feet, grabbed one of the Russian Udavs. "We'd better be going. There are bound to be more of these guards about, especially as we get nearer to Aya."

"Wait," she said.

Elley's expression turned dark. "I need to free my niece," he said. "Now."

"I understand. But the shots fired will bring more guards. This is our territory now. Best to encounter the guards here in a space we know. You won't do Aya any good if you're dead."

He looked at her, said nothing more. She was acutely aware of the change in Elley's demeanor. At first she laid it at the feet of the violence. Had he ever killed a man before this? If so, he might fall apart at any minute; death had that effect on most people, especially when you were the one who caused it. It was traumatic, to say the least. Some never recovered from it, suffered from debilitating PTSD the rest of their lives. Was Elley one of these? she wondered. If so, he would be of no use to her going forward. This was a cold mindset, one she had become inured to over her years in the field. She dealt with wet work all the time. It was a necessary state of mind in order not to turn yourself into a liability. A dead liability. Developing feeling for anyone in the field was a grave mistake. Emotionality was a weakness to be exploited by your enemies. She had to look no farther than Lyudmila and Timur to understand that.

But as it turned out, for Elley just the opposite was true. Stepping over to the corpse of the sadistic GRU officer Evan had killed, he looked down and said, "He is good and dead, isn't he?"

"Indeed he is."

Elley closed his eyes for a moment. "Good deal," he said quietly. He opened his eyes, looked down again, and then trod viciously on the dead man's face, used his heel to pry open his jaw, and spit hard into his mouth.

"How long has it been that these fuckers have worked us, kicked in our ribs, broken our kneecaps, killed and maimed our fathers, brothers, sons?" Elley was near tears. "Raping our land, hauling away everything of value." He kept on stomping now, the crack of bones breaking, the wet sounds of skin bursting, of muscle, fat, viscera broken open, exposed. At last vulnerable as Elley and his people had been vulnerable all their lives. "*Zhivotnyye*, you call us. Animals, are we? And what are you? *Muzhchiny, oderzhimyye sadizmom*. Men obsessed with sadism. What does that make you? An order below *zhivotnyye*. Many orders. What? *Nizhe dazhe nasekomogo*. Below even an insect."

Abruptly, he turned away. He'd had enough. He'd let his rage out of its cage and now he stood over the dead Russian like an avenging angel. Swiping up his weapons, his outer garments. "What that piece of shit did to you . . . and I did nothing . . . Nothing but look away. For this I am truly sorry." He made a little sound, halfway between a sigh and a groan, which was when Evan noticed he was carrying his left arm oddly, struggling awkwardly with his furred skins. His right hand gripped his left elbow.

"You've been shot." She crossed to him, saw the bloodstain widening along his biceps.

"It's nothing," he said. "I've spilt more blood shaving."

But she could tell he was in pain. She tied her scarf tightly above the wound, then felt around, making sure the bullet had missed the bone. "There's an exit wound, the bullet passed through the muscles, Elley. A major source of infection is eliminated."

He shrugged her off. "It doesn't matter. I no longer feel pain; I no longer feel anything. These monsters have taken everything from me. When I refused their infusion of money for my business they abducted my wife, raped her repeatedly before beating her to death. That's how I found her, curled on my doorstep, frozen like a piece of meat."

Evan looked up from where she crouched, going through the Russians' pockets, taking whatever she thought would be of use. "Why didn't you tell me this before?"

He glared down at her. "Before, there was no reason to do so." He gestured to the two dead soldiers. "Now death is so close I can feel its breath on the back of my neck."

Evan rose, stowed on her person everything she had found. She was about to gather up her coat and gloves when she froze.

Boot soles. Soldiers on the run, approaching. Echoing. Two, three. More. It was impossible to tell.

■　■　■

Second Lieutenant Krystov, a senior GRU officer, had a dual remit: first, to interrogate the prisoners; second, to protect the two Ninth Directorate men sent to discover how the advanced AI technology controlling the allegedly escape-proof prison had been defeated, allowing the prisoner to escape. The trouble was the leader of the tech team was uncontrollable. Mostronov was as nasty a piece of work as Krystov had ever encountered. He bullied his colleague mercilessly, and generally paid no attention to the warnings given him by Krystov himself. Therefore it was hardly a surprise that Mostronov had taken it upon himself to go exploring. But what really enraged Krystov was that the hothead stole for himself and his dogsbody two of Krystov's expensive Udavs.

As a result, when he heard the echoes of gunshots Krystov took all of his men with him to find out what possible shitstorm Mostronov had gotten himself into. To his way of thinking, if, perchance Mostronov was killed during the foray so much the better. Six steps before the doorway into the room from which the percussions had emanated he halted his cadre, held up two fingers, the sign for a two-part wave: half the cadre would rush the room, while he led the other half in seconds later.

Now, forefinger on the trigger of his Udav, Krystov watched three of his men vanish through the doorway.

■   ■   ■

Evan had positioned Elley against the wall on one side of the doorway, while she took the other side. When the GRU officers came through she was ready.

She had told Elley to hold his fire for ten seconds in order to keep them out of their own cross fire but she had no confidence that he would comply. The moment she spied movement, she dropped to the floor, fired off one shot that took the lead GRU soldier off his feet, slamming him against the far wall, too close to Elley for comfort. He had to duck to get out of the way of an arm flung wide, bouncing off the wall six inches from his head. Blood sprayed through the air, striking the floor like sleet. The second soldier stood rooted to the spot, his eyes on the two officers Evan and Elley had killed. Elley's first bullet winged him, spun him around in time for a second bullet to blast through his abdomen. Splash like a bellyflop into a pool. The third man, in a crouch, got off a shot toward Elley, who was already on the move. The bullet cracked the wall where Elley had been crouched a moment before. Chunks of cement careened through the air like mini-missiles. One of them caught Elley on the cheek, slashing a red line all the way down to the bone. Prone on the floor, Evan squeezed the trigger, nearly took the officer's head clean off.

The aftermath of silence was more a result of temporary deafness from the multiple percussions than the Udavs falling silent. But even half deaf, Evan was aware of a new assault coming through the door. She launched herself at the now headless GRU soldier, grabbed him at the shoulders to hold him upright. He was her shield. His body jerked wildly as the bullet fired by the first soldier to enter impacted his chest. Evan, covered in his blood, shot the soldier. He was flung sideways, smashed into the corner, sat down as if he were a child at play. Then he collapsed sideways.

Two left.

■   ■   ■

When Krystov saw Mostronov lying twisted on the darkly glinting concrete, ugly in death as he had never been in life, he didn't know whether to laugh or to cry. Laugh at the prick's violent demise, cry that it wasn't him who had bashed in Mostronov's exquisite skull.

Then the claustrophobic world he had stepped into exploded into gunfire. He saw his leading officer slam into the wall on the far side of the small space.

Shocked out of his stasis, Krystov made an instant battle assessment. Two shooters. They already killed four of his men. Who were these two people who knew about this prison, were able to find it, and infiltrate it via an entrance even he wasn't made aware of? His companion—the only one left of his cadre—was firing at the man running along the far wall toward the metal table, the only semblance of cover in this charnel house of a cell.

He dropped and rolled. Even so, a shot flicked concrete in his face, nearly blinding him. Twisting, he leveled his Udav at his adversary—a woman, of all things! His finger wrapped around the trigger, began to squeeze when she lashed out with her foot, sent his Udav skittering away into a pool of blood.

Still, he was unfazed, believing the man across the room had shot his men. Certainly not this . . . woman. Drawing out a hunting knife from its sheath at his belt, he rose to his knees, then his feet as did she. While she was in the process, he attacked, lunging forward, knifepoint slightly raised above the horizontal. He was going for the place between her ribs, the pathway to her heart. He expected her to defend herself, to try to fend off his attack, and he was ready for any countermove she might make.

She made no traditional countermove at all. To his shock, she allowed his attack, as he stretched forward, legs braced, to flick the knifepoint through her ribs. His weapon was only an inch away from its target when, in a blur too fast for his brain to register, she drove her combined fists straight up into his wrists. He was totally unprepared. His own hand gripping the knife shot upward with blinding speed and he was only aware of what had happened when his knifepoint sliced through his eyeball, fracturing the socket. With his good eye he saw her hands had somehow gained control of the knife, redirected it inward at him.

He gasped, ground his teeth as he tried and failed to stop her. Then the heel of her hand smashed into the butt of the knife, driving the blade into his brain.

"Oh." It was a sigh, like the air going out of a soft balloon. Down on his knees. Falling. Then only oblivion.

■   ■   ■

Evan turned, raced across the room to where Elley was losing a hand-to-hand fight with the one remaining Russian soldier, who had his hands around Elley's throat. Elley's face was almost purple, his bloodshot eyes popped, his half-open mouth gasping for air that the Russian was denying him.

Evan produced the fishing line she had bought, the ends wrapped around two five-inch lengths of wooden dowels. Dropping the line over the soldier's head, she drew it tight around his throat. At once, his head shot up, his hands came away from Elley's throat, his fingertips clawing to get between the fishing line and his skin, to intervene, to give him the time he needed to counterattack. But Evan was ready. She kneed him hard in his back and all the air left his lungs.

He wheezed, he coughed. He struggled mightily. Gasping as his eyes rolled up.

Hauling back, she finished the garroting. The Russian collapsed sideways.

The gasping she heard now came from Elley as he fought to regain his breath.

"Slowly," Evan said, pulling him up to lean against the wall. "Breathe slowly and deeply. You're safe now."

■   ■   ■

Evan led the way. They encountered no more guards on the way up. Elley's neck was red, raw-looking as an uncooked slab of meat, but he uttered not one word of protest or of pain. It was as he had told Evan back down in the killing room—he was beyond feeling pain. He lived now only for Aya's safe return. Not so very different, she thought, from her own determination to rescue Timur.

The short corridor leading out of the charnel house ended in a steep flight of stairs. There was no elevator as there might have been if this had been a restaurant. Nyurgun had had to lug the foodstuff brought to him every day via the chute up the stairs. They gave out into the kitchen, empty and silent. Whoever was preparing meals for the guards and the prisoners was not in evidence. This level was completely devoid of odors, even here in the kitchen. It was as if the interior was scrubbed clean of all human scent. The exact opposite of every other prison on earth.

After the violence they'd been through down below the absence of movement was eerie. The only sounds were the whisper of the refrigerator's compressor and the buzzing of a fluorescent light bar badly in need of replacing. As she passed, she felt the heat coming from the refrigerator, briefly warmed her hands in it.

Evan crossed the kitchen to the doorway on the far side, stood just within the shadows of its shelter. Turned her head sideways, listening intently. She felt Elley come up behind her. His heat was that of a long-distance runner almost in sight of the finish line. And there it was. If she craned her neck she could see through the clear wall to the cell where Nyurgun and Aya were being held. From what she could see they were at least alive. As best she could she looked both ways but could see no sign of any guards. Could they have killed all of them? After all, it seemed unlikely the GRU would send a large contingent in to interrogate the prisoners.

With that in mind, *I'll go first*, Evan mouthed and Elley, reloaded handgun out, nodded.

Calming her breathing, Evan stepped out into the corridor.

And all hell broke loose.

16

"So, what's next?" An Binh asked. "Are you going to try to kill me as well? I'm a witness, after all."

"Who are you going to tell?" Diti scoffed. When An Binh made no reply, she went on. "No, I don't think that would be a good idea."

"Wise choice." An Binh lowered her knife to her side. "So again I ask, what's next?"

"Now," Diti said, "we fold him, box him, and freeze him."

"Really?" An Binh lifted one eyebrow. "You brother must weigh two hundred fifty pounds."

Diti grunted. "Two sixty-six, actually." She crossed to the desk, picked up the wireless phone, spoke into it for less than fifteen seconds. "Unlock the door, would you?" When An Binh hesitated, she added, "Go on. No one's bitten you yet."

"Not for lack of trying," Nevertheless, An Binh unlocked the door.

Moments later, four men—including the brute—entered. They seemed unfazed by the scene before them and immediately got to work, moving the body, cleaning up the bloody mess beneath it. As he passed her, the brute grinned at An Binh. "I told you he liked his food too much."

"They know what to do?" An Binh asked.

Diti crossed her arms over her chest. "Believe it or not there are employees here who were not enamored with my dissolute brother's work ethic."

An Binh watched the four men as they went about their business in impeccably economic fashion. "So they prefer your style? You, a female?"

Diti turned to her. "I can be quite persuasive when the situation calls for it."

"Budiharta could attest to that," An Binh said, "if he were alive." She shook her head. "Funny, you don't look like a murderer."

Diti eyed her. "That's the general idea, isn't it?" The place where her brother died was now spotless, looking as if nothing untoward had occurred moments before. Her eyes followed the bulk of meat that had been her brother as it was folded in on itself, carted out no doubt to the crate room, thence across the corridor to the industrial freezer An Binh had spotted on her way in. "But then again you don't look like one, either. You look like you couldn't hurt a fly."

"That's the general idea, isn't it?"

That got a laugh out of Diti. "I like you," she chuckled. "I really do."

The irony of how Budiharta's body was being disposed of, while here in the office that he had meticulously rebuilt An Binh years ago had folded Ramelan into Mr. Budi Khong's massive safe, was not lost on her. She could not help smiling inwardly. Budi Khong's last remaining son had been given his just reward.

"Time to leave," Diti said, gesturing for An Binh to follow her.

And so An Binh left the offices of the resurrected Far Eastern Distributors for the last time.

■   ■   ■

"So this Lolita look you have going . . ." An Binh began twenty minutes later.

"Deliberate." Diti shrugged. "Budiharta never thought much of me, but infantilizing myself ensured no attention was paid to anything I said."

They were in Budiharta's palatial apartment. The west-facing front rooms overlooked the Malacca Strait, dark swells relieved by brass highlights as the sun began to drown itself in the water. The apartment's décor was more modern than An Binh had expected, which was not to say it was tasteful—not by a wide margin. The furniture appeared to have been chosen by a blind-drunk libertine. Nothing mixed, nothing matched. And the less said about the photos on the walls the better.

"As for the others," Diti continued, "they were too busy drooling over me to think of me as anything but a sex toy." She poured them both three fingers of Malaysian gin. "You know of this gin?" Diti asked as she handed over one of the well-chilled glasses.

An Binh suspected Diti didn't expect her to know. "Eiling Lim," she said, having spotted the bottle's distinctive label.

Diti nodded. "Malaysia's first female bottler." Her eyes never left An Binh. "This one's Pandan Predator, my favorite." Raising her glass, she said, "I apologize that it was impossible to offer you a drink before this." Her eyes sparked. "Did you think my brother would?"

"Not for a moment."

"Naturally." Diti's mouth twisted in an odd smile. "You were acquainted with the illustrious Mr. Budi Khong." She contemplated her guest. "To what shall we toast?"

"Fucking everything," An Binh said.

Diti laughed. "Yes, yes. To fucking everything." They clinked rims, swallowed the gin.

An Binh liked the bite of the liquor and said so. When Diti nodded her acceptance of the compliment, An Binh said, "I assume you're Muslim."

"I am."

"Yet you enjoy alcohol."

"Mm, I'm what you might call a lapsed Muslim—like most of my family, actually, but me most of all." She sipped again at her gin. "I admit to being more American than anything else. In fact, I'd like to switch to English, if you don't mind." She spoke English fluently without any accent whatsoever.

"Of course."

Diti kept on with a ribbon of chatter, as if she and An Binh had been friends forever, while she took them through to the rear of the apartment. She occupied a single small room, with a window that looked out on nothing to speak of.

"You may be asking yourself why this"—she spread her arms to indicate the room—"when there's so much space and opulence elsewhere in the apartment?"

"It had occurred to me," An Binh admitted. Curiously, she found it easier and easier to talk to this strange ageless-seeming young woman, who had to be close to thirty but could pass for nineteen if she wanted to. "Your brother?"

"Well, that. But mostly it's what I wanted." She snorted. "You've seen what it's like out there."

"Hideous," An Binh said.

"Grotesque," Diti said. "Just like Budiharta, who inherited it from Budi Khong."

An Binh noticed that Diti never referred to Budi Khong as "father." She could hardly blame her. It was endearing.

"As for opulence . . ." she said.

"Yeah," Diti nodded. "Hate it. Opulence attracts flies like a pile of shit."

An Binh wondered how Diti had become so canny. Then she recalled the book Diti was reading when she entered Budiharta's office. Joseph

Conrad was not your typical reading matter for a woman who intention-
ally hid her light under a barrel. She was doubtless smarter than all her
brothers put together. Now she liked her even more.

Before a full-length mirror Diti untangled her braids, brushed out her
hair, styling it into a neat ponytail. Then without a scintilla of shyness she
undressed, stood naked while she went through her meager wardrobe,
eventually sliding on a pair of black linen trousers. Like An Binh, she had
no need of a bra. "I love your T-shirt."

"Really?"

"Flower Power," Diti said. "What a time that must have been in America."

"Another world," An Binh agreed. Crossing her arms, she peeled off
the shirt.

Diti frowned. "What are you doing?"

"A gift." An Binh held out the shirt.

Diti, frowning, eyed her for a moment. Producing a tiny girlish squeal,
she drew on the tee. "Wow," she said. "That's the nicest thing anyone's
done for me. Ever." In Diti's excited exclamation An Binh heard it then,
the slight click of Diti's jaw when she voiced her pleasure. This close to
her she could see there was a slight mismatch between the sides of her
jaw. An Binh's heart broke.

Despite her best effort, Diti saw where she was looking, "My brother,"
Diti said. "He broke my jaw for an imagined slight. Ramelan tried to be
there for me, was slapped down hard for his effort."

Reaching out, An Binh ran her forefinger gently down Diti's jawline.
"Does it still hurt?" she asked softly.

Diti exhaled. "It did for a long time." Her eyes held An Binh's captive.
"Not for many years now."

A tremor of recognition went through An Binh. "But this isn't why
you killed him."

"This and too many other horrors to count."

"But there was one in particular, wasn't there?"

Diti's lips parted, her tongue moved swiftly over her teeth. "Mia and I
were in love." She said it so softly that were she and An Binh not standing
so close she might have missed it. "He sent her away to punish both of us."

Still, An Binh hesitated. She was naked, exposed. Why had she so cav-
alierly given her shirt to Diti? Now she did not want to turn her back on
her, to allow her to see . . .

"What's the matter?" Diti asked. "Just take any shirt you want."

An Bihn saw Diti's eyes open wide as she turned around and began sorting through Diti's shirts. She wanted all of them, they were all so lovely.

Diti took a step closer, reached out a hand, touched the scar on An Binh's back, serpentine, reaching from her left shoulder blade down to the upper part of her lat. An Binh froze at the touch, shivered as Diti's fingertip traced the curves.

There were more than a dozen shirts in the drawer. She snatched a midnight-blue shirt with a large image of a classic Coke bottle on the front, shrugged it on, braced herself for the question she did not want to answer. But, thankfully, the question never came.

"It fits perfectly," she said as she drew it on. This, she knew, would mean more to Diti than saying "Thank you." Sometimes, those two words were inadequate to the moment. This was such a moment. She was so grateful that Diti did not ask about her scar her eyes burned with incipient tears, even as she pushed her panic down into darkness, turned her mind to the present, turned around to face Diti, a smile on her face.

She needed to resume pursuing her primary objective. As gently as she could, she guided the conversation back onto the track she wanted. "Diti, what's going to become of the company now? Will you be able to take it over?"

"I don't know about that, but it doesn't matter," Diti said. "Far Eastern Distributors can rot for all I care. Budiharta was the only thing keeping me chained here. I'm leaving this shithole far behind as soon as I can."

An Binh frowned. "But what about Sybirsk Associates? Aren't they partners in Far Eastern now?"

Diti gave a grim laugh. "Another of my brother's lies. For Far Eastern he was an abject failure; we were going under—that's how bad a businessman he was. People were taking advantage of him left and right. We found ourselves on the short end of a string of very bad deals. No, my brother had a penchant for fucking, for snorting coke, for gambling—but when it came to business he was clueless. I'm the one who inherited my father's head for making deals. But so what?" She shook her head. "I urged him to partner the business with a multinational conglomerate, but he went ahead and sold the company. All our continued wealth is due to this company."

"Sybirsk Associates."

"Oh, no. no. We have nothing to do with them. The group that owns Far Eastern Distributors now is Kyodai."

An Binh could hear the far-off tolling of a tocsin, a warning of dire import. Kyodai was a yakuza term. It meant "The Brothers." So it wasn't the Russians who had bought out the Khong family business, it was the Japanese yakuza.

"If the Sybirsk deal doesn't exist, could the sale to this Kyodai be a lie as well?"

"Oh no, it's real. I did some digging. Kyodai is owned by the Satsuragi-kai family."

An Binh felt her blood curdling. "Satsuragi-kai. That's a Tokyo yakuza family."

Diti eyebrows lifted. "Really? Well. They seem to know all about you. Our contact informed Budiharta you were coming."

"Contact?" An Binh finished off her gin in one long swallow, shivering as the liquor raced down her esophagus, lay burning in her belly. "Who informed him? Who precisely?"

"A man named Akujin Matsumura. He's their *kuromaku*, their fixer."

An Binh's face had drained of color. "I know what a *kuromaku* is. A black curtain for the yakuza." Her voice was thin, reedy. "And I know Akujin Matsumura. He's a destroyer of human flesh."

17

Guns chattered from two different directions. Evan stepped back into the kitchen and the bullets stopped flying.

"Auto gunfire," she said to Elley.

"AK-47s?"

She shook her head. "The firing came from apertures up near the ceiling. There's an emergency response system, one that's triggered by either movement or human heat signature."

Elley looked at her as if she was crazy. "What the hell?"

"I know," she said.

His face darkened in fury. "We'll never get to Aya and the boy." His good hand clenched into a fist. "There must be a way. You have to—"

He stopped abruptly as she held up a hand. "Give me the shovel." When he handed it to her, she telescoped it open. "Watch now," she whispered as she returned to the doorway. She threw the shovel into the corridor. Nothing happened.

"Heat signature," she said, as if to herself.

"What does it mean?"

"Human beings are warm-blooded—our temperature is around ninety-eight degrees Fahrenheit. The system is calibrated to respond to that. My sense is it would not fire at a dog, for instance, or a rat. It must have the parameters of human height and weight. Anything that falls within those parameters will get its head shot off."

Elley huffed. "So what do we do? It can't end like this." He took a step toward the doorway. "If need be, I'll take my chances. Maybe if I crawl . . ."

"The sensors will pick up your heat signature whether you're running, standing, sitting, or lying down."

He ran his fingers through his hair. Despite the air-chill he was sweating profusely. Not a good sign as far as his wound was concerned. Evan knew she needed to get him to a doctor sooner rather than later. "So how do we defeat the system?" he said now.

"By outthinking it." Evan walked back through the kitchen. Something had struck her. "It's an AI, but I'm betting not a large language model."

Elley frowned. "I'm not understanding."

"The AI was made for one specific purpose," Evan said as she crossed the kitchen to where the refrigerator stood. "Within the confines of that purpose—defending this prison—it's very smart. But don't forget the prisoner here defeated it somehow. I intend to do the same."

She stopped by the side of the refrigerator, held out her hand. "You feel this current of heat?"

"So what?" He shrugged. "A unit of this size is going to throw off heat."

"Not this much," she said. "And not this dry." She moved past the side of the refrigerator, found the forbidden short corridor Nyurgun had stumbled upon weeks ago. "The heat is more intense here." She carefully stuck her head out into the corridor, saw the single aperture high up near the ceiling where an AI-controlled automatic weapon had been installed. Raising her Udav, she squeezed off two shots, wrecking the aperture.

Cautiously, she stepped out into what was clearly a service corridor, and when nothing happened, strode down its short length. The corridor ended at a door that was hanging ajar. Its elaborate electronic lock wasn't broken but clearly had been disabled. From within she felt the brush of heat. She pushed the door open. The wheeze of large fans, laboring. A wall banked with a mass of computers. The AI. The protections were nonfunctional. The Russian engineers had clearly been in the process of shutting it down. The AI was open, vulnerable. It took Evan just minutes to figure out how to open all the locks, shut down the protect mode.

"Gotcha!" she said.

■   ■   ■

They found Aya physically unharmed, but an emotional wreck. Initially, she fought her uncle, mistaking him for another one of their GRU interrogators. She was weeping, screaming, her fists beating a tattoo against Elley's chest as he tried to wrap his arms around her, comfort her. At that moment, however, she did not understand the meaning of comfort. Any man was the enemy. She was disoriented and, judging by her cracked, flaking lips, severely dehydrated. If she was bad off Nyurgun was far worse. The GRU interrogators had gone to work on him with their fists, knives, white-hot needles. He was an ugly quagmire of bruises, cuts, broken bones in two of the fingers of his left hand. He was unconscious, breathing more shallowly than was good for him. But alive. Aya, still wild-eyed and panting out her terror, nevertheless would not leave Nyurgun's side. She had tried to stanch his bleeding with strips torn her from shirt but there were too many wounds.

Evan picked him up in her arms. Aya, both hands on Nyurgun's knees, stumbled between them and Elley as they made their way through the gates, open, dead, to the deserted front entrance. No one stopped them, no one appeared. Almost all of the GRU cadre had been exterminated. She had not, however, forgotten those two glowing red eyes they had passed out front. Two more GRU guards needed to be neutralized.

Elley halted them just inside the door. He and Evan wrapped Aya and Nyurgun in the thick coats hanging on hooks where the GRU cadre had hung them. They looked tiny as infants, as vulnerable as they appeared in the clear-walled cell.

"This is on me," Elley said softly to Evan, held up a hand when she opened her mouth to protest. "No. This time you listen to me."

A heavy sense of sadness had invaded Evan's thoughts. That teenagers should be treated like lab animals weighed on her like the pressure drop before a hurricane. She felt exhausted and elated at the same time. Elley was waiting for her response. When she gave a brief nod, he slipped through the door. He moved normally, as if he felt no pain from the wound in his arm. Evan heard nothing, even though she strained all her senses. Minutes later the door opened.

"All clear," Elley said in his normal voice. There were smears of fresh blood on his animal skins. "Not mine," he said, noting Evan's expression of concern.

Evan looked around, past the irregular snow piles on the frozen ground. It was dark when they crept into the prison. It was dark now when they left. It felt as if they been inside for an entire day, but it must have been only a couple of hours. Time seemed to have lost its grip on them while they prowled through the sterile structure, while they contributed to its death throes.

Elley pointed to a thick-tired military vehicle, its engine running so the block wouldn't freeze. He ushered Aya inside. Elley climbed in after her, turned to receive Nyurgun's inert body.

Evan slipped behind the wheel and drove them away from that awful place. She stopped at the tree where their reindeer waited patiently. Elley tied them to the rear bumper of the truck, climbed back into the vehicle. Evan followed his instructions back to his house, careful to keep pace with the animals' gait. She asked Elley to call a doctor to his house and he complied. The road snaked out before her, the vehicle's massive tires plowing through the snow. As she drove, something niggled at the back of her mind. She should be elated at the success of their rescue mission, and yet a worm of anxiety roiled her stomach. They had Nyurgun and Aya. The youngsters were both alive and presumably well. She would be able to talk to Nyurgun, get information about Ilona Starkova. And yet . . . and yet. Something was off, something that danced away into the shadows when she tried to put her finger on it.

Then they were home and she turned her thoughts and actions to Nyurgun. The doctor Elley had called was waiting beside her reindeer, medical bag in hand. She nodded to Elley, frowned when she saw the state Nyurgun was in, followed them through the front door. Elley and the doctor hung up their heavy coat and skins. Elley held Nyurgun while Evan shrugged out of her coat, then returned the boy to her. He guided Aya, still wrapped, shivering, to the sofa, where she all but collapsed in exhaustion and the aftermath of terror. Dr. Kuduk tried to give Aya a mild sedative to calm her, but the girl refused. She kept asking after Nyurgun, trying to get off the sofa to see him despite her uncle gently restraining her. The doctor told him to slowly give her sips of water to rehydrate her, not to worry if she nodded off, the sleep would do her a world of good. She warned him Aya might have nightmares for the next couple of weeks or even months, but not to worry they would fade soon enough. What she needed now more than anything, Kuduk told him, was to feel safe and loved.

Elley nodded, but Evan could tell that his niece's manic condition worried him. He directed Evan to take Nyurgun to a back bedroom he used as a study. Evan lay the teenager down on a daybed, stepped away as the doctor knelt beside the teen.

After quickly cleaning and bandaging Elley's wound, Dr. Kuduk joined Evan in the back bedroom. The doctor was aptly named since Kuduk meant "well." She was short and squat like a fire hydrant with limbs. Her large round head sat atop her shoulders seemingly without the intervention of a neck. Her hands, with the long, slender fingers of a pianist or a surgeon, looked like they had been grafted onto her from another person entirely.

"How is he, Doctor?" Evan asked after Kuduk had conducted her preliminary examination.

Kuduk sighed. "The terrible things people do to each other." She looked up at her. "First order of business is to check his body more thoroughly, then set his broken fingers. After that I'll bring him around, see how he's handling the trial he's been through."

Evan bent toward Nyurgun. "Tell me about his wounds."

"Not too deep, so far as I can see," Kuduk said. "Nothing to worry about." Her fingers were moving deftly, palpating here, gliding there. She cut off the bloody strips of shirt Aya had used to wrap the fingers together. "They were intent on inducing him to tell them what they wanted to know. Killing him would have been secondary."

"It's important I speak with him."

The doctor looked up. "Why? Do you know him?"

Evan was formulating a response to that when her phone vibrated. Stepping out of the study, she walked toward the main living area where she could see Elley helping Aya sip from a glass of water. She took a calming breath, then looked down at the phone's screen. It was a second short video of Timur. Her daily update on the boy's condition. No voice component this time. He looked well, though seemingly thinner. Evan heard Nyurgun moan from behind her, was about to put the phone away when an image rose into her mind like a mote in her eye. She replayed the video and sure enough at the very end the forefinger of Timur's left hand curled around the edge of the newspaper: *tap, tap, tap.* Six times before the paper was ripped from his hands. Evan's heart thumped in her chest. A sign. Had he given her a sign? Did it mean he had forgiven her? That he understood that she had no choice in the beat down? Was he now wanting her to rescue him, even desperate to be reunited with her? Or was she merely imagining something she so wished were true? Maybe the tapping of his finger was simply nerves. A terrible sadness engulfed her, took her out of herself, locked her in a darkness deeper, more complete than starless night.

Putting her phone away she watched Elley with his niece, who was stretched out on the sofa, her head lolling, eyes and lips half open.

"How is the boy?" Elley asked when he became aware of Evan. "Has he said anything yet?"

"Still under," she said. "The doctor is splinting his fingers."

Elley put the glass to Aya's lips, got her to take a few sips before she coughed. He set the glass down on the table beside the sofa. "It's possible, maybe, that he won't recover."

There was a look in his eye that Evan strained to recognize. It was something that connected to the feeling in the pit of her stomach she'd felt in the truck driving here from the prison.

The prison . . .

Elley looking down at the corpse of the once-handsome GRU officer . . .

Saying, *"He is good and dead, isn't he?"* . . .

Acute anxiety.

"Indeed he is," Evan agreed . . .

His eyes closed for a moment. *"Good deal."*

Acute relief.

And then Evan knew what her subconscious had picked up in the killing room, what had been off. Disparate shards of memories, things she had seen and heard floated around in her head, suddenly clicked into place.

"You knew the leader," she said.

"What?" Elley jerked as if shot. "What did you say?"

"Of course," she said. "You made a deal with him. He and his man were waiting for us as we came out of the food chute. How did they know we were coming, Elley? There's only one way: you told him."

"I didn't—"

"Oh, but you did." Evan advanced toward him. "What did he promise you for my capture? Aya's release, unharmed. Yes. Your niece was his bargaining chip." *Your fatal weakness*, she thought. In hindsight the betrayal was so obvious now she could kick herself but she wasn't the masochistic kind. The only way to survive in the field was to go forward even while the ground beneath you was falling away.

But here in this moment was an anomaly she'd never before encountered in the field. Elley made no move against her, had produced no weapon. He was, instead, standing with his arms at his side, hands open, palms toward her. Peace, said everything about him. Peace.

"Why?" Evan, still assessing the situation, had no idea where the confrontation would end up. But she knew one thing: she'd had enough killing for the time being. "Why would you betray your people, ignore your own rage?"

"Have you never . . . ?" He cocked his head. "Have you never loved someone so much, so completely you would do anything—anything at all—to protect them, to keep them safe?" When Evan made no reply, he went on. "I tell you the truth, I didn't think it would be a big thing. I mean to say, you were sent—and I told the—His name was Mostronov. I told Lt. Mostronov this; I knew him through my company—he was an AI specialist but as a youngster he'd been trained as a soldier. In the event, I knew you arrived here under an alias—*you*—a woman, a female." He shrugged. "I didn't think it would be much of a loss if you . . ."

"If they killed me. Is that it?"

"But I was wrong about you, at least," Elley said. "You surprised me at every stage—riding a reindeer, the snowstorm, the bitter wind, the crawl into the prison. And then, my God! The way you buried my hammer in that bastard's head. I nearly shit my pants. It was . . . well, it was unexpected, a shock."

"What a relief it must have been to see him dead."

"Yes." He looked abashed suddenly; he hadn't picked up on her sarcasm. "I said as much, didn't I?"

"You did."

"That gave you all the hint you needed."

"As it turned out."

"And yet you went along, put your life on the line to free Aya and Nyurgun from that awful prison." He shook his head. "Look, think of me what you will. I confess I made a deal with the devil. To save Aya. Tell me you wouldn't do the same—aren't you doing the same, if you have told me the truth?"

Evan ignored the question to which they both knew the answer. "So Mostronov, your contact, is dead . . ."

"And so is any knowledge of my connection to the enemy. He never told anyone."

Evan's face darkened. "How can you be sure?"

"I know—knew—his type. Mostronov was an egotist. He would never . . . He would want the glory all to himself."

A kind of stalemate kept them rooted to their positions opposing one another. At length, Elley held out a hand, palm up. "Evan, I swear on the life of Aya that I have nothing to do with the Russians. I never will again." He scraped his scalp with his fingers. "I will never outlive my shame. Somehow, some way I will have to come to terms with it." He turned to look at his drowsing niece. "I can only pray that every time I look at her I will find a measure of solace."

"Nyurgun is awake." Kuduk had emerged from the back room. "And lucid."

Evan turned, followed the doctor down the short hallway to the small study. Already it smelled like a hospital—alcohol, Betadine, surgical tape, blood. Nyurgun half reclined on the daybed, a wad of pillows stuffed behind his shoulders. His two broken fingers were in splints, the hand swollen, empurpled. His head and neck were so covered in wounds he looked to be a victim of some terrible pox.

"Nyurgun," Evan said, "I've been waiting a long time to talk to you."

"Where is Aya?" the teen asked. "Is she—?"

"She's fine," Evan assured him.

"Just resting," the doctor followed up.

Evan came to stand beside the bed. "She's asleep, probably dreaming of you."

This brought a crooked smile to Nyurgun's face, followed quickly by a wince of pain. "You saved us, yes?"

"I did. Along with Aya's uncle, Elley."

"Thank you."

Evan dragged a ladder-back chair over, sat down. "I'm sorry the GRU put you through the wringer."

Nyurgun's eyes closed for a moment. "It was a whole lot tougher than I expected."

Evan frowned. "You expected to get picked up by the GRU?"

"Sooner or later. It's impossible to hide from them here. It was worth it, though." He closed his eyes again, for longer this time. Evan was concerned he had fallen asleep. Then he said, "Besides, she warned me this would happen."

Evan's heart rate picked up. "By 'she' you mean Ilona Starkova."

"White Wolf, uh-huh."

"So you spoke with her during the escape."

"After, actually," he said. "But she and I spoke every day when I brought her food."

"Then you can—"

"I can," Nyurgun said, "but I won't. I didn't tell the GRU anything about her and I won't do it now."

Evan, expecting this, was silent for several seconds to convey to Nyurgun that she was thinking this over, taking him seriously. Slowly, deliberately, she leaned forward. "Listen, Nyurgun, you'll understand this better than anyone save Aya. My son, Timur, is being held hostage. He's ten years old and terrified." She paused, brought out her phone, showed Nyurgun the first short video of Timur. "This video is called a proof of life. I get sent a new one every day to assure me that Timur is alive and well." She put the phone away. "But if I don't find Ilona—White Wolf—the people holding him hostage will kill him. They will make a video of that atrocity and send it to me." She sat back. "Do you understand?"

For what seemed an endless time Nyurgun said nothing. His eyes, which had focused on the moving image of Timur, now watched something beyond the walls of this room, this house, something only he could see.

"Please," Evan said softly. "Help me the way I helped you." She looked at Nyurgun, but he had Timur's face. "I am in prison, Nyurgun. Free me." She heard Elley's voice in her mind. *"Have you never loved someone so much, so completely you would do anything—anything at all—to protect them, to keep them safe?"* She scrubbed at her face with her hand. *At what point*, she wondered with a terrible surety, *will I recognize that I am living a life without friends, without pleasure? Without love?* Some emotion unknown to her passed through her like a wave of gamma rays, irradiating her without her understanding either its origin or its essence. She felt numb—number than she had while traveling through last night's raging snowstorm; drained of all volition. She had never felt so vulnerable in her adult life. Timur, Nyurgun, Aya—these young people had cracked open the armor she had painstakingly built around herself to keep out emotion, weakness, anything that could cause her incarceration, interrogation, torture. Death. She had no idea what was leaking out but she didn't like it. It frightened her in a way that adversaries never had and never would.

"Nyurgun . . ."

Both Evan and the doctor turned to see Aya standing shakily in the doorway, one thin shoulder against the frame, Elley holding her arm on the other side. Dark half-moons under her eyes, whites threaded with red from the strain she had been under.

"Nyurgun."

He sat up, said her name, a smile bursting onto his face.

Evan watched them come together. She rose, guided Aya to the chair she had been sitting on. The lovers entwined their fingers. Aya gently caressed his broken fingers with the fingertips of her free hand. "Oh, my poor love. What they put you through!"

"It was worse for you," Nyurgun said, "They forced you to watch."

"And there was nothing I could do." She was weeping now, tears rolling down her cheeks from the immensity of what she had witnessed, the relief she felt now. "Nothing."

"There, you see?" Elley watched them kissing tenderly. "This is worth everything. Everything, no?"

Yes, Evan thought. While she understood she could not forgive him—eager to throw her to the GRU, judging her because she was female. Forgiveness was not in her nature. But she understood what Elley had done and why.

"But we were saved," she said pulling her lips back from his. "These two—my uncle and this woman. We would still be in prison if not for them. Who knows what would have happened to us. You would have told them everything."

"I wouldn't have," he said hotly.

"Nyurgun, we might already be dead." When he remained silent, she pushed on. "We owe them a debt, my love. There is only one way to repay them, you know this, don't you?" She pressed her lips softly against his ear, whispered, "Open your heart as you do with me." And when she pulled away Nyurgun looked at Evan, nodded, tears in his eyes.

"All right. I will tell you what I know about White Wolf."

18

TIMUR BOUND

Had Timur been an adult his first thought would of necessity have been: Where am I? But Timur, despite a childhood that was anything but a normal—years of what had amounted to incarceration in Moscow, a terrifying flight from Russia engineered by his mother, a month of being hunted, of hiding, of Lyudmila Alexandrovna being his entire world—was still a ten-year-old child. And although he had seen more of the world than most ten-year-olds, had been in places that almost no other Russian ten-year-old had been in, his inner world was that of a child—an immensely precocious child, no doubt.

And so it was that his thoughts were these: *I have not been hurt; in fact, my captors have gone out of their way not to touch me. Only once did one of them take my chin in his hand and stare into my eyes. Moments later, I was struck across the back of my head. A verbal apology was extended to me, something that shocked me almost as much as my abduction. I have been offered a wide variety of food, fresh and deliciously prepared, three times a day, which allows me to keep track of the time—the hours, the days I have been here.*

He also wondered, more often than not, where Evan was. He tried to picture her somewhere—but where? He had no idea which, as time went on, bothered him more and more. The simple fact was he missed her. He had replayed in the theater of his mind every detail—his memory was this good—from the time he and Evan were taken aboard the pirate vessel, the appearance of the Russian spies, the hellish situation Evan had been put in, his initial reaction, childish, stupid, ignoring everything his mother and Aunt Evan had taught him. Every second ticked off in his mind like the beat of a drum.

He was ashamed of himself, and this shame was uppermost in his mind because he had been like that in the last moment Evan had seen him. He recalled with perfect clarity the desperate expression in her face, the shock and disappointment at his recoil from her. How stupid he had been! How selfish! There were times now that he could no longer stand himself, when he contemplated slamming his forehead against the wall of the small, windowless room into which he had been led. But he also knew—and this was so unchildlike—such violence against himself was not only useless but yet another form of self-indulgence. What ten-year-old comes to that conclusion? And yet that was precisely the course of his reasoning. So he did nothing, sat in a corner, his legs drawn up, chin resting on knees.

But his physical posture mimicked his emotional turmoil. He was holding back as best he could the degree to which he missed his mother and Evan. In his mind Lyudmila and Evan were fused, had become a single entity, Evan's face superimposed over his mother's, creating a palimpsest, where the outlines of Lyudmila's features, dimmed though they be, appeared like parts of an apparition within the boundaries of Evan's face.

It was this palimpsest that broke through the dam he had created, weakened by fear and loathing of his present predicament. When would he be let out? When would he be freed? Would Evan come for him? Would he ever see her again, feel her protective arms around him, her reassuring warmth, the beat of her heart against his cheek?

Fear flooded him, turning his entire body cold.

Tears started to well, scalding his eyes. He unfolded, jumped up, turned to face a rear corner of his prison cell before he allowed the tears to fall, runnels down his cheeks, dampening his collar like rain.

And then the dam broke completely. He let out a sob. He shivered, his shoulders shook, his knees grew weak. The sobs came, continued, seemed like they would never stop.

19

The vertiginously stacked neon signs of Tokyo's Shibuya district promenaded aggressively in every direction. Their size and blinding colors shouted, screamed corporate strength and virility. Their toxic maleness was designed to overwhelm, Alyosha Ivanovna thought as she strode across the vast avenues teeming with, alternately, lines of gleaming vehicles, endless rivers of pedestrians borne along on their individual currents, hurrying, never intersecting. Eat, drink, shop. Shop. Tokyo was made for spending, a late-stage capitalist's wet dream. And yet, she liked Tokyo. Liked especially its constant siren call of outsize growth through outsize profits. But then everything about Tokyo was outsized. No wonder her late father had moved here after he divorced Alyosha's mother.

Alyosha came as a teenager to visit her father. Wide-eyed and agog she had immersed herself in the frantic rush of Tokyo life. Her father took her everywhere—to gardens, vast shopping malls, tea houses, pachinko parlors, which Alyosha loved best. He also dragged her along to clandestine meetings in smoky bars, sleazy nightclubs, warehouses that seemed abandoned but weren't. At these places she sat on stools or boxes, away from the men her father was huddling with, drinking a club soda or a can of Coke. She watched the men though her father had told her not to. Even then, in her early teens, she was a student of human nature, of body types, stances, facial expressions. Once, there was an outburst of violence, silent, quickly ended. She absorbed that, too.

Now, as an adult, she saw the sprawling city, its frantic pace through a different lens. Her discipline could place all the input at a healthy distance. She moved easily through the nighttime throngs, the ceaselessly restless neon billboards, the 3-D ads for everything from electronics to films to designer fashion. American movie stars silently hawking liquor, cigars, high-end watches. Electronic fields exploded out into the air above her head.

The lights changed and she along with a thousand others entered the mammoth Shibuya Crossing. She fancied she could feel her heart pulsing against her ribs. The meeting was due to begin in less than ten minutes. This sit-down, which she privately characterized as a collision, was an affront to all her senses. Akujin Matsumura was someone she both hated and feared. He was the fixer—*kuromaku*—for Satsuragi-kai, the most powerful criminal family in Tokyo. The yakuza clan's only notable rival was Ogiba-kai, who ruled the Osaka underworld.

Matsumura and Satsuragi-kai weren't her first encounter with the yakuza, which was why Alyosha asked for this assignment, even though it meant spending significant time away from her lover. Alyosha's father, a successful businessman of questionable morals, had somehow become entangled with Ogiba-kai. This unlikely and unfortunate liaison lasted more or less three years before he wound up dead. His contact at Ogiba-kai claimed he was murdered by a Satsuragi-kai assassin, Akujin Matsumura.

And so, less than two years after her fairy-tale experience with her father, seventeen-year-old Alyosha was back in Tokyo. Like the novice she was she went to the police with this allegation. They claimed to know nothing. The officers she spoke with were as polite as they were opaque. But even though their expressions revealed nothing she could scent their underlying fear like a rancid spice. When she asked to see her father's body, they demurred. When she pressed them, they showed her one forensic photo of his torso. Knife cuts covered it like a tablet with runes. She asked to see his face; again the cops demurred. He had already been identified to their satisfaction. She insisted; she wouldn't leave until she saw her father's face. Reluctantly they agreed. They put the photo in front of her. She looked, her heart leapt into her throat. They had a trash bin waiting for her when she turned and retched, vomiting so hard she thought her stomach would turn inside out.

That night, the Satsuragi-kai quietly, terrifyingly denied the allegation to her face through the very same Akujin Matsumura she had accused. He used his muscular breadth as a silent cudgel to intimidate those he faced. Even in friendly conversation those around him felt fear. And his first and to date only conversation with Alyosha had been far from friendly.

She spoke first, before she lost her nerve. *"You murdered my father. You did more than murder him. I saw the photos."* The sound of her voice quivering almost brought the bile up again. She swallowed hard once, twice. *"I know it. I feel it. You cannot deny it."*

"You know nothing of that time. I liked your father. I did not—would not— murder him." His voice, soft and controlled, was filled with such menace it

acted like a band saw on her nerves, shredding them to the point where she was terrified to utter another word. He told her to mind her own business, that it would be best for her to leave Japan at her earliest convenience. She listened, quailing inside as he handed her a first-class plane ticket back to Moscow. She accepted this "gift" gratefully. She had never before or since felt such an acute urgency to get as far away from a human being as she had during that terrifying encounter. The first thing she did in its immediate aftermath was to find a place to relieve her aching bladder.

Now after years away she was back in Tokyo. Now she was minutes from her meeting with Akujin Matsumura, the sit-down she had been dreading ever since she deplaned at Narita Airport. She found the bar without any trouble despite the ever-changing landscape of the city that confused so many. She turned left off the avenue, then right, found herself in one of the city's myriad narrow streets, fringed on either side by shops, restaurants, and bars squeezed in cheek by jowl. It still amazed her that two blocks off the glittering ultra-modern avenues you could still find these tiny alley-like streets that had remained the same since the Edo Period, the time of the great Tokugawa Shogunate. As she stopped in front of a bar named Sonny's Place, an old woman on the floor above, knifelike elbows on the windowsill, watched her with gimlet eyes and an air of suspicion simply because she wasn't Japanese. She raised her head, grinned at the old crone. In response, she whipped her head back into the shadows of her minuscule apartment.

Inside, Sonny's Place was dim, smoky with cigarette butts and pungent with the smell of male sweat. She stepped past the bar on her right, at this hour filled with salarymen getting raucously drunk. Their next stop would no doubt be the nightclub next door, which provided many services beyond lewd dancing and karaoke.

Ignoring these fixtures of Tokyo's nightlife, she went to the back where, at the left-hand corner table, sat Akujin Matsumura. He was much as she remembered him, wide as a truck grille, a fist-like face, scarred and rippled from who knew what street battles of his youth as he made his methodical way up the ladder of the Satsuragi-kai. How many men had he maimed or killed, Alyosha wondered, as he rose, as she returned the bow, making sure it was just a bit lower than his. Not, she thought, as many as Kata surely. She presented her card with both hands. The *kuromaku* accepted hers, produced his own. The formalities out of the way, they sat down across from one another. Matsumura's back was to the rear wall, which meant she was forced to expose her own back to the front door of the bar.

Matsumura produced a smile, more reptilian than human. She saw he'd had his teeth filed to points, and she shuddered inwardly at the terrifying sight of them. He wore a charcoal-gray sharkskin suit clearly made for him. His blindingly white shirt was newly starched, his tie patterned with a traditional Japanese dragon. *I see he's dressed up for me,* she thought as a joke to keep herself calm.

"I have been waiting a long time for the continuation of our relationship," he said in Japanese just, she was certain, to test her.

"I am pleased to hear that," she responded in the same language. She was fluent, spoke without a foreign accent. If this surprised him she could not tell from his granite expression. "Please correct me if I am wrong," she said, "but at our first meeting you ordered me to leave Japan."

"Please correct me if I am wrong," he replied, "but at our first meeting you accused me of murdering your father."

"The air ticket you pressed on me was more emphatic than any verbal order you could give."

"The accusation you pressed on me was an unforgivable slur to my name, my honor."

The points of his filed teeth appeared and the menace asserted itself so powerfully she experienced it like a blow to her chest. He picked up the bottle of Japanese scotch set on the table along with two intricately incised glasses, poured them both generous portions. Alyosha recognized the brand; expensive as a nugget of gold. The glasses along with the bottle, she was sure, were Matsumura's property, stored here at the bar for whenever he decided to stop by.

"Tell me, how is dear Kata Romanovna?" he said, using the Russian form of given name and patronymic.

Alyosha did not like his phrasing, the clear implication that he and Kata were good friends, which they were not. Nevertheless, she kept her expression neutral. "Kata Romanovna is well."

"Still hasn't stuck her head out from under the rock as of yet?" He could not hide a smirk. However quickly gone, it stuck like a thorn in Alyosha's side.

"She wishes you well, *kuromaku*, in all your endeavors."

His eyes narrowed. He did not like being addressed by anything other than his name, particularly not by his title, which, in any case, was a word not to be bandied about in public. But, she thought, he had brought this barb on himself. She wondered when they would cease fencing and get down to the business at hand. They both drank, allowed the mellow burble of voices to wash over them. It then occurred to her that he might have as much distaste for what was to come as she did. If true, that was an interesting factoid she put away for future reference.

He gestured, as if flicking away Kata's greeting-by-proxy. It was at this moment she noticed the little finger on his left hand was missing, the scar tissue whitish but well healed. The result of *enkozume*, the traditional yakuza ritual of atonement. He had made a mistake in the past. This was how he was required to atone to his *oyabun*. How was it that she never noticed it before? The answer came to her, bubbling up so that she almost laughed aloud. She had been too busy being afraid of him.

"As always," Alyosha continued. "Nothing has changed."

"Everything has changed, for her—and for you." Matsumura's voice was like the heavy tread of a tank. "Kata Romanovna requested this meeting. Why? Her power base is shattered—her men incarcerated, murdered, missing. She has nothing left. She—and you—finished." His thick hand cut through the air between them. "Whatever she wants from us she cannot have."

Alyosha felt the first flutters of panic, as if the bar had tilted, its floor sliding away from her, pitching her into an abyss from which there was no escape. "We have done business for more than five years." But even to her the response was weak, and of course Matsumura was laughing in her face.

"We are not a charity. She knows this. She does not want to hear it. So she sends you in her stead."

He had prodded her once too often and, foolishly, she allowed her anger to pierce her surface calm. Before she could stop herself, she said, "You are *kuromaku*." She heard herself, could not believe what she was doing. "You are not *oyabun*." Her meaning was clear. Neither her boss nor Matsumura's had come to the meeting.

Matsumura's expression remained stony but as he shifted in his seat she saw the butt of his handgun snug in its shoulder holster, and she knew she had crossed a line. Fear lanced through her, fear that she had brought down on herself a dark consequence in which she would find her own death.

As always, every move he made, no matter how minute, was purposeful. While her gaze had been drawn to his handgun in his left armpit the fingers of his right hand gripped a push dagger. The short spade-shaped blade emerged between his third and fourth fingers, stabbed down into the table just at the web between her thumb and forefinger. Less than an inch away was the cluster of nerves that would have rendered her hand numb, useless, possibly forever.

Eyes wide and staring, Alyosha once again felt the fullness of her bladder, a pain just above the apex of her thighs. Nausea raced through her as bile filled her esophagus. She emitted a choking cough.

Matsumura watched her distress with satisfaction. His dominion over her was complete. He poured himself a refill of the costly scotch. Lifted the glass to his mouth, drank it swallow after swallow, eyes fixed upon her face.

"You will vomit now, over this pristine table. You will reveal your true self to me—who and what you are, just as your father did."

Alyosha's stomach heaved, the bile was acid in her throat, burning, burning. Her upper torso writhed inch by terrible inch.

"And then," Matsumura said, "you will be of no use to me." He grunted. "You are already of no use to me. Just like your father."

For just the space of several heartbeats Alyosha's world went black. She was sent spinning down, down into the abyss of abject failure. If she could not avenge her father's murder, then of what use was she in this life?

All at once, she opened her eyes, saw Matsumura regarding her with utter contempt. He pulled the push-dagger out of the wood. She sensed he was about to leave. Once he did that she knew she was finished. He would not come back no matter what she said or did, even if she got down on her knees and begged. A man like him, she thought, would like that—like it very much, but such a shameful gesture would only reaffirm his contempt for her.

There was only one path for her now. Perhaps it had been her path from the moment she sat down opposite him. Her father had locked her into this fate.

She folded her cloth napkin, once, twice, three times, into a padded square. Then she held out her hand.

"Give," she said.

Matsumura's face twitched, a sign she had back-footed him.

"Give it to me." Her fingers curled toward her resoluteness, her fate.

Reversing the push-dagger, he handed it over. "You are baiting me. It won't work."

She took the weapon in her right hand, laid the pinkie of her left hand on the square field of white she had made. Cushioned. "I accused you of murdering my father—to the police, to your face."

He said nothing. His face revealed nothing.

"I have shamed you. The police—"

"The police mean nothing." He shook his head. "Alyosha Ivanovna, I do not blame you."

She placed the edge of the blade along the bottom of her pinkie where it met her palm.

"You will not do this," Matsumura said in a voice that seemed strangled to her. There was something behind his eyes—something new, something she did not recognize. "You are bluffing." He reached out to take the weapon from her. "You would never—"

"I 'would never.'" She threw his words back at him with a razor's edge. "Says the *kuromaku*." The blade came down in one resolute stroke, severing the finger from her hand. Blood, but not as much as she imagined. No pain yet, just a blinding weakness. Vertigo wrapped itself around her like a boa constrictor flexing its muscles. She expelled a breath, drew in another, expelled it. With shaking hand, with great care she wrapped her finger in its white shroud, now stained red in its center.

Her head came down and she almost passed out. Black stars in front of her eyes, a hitch in her breathing, a rushing in her ears as her body struggled to accommodate to the physical insult it had received.

"Alyosha Ivanovna." Matsumura's voice was thin, hoarse.

It took all her strength to push her wrapped finger across the table to him. Absolute stillness enveloped them. Matsumura might have been dead; there was no breath in him. Then, as quickly as it stopped, movement started up again. With two hands Matsumura tenderly took up her gift, pressed the package against his forehead. His head came forward and Alyosha bowed in return.

Placing her gift in his inside breast pocket, Matsumura poured what was left in his glass over the raw wound. She tried not to wince but the pain was too much for her and she slumped in her seat, watched, weary beyond measure, as he wrapped her wound in his own clean napkin, tied it tight.

He made her drink some more scotch, then signaled to the waiter.

"You must eat now. Protein for strength, matcha for wisdom," he said gravely. "Afterward, we will drink sake, you and I."

Alyosha felt a wave of elation so strong it almost swept her away.

20

ABOARD THE *ELUSAN*, HEADING SSE,
MALACCA STRAIT, MALAYSIA

An Binh felt the vibration, a deep thrumming that penetrated to her bones. They were in the main salon aboard the *Elusan*, originally Diti's late father's yacht, for the past twenty years her late brother's.

"'A destroyer of human flesh.' That's what you said." Diti Khong's expression was both worried and frightened.

An Binh cleared her throat, changed the subject. "Where exactly are we going?"

"Port Dickson. I grabbed my chance to sell the yacht. All-cash deal. I'm delivering it to a rep of the buyer, a German company, BriteBar Metallwerks."

An Binh frowned. "Are you sure you want to sell? This boat is a nimble means of transportation."

Diti shrugged. "I don't care. I want ready cash; I don't know how much, if anything, I'll be able to squeeze out of the company now. Besides, after what you said about Matsumura, the farther I get from his yakuza clan the better."

"The clan that has controlling interest in your family's company."

Diti nodded. "So tell me now, how did Satsuragi-kai know all about you?"

An Binh's eyes clouded over. "Not a complete surprise."

"Hey." Diti put her arm around An Binh. "What is going on? You seem spooked."

"I'm fine." An Binh took more ice into her mouth, concentrated on the cold water dribbling down her throat. She knew what was coming now.

"You sure?" Diti said doubtfully.

An Binh nodded. "One hundred percent."

Nevertheless, Diti kept her arm around An Binh's shoulders. "Okay," Diti said. "Now you really have to tell me what the hell's going on. You know this guy, have a history with him, right?"

"You know what? I need some fresh air. Let's go topside."

"Right, boss," Diti said dryly as she stepped away, an uneasy smile on her face.

Diti was right behind her as they went up onto the rear deck, open to the wind and the sky. The scents of salt, brine, phytoplankton made her nostrils flare as she inhaled deeply, held the fresh air in before exhaling.

Standing by the aft railing, she took several minutes to orient herself. They were heading south down the Malacca Strait. The long snake of Malaysia passing on their left. The ship itself was huge, certainly over one hundred feet, and magnificently fitted out in rich teak and gleaming brass. Above their heads, a helipad.

"Quite the yacht," she said.

"Yes, and I can't wait to get rid of it." Diti stood close beside her. She waited several beats before continuing. "You knew Matsumura once, in Tokyo. And now clearly you're going back to find out what his masters want with FED." She raised her hand. "Don't bother to deny it. I'm already familiar with that determined look in your eyes." Briefly, she touched An Binh's shoulder. "Now tell me why else you have to go back. Why you hate this Matsumura."

Sunlight splashed against the water, sending diamonds skipping across the surface. Far behind them gulls rose and fell, searching for food, always searching.

"It seems I've been many people in my life," An Binh began. "Or perhaps I've lived many lives. In one of them I lived in Tokyo. After the incident with your father I'd had my fill of Malaysia. Not long after I found myself in Tokyo. Don't ask me why I went; I couldn't tell you. I was in Shibuya, the heart of the city, just walking aimlessly. It felt good to have such anonymity among the passing clouds of people."

Her fingers curled around the rail, knuckles whitening. "I'm half Vietnamese, half Chinese. Either way, I am an outsider in Japan; I'd never be able to penetrate its society. But at least I'm not Korean; the Japanese consider them less than." She shook her head. "Always that prejudice, always that hatred of the other." Her hand cut through the air. "Well, anyway, sometime during my first week in Tokyo I walked into a bar and sat down. I met a man."

Diti snorted. "Of course. It's always a man."

An Binh snorted. "You're not wrong, especially in this case."

"Hadn't you had your fill of men by then?" Diti's voice was unsurprisingly bitter.

An Binh's eyes lost focus as she sank deeper into memory. "I should have, that's the truth. " She sighed. "The man was Akujin Matsumura."

"Good God, no," Diti said. "Was he the one who . . . ?" She did not seem to want to go on. She reached out. "An Binh." Her voice was breathless.

An Binh nodded. "He cut me. His idea of marking me as his property."

Diti pulled An Binh to her. "I am so sorry."

"It got worse," An Binh whispered.

"Worse? Did he physically attack you?"

"No, nothing like that. Clandestinely overhearing his phone conversations, I discovered his business was highly illegal."

"*Highly* illegal?"

"The Satsuragi-kai were--are--deep into gunrunning, drugs. Bad enough. But what I overheard confirmed that they were also into moving people. Young girls, to be exact. They had them work in the nightclubs they owned, then shipped them out to God knows where."

Diti raised an eyebrow. "They were making money off girls who had already been deflowered?"

"Not exactly. Virgins are the most highly prized, it's true. Which is why this bunch had a doctor under contract. He was an expert in—how shall I put this?—'recreating' virgins."

"Pardon me while I vomit." Diti stood stock-still. She stared at the wake, the churning water, white and gray, opaque. A gull's cry pierced the late afternoon as it passed high above them. A chilly wind was rising, traveling down the strait from the north, catching up to them.

Diti stood back, took An Binh's hands in hers. "I'm getting out of my family business not a moment too soon. My only ally inside the Khong empire was Ramelan, the only one who looked out for me. After he disappeared . . . let's just say I've been surviving on my own wits since I was ten." She shuddered. "We've both had our fill of monsters."

Diti hugged her tightly, kissed her on both cheeks. For a lingering moment they were eye to eye, their breaths mingling. An Binh was drawn to Diti's heat, the contours of her body. She felt the pull of her as if magnetized to something at Diti's core. She tried to control her breathing but failed. Her heart was in her throat.

After a time, they went below, settling in the owner's salon, where they were served steaming tea and small plates of meze. Not a word was said while they drank and ate. None were required. Both of them needed to regain their equilibrium.

"You can't go to Tokyo," Diti said after an interval. "You can't confront Akujin Matsumura again."

"I have to."

"Think what he's capable of, An Binh. You know better than anyone."

"I'm stronger now. I'm smarter now."

Diti leaned forward, took An Binh's hand. "You're also different. Let the past be the past. You're here now. With me."

An Binh stared into Diti's eyes. *"And farther west on the upper reaches the place of the monstrous town was still marked ominously on the sky, a brooding gloom in sunshine, a lurid glare under the stars."*

"Conrad's *Heart of Darkness*, again. Very good. Very apt." Lips curved in the semblance of a smile, Diti lifted An Binh's hand, still clasped in hers, pressed her lips to its back. *"It is like a running blaze on a plain, like a flash of lightning in the clouds. We live in the flicker—may it last as long as the old earth keeps rolling!"*

21

"At first we didn't speak to each other," Nyurgun said. "I was too frightened and she, well, she seemed locked inside herself."

"How did she look?" Evan asked.

"They had really gone to work on her."

"Wounds and bruises?"

"Yes, those, of course. But most were already healing. It was what I saw in her eyes. I only had days, but she had months with them. They must have started with physical abuse, then tried to pry open her mind." His breath was coming fast. Too fast. "Like they did with me." Aya gripped his hand more tightly, as if she were terrified he would disappear inside himself.

This conversation was solely between Nyurgun and Evan. The others—Aya, Elley, the doctor—sat as silent witnesses, Aya because she loved him, the doctor to make sure Evan did not push him past a threshold, Elley because here was the beginning and the end of the story of which he was a part.

"Go on," Evan said softly, "if you can."

Nyurgun shot her a brief glare, then like a knife being withdrawn, smiled the flattest smile Evan had ever seen.

"Who started first?" Evan said.

"She did." Nyurgun licked his lips and Aya fed him some ice chips from a paper cup. He crunched through them, swallowed. "She asked me why I was there. 'To feed you,' I said. 'And that's all?' Her face was dark with blood. 'That's all.' I nodded to assure her.

"'Why you?' she asked me.

"I shrugged. I told her this Russian—Yuri Radik, her jailer, her interrogator here—had picked me up off the street. I had nowhere to go so I went with him to the prison.

"Then she said something strange. 'Who are you?' she said. 'Are you his or are you mine?' I was struck dumb. She said, 'Here there can be no middle ground. Choose.'

"'I choose you,' I said. I don't know why. The words just came out of my mouth. But I guess I do know why. I hated the Russians, the GRU. I hated especially Yuri Radik, who treated me like a bit of reindeer turd stuck to the tread of his boot." He took a breath. "All these things she hated, too. So there was our bond and it was unshakable."

"You came to love her a little bit," Evan said.

His cheeks flamed as he glanced at Aya. "Yes, but not in the way I love Aya. I came to love how smart she was, how courageous. To me she became like a monument. Larger than life. A symbol."

"Tell me about that," Evan said. "How was she a symbol."

"She withstood everything the Russians could think of to break her. She never broke. Her silence defeated them. In the end, they gave up. They sent her up here to live out the rest of her days. But she beat Yuri Radik, too. She found his weaknesses. She played him."

Evan sat forward. "By word or deed?"

"Neither. Her eyes . . . They're . . . I don't know, not human."

Evan's entire body stilled. "What does that mean?"

"They were colorless, but sometimes they were the palest green. It depended on the light . . . or what she was thinking."

"That sounds a bit fanciful, Nyurgun."

"You weren't there," he said somewhat defiantly. "She can look right through you. He feared her and he loved her. I could see it on his face. Plus, she told me as much. And one day he came too close to her. Like a crocodile lying invisible in the mud she waited patiently. She gouged out his eye, used it to open the electronic doors. She defeated the Russian AI as well." He took another deep breath, regathering strength. "And she took me with her when she escaped."

"Were you scared of her?"

"We ate together," Nyurgun said. "So no. Never."

"When you began to speak to each other was it in Russian?" Evan asked.

Nyurgun shook his head. "She spoke Russian to Radik. She and I spoke Sakha. She spoke it very well."

"And what did you two talk about?"

"Just little things. Nothing much." He squeezed Aya's hand and she fed him more ice chips.

"Her parents, alive or dead?'

"Dead, she said." Nyurgun considered a moment. "There was some violence in the family . . . she didn't tell me what and I learned not to ask."

"Did she tell you how she came to name herself White Wolf?"

At this, Nyurgun smiled thinly. "Yes and no. She said there were three stories bandied about on this subject. The first was that as a teenager she was out hunting red deer when she came upon a wolf. It was snowing. The wolf was covered head to toe in white. It had just brought down a sika deer. The wolf stared at Ilona, then went back to feeding. It made no aggressive move when she joined it. The second was that the name was given to her by her paternal grandfather just before he died. He looked into her eyes, watched as they changed from colorless to light green as the sunlight moved through his bedroom and called her White Wolf. The third is that White Wolf was the name her father's extermination squad gave him."

"No hint which one—if any—was the truth."

Nyurgun sat up straighter. "She said they were mirrors. Everyone who heard the stories would decide for themselves which was their truth."

"So none of them," Evan said. None of these brief histories jibed with the intel she'd received from Alyosha. Hardly surprising. She'd been well schooled by Lyudmila, who taught her never to believe anything that came out of Moscow Central, no matter how compelling. The FSB, SVR, GRU files were riddled with *disinformatsiya*, false flags, historical revisions and/or deletions due to myriad political purges, vindictive rivalries where history was rewritten by the victor.

Nyurgun just shrugged. "For me it was the snow-covered wolf she met in the forest. I liked that story best."

Dr. Kuduk cleared her throat. "I think that's enough for now. The boy—"

"I'm not a boy!" Nyurgun's raised voice startled them all.

"Ah-ah." The doctor, mouth agape, had no other words.

Nyurgun turned back to Evan. "One other thing." He spoke in a voice as if only the two of them existed in the room. "She told me about her father."

Evan felt a vein in her temple beat out the rhythm of her interest. "Her father?"

Nyurgun nodded. "Yes. Well, only that he disappeared years after some family violence."

"What happened to him?"

"That's what she was determined to find out."

Evan's pulse quickened. "How? Did she tell you?"

"I have no idea."

"Anything." There was now an urgency in Evan's voice. "Anything at all."

Nyurgun thought a moment. "No, but I got the feeling she knew where she was going."

Evan felt that she had taken another vital step toward the mysterious darkness that shrouded Ilona Starkova. "And where was that? Did she tell you?"

Nyurgun shook his head.

Evan leaned in. "She must have said something. Please try to remember, Nyurgun. You're the only one who can help me and my son."

"I don't . . ." For a moment, he looked lost and the doctor, picking up on his expression, rose. "That's enough. I really must insist."

Nyurgun appeared sad now, the sorrow carving adult lines into his adolescent face.

"I'm sorry, Nyurgun." Evan rose, too. "Get some rest."

"Wait." He closed his eyes for a moment, as if conjuring up an image. "She had a tattoo on the inside of her right wrist."

Evan drew closer. "Do you remember what it was? An animal of some sort? Maybe a wolf, yes?"

He shook his head. "No. It was odd."

"Can you draw it for me?"

Nyurgun nodded, was handed a pencil and a pad by Elley. Moments later, he turned the pad to show Evan. "She told me it's a sigil. A sign of belonging."

"Belonging to what?" Evan asked.

He shrugged. Clearly he was interested in something else altogether. A small smile spread across his ravaged face. "I said I wanted one."

"And what did she answer?"

"She'd have to take me to a place . . . in Tokyo. A neighborhood. Shee . . ." He tried to say the word but stumbled over it.

"Shibuya?" Evan asked. "Was it Shibuya?"

Nyurgun nodded.

"You're a brave one." Evan put a hand on his shoulder, squeezed gently. "You have just told me where to find her, the White Wolf."

Nyurgun closed his eyes, nodded. Tears leaked, rolling down his cheeks. Aya wiped them gently away. He took a deep breath, let it out. He looked at Aya. "I'm fine now. Perfectly fine."

Then he returned his attention to Evan. "She was kind to me. Please don't hurt her."

"I'll do my best," Evan said sadly.

He smiled, raised his hand. "Long life, Evan."

She raised her hand, the mirror image of his. "Long life, Nyurgun."

22

When Bernhard-Otto von Kleist stepped into the restaurant he had chosen, he spotted Kurt Çelik at once. For one thing, the man was unmistakable with his white hair and predatory pale eyes. For another, at this off-hour between luncheon and supper the restaurant was nearly empty. This was von Kleist's purpose in setting the time as well as the venue when Çelik had requested a meeting. Von Kleist was impeccably dressed as was his strict habit as a Prussian of the old school—his grandfather had been a prominent general in the Prussian army. As such, he had been a powerful figure in society and government. As his grandson was today. Otto von Kleist was more than a highly successful attorney, he was a master fixer. Every prominent pol in the EU came to him when they needed help of the sort only he could provide. As such he shunned the spotlight. So much so that there were few photos of him. He was also one of the three owners of BriteBar Metallwerks, whose manufacturing headquarters were here in Gerlingen, along with Bosch and many other of Germany's most prestigious electronic, machine, and auto manufacturers. Çelik was the second owner, Marsden Tribe was the third, though the names of these three or any entity that could be traced back to them did not appear on any of the papers of incorporation, contracts, bills of lading, or any other of BriteBar's public documents. All three were hidden behind impenetrable firewalls. Others, handpicked and securely vetted, ran BriteBar's day-to-day operations but it was the three principals who made the decisions.

Several years ago von Kleist had been introduced to Marsden Tribe through Evan Ryder, who had befriended von Kleist's daughter. The two men had developed as much of a friendship as the rarefied air in which they lived allowed. The main reason it persisted was that von Kleist was smart enough to know that Tribe was brilliant; trying to outsmart him was not only a fool's errand but likely to be fatal. Finally, the trio decided to start this joint venture. Tribe provided the capital and the technology, von Kleist took care of the masses of complex legal paperwork necessary for the principals to remain hidden, Kurt Çelik provided the manufacturing facilities as well as the distribution lines. In other words, they each brought their considerable expertise to the enterprise. It was, von Kleist supposed at the outset, as close to a perfect union as three businessmen could get. But humans were complex creatures, their motives opaque and, at times, von Kleist had discovered, irrational.

Çelik rose, smiling, and the two men embraced as if they were old friends, not business partners. Çelik smelled of vetiver and labdanum—smoke and leather. Like a horseman.

"Your flights from Tokyo were satisfactory, I take it," von Kleist said as he sat down.

"I arrived last night." Çelik slid back into his seat, took up the cup of coffee he'd been drinking. "Early evening, actually."

Von Kleist smiled. He was used to Çelik's question-adjacent answers, even found them amusing at times. *He must work very hard on his conversation skills*, von Kleist thought, wondering where that honed skill came from, like the sideways swipe of a cutlass through the fog of war.

The server arrived in silence. Von Kleist ordered and the server departed in the same unobtrusive manner. They were seated in a pew-like space near the rear of the restaurant, which had been in business since before the First World War. Behind them the complex copper-and-brass Kaffee machines shone, whirred, and whistled as they dispensed coffee and espresso. The smoke-darkened coffered wooden ceiling rose two stories above their heads. Light streamed in from the high cathedral-like windows on either side. Servers in long white aprons strode to and fro. Even though their customers were few they had a built-in abhorrence to looking idle, for what was a server without purpose? Unemployed, as the undying joke went.

"I assume you arrived here early in order to scope out the immediate environment," von Kleist said conversationally. "Exits, entrances, layout of the surrounding streets, that sort of thing."

Çelik's smile advertised his teeth. "Old habits never die."

"Once a soldier, always a soldier, eh?"

"I am careful about my person, always have been."

At length, von Kleist's order was set down in front of him—a triple espresso, a generous slice of apple strudel with a bowl of freshly whipped cream on the side.

He'd only begun to savor the restaurant's excellent espresso when Çelik said, "I'm calling this meeting to order."

Von Kleist unloaded a dollop of whipped cream onto his strudel, said, "Without Marsden?"

"The subject of this meeting is Marsden Tribe."

"I see," von Kleist said, though he did not see at all. A meeting called with only two of the principals was unprecedented and, in von Kleist's opinion, legally and morally perilous.

He cut a precise amount of strudel with the edge of his fork, speared it, delivered it to his mouth and chewed slowly, contemplatively, then swallowed. "I will require details," he said with no little asperity.

"I plan to give you just that." Çelik called for something stronger than coffee.

The chilled vodka arrived, the waiter pouring a generous amount into a cut-crystal tumbler. Çelik downed it all while the waiter still had the bottle in his hands. Çelik nodded to him, the waiter refilled his glass, left the bottle on the table and departed.

"When we came together to create BriteBar," Çelik said, "Tribe was one person. Now that Daedalus is ready, he is another."

"That was two years ago," von Kleist pointed out. "We are all different people, Herr Çelik."

Çelik smirked. "Not like Tribe. And don't tell me you haven't seen it yourself."

"In fact, I haven't."

"Herr von Kleist—since we're being formal with each other—I think Tribe is trying to cut us out of the product."

"And how precisely would he be doing that?"

"There's something wrong with the prototypes."

"Our labs confirm they are working fine."

"Until they don't." Çelik poured vodka into his coffee, slurped it down. "I've had some . . . how shall I put it? Some unexpected outcomes."

"Such as?"

"Subjects have gone mad—become violent, in one case homicidal."

Von Kleist sat back. This conversation was proceeding along the very lines Marsden Tribe had outlined in their recent conversation. The guy was uncanny, von Kleist thought. Scarily uncanny.

Meanwhile, Çelik was continuing with his lament. "I got so angry I had my people hack into his system."

Von Kleist held up a hand. "Hold on. You're telling me you hacked into the Parachute servers?"

"Tried to, anyway. We could only get so far. His goddamned quantum algorithms defeated us."

"Well, I should hope so." And next Çelik would ask him to betray Tribe, right on schedule. "And you want . . ."

"I want," Çelik said, interrupting von Kleist, "to kill him."

Von Kleist sat stock-still. His reaction was entirely visceral—his mind frozen solid—but distinctly odd. On the one hand he couldn't breathe, on the other his blood pounded in his ears so loudly he was certain an artery had burst.

"I don't . . ." He stopped, cleared his throat, had to start again. "I don't quite understand." Even the brilliant Tribe had not seen this coming.

Çelik's muddy brown eyes sparked like glowsticks. "If there was one thing I learned in the military it's that when someone betrays you, you burn his house down. With him in it."

Von Kleist struggled to keep himself under control. To accomplish this he took another forkful of strudel and whipped cream into his mouth, chewing it slowly, savoring the swirl of sugary tastes, swallowing before saying in an even tone, "And you want me to agree to this."

"I am offering you an opportunity," Çelik said. He sipped his coffee, his eyes never leaving von Kleist's. He carefully set his cup down. "Bernhard, what I want is for you to come down on the right side of history."

■　■　■

The right side of history. The Thousand-Year Reich, von Kleist thought, as he sat contemplating Çelik's scheme. He was almost finished with his apple strudel. He ordered another triple espresso. Being Prussian, he was descended from a long line of proud and honorable ancestors—women as well as men. The very idea of Nazism, of Fascism in any form was anathema to him. He was a capitalist in the old-fashioned sense of the word. Sadly, however, he was acutely aware of how late-stage capitalism was in the process of descending into the muddy waters of chaos. Even worse, neo-Nazism was not only on the rise around the world but had, God help us all, become fashionable. How this had come about confounded von Kleist. Increasingly, he felt more and more out of touch with the postmodern world, wanting with a fervor previously unknown to him a return to his grandfather's world, where Fascism masquerading under spurious cloaks did not exist. He felt, not to put too fine a point on it, like a man out of time, exhausted as a salmon having to constantly swim upstream without a hint of calm water ahead. It wasn't that he wanted to rest, no; what he craved was the mega-wealth of a Marsden Tribe in order to leap above the increasingly bloody fray.

He said nothing of this to Çelik, of course, who was, in any event, typing like a madman on the keyboard of his cell phone.

Von Kleist cleared his throat and, a moment later, Çelik looked up.

"Problem?" von Kleist asked, desperately wishing it were so.

Çelik put away his phone. "Already handled."

That was another thing von Kleist didn't like about Çelik, he hadn't the foggiest idea about manners. He was loud, rude, intemperate, an animal got up in expensive yet ill-fitting clothes.

With a glance at his watch, Çelik threw some bills on the table— another gesture a gentleman would never even contemplate—and slid his chair back. "Since you clearly haven't come to a decision as yet and I have a flight to catch, why don't you ride with me out to the airport? The car that brought me into town is waiting outside and I'll instruct the chauffeur to take you wherever you want to go afterward." He rose. "Sound good?"

Von Kleist nodded, rose, but his thoughts were still far away. He realized—knew this for some time, actually—that his friendship with Tribe had saved him from sinking further into his grandfather's time. He absorbed Tribe's energy and enthusiasm as if it were a tonic. In a sense his partnership in BriteBar Metallwerks had revived him. He woke up every morning excited to get to work, reveling in his part of Tribe's plan, which, he was quite sure, would revolutionize the way the world did business. He imagined that world, free of cyberattacks, state-run and otherwise, electronic espionage, site outages, enormous data breaches, extortion from very bad actors who held your information—your very patented methodology—for ransom, a large portion of the nefarious dark web.

He joined Çelik in the backseat of his sleek limo and they headed out toward the airport. After a moment, Çelik leaned forward, pressed a button that raised the thick glass partition between passengers and chauffeur.

"Now we can talk in complete privacy," Çelik said, settling back against the cushioned seat. "I think I've given you sufficient time to ponder the pros and cons of my offer." He turned his head toward von Kleist. "Your answer, please."

Von Kleist took a moment to gather his thoughts. "What you propose is no simple plan, Çelik. This a huge ask, with a great number of—"

The edge of Çelik's hand cut through the air. "Let me stop you right there, my friend. We both know that this partnership is not an equilateral triangle. You know Tribe believes he holds all the reins, believes he's better, smarter than we are. I don't know about you but I'm tired of taking orders from him. Can't you see he's using us? He could build his own factory here in Gerlingen or anywhere else for that matter. But that would take time, and it's apparent time is the one thing he doesn't have. He could, with time and a great deal of effort, replicate my contacts, but as I said, he lacks time. Additionally, establishing connections with the entities in a similar network to mine exposes him to outsize dangers to Parachute, something I know he's unwilling to do." His finger jabbed out. "But the pendulum has swung in our direction, my friend. We have the largest shipment of the bone-to-bone communicators within reach. All we have to do is take possession of them."

"Tribe will destroy us."

"Precisely." Çelik's eyes were alight. "Now you've gotten it. We need to take him off the board before he can lift a finger to stop us."

"I don't think that's possible." Von Kleist saw the chauffeur on his cell phone. He did not like when drivers used their cell phones while their car was running through traffic.

"Anything is possible." Çelik's cell chimed. He reached into his jacket pocket, withdrew not his phone but a long, thin needlelike implement that he drove into von Kleist's left ear. The pain of the ear-drum puncture lifted von Kleist off the seat, paralyzed him long enough for the poison along its tip to contaminate his brain.

Von Kleist's eyes rolled up in his head and he slumped into the footwell, not a drop of blood spilled. Çelik bent down, clicked on his phone's flashlight, pried open von Kleist's jaws, directed the light to the back of his mouth. "There you are, my pretties," he said as the light illuminated the two side-by-side molars imprinted with the Daedalus sigil. "A direct line to Tribe."

Letting go of the jaw, wiping the saliva off his fingertips onto von Kleist's expensive and immaculate right-hand cuff, he slid back the sleeve of Van Kleist's expensive bespoke suit. He unbuttoned the cuff of his Egyptian cotton shirt, turned the wrist so the inside was facing him.

"And there it is," he said with a peculiar sibilance, "the Daedalus tattoo." He bared his own right wrist where no inked design existed. He looked up. "Why were you in Tribe's inner circle and not me?" He spat onto von Kleist's aristo cheek. "You Germans are all the same—Nazis under the skin."

23

Even in the incessant downpour, Ilona Starkova had no trouble finding Studio Edo. It sat on the eastern edge of Uguisudanicho within Shibuya. Eiko was inside, waiting for her. She looked just as Ilona remembered her. Beauty in strength, Ilona thought as they bowed to each other. Then Eiko looked her over. Ilona looked back. Each was unflinching, each was mindful of the other. Eiko saw Ilona and Ilona saw Eiko.

They smiled at the same time.

Eiko was small, compact, well-grounded, as one learns in all martial arts. A thick swath of pure white adorned one side of her ink-black hair. Two other tattoo artists—both men—were hard at work on their respective clients. The air was warm, woody, slightly buzzed. "I have everything ready." Eiko showed Ilona through a door in the back of the shop, through what appeared to be a lounge area for the artists, then through another, heavier door. She handed Ilona a pair of goggles. "Even though you have these on, please keep your eyes closed. The laser is dangerous."

"Perfect." Ilona removed her wet jacket, rolled up the sleeve of her shirt to reveal the sigil. "You always do beautiful work."

"Will you be sad to lose it?"

"Not this one."

Eiko smiled, inclined her head. Watched Ilona as she climbed onto a medical table covered in a sheet of white paper.

As she readied the laser, allowing it to warm up, she said, "I never cared for this one."

"Well, it wasn't your design—or mine."

Eiko's expression darkened. "That's what I mean." She seemed to want to keep the conversation going, but apparently decided against it, instead saying, "Turn your wrist . . . Yes, just like that." Then, placing her goggles over her eyes, she began her work. The heat in the room increased, the woody odor sharp in Ilona's nostrils, soft humming in her ears. Eiko's body pressed against hers, a comforting mix of hills and glens, muscles stretched tight, a soothing balm against the insistent burn that gathered itself like sunlight through a magnifying glass.

An hour later, Eiko's work was complete. Ilona's wrist on fire. Her skin was inflamed, but the sigil was but an indistinct smudge. And still Ilona did not feel free.

PART THREE

GIRI
[HONOR; OBLIGATION]

Perception and Sight: In strategy it is important to see distant things as if they were close and to take a distant view of close things.

—*A Book of Five Rings,* Miyamoto Musashi

24

At sea, Kampung Pasir Panjung, the murder Diti had committed there, became a distant memory. There was only Diti; An Binh wanted only to be with Diti. They talked constantly—not of the twisted Khong history, not of the complex strands of Far Eastern Distributors business or how its new owner, Satsuragi-kai, would respond to Budiharta's sudden disappearance, Diti's walking away from the company. Diti feared retribution but averting that possible calamity was for another day.

They swam in the cool blue morning, made love in the orange heat of the afternoon, whispered with their legs, sticky with sweat and fluids, entwined. Diti limned by a slash of sunlight through the stateroom window. Her arms around An Binh, holding her, the heat of her body seeping through An Binh's skin, into her flesh, her bones.

An arrow of light in my life, An Binh thought, her mind drugged by sex and something else, something unknown to her but coming clearer by the second.

"You're going to leave me," Diti said with a sigh.

"I told you . . ." But An Binh, tongue thick in her mouth, could not go on. It was all she could muster, barely anything. Nothing, really. Her eyes stung, watering.

"Yes, I know. It's inevitable," Diti said sorrowfully. "You're drawn away by what you do, by who you are."

An Binh felt a stab of . . . what? Guilt? Sorrow? Brushing up against the inevitability of her fate. "What I do and what I am are separate."

"For most people." Diti's legs moved over her. "Not for you."

An Binh lifted her head, her gaze roving over Diti's flawless brown skin. *An arrow of sunlight,* she could not help thinking. *Transformed by a kind of alchemy.*

What did that mean to An Binh? Nothing? Everything? Was there anything in between? she asked herself.

The yacht lifted and fell, cleaving the water in two. Light of a different kind settled on them both. Clouds, moving swiftly, obscured the sun, bringing darkness.

An Binh learned that Diti craved the night. They never slept, instead had sweaty, grinding, increasingly desperate sex anywhere and every-where on the vessel. Diti appeared to know where each member of the crew was day or night so that they were never disturbed or spied upon when they went at it hammer and tongs in the salon, the kitchen, what had once been her brother's office. By far her favorite was under the tarp spread over the motor launch that hung from steel davits on the port side of the yacht. There, in the humid, perpetual night Diti did things to An Binh that terrified and electrified her in equal measure. Left her open-mouthed, drowned in an exhaustion that made her heart pound, her eyes roll up in her head.

■　■　■

But then, like a finger snap it was over. Waking from an erotic dream, wordlessly, a veil dimming them, they arrived at Port Dickson. They docked at the Admiralty Marina, where the *Elusan* seemed to settle un-easily, as if aware of its fate. Not long after, a meeting with the rep from BriteBar Metallwerks, the company purchasing the yacht from Diti, a re-gal blond, blue-eyed German woman straight out of the Teutonic gene pool. She didn't smile, she didn't acknowledge An Binh in any way. It was as if she were part of the sea or the sky. Diti took the German below where, Diti told her later, she did a thorough search of every nook and cranny, made a face as she watched one of the crew stripping the linens off the king-size bed in the master suite—clearly the only bed that had been slept in.

The two women, one dark, one light, one of the underclass, no matter her wealth, one uber-menschen, her birthright, returned to the deck and An Binh's sight. "I would much rather have dealt with your brother." The German, from her implied perch high above Diti, took the ownership papers from Diti as if they were contaminated with a virus.

"No, you wouldn't. He would've run you over," Diti said with a genuine smile. "Anyway, it's me you're dealing with, no one else." She grinned, an expression the German could not, under the circumstances, understand. "New world order."

"Yes, well." The German huffed, handed over the cashier's check, sniffed, said, "Now get off my boat."

Back on dry land, An Binh knew she should be heading straight for the airport where Tribe's private jet was waiting to take her to Tokyo. But her monstrous ghost memories of Akujin Matsumura awaited her in Tokyo. Diti was here, shiningly beautiful, alive and delighted; the sailing's golden glow had not worn off. An Binh found that she liked that glow. She didn't want it to fade as it surely would once she saw the airport looming in front of her.

So she postponed what she knew was the inevitable—the parting from Diti. She accepted Diti's plea to at least stay the night and informed the jet's pilot that she would be ready to leave in the morning. They took dinner at a sparkling seafood restaurant overlooking the marina. Glancing out the window between courses, An Binh watched the yacht docked, tied down, motionless. The lights were off, it looked abandoned, and this saddened her. She wished with all her heart that she and Diti could run aboard, cast off, sail back up the Malacca Strait or head farther south through the Port Dickson Strait to one of the archipelago's islands—Rampang or Galang—lose themselves in dense forest and birdcalls and moonlight. Leave everything behind. *The weight of murder, death, vengeance*, she thought, *is crushing me.*

In the suite Diti had booked in the hotel above the restaurant, they made love with a kind of fierce desperation that threatened to shatter her heart.

The morning eventually showed its flaming head, though she did her best to hold it back. Morning returned to the surface of her thoughts the one dangerous, perhaps unforgiveable secret she kept from her lover— that she had stuffed Diti's one childhood friend and protector into the company safe to die there. Also returned to her mind was her commitment to Parachute. She had thought about this long and hard during the last several days, realizing at last that her commitment had always been to Ben Butler and to Evan Ryder. When Marsden Tribe had moved to cut out Ben, to be the one she reported to, her sense of commitment to both of them increased exponentially. She had never felt comfortable around Tribe. Something about him had caused an itch to crawl under her skin. She felt protective of Ben and Evan. No matter that this remit came directly from Tribe, Evan and Timur had been abducted. Her duty was to keep Evan safe. This, in the end, provided the impetus for An Binh to leave Diti, painful as it was.

So, eyes wet and stinging, she left for the airport. Japan was waiting.

25

SHIBUYA, TOKYO, JAPAN

Oiran was the most gorgeous public space Alyosha had ever been in. The restaurant, vast, spare in the manner only the Japanese could make glorious, flowed across the entire thirty-first floor of a building that housed a bank at street level and who knew what on the floors in between. There were floor-to-ceiling windows to her left, where polished wooden tables were precisely aligned for the best views of Shibuya even as now, after dark and in the rain, with raindrops striking the glass, running in rivulets, multicolored neon smeared into shapes that reminded her of nothing so much as Godzilla and Mothra.

To her right was a long bar illuminated from below, and beyond that a free-form hinoki-wood sushi counter where diners sat on wooden stools, accepting tiny, exquisite plates of raw fish and pickled vegetables from a pair of deft sushi masters.

She and Akujin Matsumura were led to a prime table by one of the windows. Alyosha was grateful to be seated. Her damaged hand throbbed like a second heart. Though treated and bandaged by Satsuragi-kai's personal doctor she had refused the heavy painkillers he had tried to press onto her. She was in no position to have the sharp edges of her mind filed down to nubs.

Matsumura ordered sake when they sat down. The beautiful slim woman who had ushered them to their table nodded silently, vanished without a sound. Alyosha stared out the window at nighttime Shibuya. Her imagination conjured a neon Godzilla winking at her over and over. Below, the multitude of Tokyo's underclass scurried by beneath opened umbrellas, bobbing like jellyfish amid tidal waves. She felt no connection to the sidewalk citizens, divorced from them by who she was and what she did. They would never know of her, she would never know of them, an abyss between them.

The sake service arrived. It seemed far more elaborate than any she had seen before.

"Kyoudai sakazuki." Matsumura himself poured sake for both of them, which was also a first for her. The female server had delivered the sake, backed away in almost the same motion, fluid as a dancer.

"I've never heard this phrase," Alyosha said. "What does it mean?"

Matsumura smiled with just the tips of his mouth. "Literally 'Brother's sake cup.'" He nodded. "Drink."

She sipped the sake with him, her eyes never leaving his.

"We are bound now," he said, "in two rituals of tradition. First, by *enkozume*. Second, by *sakazukigoto*, the passing of sake to signify a bond between two people."

They drained their cups.

"It is done," he said. "Now we are as one."

Alyosha felt terror move through her bones like a viper spewing its poison into her system. She had crossed her Rubicon, never to return. What had she done? She was inside Satsuragi-kai in the only way possible, but she felt hollow . . . worse, filthy, as if she had just woken up from a drunken night of sex with a stranger she already despised. Or was it, she wondered, herself she despised? She realized her impossible situation: in order to complete the remit she had hit a crisis point. A decision had to be made and she made it. In the process she was forced to betray Kata. Unless she could find it within herself to successfully serve two masters. The problem: every single person she knew or had read about, attempting to thread this needle, wound up dead. She smiled at Akujin Matsumura, her benefactor, her bitter enemy, but her heart, her soul resided now in a limbo of her own making.

Desperate to jump off this toxic train of thought, she said, "They treat you here like a king. It must be because of the *shobadai* they pay you." She meant the monthly protection money businesses paid yakuza families like Satsuragi-kai.

"You would think." Matsumura laughed softly. "But no. Oiran pays *shobadai* to no one."

Now this was interesting. Alyosha narrowed her focus of attention. "Why is that?" She gestured. "This place must be worth a fortune."

"Oh, yes. It is. However, this restaurant and the hotel below is owned by Ume Linnear." Matsumura poured them both more sake. "And the rest of the building, including the bank we passed on the way in, as well as many other properties in Tokyo, Kyoto, and throughout Japan, is owned by her father, Nicholas Linnear. Two years ago, he sold his international liquid natural gas company for one hundred twenty-five billion dollars."

Even more interesting. Alyosha was close to forgetting her pain. "Are you saying this man is, what, untouchable because of his enormous wealth?"

"Not exactly. He is revered for his deep understanding of Japan, of samurai, of ninja, as well as to honor Linnear-san's mother, Cheong, who is considered something of a deity among many groups."

"Japanese?"

"Cheong is not of Japanese origin, nor is she, strictly speaking, Chinese. Linnear-san's father met her in Singapore. She might be Straits Chinese, but that's far from certain. There are those who think she was born and raised in one of the small villages on the mountainous border between China and Tibet. But, really, no one knows, possibly not even Linnear-san himself.

"In any event, each new year, Sumida Koji, our *oyabun* himself, comes here. He and Linnear-san exchange gifts."

"As a sign of respect."

"Precisely."

"He comes here instead of Linnear going to him." She shook her head. "I don't understand."

"You are not Japanese."

She knew that Japanese society was highly insular. Save for a precious few, outsiders never saw the heart of the culture, let alone were ever able to fathom the intricate levels of arcane rituals and conduct. Matsumura's comment was a slap across the face, something not unknown to her, something she could bear. But she wondered now, for the first time, whether this would always be the case. She suspected there would come a moment when a passive response to such slaps would fail her, when she would step into the unknown. When she would act.

To settle the beat of her heart she said, "A man like that must surely draw powerful enemies like flies to honey."

Matsumura, whose mien was entirely serious, even dour, as if something essential inside him had withdrawn into his secret center, nodded. "Indeed."

"Meaning?"

Matsumura's gaze, which had been wandering, returned to alight on her like a poisonous insect. "Some of Linnear-san's enemies died of old age, others perished from a surfeit of hubris. He cannot be bought and it is a fatal mistake to threaten or bully him. To my knowledge, none who have tried are still living."

"And yet . . . ?" She had heard a certain dark note in the undercurrent of his voice.

"Linnear-san has enemies still. In his world this is never-ending." Matsumura hesitated a beat. "Powerful, influential, implacable enemies. Yes, there are those set against him."

Alyosha considered this scenario. "The ones who perished from a surfeit of hubris, as you said. Did you or others act on his behalf?"

The corners of Matsumura's lips curled upward. A smile or a sneer, it was impossible for her to tell. "He never asked. Certainly, I didn't offer. No one would. He requires no one's help." His head turned. "This is the way it is with Linnear-san."

"He sounds . . . different," was all she could muster in response to this description.

"He *is* . . . different."

Was Matsumura mimicking her to make fun of her, to belittle her? With him the answer was yes. Always yes. Her eyes narrowed, but only because he was no longer looking at her.

He lifted an arm in the direction of an exquisite young woman Alyosha judged to be in her late twenties. She was dressed in an outfit that could be Japanese or Western, or neither, depending on your point of view. She glided through the restaurant as if on a cushion of air.

"That is Ume-sama, Linnear-san's daughter."

Ume glanced in their direction, smiled at Matsumura, started toward them.

"She is mixed race," Alyosha said.

"Like her father."

"Linnear—his father was . . . British?"

"Yes. His father was a British colonel, well-regarded both in Singapore and here when he joined MacArthur's staff. Nicholas was raised here in Japan; as far as he's concerned, Tokyo is his home."

She shook her head. "How can he—and his mother—be so revered here when they aren't even partly Japanese?"

He glanced at her and she felt as if a car had just missed sideswiping her. "When—if—you meet him perhaps you will understand." Matsumura seemed unwilling to continue in this vein. "We know *her* mother was American," he said without taking his eyes off Ume.

"Was?"

"Justine died some years ago. Linnear-san married into a wealthy family. Tomkin Industries. Justine's father was into construction—business and mixed-use towers in New York. After his death, Linnear took over, expanded the business through international trade, made another fortune transporting LNG—liquid natural gas. By that time, he'd returned here. Because of her—Ume. He wanted her conversant in the ways of Japanese society. Turned out she had an uncanny knack for understanding it as deeply as if she were born and raised here."

And then Ume was at their table. She was even more stunning up close. A high, graceful forehead, a swan's neck, large eyes with the iridescence of a raven's wing, slightly upturned at the outer corners. She wore her hair, thick and black, drawn back in traditional Japanese style. Alyosha counted herself dazzled. As Matsumura introduced them, Alyosha was certain Ume was aware of her injured hand but never even glanced at it, never questioned either of them about it. Her manners were as exquisite as her appearance. And yet she was also certain that Ume felt a shard of her pain, the prison of Alyosha's *giri* toward Matsumura.

Ume had turned her gaze on Matsumura. "You are summoned." Her voice was like a musical instrument, a viola, Alyosha decided.

Matsumura nodded, rose, excused himself. He did not ask Ume who had summoned him or why, but that she had used the simple phrase "You are summoned" indicated that the person Matsumura went to meet was someone of great importance. Her gaze followed him as Ume guided him to a woman in traditional Japanese dress, sitting by herself at the sushi bar. She was striking, even in profile. Older, perhaps in her sixties, though at this distance it was difficult to tell. As Matsumura bowed, settled onto the stool beside her, Alyosha turned away. She fished her cell phone out of her purse, fired it up. Scrolled to the photos of the woman whose supposed beating by Ilona Starkova she had used to help her recruit Evan. She had told Evan the woman was her sister; she was not. As Alyosha deleted the photos, unbidden cloudy shards of shattered memories, ghostly terrors of her past, attempted to rise into her mind. She instantly snuffed them out, like extinguishing a faulty flickering oil lamp.

Matsumura's return snapped her fully back to the present. At once, she sensed the change in his demeanor. He seemed somehow brittle, on edge, and she couldn't help but wonder what that woman at the sushi bar had said to him.

"Who is that?" Keeping her voice casual, as if she had minimal interest in his answer.

"Hmm?" He turned to her. "That's Kiko Ashikaga. The Ashikaga family has a long, entitled history as one of the great samurai families."

"Why were you summoned to her?" Alyosha asked this with a touch of mockery. The sight of the Satsuragi-kai's fearsome *kuromaku* answering a summons from anyone but his *oyabun* struck her as strange indeed.

"You," he said, perfectly, frighteningly serious. "Kiko-san wanted to know who you are and why you're with me."

Alyosha was stunned. "Why? How does she even know I exist?"

Matsumura grunted. "It appears she's been watching you since we arrived."

Alyosha lifted her bandaged hand. "Okay, so she saw this."

"I'm certain that was one factor," Matsumura acknowledged. "In fact, she asked about it."

Alyosha's eyes narrowed. "What did you tell her?"

"The truth," he said. "I always tell Kiko Ashikaga the truth."

"You." Alyosha huffed. "You who traffic in lies."

When, as now, Matsumura's lips curled in the semblance of a smile he made Alyosha want to back away as if like a cobra he was about to spit poison into her face.

His powerful fingers curled around the wrist of her maimed hand. "You don't speak to me that way, Alyosha Ivanovna. Never. Understood?" It was a command, not a question.

Pain in her hand, a throbbing so agonizing it made it difficult for her to breathe. That was the point, she knew. For her, the only goal was to keep that agony off her face, to keep her expression neutral, to keep her smile from being a rictus, to think about nothing but spitting in his eyes. Pain she was used to, but he had a way of dispensing it that went beyond normal boundaries.

"You obey me in all ways." The pain increased to an almost unbearable level. Her heart fluttered like an animal in a trap. Her mouth went dry, her toes curled, tried to dig into the floor through the soles of her shoes. "*Giri.*" Her obligation to him.

She conjured saliva from deep in her throat so she could answer. "Yes, *kuromaku*. I understand."

He released her wrist. "You have yet to touch on the reason for Kata Romanovna sending you here to me."

Her eyes were big around; she closed them to slits. "She wants to move her operation here to Tokyo."

Matsumura's eyebrows raised. "Seriously?"

"Under the auspices of Satsuragi-kai, of course."

He eyed her but said nothing.

Alyosha took a breath she had been holding for some minutes, sat back, folded her arms across her chest, and stared at Kiko Ashikaga. Expecting to see her profile, she was surprised to find the older woman turned on her stool, looking directly at Alyosha. When their eyes met she smiled. It was nothing like Matsumura's. In it, Alyosha saw a warmth that surprised her, and within it a touch of wistfulness.

Noting the direction in which Alyosha was looking, Matsumura said sourly, "She wants to meet you."

"Why?"

"She says it's because of her husband, Kurt Çelik. A Turk. He fired his last assistant. Japanese. He wants a non-Asian."

Alyosha, returning Kiko's smile, said softly, "I am no man's assistant."

"Pardon me, but you are—perhaps *were* is a better choice—Kata Romanovna's assistant."

She was about to retort that Kata was no man but just in time caught the malicious glint in his eye, bit back her words, understanding the double meaning of his. What pissed her off was that he wasn't wrong. In many ways Kata had more male than female traits. She felt bile in her throat, and yet he apparently did not think less of her because he knew she and Kata were lovers. And his use of the word *were* clearly implied that at the moment Kata had no organization and thus no need of an assistant.

He rightly took her silence as acquiescence. "If Kiko-san likes you— and she will, Alyosha Ivanovna, she will—this you will do for me. Her husband, Kurt Çelik, is a billionaire many times over. He is supremely influential, powerful in ways you can only dream of. It is said this is why Kiko-san married him—his power and wealth overwhelmed her. Before she met him, she and her family, like many of the old, proud samurai families, had fallen on hard times. Kurt Çelik was her way out." He let go a soft laugh, ephemeral as a soap bubble. "It couldn't be for his charm or benign personality. You being his right hand will be invaluable to Satsuragi-kai and not incidentally to me." He licked his lips. "Kiko-san does not hold me in the high regard she ought to. This perception you will change."

Alyosha took several moments to assess everything Matsumura had just revealed. Many things were now expected of her, but she was certain there were others, buried deeply, she would be required to unearth herself, even perhaps information that would give her leverage over Matsumura, iron-bound as she was to him. To *giri*. Once she had submitted to *enkozume*, the yakuza finger-cutting ritual, she committed herself to *giri*. To doing whatever necessary to get what Kata wanted. There was no escape for her. Not at the moment, at least.

Alyosha turned again, saw Kiko Ashikaga beckoning to her.

"Go," Matsumura said under his breath.

"If I do," she said, "you will take Kata Romanovna under your steel umbrella."

He nodded.

Still she persisted. This was why she had come, this was why she had bent the knee to him, maiming herself in the process. "Your word."

"You have my word," he growled. "Go now."

Hands clammy, Alyosha rose and made her way slowly to where Kiko-sama sat, aware with every step of the older woman's close scrutiny of her approach

"Sit," Kiko-san said softly.

Alyosha sat. She looked up into the warm kind eyes of Kiko Ashikaga Celik and wondered why she felt as though she were being led to slaughter.

26

SHIP TO SHORE; DAEDALUS

"You just had a meeting with von Kleist," Tribe said.

"That's right." Kurt Çelik paused. "It was unexpectedly rather awkward."

"How so?"

"Well, I hesitate to—"

"No hesitations."

"He . . ." Çelik cleared his throat. "The truth of it is he tried to pull me into some crazy scheme to cut you out of BriteBar."

He's lying, Quinton said via his Daedalus link with Tribe.

Of course he is, Tribe answered, a little too quickly, a little too sharply. *Von Kleist is dead. Çelik murdered him.*

"And what was your answer, Çelik?"

"I'm speaking to you, not von Kleist."

"Where is he?"

He is not going to tell you he killed him, Quinton said.

I already know that, Tribe snapped. For this Daedalus convo Quinton had adopted Nikki's voice, even though Tribe had expressly forbidden him to do so. It was eerily pitch and cadence perfect. If he didn't know she was dead he would have sworn they were communicating. *But the story he comes up with will no doubt be instructive.*

"Not sure," came Çelik said. "But I do know that he received a call about his daughter. She was in an accident or something. He ran off before I could get the details."

"He's not answering his cell phone, hasn't returned my voicemails."

His dead-man switch on Daedalus was activated, Quinton as Nikki said in Tribe's ear. Tribe had designed the Daedalus network to immediately deactivate upon the death of anyone on it. The moment von Kleist died Quinton knew it and informed Tribe.

"I can't help you there," Çelik said. "But good riddance, to my mind."

"It's damned inconvenient, in any event," Tribe said, wanting more than anything to reach through the connection and strangle this reprehensible felon. He had entered into the partnership with Çelik with a great deal of apprehension, but Quinton had advised him that there was no one else with the vast network of his contacts readily available. Now it had come to this. Tribe had liked von Kleist, a gentleman of the old school. He suspected had their partnership continued their nascent friendship would have deepened. "I'll have to find another person to deal with Brite-Bar's international legal logistics."

"Well, have no fear regarding the current shipment. I have all of von Kleist's paperwork. The cargo will get to its destination on time."

"It had better," Tribe said. "Parachute has a deadline to meet."

Çelik said something in return but Tribe wasn't listening. His mind—in concert with Quinton—was already working on the proper method to take Kurt Çelik out.

Let the punishment fit the crime, the resurrected Nikki said, after Tribe cut the connection with Çelik.

Indeed, Tribe replied, forgiving Quinton its trespass. It was actually comforting to hear Nikki's voice again.

In the meantime, Nikki said, *Çelik is still going to screw with you via this shipment. He's going to redirect the shipment to his Russian customer.*

No doubt he'll try.

Do you want me to—?

No. That eventuality has been dealt with, Tribe said, thinking, *Smart as Quinton is, he's not smarter than me. I have someone on the inside.*

27

The ten floors below Oiran were devoted to a hotel. When the elevator opened onto the reception level, as tradition dictated guests were required to take off their shoes. They were given *uwabaki*—traditional house slippers—in which to pad across the tatami mats to the check-in area and to wear throughout the hotel. This, then, was Nihonbashi Ryokan, a traditional inn invariably found in the countryside or the back streets of cities. Nihonbashi was the top-rated ryokan in Tokyo.

When Evan Ryder entered, the last few raindrops beaded in the folds of her umbrella, the lights within the paper lanterns were low. Setting her ankle boots aside, she found her heart lifting with the springy feeling of the tatami beneath her stockinged feet.

A young kimono-clad woman was standing in front of reception. A smile creased her face. "Good evening, Evan-sama. My name is Mariko." Her smile widened. "You are expected." She lifted an arm. "This way, please."

"I am looking forward to meeting Ume Linnear," Evan said.

"And she you, Evan-sama."

Mariko led Evan through a sliding door, down a narrow corridor. "You must be tired from your long journey," she said, and stopped, kneeling before a sliding door of wood and handmade paper panels. "The *furo* has been prepared for you." She meant the wood-fired bath. "And fresh clothes have been laid out for you. Please use them."

Evan was about to decline, anxious to meet this friend of Lyudmila's, knowing that her time to save Timur was running out—only forty-eight hours left until the lethal deadline Alyosha had pressed upon her—but she was acutely cognizant of where she was: Tokyo, the home of a revered figure throughout Japan. She was required to move at the Japanese pace, to observe all the rites and rituals of the culture. She knew full well to do so was the only way she would get to see Ume, let alone to ask for her help.

She knelt beside Mariko, the scent of cedar wafting off her. She waited, hands folded in her lap while Mariko slid open the door, first a little bit, then all the way. A puff of fragrant steam overtook them both. It smelled like fresh pine needles.

At this last minute, her anxiety got the better of her. "It is most important I speak with Ume-sama as soon as possible."

Mariko's smile never wavered. "You must be at your best when you and Ume-sama meet. Thoughts must be aligned. Your mind must be cleared of the residues of travel. Please." She waved Evan through. "Relax and unwind." She closed the door behind her.

Evan found herself in a windowless room of cedar planks and white tile. Removing her clothes, she sat on a three-legged wooden stool, rinsed herself thoroughly using warm water and a large sponge, sluicing the grime and sweat of travel off her, watching the gray water swirling down the drain between her feet. When her skin was clean and shining she stepped over to the rectangular tub. Constructed of hinoki wood it had steep sides and was deeper than a Western bathtub. Steam rose off the water. She buried her face in the fragrant steam, inhaled deeply, and sighed. Then she stepped in. The hot water closed around her, sealing her off from the rest of the world.

■　　■　　■

Slipping into the liminal place between awareness and sleep, Evan found herself back on Sumatra, her mind floating between conflated memories of her two visits there. Tropical heat, sweat, coconut oil, bronzed skin, clattering palm fronds, and the susurrus of the surf. She was stretched out next to Lyudmila, both of them happily drowsy beneath a rocking patchwork of sunlight and shade. They dreamed the same dream, of friendship and safety, as they drifted, content to be together.

Lyudmila turned her head, forearm across her forehead so she could see clearly. She said something to Evan but Evan couldn't hear her. The truth was Evan was overcome by exhaustion. She had been betrayed, beaten almost senseless, been dragged away from Timur but not from her sorrow, which seemed to drain her of energy, made it difficult to breathe.

At her side, dim in the shadows of the palms, Lyudmila spoke urgently, over and over, reached out, at last, shook Evan . . .

. . . And Evan was back inside the sluiceway beneath the Cemetery of the Drowned in Vienna. Three years ago, four? Under the water.

Hands on her shoulders, knees against her hips. No, not in the sluiceway, not in the past. She was being held down in the here and now. Someone had invaded the *furo*, someone was sitting on her chest like a night succubus. Hands against her eyes and forehead as she struggled to get her head above the steaming water.

Every time she tried to raise herself the weight sucked her back down, seemed to get heavier and heavier. The iron bars of the forearms, the legs folded at the knees, the incomprehensible weight of the torso.

Lyudmila shouting in her ear. Shouting . . . shouting . . .

And then another voice, cutting its way through the clutter and madness of the sheer terror of drowning, of having no choice but to suck the water into her lungs. For it all to end.

"*Moscow sent an* ovoshchechistka." A warning. Isobel, her former control. "*A peeler, as hellish as it gets. They've been trained since birth—no fear, no remorse, no conscience whatsoever.*"

"*Killing machines, in other words.*" Alyosha had called Evan a death-dealer.

Not now. Not ever, maybe.

The hands blinding her pushed her head all the way to the bottom of the *furo*. The back of her head struck metal, something loose in its socket. She saw stars. Her mind, disoriented, spun as if she were tied to a Ferris wheel. She was adept at holding her breath but after the incident in the sluiceway where the peeler almost killed her she had developed a fear of drowning. She thought she had beaten it down during her year in the Sumatran surf but now it had returned. Part of her knew that it would be this fear that would kill her, that would ensure that she fail at fighting back into the air.

With enormous effort she struggled through the murk of her fear into clear thought. Used her legs, jackknifing them to slam her muscled calves against the peeler's ears. Not ideal, she lacked the proper angle to gain the leverage needed to do proper damage. He only increased his grip on her head. Drawing her legs up again, this time she used her knees against his ears and felt him shiver with the suction against his eardrums. His hands lifted from her face in involuntary reaction to the attack and, using her shoulders, she pushed herself up, closer and closer to the sloshing skin of the water, to life-giving air. Almost there.

And then there was a knife at the side of her throat. She felt paralyzed as the blade bit into her flesh, drawing across her throat. But it was the raised ridge of her scar, that tough necklace she had refused to have removed, a memento of a terrible time she did not want to forget, an artifact out of her past that gave her moments more to live, moments to scrape her hand along the wooden floor of the *furo*, finding the metal inflow valve, a modern concession to tradition. Loose in its socket. Calm now, her fear all but conquered, she pulled the loose length of inflow pipe, stabbed it upward into the left eye of the peeler. Even under the water she heard his grunt. His body shook, his hands went to the pipe to wrench it out, but she was sitting up now, her mouth open, gasping for air as she concentrated on pushing the pipe through the eye. His hands fell away as his body spasmed wildly, his legs thumping against the side of the *furo*, blood, viscous, almost white, leaked down his cheek.

Evan, fully concentrated on jamming the pipe into the peeler's brain, was taken unawares by a pair of strong hands holding the pipe steady, then pushing back against her. She looked up, her eyes bloodshot, a trickle of blood ringing her throat.

"Namaste, Evan-sama." Mariko's voice was soft, soothing. Evan looked into Mariko's dark eyes. She nodded. "It's over, Evan-sama. You have him."

"I want to kill him," she rasped through gritted teeth.

"Of course you do. That is natural. But if you kill him Ume-sama will never find out who he is."

"He's an *ovoshchechistka*."

"A peeler, yes. I understand your mistake." Mariko's fingers closed over the pipe.

She blinked, started to come back to herself. "Mistake?"

"His face, his neck."

She looked, saw a face that was definitely Japanese. She looked lower, saw the tattoo of a growling tiger working its way up from the assassin's chest, the serpent curling around his right arm.

"Yakuza."

Deftly, Mariko slid the pipe from her hands, set it down beside the tub. Now she had a towel in her hands. She helped Evan up, wrapped the towel around her.

"Let's get you cleaned up."

Evan stepped out of the tub. Mariko had entered the room without Evan picking her up by either sight or sound. This registered. She was in bad shape. As Mariko reached her arm around her shoulders, she looked back. The yakuza's torso and head had fallen back against the side of the tub. Evan, regaining her breath, wiped water and sweat out of her eyes, gazed down at him as if he were part of another world, another time, another place. The peeler in the sluiceway. But this was someone else. Not Russian, not a peeler. But a professional assassin, just like the peeler.

"I will take care of you, Evan-sama. I have contacted Ume-sama. She will deal with your would-be assassin." She cocked her head. "If that is to your satisfaction."

Evan nodded, still half dazed. "Of course. Yes. I am in your hands."

Out in the corridor, Mariko led her into another room, warm, scented with pine and jasmine. Tiled floor and walls. A walk-in shower, Western style.

Evan stood in front of the shower as if rooted to the spot. She felt death very close, the sensation like ants crawling over her skin.

Mariko bowed slightly. *"Mizu ni nagasu." The water flows. Let it go.* Stepping forward, Mariko turned on the shower. Water streamed and steam billowed. As Evan was about to step in, she turned, handed Mariko the towel.

"There's water on the floor of the *furo.*" She was still half dazed. "Apologies."

"After the *furo,*" Mariko said so softly it was almost a whisper, "there is always water on the floor."

Evan took a breath, let it out. She entered the shower. Blood flowed along with the water, then vanished down the drain. *Mizu ni nagasu.*

28

AZABU JUBAN, MINATO WARD, TOKYO. JAPAN

Kurt Çelik and Kiko Ashikaga owned an enormous triplex apartment in a residential high-rise in Azabu Juban, one of the five sections of Minato Ward, home to the fabulous and uber-wealthy including Tadashi Yanai, the founder of Fast Retailing; Masayoshi Son, the CEO of Soft-Bank, the high-tech investment company; and Senjuro Kono, a high-ranking member of the oxymoronically named conservative Liberal Democratic Party.

Alyosha stepped in to what struck her as an unsettlingly unharmonious main floor. As Kiko led her around she saw that one half was Western— ugly as sin. Everything at maximal level: over-velveted, over-gilded, over-tasseled, pretty much over everything. Fortuny fabrics covered every piece of furniture, and above them a Murano glass chandelier, looking like three octopuses entwined. And the colors! *My God*, she thought. *Wearing sunglasses wouldn't be out of order in here.*

"Am I to be interviewed by Kurt Çelik now?" Alyosha asked.

"Soon. He is lately returned from Germany and is currently otherwise engaged." Kiko smiled. "But first . . ." She raised an elegant arm. "Please. This way."

■   ■   ■

The other half of the vastness was all subdued shades of gray and ocher. Simple lines, spare without being in the least bit stark. Though there were expensive carpets rather than tatami mats on the floor, this part of the apartment was unmistakably Japanese. Kiko Ashikaga's space, soothing and serene, the one decoration being a magnificent bonsai pine. The air smelled of cedar and fresh-pressed linen.

She was guided to a small tatami room, a raised tokonoma against one wall on which rested a bronze Buddha and a slim celadon vase holding three red peonies and a twisted branch artfully arranged.

Shoeless, they sat on either side of a low table. Kiko poured from a teapot iced vodka, a welcome surprise for Alyosha.

"Thank you," she said, after taking a demure sip as was required by custom.

Kiko briefly inclined her head in acknowledgment. "So, you are Akujin Matsumura's emissary."

"I am here, Kiko-san, at your beckoning."

Kiko's gaze darted downward like a dragonfly skimming water, taking in Alyosha's bandaged hand. Her eyes found Alyosha's. "You are bound to him now."

"*Giri*," Alyosha said.

Kiko's eyebrows lifted slightly. "It astounds me that a Russian understands the meaning of *giri*."

Alyosha felt a stab of the other's condescension. "Have I disappointed you, Kiko-san?" she said almost sharply.

Kiko's soft laugh settled Alyosha somewhat. "On the contrary. I am extremely pleased." She took a sip of her vodka. "You know, don't you, that my husband does not like Akujin Matsumura."

"And why is that?" Alyosha asked.

Kiko leveled her gaze like a silent weapon. "He doesn't believe that Akujin Matsumura can be trusted."

"Nor do I."

Kiko pursed her lips. "Again, you surprise me, Alyosha-san."

"I hope to do so many times in the future."

Kiko raised her forefinger. "I like you, Alyosha-san. I find I like you very much."

Alyosha was acutely aware that this was the first time Kiko had addressed her in the Japanese manner and despite herself she felt a hot flush rise up from her throat into her cheeks. She bowed slightly.

"Akujin Matsumura claims he has never lied to you," Alyosha said.

"I'm hardly surprised," Kiko told her, "but that itself is a lie."

"So." Alyosha waited several beats. "Which one of you is the liar?"

Kiko produced a scimitar smile. "I imagine he also swore he did not murder your father when you accused him of it."

"That's right."

"And you did not believe him." When Alyosha did not answer, Kiko continued. "And that's why . . ." Her gaze swept over Alyosha's bandaged hand. Still, Alyosha remained silent. Kiko sighed. "My dear, you are brave and foolish in equal measure."

Alyosha's blood was throbbing in her neck, pounding in her ears. "I have a job to do."

"And you're still doing it." Kiko laughed a little. Very little. It was sharp-edged, yet there was a sadness to it. "I know why you're here, why I 'beckoned' you, as you put it. Akujin Matsumura is attempting to use you to get to my husband." She lifted a hand. "Please don't bother to deny it."

"I wasn't going to," Alyosha said. "That's exactly what he wants me to be—a mole inside your husband's business."

Kiko ran her finger along the edge of the table. "Since you've shared a truth with me—one that will be beneficial, perhaps even profitable—I will return the favor." She rose. "Excuse me. I will only be a moment."

Good as her word, Kiko returned with a laptop in one hand, a thumb drive in the other. Without a word, she sat, opened the laptop, plugged in the thumb drive. With one fingertip she navigated to the directory, the file she wanted on the thumb drive, turned the laptop around so that it faced Alyosha.

"You need only hit Enter." Kiko watched Alyosha staring at the blank laptop screen. "The file is audio only."

The offhand manner in which she said this sent a bead of icy sweat down Alyosha's spine. Reaching out, she depressed the ENTER key. There were several seconds of ambient sound, followed by a deep voice. "Is it done?" the voice asked.

"It is." Even with those two words, Alyosha recognized the voice.

"Tell me."

"As you wished, *oyabun*," Akujin Matsumura said, and Alyosha closed her eyes. "His death was not an easy one. I spent over six hours cutting him, bleeding him. Then I severed his genitals from his body, stuffed them in his mouth."

Another several seconds of ambient noise. The clink of the rims of two glasses coming together sounded like a gunshot.

Kiko's voice, soft now, velvety. "The deeper voice belongs to Sumida Koji, *oyabun* of Satsuragi-kai."

Alyosha's belly felt as if it had been invaded by a nest of serpents writhing their way up her intestines. She tasted bile, quickly drained her cup of vodka to keep herself from vomiting.

"And did you enjoy this, ah, venture, Matsumura-san?"

Alyosha held her breath. Her head swam; dizzy as if she had been lifted bodily by a tornado.

"I always enjoy the time before death," Matsumura said. "Whether it be days, hours, or minutes the feeling is the same. Like a sexual orgasm."

"But better," Sumida Koji opined.

"Indeed. Stronger, longer. A high like no other."

A moment later, the file ended.

29

Ume Linnear stood over the *furo*, now drained of water. She held the plug pipe in her hand, the implement Evan Ryder had reinvented as a weapon to save her own life. *How clever*, Ume thought. *It appears everything Lyudmila told me about her is true.*

Ume stared down at the shivering yakuza. One hand was over his destroyed eye, the other was pain-clenched, knuckles white. Blood dripped slowly from the bottom of his hand, down his cheek, poised on his chin before each quivering drop let go, fell to his lap.

Mariko would take good care of Evan, get her throat cleaned and bandaged, salve massaged into her bruises. Her attention fully on the yakuza, Ume removed his soaked socks, stepped into the tub so that one foot pressed against the yakuza's crotch. The man started but his face remained impassive. He would not easily give up information: who he was, what family he was affiliated with.

Her gaze locked onto the yakuza's good eye, swollen, bloodshot. "No need to guess. You are from Osaka." Her foot pressed down hard enough for the man to wince. "Ogiba-kai."

When the yakuza said nothing, Ume put all her weight onto her foot. The man let out a puff of air. His teeth ground together. Crouching down, Ume pulled open the discolored eyelids of his good eye, held them open. The yakuza tried to blink, could not. When the eye began to tear, Ume wiped the moisture away, over and over, until none remained. The yakuza gasped, squirmed, trying to free his eye and his crotch without so much as a single degree of success. His eyeball rotated wildly in its socket.

"This won't get any better," Ume said softly. "I can do this all night. How about you? When will you break? And more important, what will you be like at that point?" Ume leaned in, her voice lowered to just above a whisper. "I can tell you. There will be nothing left. Your mind will have emptied out. You will be a shell."

All at once, she sat back, took her fingers from the yakuza's eyelids, her foot off his crotch.

"There are so many ways to go about this," she said conversationally. "But here's the thing. You went after my guest. In my house." She shook her head. "That is inexcusable. So . . ." She pulled the yakuza's hand away from his ruined eye and in the same moment plunged her thumb into the socket. The yakuza jumped as if she had put an open electric wire to him. He bit his lip so hard it began to bleed. Ume pressed her thumb in deeper. The yakuza squealed like a frog on a dissecting table.

"All right, all right." His voice was thick, coarse. He coughed up pink phlegm.

"What is your name?" Ume said.

"Arata Sazama."

"Your family?"

"Ogiba-kai. As you said."

But Ume was already shaking her head. An ominous feeling like a storm cloud occluding the sun gripped her, and she thought, *Shimensoka. We have been betrayed and we are now surrounded by enemies.* "No, Sazama—if that is your real name. You do not speak with an Osaka accent. You are from here—from Tokyo." She ground her thumb in a semicircle. Sazama's entire body, spasming uncontrollably, lifted off the bottom of the tub.

"Who sent you, Sazama? Who ordered you to kill Evan Ryder?"

The yakuza licked his peeling lips, tasting his own blood. His teeth were red, as if he had lacquered them like a shogun's bride.

"I am ronin." His voice was clogged and he spat more bloody phlegm. "Unaffiliated."

"A ronin." Ume did not let up her grip. "Who ordered this atrocity?" she said. There was a fire in her heart, a stretching of ancient knowledge she hadn't experienced in years. She thought of her father, of Nicholas. He'd told her he was done with all that, but no, with a sudden stab of insight she realized he would never be done with that part of his life. Was that a good thing? She couldn't be sure, she only knew that now it was setting her on his dark and perilous path.

Sazama was trying to cry but there was no fluid left in him. He was dry as a wind-scoured bone. He made ugly sobbing noises instead.

"Matsumura," he whispered. "Akujin Matsumura."

It was the last thing he ever said.

∎ ∎ ∎

"He's lying," Ume said.

"Why would he do that," Emiko said softly, "after what you put him through?"

The two women sat at the table closest to the door of Oiran, their voices soft so as not to carry. Ume noticed that Matsumura was alone now, and had switched from sake to high-end Japanese scotch, judging by the half-empty bottle in front of him.

"Good question." Ume sighed. "Answering that is my first order of business."

"And the second?"

"Close the breach that allowed him to enter the *furo*."

Emiko lowered her eyes. "The fault is mine. I did not see him enter the hotel."

"You cannot be everywhere, Emiko-san. This is why my father installed the CCTV camera network."

■   ■   ■

Emiko bowed in acknowledgment of Ume's understanding. "Mariko-sama is with Evan Ryder now. She and Lyudmila-sama were connected, even though one is American, the other Russian. Lyudmila-sama was a unique individual," Emiko said. "Like you, Ume-sama."

Ume took the compliment in stride. "Why is Evan Ryder here? What does she know? Or want?"

Emiko nodded. "It's time you spoke with her."

"Soon. Now I have another task that cannot wait." Ume rose, silent, like day turning into night.

30

"For nightlife, Roppongi is zone zero," Eiko said as she led Ilona Starkova through the pattering rain, picking her way amid the throngs at Roppongi Crossing. "And zone zero in Roppongi is E-LIFE."

The dazzling club took up three stories in an otherwise unremarkable building. Lines around the block, VIPs exiting limousines drawn up outside, golden ropes, and three burly doorstops checking off names on a list before they let anyone in. Eiko must have known someone high up the E-LIFE food chain because she went straight to the head of the line. She took Ilona's hand. The three-headed dog knew her, ushered the two of them in with a lifting of the golden rope and deferential nods. Neon lights bounced off their bald heads like sunlight off steel siding.

They danced for a while to blasting EDM, drank a few beers, then Eiko indicated a door on the far side of the dance floor. They pushed through it. The moment it closed behind them the sound was cut off as if it never existed. Ahead of them wound a spiral staircase whose glass treads appeared to float on air. At the top, another door—baize, padded leather, soft as the skin of an inner thigh—pushed through into another world.

This was the lounge floor, quiet as a library. A bar ran along the inner wall, round tables, lit by small, shaded lamps, and comfortable leather chairs sprinkled at discreet distances on the opposite side lent the place the sensual intimacy of a modern-day bordello, heightened by the number of slim, tall, busty women, all Western, occupying tables opposite Japanese salarymen.

They were shown to a table by the window and, as Eiko requested, as far from the entrance as possible. Eiko ordered sake but Ilona ordered green tea. "This is for you." Eiko drew out a small round container, opened it. "Come here," she said softly, and applied a cooling cream to Ilona's inflamed inner wrist. She handed over the container. "Twice a day; it will heal in no time."

The drinks arrived and they toasted each other, sipped. When they were alone again, Eiko sat back. "I know you a long time, Ilona. I've done all your ink, but this one . . . well, it's somehow disturbing and now that it's no longer part of you . . . you know I make it a habit not to ask my clients the meaning behind the tattoos they want."

"That's a good habit."

"But this one . . . Ilona, please tell me what that sigil means." Eiko stroked the back of her hand, but Ilona was already shaking her head. "Come, then. I will make you happy."

Ilona gave her a mournful look. "I don't want to be happy."

Eiko cocked her head. "No?"

"I want revenge."

"Why? Revenge is a little death."

"Not for me." Ilona shook her head. "Without revenge there is no life."

31

SHIBUYA, TOKYO, JAPAN

Ume watched Akujin Matsumura struggle to keep his expression under control as she approached his table. Matsumura, so fearsome and intimidating with everyone else, held Ume, as Nicholas Linnear's daughter, in such reverence that his façade was thin as tissue paper. Only once had Matsumura come to Ume's dojo. Only once had he watched Ume demolish her opponents on the aikido mat. Catching him in the corner of her eye, Ume held the suspicion that Matsumura had come to oppose her in a match, but one viewing was more than enough for him; he never returned. She had completely bedazzled him, and this filled him with unease. His love for her caused him such agony that he tossed and turned in his bed at night, wishing her beside him, knowing she would never accept him.

Now he rose as Ume stepped to his table. They bowed, exchanged formal greetings.

Ume lifted an arm. "Walk with me, please."

"*Hai.*" Yes.

Ume led him to the rear of Oiran, through a double door into the gleaming kitchen, past service and cooking stations, the cold storage that kept vegetables, fruit, and fish delivered in the dead of night fresh for the following evening's meals. Nothing was ever kept any longer.

In one corner of the kitchen was a square door. Ume pressed a button and the door slid open, revealing a stainless steel interior. The floor was a platform that moved up and down like an elevator.

Standing aside, she gestured. "Please, Matsumura-san, get in." When Matsumura hesitated, Ume said, "No harm will come to you. I give you my word."

Still, the *kuromaku* hesitated. "Is this necessary, or even wise?"

"Either you trust me," Ume said softly, "or you don't."

The implied threat was too much for Matsumura. Without a sound he folded up his body so that he was fully inside the interior. "I trust you're not claustrophobic. In any event, this will only take a moment."

She closed the door, pressed another button. A soft humming could be heard over the almost library-level silence in the kitchen as the chefs and sous-chefs went about their duties as if they were monks.

Three minutes later, downstairs in one of the ryokan's service areas, Ume stood before another door, pressed another button. The door opened, and she indicated that Matsumura should unfold himself.

"Interesting," he said as he brushed wrinkles from his suit. "Like an origami." He looked Ume in the eye. "But what was the point?"

"We are now in the hotel below Oiran," Ume said. "This is how the hotel was infiltrated. From the restaurant's kitchen to the hotel's service area." She looked hard at Matsumura, who said nothing, gave away nothing. Apparently he had regained his iron-bound composure.

After an increasingly tense silence, Ume turned on her heel. "This way." Ume took him out of the service area, down several corridors. Mariko, kneeling, awaited them in front of a sliding door. When they both had removed their shoes, she leaned slightly forward from the waist, slid the door open. Then she rose and without a word vanished down the corridor.

Ume ushered Matsumura into the *furo* where the violent attempt on Evan Ryder's life had occurred earlier.

"Who is this?" Ume pointed to the now-lifeless body of Arata Sazama lying tangled at the bottom of the *furo* tub, his eyes black, his mouth hanging open.

Matsumura flinched. "What happened to him?"

"He was the one who made the mistake of infiltrating my ryokan." Ume stared at Matsumura. "So."

Matsumura spread his hands, palms up.

"Really." Ume brought the *kuromaku* a step closer to the corpse. "Didn't you send him here?"

"What? No!"

"Curious. He named you." Ume's voice was low and hard. "I asked him who sent him here. 'Akujin Matsumura,' he said."

"He lied," Matsumura said. "I've never seen him before in my life."

"Why would he name you in particular?"

"Desperation? I have no idea."

Ume changed to a parallel track. "So you're telling me that he's not a member of Satsuragi-kai."

"He is not." Matsumura was adamant. He bent at the waist, turned on the water faucet, washing the blood off the man's body. He ran his fingertips along the tattoos of the tiger, the serpent. "In fact, I very much doubt that he's a yakuza at all."

"Why would he pretend to be?"

Matsumura was taking a closer look at the body. When he stood up, he turned to Ume. "This man is *johatsu*."

The literal English translation of *johatsu* was "evaporation." *Johatsu* were men who, having failed in their jobs, their marriages, were carrying too much debt—the pressures of life in Japanese society—hired so-called Night Movers, companies that specialized in allowing these men to leave their pasts behind, relocate them, even change their identities.

"All right, then." Using her cell she took shots of the *johatsu's* face. "Forget about who he is. What I need to know is which Night Mover he used and who paid for his disappearance."

Matsumura stood up. "There are only so many Night Movers in Tokyo." He had already punched in a number. "Send me the photos and I'll find out which one is responsible."

32

TIMUR BOUND

It wasn't only Evan he missed, he realized, but running. On Sumatra, at Marsden Tribe's estate, he and Evan ran every day, building up his legs as well as his stamina. It was hard work, and at first he struggled, having had such a confined existence previously. But he soon found the sweat rolling off him pleasurable, the pain in his knees and quads turning to an ache, then into pleasure as his muscles expanded, breathed. At some point during the process he realized that his body was becoming an instrument, one that Evan was expert at fine-tuning. His first decade of life had been lived almost entirely in his head, reading, writing, taking the exams his tutors put in front of him. He'd had no attention paid to his body, no inkling that it could do the things Evan pushed him to try, to do. It was an awakening of sorts, in many ways similar to the changes he would soon enough experience, those that adolescents find happening to their physical selves when passing into adulthood.

Timur's crying jag was long over. It had lasted, on and off, for several hours, after which, utterly exhausted, he'd fallen into a deep, dreamless sleep on the floor where he'd been standing. He had awakened in his bed, covered to his neck in a sheet and blanket. As to who had moved him, tucked him tidily in he had no idea.

His bladder was full, aching, and he called out as he was told to do. Almost immediately the lock clicked and one of his jailers stood in the doorway. A Russian. They were all Russians so far as he could tell. Russian was what they spoke to each other and to him, but if he spoke in English they understood him perfectly.

"Why do you have to pee?" the Russian said with a laugh. "Aren't you all cried out, *tsypochka*?"

Calling Timur a chick, as in baby chicken, had become something of a pastime with this crew. Timur had winced the first couple of times he was faced with this epithet. But as with everything else here he soon grew numb to the humor.

"That's so played," Timur said, in English.

The Russian's brow crinkled. "What?"

"That name's old already."

They were out in the hallway now, on the way to the toilet. The Russian laughed some more, ruffled Timur's head good-naturedly. Then his nose wrinkled. "You stink, *tsypochka*, so maybe you're right. Hm, let's see." He tapped a forefinger against his lower lip. Then his face lit up. "Ah, I have it. In honor of your stink from now on we shall call you *porosenok*."

Piglet, Timur thought. *Lovely*. "I shall be proud to be called *porosenok*," he said, "but only if you tell me *your* name."

The Russian grabbed Timur's arm, swung him around just outside the door to the toilet. For just an instant Timur's nerves fired. As Evan had taught, he could flip this Russian pig, he could slam a knee into his throat. Just as Evan instructed, over and over, until he almost burst into tears at the repetition, her harsh voice snapping like whiplashes until at last—finally—he had absorbed the move into muscle memory. No thought needed. But now in this place, at this time he stopped himself.

"Is it you giving me orders?"

Now was not the time. Not yet. But soon. He smiled at the Russian and the Russian's expression lightened.

He laughed. "You know, *porosenok*, you are a smart fellow. Pigs are smart, did you know that? A lot smarter than chicks, that's for certain. So I have hit on the right name finally." He twisted the doorknob, kicked the door so that it swung inward. As Timur stepped across the threshold, onto the tiles, the Russian said, "Grisha. My name is Grisha." He gestured. "Now go grab your *kher* and pee."

Grisha's gruff laughter followed Timur all the way across the bathroom to the toilet.

33

"I am Ume, Nicholas Linnear's daughter."

The room Mariko had led her to following her long, hot shower was entirely Western in nature, with sleek furniture—a sofa, two chairs facing each other, a low table between them. The walls were adorned with ukiyo-e Japanese woodblock prints, Hiroshige's depictions of *The Sixty-nine Stations of the Kisokaido Road*. The Kisokaido was one of the five main roads connecting Edo, the seventeenth-century capital, now Tokyo, with Kyoto.

"Ume . . . how lovely. Plum," Evan said, thinking, *This is the most exquisite woman I've ever seen.*

"Among other things." Ume bowed slightly. "How do you feel?"

"Like I've just been saved from drowning." Evan ached all over and her throat felt scrubbed raw. Mariko had treated her wounds, given her water, and discreetly left Evan to dress herself in a soft cotton top and a pair of wide-legged trousers. The fabric lay against her skin now, soothing as silk.

"Please." At Ume's welcoming gesture they sat facing each other on the thickly upholstered chairs.

The door opened and a young woman in a kimono set a tray of tea and small plates of food on the table between the two women. She poured green tea into two hand-thrown cups, set the teapot down, bowed, and left.

"I apologize for my father," Ume said, handing Evan one of the cups. "He is attending to urgent business, but he assures me that he is greatly looking forward to meeting you." She took up the second cup, inhaled the steam from the tea, smiled at Evan, encouraging her to drink without saying a word. "Lyudmila told him a great deal about you."

Evan's heartstrings shivered at that name. She took a breath, let it out. Part of her was still struggling underwater. All at once, as the last of the adrenaline flowed out of her veins, she felt enormously tired. She drank her tea gratefully, feeling the delicious liquid warm her. Suddenly famished, she ate food from two of the plates. Ume, sipping her tea, watched her.

When she was finished, at least for the time being, Evan sat back. "I'm curious as to how your father knew Lyudmila."

Ume nodded. "As in all things in life, their connection is simple yet complicated." She lowered her upper lids for a moment. "A favor was asked, a favor was given. How the world works."

Evan waited, sensing that silence was what Ume sought.

At length, Ume began. "You recall Lyudmila's fall from grace."

"I do, of course. She was purged from the politburo."

Ume nodded. "For being female, for becoming too powerful."

"Most definitely for that, yes. But as it happened there was another reason." She took out the sat phone, showed Ume the last vid of Timur sent to her daily. In response to Ume's raised eyebrows, she said, "His name is Timur. Lyudmila was his mother. His father was the late Sovereign of the Russian Federation."

Ume let out a breath. "And he is being held now against his will."

"He and I were abducted at the behest of a small Russian cadre—I don't know their affiliation, but I'm all but certain they have no official affiliation." Evan kept watching Ume's face for any sign this was not news to her, found none. "Timur is being held hostage at an undisclosed location. I have been given an assignment. If I'm not successful he will be killed."

Her expression utterly composed, Ume leaned forward, refilled their cups. A time-out was obviously called for. Evan sipped her tea. Her hunger had vanished the moment she recounted Timur's situation. Ume was not one to look away. The two women gazed at each other in the silence enjoyed only in an atmosphere of trust.

"Thank you," Evan said softly.

Ume slowly, deliberately lowered and raised her lids again. "Please know you are always welcome here, Evan-sama." She put down her cup, did not refill it. "Lyudmila came here to ask my father for help. This was immediately following her expulsion from the politburo—from Moscow itself. She left Russia and flew here."

"What did she want?"

"Lyudmila's training was in weapons of all sorts," Ume said. "As you must know she was quite skilled." She pressed her palms together as if in greeting or prayer. "Still, she was in mortal fear for her life. She asked my father to teach her how to use her hands, her feet. She asked him to help her body to become a weapon."

"Martial arts."

Ume nodded. "Jiujitsu, karate, Muay Thai, aikido, which is my father's preferred martial art." She shrugged. "But of course she didn't have decades to learn, even years. So my father concentrated on teaching her aikido."

"I'm certain she was an exceptional student."

A smile, a memory warmed Ume's face. "Indeed she was. An excellent one. Her muscles eager, her concentration absolute. Her body responded immediately, even, I would say, joyously. It was a happy time for us."

"Happy, yes." Evan felt a twinge of jealousy. "I imagine it was."

"And your time with her," Ume said, "it was also joyous."

"Until the end." Evan set aside her tea cup. "As she lay dying in my arms I made her a promise that I would take care of Timur as if he were my own child."

"And now . . ." There was no need for Ume to continue; she had seen the video of Timur. "What happened?"

Not for the first time a stab of guilt went through Evan. "I was taken off guard. Timur and I were swimming. We were in Sumatra, at one of Marsden Tribe's villas he has strewn all over the globe. I was on hiatus. I was taking care of Timur, making good on my promise to Lyudmila. It wasn't difficult; he's a great kid, learned everything I taught him, soaking information up like a sponge." Her eyes grew big as tears rolled from them. "He's got the mind, the quickness, the instincts of someone a decade older than him." She paused, feeling strangled. Her heart rate was elevated and she went into *prana*, slowing, deepening her breathing.

Ume, tuned in to what Evan was going through, said nothing, waited patiently for Evan to return to herself. She was there if Evan needed help. She didn't think that would happen and she was right.

Evan cleared her throat, wiped away her tears. "They caught us in the water. There was nothing I could do. A group of Malaysian pirates but armed with Russian and Iranian weapons. They brought us back to their ship, where the people controlling them were waiting."

"Who were they? Do you know?"

"Oh, yes." Evan nodded, eyes narrowing. "Russians."

"SVR?"

"Ex-SVR. Now a rogue cadre commanded by Alyosha Ivanovna."

Ume's audible intake of breath stopped Evan in her tracks. "What? Have you heard of her?"

"More than that," Ume said. "I've met her."

Evan's brows lifted. "You've—"

"Yes, yes." Ume was animated now. "A little more than an hour ago. She was upstairs in my restaurant. She was accompanied by an underboss of the Satsuragi-kai, the most powerful yakuza family in Tokyo—a *kuromaku* by the name of Akujin Matsumura. You know this word, *kuromaku*?"

"I do. He's the Satsuragi-kai's so-called 'black curtain,' a fixer of sorts. Very powerful in his own right."

Ume nodded. "She left perhaps thirty minutes ago with the wife of Kurt Çelik, a wealthy Turkish businessman."

Evan's mind was working at warp speed. *Alyosha is here,* she thought as another piece of the puzzle fell into place. *Tokyo is the end point—ground zero, for Alyosha, Kata, and most likely Ilona Starkova, too. Something here is drawing them like the magnetism of true north. This is where Kata means to set up her new base of operations. Not a bad choice—she's in bed with yakuza and perhaps this Turkish businessman, which means one or the other ordered the abduction in order to coerce me into finding and killing Ilona Starkova. But why? What has Ilona to do with the Satsuragi-kai or Kurt Çelik? Neither connection makes sense. Not yet, anyway.*

Ume rose. "Excuse me while I make some calls. I will find out where Alyosha Ivanovna went with Kurt Çelik's wife. You and I will find her. You will talk to her. You will get the answers you require." Her face was tranquil, even though her words turned dark with menace. "She will answer any questions you put to her, believe me."

She left as silently as she had appeared, leaving in her wake the subtle scents of sandalwood and pine. Evan was left with her sat phone, on which three—soon to be four—proof of life vids lived.

Scrolling down, she opened the second one. The one that had been sent to her when she was at Elley's, questioning Nyurgun. There was something there she hadn't fully understood. She was sure of it. She zoomed in on his left hand, curled around the side of the newspaper. Yes, there it was. Unmistakable only if you were looking for it. The pad of his forefinger was tapping the newspaper, just discernable through the grainy, low-light vid; and, of course, the vid got grainier the more she zoomed in. But still, there they were—the fingertip movements she'd seen the first time, so hoping it was a coded message from him, but convincing herself it wasn't. But now her heart rate sped up and her pulse was heavy in her ears. She'd been wrong. It *was* a message. Timur was reaching out to her. He didn't hate her. She watched, backed the vid up, watched again. And again. The third time through she had it: dot dot dot/dot dash/dot/dash dash dot. Morse code. Yet another old-school trick she had taught him. She went through it a fourth time just to make sure she had the sequence right: S A E G.

What could SAEG mean? She knew that Timur wasn't given a lot of airtime and apparently he knew it, too, so he wasn't able to transmit a full word that would help her discover where he had been taken. She had to assume this was why he was using the code.

Not seeing the meaning in SAEG, she pulled up the third video that she'd received today while in the cab from Narita to Nihonbashi Ryokan, the one she'd shown to Ume. Again, Timur stood with the same masklike face, the day's paper held at chest height. This time she zoomed in as soon as the vid started. The pad of his forefinger at first was still. But then it began: two dots, then three dots, finally dot dash dot dot: I S L.

This sequence seemed to her easier to make sense of: ISL = island. This could mean that Timur was on an island. But where? So many islands in the world. Then she put the two messages together: S A E G, I S L. Could the first part be the South Aegean Sea? Timur was being held on an island in the South Aegean? But again which island? The Cyclades, the major group in the South Aegean, off the Greek Peloponnesus, consisted of a huge number of islands—over two hundred in fact.

There was more, but at that moment, Ume returned, opening the sliding door. She had changed into Western clothes: close-fitting black jeans, a white man's shirt under a long black rain slicker, belted at the waist.

34

SETAGAYA, TOKYO, JAPAN

In the citrus-steeped dimness of Eiko's tiny apartment, the shadows made diagonal stripes across their naked bodies. They were in Setagaya, a relatively untouristed, mainly residential neighborhood, where the prices for apartments were more reasonable than in Shibuya to the west or Shinjuku to the northeast.

Sitting on Eiko's curved sofa, they drank tea she had mixed especially for her, imported from the mountains between China and Tibet. It was bittersweet, dark as the ocean at night. They sipped and talked, almost as sisters. Ilona learned that Eiko had been with two lovers since the last time they had been together, neither of whom had been fulfilling or even satisfactory.

At length, Ilona set down her cup, drew something from a small suede bag. Turning back to Eiko, she held out the two molars she had extracted from Yuri Radik's mouth, dropped them into her friend's cupped palm.

Making a low sound in the back of her throat, Eiko padded over to a small desk along one wall, snapped on a powerful light, swung a jeweler's magnifier over the teeth as she sat down. She rolled them in her hand for a moment, then grasped them between the tips of two fingers and her thumb.

"Huh, the same sigil I tattooed on you." She looked up. "Now will you tell me?"

"Yes." Ilona rose to stand beside Eiko. "I told you about my childhood, so you know I was powerless. Powerless to save my mother, to avenge her. I lost my sister in the crowded city streets. I was powerless to find her. Long years in the wilderness at the fringes of the city, taking odd jobs, being robbed, twice raped, always hungry, always filthy. Nothing to live on but my vision of the future. One way or another, I promised myself, I would have power. And then I would get my revenge. I would find my father and I would make him pay for his sins.

"I made my way out of Russia, slowly and painfully, and started traveling—southwest, always southwest until I reached Istanbul, that beautiful historic bridge between East and West. I stayed on the Asian side, keeping to the run-down streets, losing myself in markets where few tourists ventured. And that was where, one night, I came across Marsden Tribe."

Eiko let out a tiny shriek. "*The* Marsden Tribe, the multibillionaire?"

"The same."

"What was he doing in the Asian side of the city?"

"A walk on the wild side, or so I said to him."

"Where did you meet?"

"Well, that was the joke. We sat at adjoining tables at Fazil Bey, a famous coffee shop, one of the safest places in Kadikoy. You're more likely to be gifted a second cup of Turkish coffee from the people sitting next to you than having a gun waved in your face."

He was with a group of businessmen, she was there by herself. He kept glancing sidelong at her, which she didn't like, made her suspicious. She was on the point of getting up and leaving when he leaned over and said that he was a great admirer of her work. Then she did get up, slapping down some bills and striding away from him.

"He came after me, introduced himself," Ilona said. "Of course I knew who he was. I'd seen his face and quotes in print and online. What I couldn't figure out is what he was after. If he was coming on to me his opening line was way off in outer space. But then he said something that stopped me in my tracks. He said, 'You're attracted to danger. Just like me.'"

She looked at him in a different light. He wasn't coming on to her. He wasn't a threat. But he hadn't yet made it through her vetting process. Still, this was just between the two of them. "You've mistaken me for someone else," she said.

Then he smiled a real smile. She realized she hadn't seen one in a long time. "You mean you're not going to take credit for igniting that Nigerian general's headquarters last week? Breaking three electronic security rings, without triggering them, that was brilliantly done."

She did not know what to do with this and was for a moment at least at a loss for words.

"By the way," he went on, "who paid you for that?"

That's when she laughed, laughed so hard tears came to her eyes. "I don't want credit," she said.

"Of course not. You did it for the danger."

"He was right, of course," Ilona said to Eiko. "He had me pegged, or thought he did, anyway. I wanted to cement his assumption, give him what all men want, a feeling of superiority. I was opaque to everyone but him. What could make him feel better than that? Nothing. What else could make him lower his guard? Nothing. It's funny, don't you think, how transparent men are? So I told him, 'What is life without danger? I eat danger for breakfast every morning and shit it out at night.' He liked that; I could tell because something in his face came alive, something that wasn't there before. It was something a man would say. And I knew him, then. He is a man who is attracted to strong women—strong women on whom he can impose control. That's how he gets his kicks. In this vein, I said, 'Being in danger is the only way I know I'm alive.'"

"I knew it," he said. "You're addicted to it."

She lifted her head to him. "Like you."

He grinned. "On the edge, always."

"So, what?" Eiko said. "You went to work for him?"

"I did, yes. Eventually."

"But why would you do that? Enslave yourself to someone like that?"

Ilona stared up at the ceiling as if seeking an answer there. "I've asked myself that same question a dozen times or more." She sighed. "My father was an out-and-out shit. He was violent, a murderer who knows how many times over. On any other level he was unknowable. He was hardly at home; his work in the GRU took him many places, even sometimes outside Russia, I think. Anyway, he and my mother had a difficult time of it. He was at best indifferent to her. And to us—me and my sister—he was like a porcupine. If you tried to get near him you'd find yourself damaged in some way—physically, emotionally, often both."

Eiko let out a breath. "So . . . what? You saw this man, this powerful man who would subjugate you as a father figure? You were following in your mother's fucked-up footsteps?"

Ilona closed her eyes.

"Then the relationship was doomed from the start."

"I suppose that's what I wanted; he was a spectacular lover, though, as it turned out, he knew nothing about love. I think also I thought I could control him in the ways women have learned to control men down through the centuries—soft control. But now, three years later, I'm in too deep—into something I don't understand."

"Okay, but what does this have to do with your tattoo?"

"'If you want to work for me, do what I ask without question,' Marsden told me. 'I'll throw all my resources—'

"'Considerable resources.' I was keeping eye contact, willing myself not to blink. You know how good I am at this."

Marsden gave her a small deprecating smile and she saw within it a softness he never allowed himself to feel. Too busy growing up, too busy building things, microcircuits, to begin with, then algorithms, later, the irresistible glimmer of advanced quantum theory, AI in his eye. She got this part of him now. He lived in the future. No time to say hello, goodbye.

"Everything I own is considerable," he said, his first, but certainly not his last, verbal mistake with her. He'd shown her a sliver of vulnerability.

"I bet," she said, playing along. "So everything I read about you is true."

"Not at all." He frowned. "I doubt it. If you read it on the internet it's best to take the revelations with a pound of salt." He blinked. "Sound okay so far?"

"Sure."

He stepped toward her. "You're going to get inked," he said. "I'll send you to Tokyo. The best tattoo artists are there."

"In Shibuya," she told him. "Yes, I've been there. I know someone." She showed him the small rose entwined with thorns Eiko had done for her. He was duly impressed.

"Why?" she asked him. "Why do you want me to get this tat? It's not a number or anything."

He stared at her for a second and for an instant she thought he was going to turn on his heel and walk away. "It's a sigil of my design," he said softly. "Do you know what a sigil is?"

"It's a kind of symbol."

He nodded. "Close enough. This sigil is a sun caught between the arms of a caliper. Its rays almost touch either arm. It's a 'symbol' as you put it of communication. But a sigil is more. It's a representation of a close-knit clan."

"The sigil," Ilona concluded to Eiko, "is also, as it turns out, a sign of power. Great power."

Eiko, frowning, looked up at her. "What kind of power?"

"That's what I've come to Tokyo to find out. I was meant to send these"—she pointed at the teeth—"back to him via a secure courier service once I was out of Russia. But now I have them, I want to keep them—I want to know what he's been keeping from me. I want to unlock his secret."

"Maybe this can help." Eiko gestured. "Take a look."

Bending over Eiko's shoulder, Ilona studied the tops of the molars, saw that what she had mistaken for a simple etching at first glance was actually a narrow channel incised deep into the enamel. More than that, something filled the channel.

"See it? That's not ink."

It had seemed black to her with the naked eye but now, under the lamp and the magnifier, she saw that the channel was filled not with some sort of solid material, but with a series of ultrathin metallic strands.

"What the hell am I looking at?" Ilona said.

"Good question." Eiko sat back. "I can't be certain—it's not my expertise—but the sigil looks like a part of a microprocessor. If so, it's an astoundingly sophisticated one."

"How can I find out?"

Eiko dropped the molars into Ilona's palm.

"There's a woman named Chiyoko. She might know."

"An artist, like you?"

"An artist, yes." Eiko smiled. "But not like me. Chiyoko is an electronics genius, specializing in miniaturized circuits."

"Can you arrange for me to see her?"

Eiko stood up. "I can do better than that." She stood, began getting dressed.

"At this time of night?"

Eiko laughed softly. "These hours are when Chiyoko does her best work."

They hurriedly dressed and left the building. The rain struck the pavement so hard the drops bounced like steel BBs. Eiko held Ilona back for a moment. They stood very close.

"A word of warning," Eiko said over the hiss of the rain. "Chiyoko is not a friend. Also, she's not like other Japanese."

Ilona wiped water off her brow. "What does that mean?"

"You'll see."

35

Through slivers of rain, An Binh watched Alyosha Ivanovna being led into a posh ultramodern high-rise in Azabu Juban. She was accompanied by a handsome Japanese woman, several decades older than the Russian agent, though, An Binh had to admit these days it was becoming more and more difficult to judge the age of either gender simply from their faces. *Ah, the miracles of the latest cosmetic surgery procedures,* she thought, *where stem cells are being used to rejuvenate aging tissue.*

Earlier, she had stationed herself across the street from Oiran, Aku-jin Matsumura's favored nighttime hangout. Of course, she could have exited her rental car, gone up to Oiran to look for him, but she felt stuck to her seat, unable to pull the trigger on confronting him. So there she remained, eyes glued to the doorway to the right side of the darkened entrance to the street-level bank. She already knew Evan Ryder was in Tokyo; she had used one of her Parachute-created aliases at Immigration. It had shown up on An Binh's company cell phone. What she didn't know was how to get in touch with Evan—Evan's company cell was down, perhaps permanently. In any event, she knew Evan was alive, knew she had somehow escaped her abductors. This intel she passed on to Marsden Tribe via encoded text message. Maybe he'd have some way to find out where Evan was and what she was up to. The fate of the child, Timur, never crossed her mind; she assumed, incorrectly, that Evan had taken him with her when she absconded from wherever her abductors had taken them. In any event, as Tribe made abundantly clear, Timur was not part of her remit.

Neither was Alyosha Ivanovna, but an hour into her vigil she spied the Russian agent emerge from the building's entrance alongside the Japanese woman and, presumably, the woman's bodyguard. They hurried into a large navy-blue Mercedes, which almost immediately nosed out into traffic. An Binh had followed, keeping a discreet distance. She wondered what Alyosha Ivanovna was doing here; she recognized her immediately from the intel regarding the failed coup against and assassination of the then Russian Sovereign over a year ago, a coup in which Alyosha and her boss, Evan's sister Kata, had been major players. Now the women were personae non gratae in the Russian Federation. Maybe she was attempting to establish a foothold here in Japan.

An Binh peered out through the rental car window at the residential building across the avenue from where she was parked. Nothing was happening; nothing was going to happen, and she thought, *What am I doing?* The fact was she was miserable, an emotional state with which she was not accustomed. Leaving Diti Khong had rent something inside her—something vital. It had come as a shock to her. Being with Diti had changed her. She was no longer the arrow of justice, seeking revenge. She had taken her revenge, twice over, but rather than freeing her revenge had hollowed her out.

The rain had let up now, sprinkling intermittently, silver and gold in the lights from the street and the businesses. The dank whisper of the passing traffic, the streets slick and dark, shining like spilled oil. Then the downpour began again, heavier than ever, obscuring the street, pushing her further into herself.

What was she doing, she once again wondered, sitting here in the rain, waiting for another glimpse of Alyosha Ivanovna? The fact is, she didn't care about Alyosha Ivanovna, she didn't even care about her remit. What she cared about was Diti Khong, who had climbed into the hollow inside her, filling it with light and love. *When*, she asked herself, *have I ever felt pleasure like I do with Diti?* Never. Never before.

It occurred to her now that she had never before experienced love, never before felt filled with another person's light, never felt attached and wholly herself all at once. It was a wonder that stopped breath, stopped time, stopped her constant striving. For what? For what? She'd had a lifetime—several lifetimes, to be honest—of death and destruction, of living in the shadows at the edge of the world, alone, her heart dark, contracted with hate.

It was at that moment that a sleek, dark-colored sedan pulled up behind her and parked. She glanced at her rearview mirror. The driver was alone, drenched in shadow. Then the headlights from an approaching car picked out the driver's features and at once the electric shock of recognition passed through her like a lightning bolt. Akujin Matsumura. But he was not looking straight ahead, had no interest in her. Instead, his gaze was fixated, as hers had been, on the entrance to the apartment building

into which Alyosha Ivanovna and her companions had disappeared forty
minutes ago.

Now was her chance at retribution for all the pain and suffering he
had caused her. Now was her chance to strike, to kill. Fate, she was certain, had gifted her with this chance. She opened her car door, swung
her feet around until her shoes touched the curb. Rain fell into her lap,
ran down her shins and into her shoes. For what seemed a long time she
sat like this, immobile, her head turned so that Matsumura's silhouette
remained in her view. Still as a wall of water caught in time, she shuffled
through the manner in which she could inflict pain on him before she
killed him: knife, scarf, wire, bare knuckle, the tip of her thumb neatly
placed in the space where the side of his jaw met his neck. *Push!* And
again. Again. She imagined his eyes open wide, the magnificent rictus
of his face, his powerful hands scrabbling for purchase somewhere—
anywhere—on her face or body. Scratches scored, blood streaming, his
mouth open in a howl, quickly stifled by her fist, fingers down his throat
like poisonous tentacles. Satisfaction as he died?

And yet, not. The images blew through her like chaff in the wind, odor-
less, tasteless, a complete blank. Why? Rain soaking her thighs and feet.
She knew why: in the new light of her life, she wondered whether this
moment in time was a chance at all. Perhaps she was being gifted with a
choice: continue down her familiar moonless path of death and destruction or create a new path for herself with Diti. A new life, filled with sunlight, with joy, not hatred. For so long she had lived among the ghosts and
ravens, all of them plucking at her, wanting pieces of her. For so long this
was the only life she knew, the only one she could conceive of.

Against all odds, at the exact moment when An Binh's rageful soul
turned black again, Diti had come into her life. Diti, the daughter of Budi
Khong, the man she had murdered. Diti as a child, grateful and adoring
of her older protector Ramelan, the man who had seduced An Binh and
broken her young heart, who she had, in turn, stuffed into the Khong
family safe before she set the building on fire. Diti, her own personal
Virgil, sent to show her the way past the ferocious she-wolf, out of the
Inferno.

Into her mind now swam the quote from Conrad's *Heart of Darkness*
Diti had recited to her just before she left the *Elusan*: "*We live in the flicker—
may it last as long as the old earth keeps rolling!*"

It *would* last.

Settled now, she swung her legs back into the car, pulled the door shut.

She no longer stared at his silhouette. *He is nothing to me*, she thought as she keyed the ignition, eased into traffic. Stopped at a light, she chartered a plane—hugely expensive due to the last-minute booking, but no matter, it would be the last charge she would make on her Parachute black card—and headed for Narita.

Ninety minutes later, she was twenty thousand feet in the air, winging her way back to Port Dickson.

Back to Diti.

36

Evan and Ume were just over halfway through checking out the tattoo parlors in Shibuya when they stepped out of the rain into Studio Edo, a small, well-kept business. Like the others, the walls were covered with the best examples of the ink master. There were four tables, one of which was occupied by a young, muscled yakuza. His full back ink was near completion. It must have been a year since it was started—the phoenix rising out of flames, the twin tigers rampant on either shoulder, roaring, claws of their front paws held forward. Only one small patch was left, the female artist filling in the color using the traditional by-hand method of bundled bamboo needles. Male ink masters were cleaning up beside two other tables. No one was at the fourth table.

The two male artists were a study in contrasts. The older one, gray streaking his temples, moved with the deliberate grace of experience, his own arms decorated with fading traditional designs. The younger wore sleeve tattoos of contemporary geometric patterns, his movements quick and precise as he sanitized his workspace. The female artist was petite but muscular, her black hair pulled back severely, revealing a hummingbird that curled around her neck. Her hands never hesitated as she worked, each strike of the bamboo needles precise and purposeful.

Evan pulled the folded paper from her pocket, the drawing Nyurgun had made for her of the tattoo on Ilona Starkova's wrist, smoothing it carefully before showing it to the male artists. The design was simple but unusual: a blazing sun caught between the sharp steel jaws of a caliper. Both men studied it, then shook their heads. She waited for the female to re-dip her implement, showed her the drawing. The girl shook her head, but to Evan's mind, turned away a beat too quickly.

"Who uses the fourth table?" Ume asked, gesturing to the empty station.

"Eiko's table," the younger artist replied, not looking up from his cleaning. "But she's not here."

"When will she return?"

A shrug. "Who knows? She comes and goes as she pleases."

Throughout the exchange, Evan caught the female artist glancing her way between strikes of her needles, her eyes darting up and then quickly back to her work. There was something furtive in those looks, something that made Evan's instincts prickle.

They left the shop, stepping back into the rain. They'd barely made it three steps when Evan said, "Hold on," her head cocked. The door chimed behind them.

"Wait," called the female artist, slightly breathless. She had unfurled an umbrella over her head. She glanced back at the shop, tilted the umbrella to block the view of anyone looking out through the door. "I know that design," she said in a low voice. "Eiko did it. The customer—she was here earlier today."

Evan asked her to describe the customer. Her heartbeat quickened. It was Ilona Starkova, all right. "Go on," she said kindly.

The artist's hands twisted together as she spoke, betraying her agitation. "Eiko took her to the laser room in back. I . . . I followed them. Through the lounge where we take breaks. I shouldn't have, but . . ." She looked down. "The truth is I was jealous. If they were going to have sex I wanted to know. Eiko doesn't care about me; she only has eyes for her. For Ilona." She took a breath, glanced back at the door to the shop. "But that wasn't it at all."

She touched her neck, where the hummingbird's wing rose over the hastily thrown-on jacket. "When they came out, I could see it. The redness where the design had been. Eiko had lasered it away."

37

KABUKICHO, SHINJUKU, TOKYO, JAPAN

Dokoni Mo, hidden like a feral creature in its den, inhabited the second story of one of the ramshackle row buildings that lined so many of Kabukicho's narrow alleys, replete with tiny restaurants, one after another, their colored paper lanterns illuminating their fronts, all appearing more or less the same but turning out a minuscule menu of dishes unique unto themselves. This particular alley, like the others that made up this neighborhood off the wide, modern, neon-lit avenues, remained anonymous even to seasoned Tokyo residents, bellies full of udon, skewered pork, pan-seared shrimp, pickled daikon, beer, and sake who often lost their way. A smattering of small dive bars where salarymen could pick up girls along with their Suntory whiskey peppered the street, lights twinkling, both a signal and a lure.

"*Dokoni Mo.* Nowhere," Evan said. "An apt name for a company that plucks you out of a miserable life, places you in one of anonymity."

"Isolation seems to be the preferred state of the modern-day Japanese," Ume said. "Our traditional groups have gone by the wayside."

Matsumura had phoned Ume the directions to find Dokoni Mo's address, in the insane maze of this part of Shinjuku. There were no building numbers, rather landmarks as if they were hiking through a forest. And they were. An urban forest.

The rain had abated, the alleyway shone with inconstant reflected light. Walls wept, lanterns shed their tears. Graffiti was everywhere. The stairs—wooden, narrow, creaky—led up into a darkness that foretold abandonment or peril. But at the top, they opened a door with an opaque glass panel like that in an old-school detective agency. Very noir.

Inside they found a long narrow space lit by two standing lamps and one gooseneck lamp crouched on one corner of a beaten-down desk that looked like it had been flayed by a pirate captain. To the left was a broken-back sofa, to the right two uncomfortable-looking ladder-back chairs. Totally Western. Red, green, blue light dribbled in through blinds so dusty they had taken on an unearthly color. Bad reproductions of two Japanese woodblock prints hung on the walls. The one between the two chairs was a sad tattered replica of an original that hung in Ume's office—part of the *Sixty-nine Stations of the Kisokaido Road* series depicting a journey along the famed footpath. A fitting accent for a company sending men on their way to a new life. The other repro was of the most famous shunga erotic woodblock: a woman with her kimono open, being serviced in every way possible by two obliging octopuses. The rapturous expression on her face said it all.

Sitting in a swivel chair behind the desk was a Japanese man so heavy his age could not easily be determined. He might have been a retired sumo wrestler. He did not look up when they stepped into the office, seeing as he was in deep contemplation of a magazine featuring young naked women ritually—some might say artistically—bound in knotted red silken cords. Some lay on tatami, others knelt. Still others hung from the ceiling, their legs tied back at the knees. There was no hint of pain or suffering on their faces, not at all. This was Shibari: modern-day rope bondage—one of many Japanese sexual kinks, the idea being to look, appreciate the positions, knots, ingenious binding patterns, and possibly to engage in sex.

"You in charge here?" Evan asked.

The man turned a page, did not look up. "Who's asking?"

Ume answered. "Ume Linnear."

That caught the man's attention. Like a fish on a hook he squirmed, closed the magazine, shoved it into a desk drawer, slammed it shut, and directed his attention to them.

He spread his hands, "I am as you see me, Ume-sama, but a humble servant of this fine establishment."

Evan restrained herself from laughing in his face. How many Raymond Chandler books had he read? Had he memorized all the hardboiled dialog?

Now he studied Evan, gimlet-eyed. "You brought this person here to be disappeared? Strange. It's always men who need to walk away from the rubble of their lives."

Ume said, "We're here to discuss Arata Sazama."

Sumo's eyebrows raised. "Who?"

"He's a client of yours. Recent, I imagine." Ume's voice was velvet, but if you listened closely you could feel the rip current building. "One week, two at the most."

Sumo pursed his lips, his melon head swinging back and forth. "Never heard the name."

Evan stepped forward. Ume whispered, "No," under her breath, but Evan was right up against the desk. She reached out, grabbed Sumo's ears, slammed his face down onto the desktop.

He groaned as blood splashed over the desk. Without turning her head, Evan said, "Apologies, Ume-sama, but my time is running out. I have no time for patience or ritual."

Picking Sumo's head up by his ears, she ignored his ruined nose. "How about now? You know Arata Sazama."

"Sure, sure." Sumo's eyes were bloodshot. He wiped his nose with the cuff of his shirt, winced. "Came in maybe eight days ago. We gave him that name, new address, you know, the whole deal."

"How did he pay?"

"Well, that's the odd thing. Usually clients come in and, you know, pay in cash, the last of what they were able to swipe before they left their old life behind."

"So Arata Sazama didn't pay cash?"

Sumo spread his hands. His face was starting to swell—cheeks, lips, eye sockets. "He didn't pay at all."

"What? Why would he get a free ride?"

"Well, he didn't. I mean, he wasn't the first one not to pay. Pay me, that is. Arata Sazama, like a couple others before him, had some kind of deal with Bando."

"Who is Bando?" This from Ume, who had stepped up beside Evan.

"Bando Shinji," Sumo said, coughing. "He owns the business."

"And where might we find Bando?" Evan said. She still had hold of Sumo's ears. Tears were leaking out of his eyes.

"He'll kill me."

Evan slipped her pinky into Sumo's ear, all the way to the eardrum, twisted. "Not before I do."

Sumo shuddered, his eyes screwed up. A horrific squeal emanated from his open mouth. Blood covered his teeth and gums. "Okay, okay. He's at his club—Hiromaru." The English translation was Spread. "It's a strip joint one street over. You can't miss it, the entire front glows pink like a girl's—"

"Lovely," Ume spoke over him.

Now the shunga print made sense. Evan let go of Sumo's ears. "Cell phone." She snapped her fingers. Reluctantly, he handed it over. Evan opened it, took out the SIM card, crushed it beneath her heel, did the same for the phone itself to ensure Sumo wouldn't warn his boss they were coming the moment they left the office.

"Time for you to take a vacation," Ume said in her soft, soothing voice. "Now, tonight. Do not wait."

38

KABUKICHO, SHINJUKU, TOKYO, JAPAN

Hiromaru lay at the end of the next street over, Sumo hadn't lied. The alley was, if possible, even narrower than the one they had just left. Rain had started up again, a drizzle so fine it was almost a mist, but it was steady enough. Though they entered the alley from the opposite end the club's bright pink neon blared through the night, the tiny droplets only picking up the glow, repeating it so that it filled the entire street.

Ume stopped Evan before they neared the club. "I think it best if you go in alone."

Evan nodded. "All right. And what, you'll stay out here in the rain?"

"I?" Ume smiled. "No. I'm going to find the rear entrance to the club."

Down five steps, through a curtained door, the garish Pepto-Bismol pink was all consuming, everyone gifted a cartoon complexion. Adding to the unreality was the bar area, which resembled nothing so much as someone's 1930s idea of a spaceship. And sure enough, in a niche on the wall surrounded by bottles of whiskey was a framed photo of Buster Crabbe as blond-haired Flash Gordon. Right beside it was another copy of the shunga print of the maiden getting serviced every which way by the octopuses. No one, so far as Evan could tell, was paying the slightest attention to either; they were too busy guzzling Suntory, trading off-color stories, laughing at lewd jokes, slapping the butts of girls squeezed in between them. A pair of female bartenders who looked like twins kept the whiskey flowing, the tabs growing exponentially. No one seemed to care about the rising cost, either.

Beyond the bar a miniature theater in the round was crowded with salarymen. They pushed and shouted encouragement to a young woman currently writhing athletically around a chrome pole to the thumping beat of electronic music. Upside down, one leg wrapped around the pole, her thick black hair, threaded with multicolored strands that glittered beneath the spotlights, hung down across her face, tips sensually caressing the floor. She wore a gold micro-bikini with paste red gems meant to be rubies highlighting nipples and her cleft.

Evan worked her way around the periphery of the stage, which slowly rotated so everyone could get a look at the performer, if only for a moment or two, hanging on for the next revolution. By the time Evan reached the far side of the theater the girl had slid to the floor, legs wide apart. She whipped off her top, then her bottom, her sex hidden only by the chrome pole wedged between her thighs.

While the heaving audience clamored for more, Evan found a door almost completely hidden by deep shadow in the far left-hand corner.

Through the shadows, Evan made out two figures flanking the door, their stances betraying them as yakuza. The shorter one's jacket pulled tight across his shoulders, revealing the telltale bulge of a shoulder holster. The taller one kept his right hand tucked inside his suit jacket—ready.

The pounding bass from the theater in the round provided cover as Evan edged closer, analyzing her options. The security men's positioning left no blind spots. A direct approach wouldn't work—she needed a distraction.

. . .

Outside in the rain-slicked alley, Ume moved like a ghost between the shadows of air-conditioning units and electrical boxes. Years of training had taught her to spot the telltale signs—the fresh scuff marks on the pavement near a steel door, cigarette butts clustered where guards took their breaks. The rear entrance would be heavily monitored, but there was always a weak point.

She found it in the form of a rusty fire escape. Above it, a window sash was raised to accommodate a makeshift metal vent from which food-scented smoke rose, trembling through the rain. A certain fire hazard, Uma thought, as she mounted the lowest rung on the fire escape.

. . .

Evan noticed one of the bartenders heading toward the door with a tray of oversized glasses and three bottles of premium Suntory whiskey. Perfect. As the woman approached, Evan stumbled forward, apparently drunk, colliding with her. Bottles crashed to the floor, drawing both guards' attention.

"*Gomen'nasai, gomen'nasai.*" So sorry, so sorry, Evan slurred, making a show of trying to help clean up while actually positioning herself closer to the door. The shorter guard stepped forward, reaching for her arm to escort her away. It was the opening she needed.

Evan's elbow connected with his throat as she spun, following through with a palm strike to his nose. Before the taller guard could draw his weapon, she was inside his reach, driving her knee into his solar plexus. Both men crumpled silently, the thundering music drowning any sound they might have made. She pulled the door open and slipped through, finding herself in a narrow corridor lit by flickering fluorescent tubes. The walls vibrated with the bass from the club, but another sound caught her attention—a male voice from above. The music made it impossible to hear individual words, but she was betting it was Bando Shinji she was hearing.

■ ■ ■

Ume reached the window, her fingers finding purchase on the wet sill. The smoke forced her to keep her eyes slitted. Inside, steam and the clatter of dishes in the kitchen. Two cooks worked with their backs to her, focused on great iron woks. Pushing the makeshift vent, she climbed through, landing silently on a stainless steel counter. The heat was intense.

■ ■ ■

On the floor above where Evan crouched was Bando's office. His voice was raised. There was no second voice, indicating he must be deep in a phone conversation. All she needed was for him to reveal one name—who had paid for Arata Sazama's new identity. The answer would unlock the question of who had tried to murder her—someone local it seemed, not the FSB or the GRU; another enemy. She moved forward.

A stairwell at the end of the corridor led upward. The voice was clearer now—an argument in rapid-fire Japanese but there was still too much ambient noise to make out its nature. The tone, however, was unmistakably acrimonious. Up above, a door opened and closed. Footsteps descended toward her position.

Evan pressed herself against the wall, letting the shadows swallow her. The footsteps grew closer—two sets, heavy, purposeful. Male voices muttered in the stairwell about "gaijin trouble." The fluorescent light caught their weapons—long-bladed knives, not surprising since any gunfire within Bando's inner sanctum would be strictly forbidden. It seemed that Bando's premises was a hive of yakuza activity. Evan waited until they passed, then slipped up the stairs, her boots silent on the worn wooden treads.

· · ·

Ume moved like water between the kitchen's prep stations, staying low. A delivery door at the far end stood open, and through it she glimpsed a private elevator—the kind high-end clubs installed for VIP clients who preferred discretion. More importantly, she spotted the card-reader controlling access. This would be Bando's personal escape route. The cooks were too concentrated on the contents of their woks to notice a skittering shadow behind their backs. Ume plucked two knives off one of the racks, reached the elevator without incident, stepped in. The door closed without her making a move. The light above her head went out, plunging her into complete darkness. Reaching out for the door, she tried to open it without any success. Her fingers moved to the right, found a vertical line of four buttons, pressed each one. Nothing.

The good news: the cab was small enough for her to reach up to the ceiling. The bad news: the cab was so small that it had no maintenance hatch she could pry upward to get out.

She was trapped.

· · ·

Evan reached the second floor. Carefully, she peered through an open doorway to her right. Four yakuza sat around a low table, playing Oicho-Kabu, a card game not unlike baccarat. They had removed their shirts, tying them around their waists. Their muscled torsos naked, they displayed their full-body tattoos to each other. Other than when they bathed in a communal *furo* this was one of the few times that yakuza displayed their tattoos, as they normally kept them concealed in public.

Down the hall to her left the male voice—again, she suspected it was Bando Shinji's—grew in volume, the tone more heated. The conversation had morphed into an intense argument. Creeping closer, she could finally make out what Bando—she was sure it was Bando now—shouted: "The Americans are asking questions about Sazama! You promised this would never come back to me!" Pause. "No, it's not my problem. It's our problem now." Pause. "Is that a threat? Really? I would think twice before I said one more word."

Evan heard the sound of a cell phone slammed down on wood—no doubt Bando's desk. Almost immediately the cell began to ring.

The door handle began to turn. Evan coiled herself, ready. From below, a high whine rising up through the building.

Inside Bando's office, his cell stopped ringing. His voice cracked: "What? I—wait, what? The elevator? But how—?"

At almost the same moment the door swung open inwardly, away from Evan, and a tall figure in a charcoal suit stepped out, nearly colliding with her. As the door swung shut again, she drove her knee up, but he was faster than she expected, blocking and countering with a strike that would have crushed her windpipe if she hadn't rolled with it.

Her attacker's suit jacket ripped as he twisted away from Evan's strike, revealing the vibrant scales of a dragon tattoo writhing up his forearm. Pure yakuza. His technique was raw, brutal: the street-hardened fusion of karate and dirty fighting that marked a *kobun*—a yakuza underling.

He lunged forward, trying to trap Evan against the wall. "Gaijin bitch," he spat in Japanese, "you have no idea what temple you've desecrated."

Behind the office door, Bando had stopped sputtering into his phone. Instead came the distinctive sound of paper feeding into a shredder. Evidence disappearing by the second.

The yakuza's next attack drove Evan back a step, but she'd faced his kind before. These men lived in a world where reputation and intimidation usually did their work for them. When that failed, they relied on overwhelming force. But underneath the dragon tattoos and practiced ferocity, they could be surprised.

She let him think he had her pinned, waited for him to commit to his next strike. When it came—a vicious hook meant to cave in her temple—she wasn't there. Instead, she flowed inside his guard, years of aikido training taking over. His own momentum became a weapon. The yakuza lifted off his feet, crashed hard against Bando's doorway. The impact splintered the frame.

The yakuza started to rise, reaching inside his jacket. Evan's kick caught him under the chin, snapping his head back. This time when he hit the floor, he stayed down.

Through the broken doorframe, she could see Bando frantically feeding papers into an industrial shredder. His suit, so impeccable in the club photos downstairs, was sweat-stained and wrinkled. When he saw her, his face went slack with terror.

"Please," he said in English, "you don't understand. If they find out I talked—"

"The Satsuragi-kai?" Evan kept her voice neutral. "Or someone else?"

Before he could answer, Evan was yanked out of his office by two of the four yakuza who had been playing cards in the room nearby. They dragged her down the corridor, hooded her. Knife at her throat. She stumbled, a hand grabbed her left shoulder, pulling. She went with it, using his own strength against him, jamming her shoulder into what she expected was his chin. The grip on her loosened. She grabbed the wrist, twisted it so sharply she heard the bones snap. He grunted, his grip on her gone. She swung him around in time for his throat to be slashed instead of hers. Blood spurted. She felt the others instinctively back away, the other two cardplayers having emerged from the room as well. She grasped the hood, jerked it off.

She saw the layout immediately: five bodies, including hers. The dying yakuza was hard against her chest, becoming heavier by the moment. She backed away from the remaining three yakuza, dragging her dying hostage with her. Crossing the corridor, she entered the game room, the trio crouched, ready to spring, following her, eyes intent, searching for a flaw in her defense.

With the edge of the low table against her calves she stopped, whirled, slammed the yakuza's body down on the tabletop, scattering cards every which way. The table groaned, cracked, splintered.

The trio were advancing now. All three had tantos out, the short blades' tips gleaming in the overhead lights. Evan crouched, drew out a table leg from the rubble, swung it up toward the first advancing yakuza. The tanto followed her strike, but it was a feint. She struck low instead, cracking the table leg into first one knee, then the other. The yakuza howled, crashed forward, face-planting on the floor in front of her.

Scooping up his tanto, she threw it point first into the oncoming yakuza's chest. He staggered, his expression uncomprehending. His fingers curved around the hilt but they had lost all strength. His eyes rolled up and he collapsed.

The room was now a maze of bodies, wood shards, blood. The remaining yakuza, muscular torso glistening with sweat, approached her in a wary fashion, witness to what she had done to his comrades. He stepped as carefully as if crossing a minefield, eyes fixed on her and only her. He stood still, silent, scarcely breathing then launched himself not directly at her but toward her left side.

She realized his tactic an instant too late. His forearm connected with her side just above her hip bone and she doubled over, the wind taken out of her. He was on her in a flash. His fist slammed down on her throat, her legs curled up reflexively, her back arched. He drew his fist back to deliver the killing blow, her mouth opened and the vomit rising up her esophagus spewed into his face. She used his recoil, jammed the heel of her hand into his chest over his heart. He rocked back, she twisted, rolled him off her. She was still seeing stars, the edges of her vision black, roiling. She was saved by automatically going into *prana*, breathing deep and slow, resisting a gasp that would bring her only minimal oxygen and her body needed oxygen more than anything else.

The yakuza was using his forearm to clear his face. Rearing up on her haunches, teeth bared, she grabbed the broken table leg, slammed it down on his forearm with such force all the bones splintered. The yakuza's head flew backward, mouth open in a silent scream. Turning the leg, she jammed the splintered end into his mouth, down his throat.

She rose then, for a moment unsteady on her feet. High-stepping between the corpses, she rested against one wall, gathering her strength, returning her interior to a semblance of normalcy—as normal as she could get covered in blood and vomit, with the agony of her side and throat pulsing up behind her eyes.

Out in the corridor, into Bando's office, which was predictably empty; he wasn't about to hang around. She turned, saw him frantically pushing the button of the elevator at the far end. He must have heard her coming because he whirled, leveled a pistol at her.

"Don't come any closer," he warned.

His eyes were opened so wide she could see the whites all around. He was sweating like a horse lathered after a long gallop. *Terrified*, she thought. *His mortal coil brought up against the black wall of death.* Therefore she knew she had to be careful, had to treat him like a skittish animal, that's what he'd been reduced to. In this situation some men grew defiant, dangerous, unpredictable. Others had their innate cowardice burst through the walls of the hard-man shell they had constructed. Bando, she knew now, was a coward; he did not want to die, but the tremor in his gun hand told her he could not shoot her.

She held up her hands, palms toward him. "I mean you no harm, Shinji-san. Trust me."

"Trust you?" His eyes widened even more, rolling in their sockets. "Look what you've done!"

"I was attacked, Shinji-san." Took a step toward him. "All I did was defend myself. You wouldn't expect less of me." Another step.

"Who are you? What do you want?"

"Who I am is irrelevant to this conversation." Third step; the muzzle of his gun was close now. "What I want is all that matters. Someone paid you to hire Arata Sazama to kill Evan Ryder." She cocked her head. "Who did that, Shinji-san?" She was careful to keep his gaze on her face. Fourth step. "Give me a name and I will leave you to your rackets."

"I don't—"

At that moment the elevator pinged, the doors opened, out stepped Ume. Shinji turned his head, Evan slapped his gun hand to the side, wrested the weapon out of his slackened grip.

"Who is . . . ?" He turned back to her. "I . . . I can't tell you. He'll kill me if I tell you."

"Bando, Bando, Bando." She put a hand on his shoulder, felt him flinch. He licked his dry lips. He emitted a tiny moan as her hand moved to the nape of his neck. "I meant it when I said I mean you no harm. But the fact is I must have that name. If you don't give it to me . . . ." She shrugged as her fingers tightened around his neck. "Why, then, you will leave me no choice."

Fingers clenched. Shinji's body began to tremble. Ume stood silent, unmoving as a statue. Observing closely the byplay, no expression on her face, not even at the wretched state of Evan's clothes, the stink rising off them.

"I came in peace, Bando. It was you who decided to declare war. What-ever happens now is on you." Her fingers worked around to the nerve cluster at the joining of his neck and shoulder. "Live, Bando. Live or die."

A wet stain spread down the crotch of Shinji's trousers. "Çelik." His voice trembled. "His name is Kurt Çelik."

39

Alyosha followed Kiko back to the Western half of the apartment. The atmosphere had changed radically. She sniffed burnt almond and black tea, so strong it was almost overpowering.

"Alyosha-san, here is Kurt Çelik, my husband."

A large shadow emerged from one of the Western rooms. Her first impression as she took Kurt Çelik's hand with its surprisingly long fingers was of a pair of eyes large, muddy brown. Below them his aggressive nose, above a wide forehead, a shock of white hair, thick and lustrous, though Alyosha judged he must be well into his sixties. She could tell he'd had work done on his jaw, throat, and cheeks; the skin stretched over his bones in those places was sleek, almost poreless. He wore a Western suit but, though clearly expensive, it did not sit well on his frame. His one piece of jewelry was a dark silver ring, thick and wide.

He had a grip of iron, this man. He held himself ramrod straight, and with his athlete's body that time had only delicately eroded around the edges, he once might have been a horseman.

Çelik stared directly into her face. She saw his hands, large, rough-looking, as if he'd spent many years outdoors. "Alyosha Ivanovna." He smiled warmly. "I am delighted to meet you."

He did not invite her to sit down and he himself remained standing. His gaze drifted to her bandaged hand. "I see you have met Akujin Matsumura."

Alyosha tried not to wince. "Not for the first time."

"No, of course not." When she gave him a questioning look, he added, "I know Akujin Matsumura better than he knows me." His smile tightened. "Which is, I believe, why you are here."

"At your wife's behest."

Çelik lifted a hand, indicating the doorway from which he had emerged. "Join me, if you will."

They crossed the threshold into a square drawing room filled with books on shelves along the side walls.

"Do you enjoy your time with my wife?"

"Very much," Alyosha said. "She's an exceptional hostess."

"I trust you found the visit educational."

"Extremely."

They passed through the drawing room and entered a short corridor with a marble staircase off to the right.

"Quite palatial," Alyosha said. "I see there's more than one floor."

"Three, in fact," he said in the offhand, almost bored manner of the very rich.

They arrived at a set of carved heartwood double doors that her host opened, waving her inside. He closed the doors behind them.

They were in what appeared to be Çelik's study. Before her a large desk, behind which was a swivel chair and behind that another wall of bookshelves filled with leather-bound volumes. Prints of horses, some with riders, others not, adorned the walls. Or were they photos? In the low light Alyosha couldn't tell.

He bade her sit in a comfortable upholstered chair, pulled up a has-sock opposite. To one side was a small wooden table, a goosenecked floor lamp, which he drew close.

"I trust the education my wife provided did not prove overwhelming."

"Not at all," Alyosha said. "Revelatory would be a more appropriate adjective."

"Good, good." He nodded. "Now you know the breed of man you are dealing with."

"I am bound to him, Mr. Çelik," she said, lifting her wounded hand.

"*Giri.* Yes, I'm well aware." He smiled at her as he placed the low table between them. She could see that it contained a single deep drawer. "You have received a wound. May I take a look at it to make sure it doesn't become infected?"

Without a word, Alyosha placed her bandaged hand palm up on the table. Çelik opened the drawer, took out what appeared to be an old-fashioned pigskin doctor's bag. This he opened, unraveled a well-worn flannel, revealing a precisely aligned set of implements. She recognized the shapes and style immediately.

She looked up into his face, saw despite his clever surgeries the Slavic influence. "*Ty ne turok.*" You are not Turkish.

He made no comment, instead took up the first implement, a chrome bandage scissors. With extreme care and a gentleness that surprised her he cut through the bandage, slowly and deliberately freed her hand. Beneath was the wrapping of the stub of her little finger.

"*Bol'*?" Pain? he asked as he cut through the inner bandage.

"*Bol', to poyavlyayushchayasya, to ischezayushchaya.*" Twinges, off and on. Thereafter, they only spoke in Russian. Alyosha stared at him. When he spoke Russian—his native language—his voice changed. It was deeper, rougher, that of an army officer, perhaps.

This conversation was going in a direction she never even contemplated. But then ever since Kiko had played her the tape of Matsumura admitting to his atrocities on her father a certain unreality had crept into her world. She no longer knew where she stood or who she was talking to. "*I trust the education my wife provided did not prove overwhelming,*" Çelik had said. She wondered whether he had sensed the lie of her answer. Of course she was overwhelmed. How could she not be?

What was left of her ravaged pinky was darkly stained, crusty with dried blood. The flesh was red and swollen, ugly as sin. She felt the prickle of tears in her eyes—she couldn't tell if they were for her poor pinky, or an unexpected reaction to his touch being so gentle. He might call himself Kurt Çelik but that was an alias. Who was he, and why had he chosen to reveal himself to her?

"I thought as much." He shook his head. "These doctors the yakuza employ. They don't know how to properly dress a wound." He irrigated the stump with a disinfectant; she sucked in her breath at the sudden flare of pain. "So what will you do now," he said, "go off and tell your new master what you have learned here?"

"There is nothing I learned here he needs to know." She wondered again, this time with a strange uneasy sense of urgency, who Çelik really was, and why he deliberately chose to reveal himself to her. "Nor is there anything I've learned here I wish to tell him."

Çelik dabbed the stump with a sterile pad so tenderly they felt like kisses. "Aren't you bound by duty to tell him?" he asked. "*Giri.*"

"Either you feel *giri* or you don't. So I've been told." She watched him apply an antibiotic ointment to her wound, then begin to wrap it. "I am neither Japanese nor yakuza."

"No," he said. "You are GRU."

That brought a flicker of a sardonic smile to Alyosha's face. "I used to be, once upon a time."

"Ah, yes. You report to Kata Romanovna—the assassin, the outcast, the pariah. The criminal in hiding."

It was true. But Alyosha realized she and Kata used to call Lyudmila *the criminal in hiding*. Somehow, weirdly, now that Lyudmila was dead, Kata had taken her place. An actual shiver ran down Alyosha's spine.

"Keep still, please," Çelik admonished her softly.

Unlike the yakuza doctor Matsumura had taken her to, Çelik's work was considered, methodical, precise. She found that she liked being in his care and this shocked her. It also prompted her to ask, "You haven't told me your real name."

Çelik paused. He had been wrapping her stump as if it were a Christmas present he was going to gift her. Looking into her eyes, he said, "You haven't told me yours."

"What do you mean?" A frown caused a vertical line to appear above her eyes. "You know my name perfectly well. Alyosha Ivanovna Panarin. My father was Ivan Vladimirovich Panarin."

Çelik's hands returned to the open pigskin bag, pushed some things out of the way, brought out a black-and-white photo in a silver frame. By the look of it the photo was quite old—two decades at least. He handed it over to Alyosha.

What she saw was this: a family portrait—mother, father, two prepubescent children: daughters—in a bucolic setting. No, not rural, but a leafy park and beyond it the tall houses of St. Petersburg. The season was winter, the father bundled in a greatcoat with military shoulderboards. The mother and daughters cocooned in fur-collared winterwear. The father and mother wore gloves, the girls mittens.

The portrait under the intense light of the gooseneck revealed the family's faces. The mother was beautiful with a slender face, wide lips, big, slightly uptilted eyes. The father's eyes were his most prominent feature. Even in black-and-white their uncanny paleness was unmistakable—they could have been made out of chips of ice. Alyosha looked up, saw Çelik cup one eye, then the other, fingertips popping out colored contacts. Those same uncanny pale eyes from the photo stared back at her.

"You," she said.

Çelik nodded. "The family."

"Why are you showing this to me?"

"Isn't it obvious?" Çelik said. "No? Take another look."

Then her heart seemed to skip a beat. Blood rushed violently to her head, causing a moment's vertigo.

"What are you saying?"

Çelik watched her carefully. "Our family," he said softly. "In happier times."

"*Our* family?"

His forefinger pointed to the younger daughter. "That's you, Alyosha."

"Bullshit." Her head seemed to explode. "What are you doing?" She jumped up. "Trying to manipulate me?" Hands on hips. "Why? What's your deal, anyway?"

Çelik looked up at her. "Look at the color of my eyes. Study my face in the photo. Look in a mirror. I'm telling you the truth. You take after me."

"What? No." Her head was spinning. Her lungs seemed to have forgotten how to work. She whirled around. "Air. I need air."

As if this were a command, Çelik rose, took her by the hand, led her to a pair of French doors. Opening them, he took her out onto a narrow cement balcony. They stood side by side beneath the overhang as the rain spattered their faces and shoes. By this time she had pulled her hand away from his, explosively, violently. She rubbed it now with her other hand as if his grip had caused her pain. But it was his words—lies? Truth?—that had wounded her.

"I know this is difficult to take in," Çelik said softly.

"Shut up," Alyosha told him. "Just shut up." She pressed her fingertips to her temples, as if to push out everything he had said to her in his study. *My God*, she thought. *My God. I can't . . .*

She turned on him suddenly, in her mind a battle stance, her body ready to pummel him, take hold of him, heave him over the rim of the balcony. She imagined his back breaking as he hit the pavement far below, his head cracking open like a melon, all his hateful words spilling out, liquifying, drained away by the rain.

"I don't believe you." Her throat was clotted with emotion. "What you're saying can't be true. I had parents who loved and raised me."

Çelik never took his eyes off her. "Not from birth." He held out a hand. "Alyosha, listen to me."

"Fuck you." She turned and fled back through the French doors, the agitation of her rush through his study lifting the photo off the table, spinning it, settling it to the floor as she ran through the short hallway, out into the living room—Çelik's hideous overdecorated living room, so very Russian now that he had revealed himself, now that she saw it through the eyes of his hidden past.

40

KURAMAE, TOKYO, JAPAN

Chiyoko's lab was located in Kuramae, an up-and-coming riverside neighborhood of Tokyo. Bursting with small artisan and designer workshops, recently established distilleries, tiny restaurants, and warehouses being rehabbed. Here wound thickets of narrow backstreets, shadowed, shabby, proud still of what they had been three hundred or so years ago, filled now with young people fueled by an entrepreneurial spirit. Telephone lines crisscrossed over Eiko's and Ilona's heads while behind them neon kanji seemed to float down with the rain. The narrow streets awash, water rushing along the gutters. Along one such street, in one such rehabbed building, Chiyoko labored through the nighttime hours making her bleeding-edge commissions.

Eiko stopped in front of a building with no signs whatsoever. But it did have a CCTV camera pointed at the entrance. She pressed a bell and, after a moment, they were buzzed in.

"Don't say a word," she told Ilona. "Let me do the talking." She held out her hand and Ilona dropped the teeth into her palm.

Unlike Eiko's apartment, which was meticulously neat and spotlessly clean, Chiyoko's workspace was a jumble of mechanical and electronic equipment that climbed the wall behind her from floor to ceiling, the functions of which were entirely opaque to Ilona. The room was as cold and dry as an operating theater.

Chiyoko, tall for a Japanese, let alone a woman, sat bent over her worktable, a band holding a tube of light around her head. She looked like an angel, halo and all. She glanced up momentarily when the two women entered. Her left eye was out of whack, roaming the space between her two guests as if it had a mind of its own.

"Don't touch a thing," she said. "Everything is precisely where it's supposed to be."

Ilona glanced around at the masses of books, papers, printouts, implements, orphaned dials and switches wondering how this could be so. The air was filled with the ghosts of metal, cold coffee, the smoke of solder thick, depriving the room of oxygen despite the whirr of water-cooled fans.

Chiyoko gestured without looking up from her work. "Sit. Now."

They pulled up metal chairs, dusted them off. Ilona noted a thick, incomprehensible manual composed exclusively of equations spread across an adjacent table as she lowered herself into what seemed the most uncomfortable chair she'd sat in since her interrogation in the Lubyanka in Moscow. As Chiyoko raised her head again, stared into her eyes, it occurred to Ilona that the electronics expert did not enjoy company. The chairs clearly were designed to get visitors up and out of her lab as quickly as possible.

Chiyoko held out a hand, fingertips oddly silvered as if they were mechanical rather than flesh and blood. "You have brought something for me."

Eiko rose, handed her the teeth. As she did so Chiyoko's good eye seemed to stab Ilona through the heart. Something inside Ilona flinched; outwardly her expression did not change. She thought of Eiko's warning: *"She's not like other Japanese."*

Chiyoko weighed the teeth in her cupped palm but did not so much as glance at them. Instead, her fixed eye still upon Ilona, said, "You're Russian."

Ilona sat absolutely still. "You can't know that."

"I don't like Russians," Chiyoko said to which Ilona simply shrugged.

Now Chiyoko looked down at what Eiko had given her. Her head bobbed as if she had been delivered a blow. Setting her magnifier in place she studied first one tooth, then the other. Lastly, she put them together in what Ilona could see was the proper order. "German made," Chiyoko said. "Meticulous craftsmanship surrounding the key element."

Despite Eiko's warning Ilona couldn't help herself. "Which is . . . ?" She pointedly ignored Eiko's anxious rustle.

Chiyoko lifted her head up. "How does a Russian come into possession of these?"

"What are they?" Ilona pressed. "What are they meant to do?"

"Meant to do?" Chiyoko's roving eye now alit on Ilona and Ilona felt an eerie kind of clawing at the flesh around her eyes and ears. As Chiyoko lifted the teeth she smiled a crooked smile, thin as a razor blade. "Madam, these teeth are a communicating device."

Ilona's lips pursed. "I beg your pardon?"

Chiyoko expelled a corrosive laugh. "Bone to bone. Totally sealed end to end. No one, nothing can eavesdrop on the conversations using this ingenious device. Directly, no matter the distance between users."

Chiyoko plucked a cigarette from a gold case. The top was incised with a snarling dragon. Placing it between her lips at one corner of her mouth, she lit it with a beautiful Dunhill Rollagas palladium-and-leather lighter. For some time she sucked smoke into her lungs, shot it out into the air. She studied Ilona through the bluish haze, her gaze steady, unblinking, giving away nothing.

Ilona's hands curled into fists.

"There are always two teeth, as you see," Chiyoko said, ignoring her. "Molars, of course. One is the sender. This one." She held up one of the teeth. "The other is the receiver." She sucked in more smoke, let it out in a leisurely hiss.

Chiyoko shrugged. "These are yours," and handed the molars directly to Ilona.

Ilona rose for a moment to take them. Chiyoko grabbed her wrist with surprising, almost superhuman strength. Ilona immediately felt this, did not try to break free.

"Tell me again that you didn't know what these are."

"If I did know," Ilona said, "I would not have needed to come here, I would not have needed you to explain their use to me."

"But you are Russian."

"Stating the obvious." Ilona was becoming annoyed. "Repeatedly."

"Madam, these were manufactured by BriteBar Metallwerks in Gerlingen, Baden-Württemberg, Germany."

"What's that got to do with my being Russian?" Ilona snapped, eschewing all sense of courtesy. This woman rubbed her the wrong way from the moment they locked eyes.

"Everything." Chiyoko abruptly let go of her wrist. "Everything."

Eiko, trying to defuse the escalation in volatile tempers, broke in, "These teeth seem like a rather . . . baroque method of communication."

Chiyoko's gaze turned on her. "Clumsy, too, I suppose you'd say."

"I would, yes."

Chiyoko stared at the lengthening ash end of her cigarette, stubbed it out in a small brass plate. Her gaze rose to Eiko's. "That is because you are inexpert. Not to mention ignorant." She sat back. "These days no communication is safe from hacking. You should know this."

"I do," Eiko said, feeling as if she was a child being upbraided by an

adult who knew so much more than she did. "All communication is vulnerable in one way or another even when claimed otherwise. The hackers
are already one step ahead."

"You are right—but also wrong." Chiyoko's expression was smug, her
voice condescending. "Those teeth represent a system that is hack-proof,
no matter how fast bad actors evolve their systems. Bone to bone, Eiko.
Bone to bone. Unhackable."

"Is this true?" Eiko's eyes open wide, turned to Ilona. "You're sitting
on a potential gold mine."

"You're getting ahead of yourself." Ilona's brow wrinkled in annoy-
ance.

Eiko shrugged, a disinterested expression on her face. Or was she
merely feigning indifference? Ilona was abruptly on alert.

"Now the secret is out," Chiyoko said to Ilona. "You should have sent
her away. Instead, you allowed her to stay. This is on you."

Eiko startled. "What? Ilona, what is she talking about?" Her mouth
hung open in shock as Ilona advanced on her. "What? Ilona, you wouldn't.
You couldn't. You know me. Your secret is safe with me."

"Secrets," Ilona whispered, "are best served hot. The colder they get,
the older they get, the more the danger."

"But I—" The breath went out of Eiko as Ilona buried her fist in her
solar plexus. Making short, sharp barking sounds like a seal in distress,
she sat down, her back against Chiyoko's desk. Tears overflowed her eyes,
ran down her cheeks, dripped onto her chest.

"But, but . . . but you love me. We love each other."

"Love." Ilona crouched down in front of her. "Love has nothing to do
with this."

"How can you say that?" Eiko was sobbing. "How can you *think* that?"

"I think," Ilona said, "because I can." She shook her head. "But love . . .
love exists on another stage altogether. I don't know that stage; I never
have."

"But you . . . we made love, we were so tender with each other."

"Lamb is tender. Veal is tender. That is what tender means to me."

"You're cruel." Eiko tossed her head from side to side. "How could you
be so cruel?"

Ilona reached out, took Eiko's chin between thumb and fingers. "Oh,
Eiko, I'd have to be alive to be cruel."

She stood up abruptly. "It won't hurt, that I promise."

Behind her desk, Chiyoko lit another cigarette, kept her head down while she studied an engraving she was making in a ring for Kiko Ashi-kaga, a present for her from her husband, Kurt Çelik. She took a puff, set the cigarette down in an overfilled ashtray, took up a tool, started working on the intricate scrollwork, studiously deaf to the desperate high-pitched mewling rising from the space in front of her workspace. A sharp crack and the mewling stopped.

Chiyoko continued with her delicate work. "I suppose," she said, "that you will kill me next."

Ilona took the cigarette Chiyoko had set down, put it between her lips, sucked down smoke, then ground it out in the ashtray. On the exhale, said, "Give me a reason not to."

"Kurt Çelik is a powerful Turkish businessmen, who lives here in To-kyo. He is one-third owner of BriteBar Metallwerks."

Ilona shook her head. "This information concerns me how?"

"He's married to Kiko Ashikaga. The Ashikaga are one of the better-known families of illustrious samurai dating back to the era of the Tokugawa Shogunate."

Ilona took a step toward her. "I'm running out of patience, *madam*."

At that stroke of anger, Chiyoko looked up. "I perceive that you pos-sess a transactional personality. So I propose a trade. Information for my life."

"You're something of a bitch," Ilona mused. "I don't like you, but I'm beginning to admire you. Go ahead."

"Oh, no," Chiyoko said. "I'll tell you the beginning, then you make your promise."

"How do you know I'll keep my promise?"

Chiyoko gave off a thin smile like the radiance from a faraway light. "We are both transactional creatures. This I know. This I trust."

Ilona huffed. "You're used to being the smartest person in the room."

"It's a failing of mine, I admit."

This produced a laugh from Ilona for whom laughter was an alien thing. She nodded. "The beginning, then."

Putting down her engraving tool, Chiyoko lit yet another cigarette, took a long pull at it. Head wreathed in blue cloud, she said, "Kurt Çelik is as much a Turk as you are, Ilona Starkova. In fact, in one sense you and Kurt Çelik are the same. You're both Russian."

Not many things startled Ilona, but this revelation did. "How do you know my name? Eiko didn't introduce me."

That smile again, slender as a crescent blade. "I know many things,

Miss Starkova. I hold in my head many secrets. A number of them useful to you." Her eyes opened wide, eyebrows raised.

She was looking for Ilona's promise. Ilona gave it. "You have my word I will not touch a hair on your head." Her eyes narrowed. "I value you too much."

"And the secrets I keep."

"Being transactional, yes, of course."

Now it was Chiyoko's turn to laugh, a sound not unlike metal on metal. "Yes, I see that now. This, I believe, would be a good thing—for both of us."

"My word is law," Ilona said. "Time to share this secret."

"I know many things about Kurt Çelik others do not." Chiyoko took another hefty drag on her cigarette. "Perhaps his wife, but none others." Smoke rolled out from her nostrils like the exhalation of some mythical creature, half human, half animal. "As I said, Çelik is one-third owner of BriteBar Metallwerks, along with a German of no consequence to you, and Marsden Tribe."

"Tribe," Ilona repeated. "I am meant to deliver these teeth to him."

"And yet, you're here."

"I needed someone to tell me what these teeth are."

"Me."

"Yes."

"There's something else. Something more important to you." Chiyoko ground out her cigarette. "Çelik is Russian, as I told you. You are Russian. Even more curious, you have the same family name. Çelik has been hiding here in Tokyo for some years, has had plastic surgery, wears contact lenses to hide his pale eyes. Your eyes, Ilona Starkova.

"His name is Rachan Dmitriyevich Starkov. He is your father."

41

TIMUR BOUND

It wasn't the incarceration that was getting to Timur—he'd only been in this cell for a little over three days by his admittedly inaccurate accounting. After all, he'd spent most of his early childhood in Moscow and Cyprus—if not incarcerated then certainly restrained within a very fixed and small boundary. He'd never been allowed outside his father's various heavily defended compounds without a veritable phalanx of wide men with the fixed expressions of a wax figure.

He remembered with a combination of chagrin and amusement the time when he was four, stamping on one of the wide men's shoes in order to get him to change his expression. All he received for his effort was an aching ankle.

No, what was bothering Timur was the change in atmosphere among his captors. They were, to a man, more anxious, short-tempered, querulous. Gone were the games of chess and backgammon, the faint strains of abrasive Russian rap music. Not an hour ago a fistfight broke out just outside his door. With his ear to the metal Timur heard it all—the heavy exhalations, grunts, curses, wet-sounding smacks, what sounded to him like the snap of twigs but must have been the crack of bones breaking.

Thirty minutes later, with his bladder's fullness smacking a headache behind his eyes, he beat on the door with his fist. Moments later, a key grated in the lock, the door swung open halfway, revealing Grisha's black eye.

"Not a word," Grisha growled. As Timur stepped out he became aware of a large bruise darkening the side of Grisha's thick neck.

"I hope the other guy—"

"You see the other guy," Grisha said through grinding teeth, "it'll make you want to run to your mommy, hear me?"

Timur nodded. As they began their walk down the windowless corridor toward the bathroom, Timur smelled a commingling of blood and bleach, an unmistakable combo that made him want to retch. He reached his tongue up to his palate, massaging it to keep down the restless bile.

"When am I getting out of here?" He hated himself for asking but he could no more stop the words tumbling out of his mouth than he could knee Grisha in the groin, not after hearing that fistfight. He'd have no chance against this bull.

"Two days, *porosenok*," Grisha said darkly. "Or not at all." He might have won the fight but it had done nothing for his mood.

Timur looked up at the wide Russian. "You wouldn't kill me, would you, Grisha?"

Grisha grunted, which could have meant anything from "Never," to "I'm considering it right now, you chattering little shit."

Timur spent the next five minutes, one of them urinating, racking his brains for a way out of here. Hearing that fistfight, seeing its aftermath on Grisha's face, had terrified him. How stupid was he to even consider attacking the Russian. He wasn't in a Marvel movie—one of the few Western entertainments he'd been allowed to access during his childhood—he didn't have a cadre of SFX techs working to help him get free. This was real life. By the time Grisha banged on the door he'd concluded his situation was hopeless.

He opened the door, stepped out into the corridor, and was immediately met with lewd laughter, the wet sounds of bare flesh smushed against bare flesh. He pointed to his right. "What's going on there?"

Grisha huffed. "The boys have ordered in some female entertainment. They were going nuts with boredom. I imagine you heard the fistfight outside your door. Well, that would have been the start of many others if the girls hadn't been brought in to ease the tension." He gripped Timur's shoulder. "And here I am babysitting our own little *porosenok* on his piss break."

Timur's brain lit up like a flare in the night sky. "Why don't you go on over and join the party?"

Grisha glowered, his grip on Timur became painful. "Because of you, you shit-faced princeling."

"Take me with you."

Grisha's heavy eyebrows lifted. "What is it you say?"

"Take me with you." He struggled out of the big Russian's vise, took his hand, attempted to pull Grisha toward the increasingly lewd sounds of the party. "Come on, Grisha. You don't want to miss all the fun, do you?"

Timur now was praying that he was right, that Grisha didn't want to miss the fun. That he'd been angry over his ill fortune ever since the girls had been ordered in. And now they were here, now that his compatriots were partaking of the voluptuous flesh, Grisha was goddamned if he was going to miss a minute more.

Bingo.

"Fuck me," Grisha rumbled, leading Timur down the corridor. "Let's do this thing."

The place smelled strongly of cigarette smoke, perfume, sweat, and something thicker, musky, that reminded Timur of the rutting animals he'd come upon in the forest surrounding one of his father's dachas. The atmosphere made his eyes water; he resisted the urge to cough. He was exceedingly careful not to make any sudden move, to keep to Grisha's side. Biding his time. All the girls were either naked or on their way, slithering out of their provocative clothes. All the men's eyes, hands, mouths were on their exposed flesh. So far as Timur could tell the girls were Japanese, and young—very young; maybe fifteen or sixteen. Oddly, they all had Western names.

The plan had formed in his mind the moment Grisha had told him about the girls. Now was the time to put it into action. He waited patiently, his heart pounding wildly in his chest, as though seeking to break through his rib cage. He thought of his lessons with Evan and he made his breathing slow and deep. Oxygenating his system. Calming his heart.

A girl broke away from the throng, older than the rest, though by no means old—still in her teens—headed directly for Grisha, making her intentions known through both her expression and the exaggerated sway of her hips. Timur, on high alert, was aware of Grisha's immediate attraction. Grisha's mouth hung half open; he seemed magnetized. Timur waited, waited, continuing to breathe slowly, deeply.

When the girl came within arm's length, when she spoke to him in a low, smoky voice, Grisha reached for her narrow waist and Timur turned on his heel, sprinted through the open doorway. He heard one voice, then others raised behind them, with great concentration paid them no mind, continued down the windowless corridor, turned left at an intersection, then right. He had only a vague idea where he was going, of course. The place was a maze. He thought of the Minotaur—half man, half bull—at its center. He thought of himself as the Minotaur. Tall and strong and this lent him strength as well as courage. He always liked the Minotaur from the first time he read about the creature—supposedly grotesque but to Timur beautiful in a somber, almost lordly, way. He, incarcerated within his father's dacha, found common cause with the monstrous being. *If I was as tall and strong as the Minotaur,* he used to tell himself, *I could break out of here, swat down all the security men who bend the knee to my father—a father who never comes to visit, even to say hello.* Like the Minotaur, Timur both existed and didn't exist, tied to a place he despised.

Turning left now, another right fifty yards on. There was no one about; they were all getting their "swords polished" as Grisha had told him with a lewd smirk.

He was getting close now; he could feel the pull of the sea, the sharp mineral taste in the air. He was smart enough not to head for the door, which would surely be locked. What would Grisha do to him if he caught up to him? Timur put the thought out of his mind. At this moment he was free; he would remain free. A window; he needed a window. Another turn and there it was, the frame old, paint peeling, the pane salt-stained, thin. Stepping over to it he tried to lift the lower half of the window but there was no grip. So many layers of paint covered the sash it was impossible for him to open the window, no matter how hard he strained. He was wasting time; he knew—he heard—he had precious little of it.

He needed something to break the glass. Was it even thin enough to break? Turning on his heel, he spied a chair. That would do quite nicely—he hoped. Picked it up. Now he heard voices rising on an angry tide. Boot soles pounding the stone floor. Fingers crossed.

Timur hefted the chair, stepped to the window, swung it around and let fly, the junction of back and seat smashing through the glass. With the shards still glittering around him, he leapt, but before he could make it through a pair of hands like meat hooks gripped his leg, started to draw him back inside. Whipping his head around he saw Grisha, cheeks red, lips drawn back from his nicotine-stained teeth.

"Get back here, you little shit," he growled. "Where d'you think you're going?"

Timur sucked saliva into his mouth, spat it straight into Grisha's left eye. Grisha's head lifted up in response and Timur, praying that the angle was right, tried to smash the heel of his hand into Grisha's nose. But Grisha was too quick and Timur's hand pushed only air.

The big man gripped Timur's hips, pulled him back inside the building, spun him around.

"If you were anyone else . . ." Put his face so close Timur got an unwanted whiff of his foul breath, like a feral dog with shreds of meat decomposing between his teeth. "You'd be well fucked up by now." Nevertheless, he cuffed Timur on the back of the head, grabbed him by the scruff of the neck, frog-marched him back to the room where all the co-ed exercising was still in full swing. Timur caught blurred glimpses of bared butts and breasts, the musky scent of animals in heat. The men grunted, the women stayed silent.

One of the women rushed up to Grisha but her eyes were on Timur. "What did you do to this little darling?" Crouched down in front of Timur, she used some of the tissues all the women carried to wipe their nether regions at the end of their sessions to clean blood off his right cheek. He had been cut by a piece of glass as Grisha hauled him back through the broken window.

"Brute. Animal," she snapped at Grisha as she worked on stanching the blood flow. "He's only a little boy."

"He was trying to escape, Dahlia," Grisha said lamely.

"Where to?" Dahlia's lips twisted, her fingers already working expertly at Grisha's crotch. "There's nothing out there but sand and salt water." When she felt him grow hard, she parted her lips, ran her tongue over them, making them glisten. "I can't wait." A little moan just for him. Abruptly, she turned her back to him, drew Timur to her. "Oh, come here, honey." She looked accusingly back at Grisha, whose eyes were now half glazed with lust. It had been weeks since he'd been with a woman and the need had grown to outsize proportions. "He's crying now. See what you've done?"

She rose with Timur in her arms, put herself between him and Grisha, moved a little away, in the general direction of the door.

"Go," she whispered in Timur's ear. "Run as fast as you can. I'll keep him occupied."

She put him down, turned back to Grisha. "Daddy's been a bad boy." she said in a throaty voice. "Look what I have for Daddy." Unzipped his fly, took hold of him, fingers sliding up and down. "Daddy needs to be punished." Clamping the head so hard Grisha's eyes watered. "Daddy needs to be punished now."

■   ■   ■

Timur fled at full speed. He had by now memorized the different routes to the window he had smashed. There were three; he chose one. Arriving at the window, he leapt over the sill, curled himself into a ball, as Evan had taught him, practiced every day under the broiling Sumatran sun until he felt like a puddle of sweat. But that practice served him in good stead now. He came out of the roll and began to run, directly toward the

tree line. Beyond that, the ocean. He could hear it, the soft suck and release of the waves rolling endlessly in.

Amid the maritime pines, twisted, stunted by the salt wind, heading
left to get himself as far away from the prison-house as he could before
his energy ran out. He had run with Evan every day, longer and more
difficult routes. She had driven him hard and now he was most grateful.
On the other side of the ledger he had no water with him, was semi-
dehydrated already. So the balance was more or less even. They could
still catch him, he knew. They were fast and persistent and determined
and they would have flashlights when darkness fell. He knew all this,
and yet was able to swipe the thoughts aside, concentrate on all the ways
to elude them, ran through them in his mind.

Two miles from the prison-house and he hadn't yet been caught, had
neither seen nor heard a whisper of pursuit though he knew they must be
out there somewhere. He quit the trees, stepped down through the slop-
ing sand and into the surf, sluiced the sweat off himself, dunked his head
several times to refresh himself. By that time, all traces of blood had been
washed away. Stooping, he picked up a branch, used the brush-like pine
needles to erase all footprints between the surf and the tree line, and back
again. He finished at the water's edge and then walked just inside the
creaming surf where his footprints vanished as soon as he made them.
Even if they hired dogs the animals would lose his scent in the water.
He was stunned now at how so much of what Evan had taught him was
saving his life now. During the few days of his incarceration—which had
passed with the slowness of months—he had ceased to think of her as a
living human being. She loomed large in his consciousness as a cutout
figure, a silhouette, a shadow without substance. She had faded, not part
of his new existence, but now she was with him again, whispering in
his ear, all the training she had gifted him coming into play. He began
to laugh—the exhilaration of his freedom hitting him at last. All at once
he collapsed, the gentle waves washing over him. His laughter was gone,
replaced by deep-felt shivers running through his body. The tears came,
hot and biting, turning his cheeks red. Hours passed or they might have
been minutes; he had lost all sense of time. Nighttime was making swift
strides across the sea from the east. The sky indigo, pinpricks of stars
shyly showing themselves. The blinking lights of vessels far out on the
Aegean—too far for him to signal, let alone swim to.

He knew he should keep moving but his exhaustion—thirst and now
hunger combining to debilitate him—kept him in place. The most he

could manage was to crawl out farther into the water until he was immersed up to his shoulders. Floating, his weightless body soothed by the incoming tide. Rocked to the eternal rhythm of the sea his eyelids began to lower, his sense of place vanishing into the green depths of the ancient Aegean, home to Theseus, the Minotaur, so many others, part of the sand through which he had so recently stepped.

And it was with the tears rolling freely, his heart aching, that he heard the distant *thwop-thwop-thwop* of a helicopter.

PART FOUR

WOLVES

The wolf may change its appearance, but never its intentions.

—proverb of unknown origin

42

Ume pulled the electric Toyota to the curb opposite Çelik's building. "Up there," she said, pointing. "The terraced triplex apartment."

Ume had taken Evan back to the hotel, waited while she showered. Mariko threw out her soiled shirt and trousers, had new clothes waiting for her, along with a brand-new, fully charged cell phone. Twenty minutes later, they were back in Ume's car, headed for Azabu Juban.

"Okay," Evan said now. "I'll take it from here."

Ume turned to Evan. "Translation, please."

Evan smiled thinly. "I'll be getting out here. Alone."

Ume made no comment, her eyes straight ahead at the rain sliding down the windshield.

Sensing her tension, Evan went on. "Ume-sama. I am heading into a situation that's extremely dangerous. This is my fight."

"Do you think I can't take care of myself?"

"On the contrary. Even if you weren't Nicholas Linnear's daughter I know you can. Still, I don't want you involved."

"You came to me." Ume's voice was soft but Evan felt the steel beneath the silk. "In my ryokan you were assaulted, nearly killed. In my hotel, an extension of my house. This is an intolerable offense. The moment you stepped through the door you were under my protection. In that I failed."

"It's not your fault."

Ume turned to look at her again. It was very quiet inside the car, very still.

"Evan-sama, I owe you a debt I can never repay."

"*Giri.*"

Ume nodded. "There is no choice, you see. There is only what is here before us both. This is the now we must navigate. Together."

Evan nodded. She understood. She didn't like it but also knew there was nothing she could so about it. This was Japan. A debt like Ume incurred was sacred; she accepted that. That was her duty.

"All right." She looked out the rain-slicked side window. "How do we know Alyosha is still with Çelik and Kiko Ashikaga?"

Ume pointed. "You see that car parked just down the block? It's waiting to pick her up."

Evan squinted through the windshield. "How can you possibly know that?"

"It's simple enough." Ume smiled. "That car belongs to Matsumura. She belongs to him now. Except when she's with Çelik, like now, he'll make sure she's with him."

"Okay, do you know how we infiltrate Çelik's apartment?"

"We don't."

Evan gestured. "I can get in anywhere."

"Not this place. Çelik and Kiko have the top three floors. I myself have done recons. I know how to get into the building, get up to the entrance to their home, but then . . ." She shrugged. "They have made their home into a fortress—secured by an electronic web of overlapping safeguards. You can't even cut the power; there are redundancies within redundancies. The only access is via a prestored thumbprint. And before you say anything, the reader is photonic, not haptic."

"So no fooling it with Alyosha's print lifted off a glass or surface."

"Correct."

"Nevertheless we have to try," Evan pressed.

"Have a bit of patience."

"Ume-sama, I don't have the luxury of patience. My five days to find the White Wolf are almost over."

"Nevertheless."

Evan had never encountered anyone who could convey so much with a single word. Against the push of urgency in her mind she settled back, took out her new cell phone. "If you would, please send the results of your recon to this lovely new phone you've gotten for me."

"Evan-sama."

"'Have a bit of patience,' I know. Please."

Ume smiled subtlely and nodded, busied herself with the transfer.

It was almost time for the fourth vid from Timur, reminding Evan that she hadn't yet revisited the third vid. Timur's first clandestine message in Morse code was SAEG, the second was ISL. She opened the sat phone and showed these to Ume, who became immediately excited.

"If I've interpreted these codes correctly, Timur is being held on an island somewhere in the South Aegean."

Ume sucked in a breath. "Do you know how many islands there are in the South Aegean?"

"There are two hundred twenty islands in the Cyclades group," Evan said. "But only thirty-three are inhabited."

"Thirty-three? That might as well be three hundred thirty-three."

"But wait. There was more than I didn't get to decode yet." Evan scrolled to the third vid, zooming in on Timur's left hand. Again, she just managed to discern the tapping through the grainy picture. She read off the letters as Timur spelled them out in Morse: I S L S U N F."

"S U N F," Ume said. "What could that mean?"

As an answer, Evan took up the cell phone and brought up a map of the southeast Aegean on Google Earth, let her gaze rove over the area as a whole, then started to zoom in on different sections, three or four islands at a time.

"It's of course possible that they would have brought him to one of the uninhabited Cyclades," Evan said, "but highly unlikely. They need to keep him in a safe place, a permanent house of some sort, not a makeshift shelter." Her finger kept the interactive map moving. "If I stay with the inhabited islands . . ."

"But S U N F? What does that tell us?" Ume said. "What is he trying to say?"

"There!" Evan's finger stopped over the island of Naxos, one of the largest Cyclades. "What does the outline of Naxos look like?"

Ume peered closer, breathing, "S U N F," like a chant. Or a prayer.

"A sunfish!" Evan cried. "Look at the squat, rounded shape of the body of the island, the large 'fins' at top and bottom."

"You're right. SUNF is sunfish." Ume shook her head, marveling. "What a clever, clever boy."

"He must have caught a glimpse of it as they were flying in."

"He should have been blindfolded," Ume pointed out.

"He's a little boy. Apparently, they didn't even think of hooding him. Maybe they didn't care."

Having gone through the third vid she checked the time on her cell phone. Her heart constricted painfully in her chest. There was a roaring in her ears she struggled to quiet. "Ume-sama, it's past the time when Timur's next vid was due."

"Evan-sama, there could be any number of—"

"No, no, I made this quite clear to Alyosha—a proof-of-life vid every evening at this time. Something's happened, I know it. If he's been hurt in any way I'll never be able to forgive myself. I've got to get to Naxos, get him out of harm's way him as soon as possible. I mean now."

"But you can't," Ume said. "Not when you're so close to finding Alyosha. Both she and Ilona are here in Tokyo. You need to get to them, find out why this five-day deadline is so crucial."

But Evan was already shaking her head. "No. I promised Lyudmila I would protect her son while she lay dying in my arms." Her eyes were bright with incipient tears. "*Giri.*"

Ume nodded. "I understand. But think this through. The fact that no video showed up tonight is only an indication that Timur is not available."

"That's what I mean."

"Calm, Evan-sama. Calm. I know you love this child, I know you feel an obligation toward him. But take a step back, see the situation more clearly. My first reaction to the lack of tonight's video was, there was a technical issue. But now what comes to my mind is this: you have been training him for a year. He's clearly an exceptionally bright boy. Not only did he figure out where he was being held, he found a way to tell you. So—what if he is also clever enough to have escaped his captors? It's very possible, don't you think?"

Evan said nothing for some time. She watched the rain sliding down the windshield, saw wind-blown leaves skittering beneath the trucks rumbling past. Took a deep breath, then another. In this way she cleared her mind of the clutter of whipped-up emotions. And immediately she realized that Ume was right. It was more than possible that Timur had managed to escape. In fact, considering everything she had taught him, she'd bet on it.

Ume watched her steadily, said in her softest tone, "You have already made good on your promise. You found where they've hidden Timur; no one else could have done that. Consider: you've solved the riddle. You're needed here, you know that."

"But even if Timur has escaped, he's all alone on this island with his captors looking for him."

"My father has people in Cyprus. In three hours they can be in Naxos without anyone knowing. They will search and they will find Timur."

"I can do that as well."

"Not within three hours you can't. Not from here. No one can. It's a nine-hour flight even on my father's Cessna Citation X+." She shook her head. "And what about Alyosha and Ilona? What about Kurt Çelik wanting you dead? Think, Evan-sama. Your attachment to Timur, your guilt at not having protected him from his abductors are keeping you from looking at the situation pragmatically."

Evan was about to protest, to continue opposing Ume's suggestion when she stopped herself. "I am looking at it as I was trained to do."

"Yes, of course," Ume said. "But consider this. Everything in life is a pattern. Remits are no exception. At the moment you are understandably inside this remit's pattern. But if you can find it within yourself to step outside it, you will find another pattern—one that yourself are making."

She realized that Ume was correct. She felt mired down, enmeshed in and confounded by this remit's twisting pattern. Of course all field missions morphed into something else, were fluid, ever-changing when complications arose, which they always did. And especially, she reminded herself, when the mission was forced on her by the enemy. It occurred to her now that she had no real idea of Alyosha's—and by extension, her sister's—motive for wanting her to neutralize Ilona Starkova. She had been forcefully recruited to be their stalking horse, cannon fodder sent into the front line blindfolded. On field missions the agent was never given the big picture, for obvious reasons—security, distractions, etc. That was for the handler to know. But Alyosha wasn't Evan's handler, she was her oppressor.

Ume, taking Evan's silence for reluctance, said, "Listen to me. I will tell you something I've never told anyone. When Lyudmila Alexeyevna came here to train with my father, he fell in love with her. Please understand, he hadn't been with anyone since my mother died, never seemed interested. My mother had a hold on him even from beyond the grave. That was okay. She was an exceptional person. I could not have loved her more. But then Lyudmila Alexeyevna was dropped seemingly out of nowhere into our lives. You knew her so well—the two of you were like sisters, weren't you?"

Evan nodded, not trusting herself to speak.

"She had charisma. My mother had charisma, too, but it was of a different kind. Lyudmila did nothing to attract my father—she didn't flirt, wasn't coquettish around him."

"She was incapable of that."

"Precisely."

They were briefly illuminated by a passing truck's headlights, and then the Tokyo night returned.

"But Lyudmila was Lyudmila," Ume went on. "She withheld secrets from even the ones who loved her most." Evan nodded, knowing it to be true. "This was her innate nature. We never knew she had a son—not until you told me. But Lyudmila talked about you—a lot. There was a connection between the two of you that was most special. The same held true with her and my father. They were—what's the word?—sympatico from the outset. I watched their relationship blossom and was so happy for the both of them. But their time was so short, Evan-sama, so very short. A matter of months. But we knew this from the beginning—she told us. She was on a strict schedule. But so strong was their bond her timetable was forgotten. Until it wasn't. I felt bereft when she left."

"And your father?"

"My father is very devoted to Japanese tradition—in many ways he is more traditional than I am."

"Stoic."

"He's a warrior, first and foremost. But I knew inside he was hurting. The two women he ever loved were taken from him. And then when word came to us that Lyudmila Alexeyevna was dead, well . . ."

Ume took a breath, let it out. "Truth be told, I think the reason you haven't met him yet is it would be too painful for him."

"I think I understand."

Ume smiled. "Somehow I knew you would. You will meet him—that's a given."

"In time."

"Just so," Ume said. "So, you see, I want to take on this burden—this mission. All my father's people are trustworthy. They're the best at what they do."

"And what would that be?"

"To find Lyudmila Alexeyevna's son, of course. Please let us do this—for you, for Lyudmila Alexeyevna. For Timur."

Evan took a moment. She still felt the gnarly threads of this mission winding all around her, but now she knew she wasn't alone. If she couldn't be in two places at once, well, she trusted that Ume and Nicholas would make it seem as if she was. But still she required more from herself and from Ume before she could accede to the plan.

"Ume-sama, I know I'm mostly in the dark. This remit I was forced to take on has become a maze of lies and secrets. Without confronting Alyosha I'll never find the way to the center."

"And if you leave, if you go after Timur now, you'll never know," Ume said. "Both Alyosha and Ilona will remain at large and who knows what chaos they will cause."

"All right." Evan nodded. "Do it."

Nodding, Ume made two calls. When she was finished, she handed Evan the keys to the car. "I will be picked up within two minutes. The rest is up to you." As she opened the door, she turned back. "Remember, the way to Ilona is through Alyosha Ivanovna. The way to her is through Matsumura."

Then she was gone, stepping lightly along the sidewalk behind the car. Evan watched her walk to the corner of the street. Despite the rain she did not turn up her coat collar, did not hunch her shoulders or keep her head down. A warrior just like her father. A sleek new-model Mercedes appeared at the corner. Ume stepped into it and at once the Mercedes took off down the rain-slicked street. Evan was on her own.

Just the way she liked it.

43

Rachan did not pursue her; he didn't have to. Kiko Ashikaga was standing in her way, face serene, body relaxed, hands pushed into the wide sleeves of her kimono.

"He told you," Kiko said softly.

Alyosha nodded, for the moment unable to utter a word.

Kiko sighed. "He said he would." A watery smile appeared for a moment, then was gone. "For what it's worth, I cautioned him not to."

"You didn't want him to lie to me. I appreciate that."

"No." Kiko shook her head. "You misunderstand. I didn't want him to tell you the truth."

Alyosha stood stock-still, scarcely breathing.

"Kurt *is* your father, Alyosha, whether you choose to believe it or not."

The same storm that had nearly overcome her in the study now resurfaced. "He can't be. My name is Alyosha Ivanovna Panarin."

"Panarin was a criminal."

Alyosha whirled to see Çelik standing in the doorway to the living room. "I told you to shut up." She was trembling with rage and fear.

"Panarin was a liar, a thief, a con man who got caught out here and was killed for his transgressions." He had returned to speaking Japanese; his voice lightened, less authoritarian. "Do you remember when he found you wandering St. Petersburg, when he took you in?"

Alyosha pressed her palms to her ears. "No, no, no, no, no." She yelled the denial, over and over, as though through sheer volume and tenaciousness she could render Çelik's words untrue.

"You know," Çelik said, "you have a sister. Three years older than you. You saw her in the photo. Her name is Ilona. Do you remember her?"

Alyosha stared at him. Her head seemed full of concrete. Did she remember a sister? She shook her head. There was no sister; no being found wandering the streets of St. Petersburg; no empty space in her mind where her childhood should have been.

"The two of you loved to play in the fountains of Peterhof. Your mother was frightened you'd fall in and drown. Remember? No? There was one gilded statue your sister loved but frightened you. She used to drag you over to it, plunge your hand into the water."

Çelik's pale eyes were like a wolf's beneath a full moon. They seemed to penetrate to the muscles beneath Alyosha's skin, deeper, to her heart and lungs.

"This statue that scared you was of a merman, strong, powerful. He was reared up, his muscled arms holding open the jaws of a giant alligator. Water fountained out of the sea monster's throat." He cocked his head. "You had nightmares about that creature. The open jaws terrified you."

Alyosha closed her eyes. She remembered being on the streets, terrified of large dogs—large enough to be wolves.

"My sister," she said in a perfectly modulated tone, "was a figment of my imagination. She never existed, my father told me so, more than once."

"I told you he was a liar." Çelik stepped out of the hallway gloom into the living room. "He lied to you. He lied to the people he did business with here in Tokyo."

"Yakuza." Alyosha's voice was a dry rasp.

"Of course you know this." Çelik nodded to his wife. "Please fetch my daughter something to drink."

"Water? Tea?"

"I was thinking more along the lines of Yamazaki single malt.

"You look faint," Çelik said, almost tenderly, turning back to Alyosha as Kiko crossed the carpet to the side bar.

"I'm perfectly fine," Alyosha said, but her voice betrayed her. Her mouth felt wadded with cotton. She accepted the old-fashioned glass from Kiko. She had meant to take just a sip but she drowned herself in one go. Her throat burned but the heat radiating through her drove the weakness from her.

Çelik stepped to the sofa and settled himself onto a cushion, watching her with kind eyes the whole time. Her mind was spinning like a merry-go-round filled with wolves instead of horses. She, too, needed to sit, to gather herself. To try to calm her mind.

As she lowered herself into a chair across from where Çelik sat, Alyosha realized that Kiko had vanished. This was to be Alyosha's time alone with Kurt Çelik, again. They were not done. "So your real name would be . . ."

"*Belyy Volk*," Çelik said. "Does that mean anything to you?"

"White Wolf."

He nodded. "That's what they called me when I was in the service. Ra-chan Dmitriyevich Starkov." He shifted and she tried not to cringe. "Al-yosha Rachanyevna Starkova." He pointed. "This is you, my daughter."

Alyosha just shook her head. She got up, determined to leave, but stopped short, her mind whirling. Of course White Wolf meant some-thing to her, and so did the name Ilona. What, she asked herself, if this is all true, and that she, all unknowing, was sent to kill her sister, who may not have been a figment of her imagination? She was brought out of her terrifying train of thought by the reappearance of Kiko, holding a cut-glass perfume bottle in the palm of one hand. Fingers of the other hand about to pluck the top off. Alyosha squinted, saw the Guerlain shieldlike hallmark and under it in large letters . . .

Her heart skipped a beat, her knees felt weak.

JICKY.

What did Jicky mean to her?

Kiko stepped forward. "Here, my sweet." She waved the open bottle under Alyosha's nose. A complex amalgam of citrus, aromatic herbs, va-nilla rushed into Alyosha's system, so familiar she started to swoon.

"Catch her," Kiko said as Alyosha's legs turned to liquid. Alyosha's world canted over and she would have hit the carpet if Rachan Starkov hadn't caught her under the arms, held her as he placed her back on her feet.

Images, long withheld in the deepest recesses of her mind, careered through her conscious mind like a pack of ravenous wolves: She was in her mother's boudoir, hands reaching for the cut-glass perfume bot-tle . . . inhaling her mother's signature scent . . . her sister staring into her mother's mirror, eight-year-old Alyosha standing aside, her body shaking, her face white with terror, her mind stuck on the gunshot, the red hole over her mother's heart, blood pumping out as her mother collapsed . . . her sister grabbing her, running with her . . . running, running, running . . . outside in the wide St. Petersburg streets . . . los-ing her sister amid the dense crowds on the English Embankment . . . looking . . . searching . . . panicking . . . where are you, Ilona? Gone . . . gone . . . gone . . . What do I do now?

Alyosha was slumped in a chair, eyes closed, hands over her face, tears streaming down her cheeks, wetting her hands, dripping off her chin.

Rachan's voice: "Alyosha . . ."

Kiko's voice: "Leave her be, Rachan, Give her space."

Rachan's voice, softer now: "You were right, Kiko-sama."

Kiko's voice, soft as velvet: "Scent is the most powerful method of unlocking trauma. What happened that evening was so hideous she suppressed all memories of it. The smell of Tatiana's perfume crashed through the walls she had built and the memories have come flooding back."

Alyosha's mind had become a memory palace. Isolated images of the past came flying together as if in a film run backward. When the whole was achieved she flinched at a deafening noise inside her skull. She saw her mother out of her eight-year-old eyes, mouth open, cheeks blanched, arms held in front of her as if she could ward off the bullet that had already penetrated her clothes, her flesh. Her heart.

Blood. All was blood.

Alyosha's hands dropped to the chair's arms. Her eyes opened. Magnified by her tears, they appeared enormous.

"'Anya, you bitch!'" she cried, launching herself out of the chair.

"What?" Kiko moved around to her side.

Rachan stood before her, his expression resigned to the terrible moment.

Alyosha flared, memories like daggers, jagged, agonizing, assailed her. The stump of her finger began to throb painfully. "That's what you said, just before you pulled the trigger." Her voice was rising in pitch and in volume. "You psycho sonuvabitch, you shot my mother. Your wife." Her hands rose, nine fingers balled into fists as though she might attack him, though that pained her even more. "Don't deny it. I know. I was there."

"Yes. Yes, you were, Alyosha, along with your sister, Ilona. But I killed her because—"

"There's no because!" Alyosha shouted. "There is no reason in the world—"

"I had no choice," Rachan said softly, sadly.

Alyosha took a menacing step toward him. "Of course you had a choice."

"She gave me no choice," Rachan said. "She had betrayed me and her country."

Alyosha weaved on her feet like a drunk, trying to remember without going crazy, trying to absorb his words. The cords stood out on her neck. "Tell me the truth."

"Slowly, Rachan-san."

Silence as Kiko reached out to Alyosha, stroked her arm and back. Silence, only the minute sounds of the apartment breathing steadily, like clockwork. "Your mother . . ." Kiko released a sigh. "Alyosha, your mother was a spy working for the Americans."

"Lies," Alyosha breathed. "Impossible."

Rachan ran a hand across his eyes. "Unfortunately, all too possible. Her grandfather was a White Russian. He despised the Soviet revolution and everyone it swept into power. His life—his very way of life—was nothing more than ashes, thrown onto a trash heap. My wife—Tatiana, your mother—had come under his sway at a very early age. He taught her, he schooled her. She became his living legacy. And so, inevitably, the American spy network sought her out, recruited her. She gave them all my secrets."

"And you killed her for it."

"I did her a favor."

Alyosha could not suppress a bark of bitter laughter. "Please."

"The alternative," Rachan said, "was arrest, the Lubyanka. You're of course familiar with the infamous political prison. She would have been tortured. Your mother was a strong-willed woman. Tough as shoe leather. But no one survives the interrogators of the Lubyanka. I couldn't allow them to get their hands on her. Even after her betrayal I wasn't going to do that terrible thing."

"You could have spirited her away."

But he was already shaking his head. "There was no way. My men were with me. I was a kind of . . . how would one put it? I was a kind of a celebrity within the Kremlin, you might say. Too much in the spotlight, too many eyes on me."

"He could have exposed her, let them have her, you know," Kiko said in almost a whisper. "A major catch like Tatiana would have accorded him anything he wanted for the rest of his life. More medals, more money, a dacha of his own on prime land, more men under his command."

"He would also have come under suspicion," Alyosha pointed out.

Rachan shook his head. "I still came under suspicion. Even celebrities—I should say especially celebrities—well, you know as well as I do. After all, that's what's happened to Ilona."

Alyosha scarcely heard him now. Her mind rushed at Ilona—White Wolf—her older sister, who was supposed to take care of her. What had happened after they were separated? Did she look for Alyosha, did she even try? No matter. She had forgotten all about her.

She felt the truth wrap itself around her like a shroud, sink into her bones, become part of her. Changing her . . . but into what? Who had she been? Who was she now? She had no idea. Walking backward, she sat down hard in her chair. She felt as if she had been run over by a truck, the wind knocked out of her.

"My God," she whispered. "My God."

"God is dead," Rachan said with the finality of a judge.

44

CONVERSATION IN THE RAIN,
AZABU JUBAN, MINATO WARD, TOKYO, JAPAN

"Is the deal with Akujin Matsumura consummated?" Kata asked.

"Nearly done," Alyosha said. She was standing on the corner of her father's street beneath a narrow concrete overhang, almost fully shielded from the rain. Drops spattered off the sidewalk, building up on her shoes.

"Matsumura is a tough nut to crack, which is why I sent you."

Alyosha stared unseeing at a passing car. "I've met with an accident."

"What kind of accident?" She could tell nothing from Kata's voice. "Are you all right?"

"It's easy enough to make do with nine fingers," Alyosha said. "I hardly miss the little finger of my left hand."

"I'm sorry for your loss."

Was that a joke? "The price of doing business," Alyosha said, deadpan. "The price of us being accepted here."

"So I will be able to exfiltrate myself out of this hellhole. Say *adios* to the Chechens."

"Not yet," Alyosha said. She shook her right thumb, which she had pressed into the photonic reader of the Çeliks' security system to store it. Unlike a haptic reader, which used pressure, this one used light. And that particular light was hot as a laser. *"But far more secure,"* her father had told her.

"There is one loose end yet to be tied up," she said now. She had had no intention of telling Kata about her father but suddenly she blurted out. "And I met my father. My real father."

Kata laughed. "Yes, of course. That's the second reason I sent you."

Alyosha felt the pavement drop out from under her. "You knew?"

"Of course I knew. Do you think Akujin Matsumura bringing you to Oiran at the same time Rachan's wife sat at the sushi bar was a coincidence?" She laughed again. "Life hardly works like that, darling. It takes work. Planning. It's all a chess game, as I've told you more than once."

Alyosha could hear how Kata's voice flattened out. "Why did you want me to find my father?"

"Because he's important to me—to us."

"We have Sumida Koji, *oyabun* of Satsuragi-kai—or will soon enough."

"Listen, I'm trusting Koji because I have to. But he's yakuza. We can't know his future plans—whether or not they include us. I'm hoping they do, but building the future on hope is not an ideal business plan. So I have devised a backup."

"Rachan."

"Rachan Dmitriyevich is one of us. Russian. Him I can trust. He's the one who will help us establish our beachhead in Tokyo. Plus, because of me he now has his daughter back. You're important to him. He owes me."

Alyosha stepped out from under cover into the rain, now only a misty drizzle. It made her lashes heavy, her cheeks and upper lip wet. Or were those tears? Her tongue flicked out. Salt.

"You're a long way from home, Kata," she said.

Silence at the other end of the connection. Alyosha looked up at the sky. Through the mist, through the ever-present neon halo in the Tokyo night sky, she thought she could make out one star. One glimmering among the billions yet unseen.

"Why won't you say it?" There was a catch in her voice that made her ashamed.

"Say what?"

Alyosha took a breath. "That you miss me."

"Is that what you want?" Kata said, her voice like static, like some machine click-clacking far away. "Is that what you need?"

Alyosha swiped her phone off, stowed it away, then she breathed. Just breathed. Into her mind came a section of a book she had picked up on the sly while she was in FSB SIGINT training, about relationships, of which at that time she had none. She had read that relationships consist of the Lover and the Loved. There was always a power imbalance between the two. And she suddenly saw herself so clearly as the Lover in her relationship with Kata, who she loved—and perhaps now coming to realize that she had always loved more than Kata loved her. Kata, who was, after all, a borderline psychopath, always at a remove, even when they were entwined in bed, the essence of her out of reach. It took her being this far away from the Loved one for her to understand this sad, irrevocably damaged dynamic. Her heart grew heavy. She tasted the salt of her tears through the rain. Lifting her head, she wiped away her tears along with her moment of self-pity. Both now were gone.

Breathing deeply, she strode across the street, got into Matsumura's car, closed the door behind her.

"How did you know I'd be here?" he asked. When she remained silent, her eyes directed ahead at the street, he sighed, said, "So how did it go with Kiko and Kurt?"

"Drive," she said.

45

Evan drove, keeping several cars behind Matsumura. Her body still tingled with the electric current that had raced through her upon seeing Alyosha Ivanovna again. Every moment of the abasement the Russian had put her and Timur through aboard the Malaysian pirate ship ran through her mind as if on an endless reel.

As she maneuvered around traffic she punched in Marsden Tribe's private number. He would not answer, of course; the generative AI monitoring the line would not recognize the number of the cell phone Ume had given her. But it did allow her to input her alphanumeric code. She disconnected, waited for him to call back. It wasn't that she didn't trust Ume, but she was desperate to find Timur and, as she considered it, even three hours was too long to wait. Only Marsden had the wherewithal to get people to Naxos even more quickly. The cell buzzed and she heard his voice. He sounded very much himself; she realized she missed that. It was a comfort, in a way she could not explain even to herself.

Succinctly, in the way he would respond to best, she told him what had happened, what she was being forced to do—find Ilona Starkova, aka White Wolf, whose existence of course he knew of; by whom—her sister, Kata Hemakova, confirmed by Marsden to have masterminded this entire nightmare and sent her lieutenant, Alyosha Ivanovna, to carry it out. She told him where she was, how close to Alyosha she was. All this before telling him where Timur was. "Alyosha's Russian cadre took him to Naxos. Now I think he's escaped. I'm asking you to find him, keep him safe."

"You only have to ask once," Tribe said. "Are you—?"

"I'm fine. Really."

"I take it you don't want help."

"Only for Timur."

"Got it," he said. "Stay safe."

She felt better now, knew he wouldn't fail her. Timur was as good as safe now.

"One more thing," Tribe said. "I need you to do something for me off the books."

Evan almost snorted. "Everything I do for you is off the books, Marsden."

"This is on another level."

She said nothing, watching the road, the hastening car she was shadowing.

"Are you listening?"

"Of course."

"I need you to find someone in Tokyo and kill them."

"Yes?"

"His name is Kurt Çelik."

Her surprise, tinged with the innate suspicion her profession fundamentally demanded of her, set her heart pounding against her ribs. "What's Çelik to you?"

"I'd say it's none of your business but in this case I'm going to make an exception."

"Marsden, what the hell is going on?"

"Çelik murdered a friend of mine. In fact, you met him several years ago. You're friends with his daughter, Ghislane."

Evan's breath caught in her throat. "Bernhard-Otto von Kleist? He's dead?"

"Unfortunately."

"I liked him."

Tribe sighed. "So did I."

"Marsden, really, what the hell? Both Ilona Starkova and Alyosha Ivanovna are here in Tokyo. Alyosha was in Çelik's apartment until five minutes ago. There must be something connecting them all."

"There certainly is. Çelik is a legend the man took when he fled Russia. Kurt Çelik is Rachan Starkov."

"Ilona's father?"

"Also Alyosha's. They're sisters."

"What? You must be joking."

"I'm perfectly serious."

Evan took a moment, trying to digest this monumental news. It was decidedly difficult getting her head around everything Tribe had dumped on her at once: Kata had ordered the abduction and subsequent coercion, Çelik was in reality Rachan Starkov, Alyosha and Ilona were his daughters.

She took a breath, then another. "One more thing. Ilona had a weird tattoo on the inside of her right wrist—a blazing sun caught between the jaws of a caliper. You know anything about that?"

"Why would I?"

"A shot in the dark. Well, anyway, she had it lasered off yesterday."

Now there was a silence on his end. Finally, "Are you sure about that?"

"Absolutely."

Another silence. "Listen, Evan, I'm trusting you on this. Ilona stole something that belongs to Parachute, to me. You get that for me. No one else can."

A sharp indrawn breath. "You didn't tell me you *knew* Ilona Starkov."

"You only asked me if I knew *of* her."

Evan felt the urge to leap through the phone and throttle him. Why was he being so obtuse, so damned secretive? "What is it?" she managed to rasp through her anger. "What did she steal?"

"A pair of teeth. Molars."

"What?"

"They're imprinted with the same sigil Ilona had lasered off."

"You just told me you didn't know what that sigil was."

"At that moment lying seemed the best course."

Again and again, Evan thought. *What's changed? Or has he been lying to me all along?* She thought she knew but required confirmation. "The conversation changed when I told you Ilona had the tattoo lasered off her wrist."

Tribe made no reply, which, knowing him as she did, was all the confirmation she needed.

She ended the call, slid the cell into the pocket of her coat, and returned her full attention to the car racing ahead of her while her mind continued to work over the core mystery. Alyosha and Ilona—both had ended up here in Tokyo. So it was ground zero. But for what? And why had Kurt Çelik hired someone to have her killed? What was the big picture she was missing?

• • •

Alyosha was no longer afraid of Matsumura, or perhaps she had stepped beyond her fear, thought of him now as simply a thing, an impediment to her happiness. Alyosha, staring straight ahead through the rain being whisked away by the relentless swipes of the wipers, found that notable. With a jolt of adrenaline she realized that being with her father and step-mother had changed her irrevocably. Being with people who didn't lie to her on a constant basis was, frankly, revelatory. That she had a family now—a real family, blood family—had turned her life around, or upside down. Or, she thought, more accurately turned her life right side up. Now she had to play it as it lay and not make a mistake with Matsumura, this cultured murderer with a heart black as carbonized wood.

"I'm in with Kurt," she said. "He bought every lie I told him."

"You sold it," Matsumura said. "I knew you would."

"Then we're good with Satsuragi-kai? You'll recommend to your *oyabun* that the family will accommodate Kata and our people here."

"I gave you my word," Matsumura said shortly.

Alyosha nodded. "Then it's done."

Matsumura kept his eyes on the slick road as the rain beat ceaselessly against the windshield, the roof of the car. He switched his wipers to high speed.

During this brief exchange Alyosha had surreptitiously slid her right hand into her coat pocket, curling her fingers around the weapon her father had given her. *"What you do with the information Kiko revealed to you is up to you. Act or don't act,* dorogaya doch'—*darling daughter—that is up to you."*

"And if I do act?"

"Vy budete zashchishcheny." You will be protected.

Alyosha sat back in the plush seat of the Mercedes. She trusted Kurt, she trusted Kiko. Part of her sighed inwardly. It was as if an iron bar thrust through her lungs had been excised by a clever surgeon. She still hurt, but it was a dull ache, rather than a sharp pain interfering with her breathing.

"Where to?" she said.

"Are you hungry?"

"I need to let off some steam. I want to play pachinko."

■ ■ ■

The car Evan was following headed into the thick nighttime Tokyo traffic, made up of mostly trucks. In Tokyo deliveries were made at night. She switched on the GPS, tapped the Language button out of Japanese, into English. While she was fluent in Japanese the extra millisecond it took her to read the kanji might mean the difference between keeping

Matsumura's car in sight and losing it as it sped around the slower traffic and the large trucks.

After a time, constantly checking the map on the GPS, it became clear to Evan that he was heading for Akihabara, the techno/anime hub of the city. She braced herself. Amid the area's densely packed streets, the noise and strobing colors of the pachinko arcades, it would be all too easy to lose them.

While certain of Matsumura's destination, something felt wrong—a nagging in a far corner of her mind. It was her trained habit to glance at the rearview mirror every thirty seconds or so, but she had been so concentrated on her target that it wasn't until they were closing in on Akihabara Station that she noted, like a mote in her eye, a neon-green Kawasaki Ninja ZX-25R motorcycle several cars behind her. With a liquid-cooled inline-four that spins at up to 17,000 rpm—about 2,000 rpm faster than a modern Formula One car—she knew she could never outrun it. Whoever was driving that beast knew what they were doing, as it kept varying how many vehicles it allowed between them. She felt a quick stab of fear as she wondered if she was being followed.

Akihabara Station came up very quickly. Matsumura's car swerved into a parking garage, and she followed. She parked on a low level, waited in the shadows for her quarry to descend. She also kept an eye out for the Kawasaki but it never appeared. Perhaps she had been wrong. Seeing Alyosha here had triggered a paranoia inextricably entwined with the horror show she had put Evan and Timur through aboard the pirate vessel. And there was the added tension of knowing that Alyosha was the closest person to Kata Romanovna Hemakova. Evan felt both elation and terror at the possibility of meeting her sister. So many life-changing events had occurred since she last saw Bobbi. In many ways, it was as if Kata was her sister in a past life, dimly remembered, large terrifying gaps in those memories, as if the sisters had been together only in a dream or a nightmare of Evan's.

She saw her, then—Alyosha, striding by Matsumura's side. She felt her pulse in her throat, the surge of adrenaline so powerful she was for a moment dizzy. Timur's image rose in her mind like a specter. She had to trust Tribe would get to him faster than Ume's people could, would find him before Alyosha's Russian cadre did. Gathering herself, she followed the pair as they headed northwest on Kanda Hanaokacho toward Kanda Sakumagashi, then turned left onto Sotokanda 6-chome.

The neon-drenched street, lined on either side with pachinko arcades, blurred into streams of liquid light as Evan shouldered through the crowd. Even this late at night, right into the early morning, most of the arcades and pachinko parlors were bright as electronic noontime; Tokyo was a city that never slept. Evan observed the pair as they darted between a cluster of drunken salarymen with their sleekly dressed paid escorts, whose high squeals of hilarity briefly drowned out the cacophony of arcade sounds spilling from the various rainbow-hued parlors. They paused perhaps a third of the way down the street, Alyosha nodded her head in the direction of a parlor entrance, they went in.

The interior of the parlor was an all-encompassing sensory assault. Hundreds of vertical machines lined up in soldierly rows, their LED displays painting the faces of the gamblers in ghostly blues and reds. The metallic chorus of thousands of tiny silver balls created a percussion that thrummed in Evan's chest.

She watched them choose their machines, sit side by side, slide money into the proper slots, begin to play. Considering Alyosha's bandaged left hand Evan found it curious that they chose to play pachinko, where she surely was at a disadvantage. Had Matsumura devised this as some kind of initiation or even punishment? She couldn't make out the nature of their relationship. Whatever it was, she decided, it wasn't cordial.

Rivers of silver balls cascaded down, knobs turned, buttons pushed, balls flew across the playing field, lights strobed, electronic tones shouted, theme songs blared. Stars of anime and film arrived on screens—Motoko Kusanagi and Batou from *Ghost in the Shell* on Alyosha's machine, Godzilla battling King Kong on Matsumura's. He won, she didn't. In the rematch, she broke even, he won, but just barely. This went on for a time, two people within rank after rank of humanity concentrated on winning, almost always losing. Thirty minutes later, they paused. She wanted to play another game, he shook his head. She rose, stretched hugely, glanced to either side of them. All the seats were filled. An army fixated on the lights, bells, whistles in front of them. Matsumura sat facing his machine for perhaps thirty seconds—to prove, what? Evan wondered, because she was sure every move he made was calculated to an agonizing degree.

At length, he rose. Neither had amassed enough balls to exchange for any tokens, which in any event involved a typically Japanese convoluted process, since gambling is illegal in Japan.

"That was fun." Not that she could hear Alyosha over the constant racket coming from all directions at once, as if the entire place was one giant pachinko machine, but she had no trouble lip-reading. It was not what she said, but her demeanor as she said it—like a little girl out with her daddy. Matsumura merely shrugged. Clearly, he had more important matters on his mind other than babysitting a young Russian woman no matter how useful she was to him. In fact, he looked bored. The hairs at the back of Evan's neck stirred. Studying Alyosha's face she could just discern the hint of a smile curl one edge of Alyosha's lips. Evan knew that look from their violent shipboard encounter. Alyosha had maneuvered Matsumura into this state of casual inattention. She had something in mind, Evan was sure of it. But what?

■ ■ ■

"Place and time," Rachan Starkov had told his daughter before she had left his apartment, had had her fatal conversation with Kata. He had given her two weapons to use, each for a different contingency because, as he reminded Alyosha, *"Nothing ever goes smoothly in the field. You must be prepared for all possibilities, at any instant you will sense them becoming probabilities. Moscow rules."* These instructions were, of course, hardly new to her; she had been taught them even before she had come under Kata's training.

"Moscow rules. You must choose the place as well as the time," her father had told her in his overbearingly earnest way. Alyosha forgave him that; Rachan Starkov had been Kurt Çelik, and she, Alyosha Starkova, had been Alyosha Panarina for so long, they both needed to edge their way back to each other over particularly rocky terrain. She saw how he came alive shedding his brilliantly realized legend. He became who he had always been beneath the constraints circumstance imposed on him—Rachan Starkov. *"For tonight I think the proper venue will be a pachinko parlor—a particular one, I'll give you the address, such as it is around here. So. You want a "Ghost in the Shell" machine. This place has them. Lull him into a sense of complacency. I chose this parlor for you. It is attached to an anime-themed hotel. By the time you arrive there, none of the CCTV cameras will work. Once you're in the hotel you'll feel your way. I have given you the right place, you will choose the time. Keep your options open: Moscow rules."*

He kissed her on both cheeks. *"When it's done come back here. We'll be waiting."*

■ ■ ■

Evan watched Alyosha and Matsumura thread their way down an aisle between the rows of machines. Once she realized they were headed for the rear of the parlor, Evan followed. According to a sign, the double doors they were approaching led to a restaurant and, above it, a hotel. They pushed their way through the doors, Evan shadowing them, but just as she reached the doors, someone gripped her shoulder from behind. The muzzle of a pistol jabbed her side, bringing her to a complete halt. She tried to turn, to get a look at her assailant but received a punch to her kidneys for her effort. The air went out of her lungs and she faltered. Grabbed from behind she was stood up straight.

"You speak Russian?" a voice said in her ear. Whoever was behind her stood very close. When Evan nodded, the voice—it was female—said. "Good. We will speak Russian."

Evan inhaled the odors of metal and exhaust. "You must've loved your ride on that Kawasaki Ninja."

The woman behind her barked a laugh. "How're your kidneys feeling?" And roughly shoved Evan through the double doors.

46

These things happened in a slow, horrifying parade: Diti did not show up at the airfield even though An Binh had texted the flight number and arrival time, even though her plane landed as scheduled, just before three AM. Diti did not answer her cell; did not return An Binh's texts.

A hot wind blew in An Binh's face as she left the deserted airfield. She walked to a darkened taxi, the driver asleep, mouth open, snoring. She slammed her fist so hard against his window he jumped as if electrified, eyes opened wide in terror.

She slammed her fist against his window again and he said, "Get in."

The interior smelled of curry, beer, stale sweat. She rolled down the window, stuck her nose out, listened to the whisper of the wind while she drank in the scents of the sea, tamped-down earth, concrete dust.

It was that time of the night when no reds or greens existed on the roads, lights blinked yellow or not at all. An Binh felt herself rushing as if pushed by a gathering tsunami high above her head, a towering darkness, deeper than the night. She felt outside herself, lifted from her body, watching it inside the stinking taxi. She was here and not here, and this disturbed her, caused anxiety to stick to her palms, the back of her neck like warm tar.

The marina hotel loomed up and it took her until they were stopped at the head of the driveway to recognize it. The world tilted further from her.

When she emerged from the taxi she stood just outside the hotel's front door, stock-still. When the doorman opened the door to allow her entrance, she shook her head. She did not know why. She cocked her head. Something was different. In the hours she had been away something had changed, the world seemed just off its axis.

After a time, she went inside. Diti had not left her a key to the suite where she and An Binh had spent last night even though An Binh had texted her to do so if for some reason she couldn't make it out to the air-field. After ascertaining that Diti was not answering her room phone, An Binh had one of the uniformed bellmen stow her overnight bag. For the fourth time she dialed Diti's cell phone and again the line went straight to voicemail, which meant that Diti had her phone off. It had been off for hours now. A sinking in her stomach made An Binh feel as if she was in a free-falling elevator.

She sat in the hotel lobby, waiting, cleared her mind of expectation, instead stared into the clear pool of each moment as it passed. When Diti emerged from one of the elevators into the corner of her eye, she came alive. By the time she put away her phone and turned she saw only Diti's re-treating back. She wore a suitably Diti sexy outfit: shockingly short skirt, HAZZARD T-shirt, shiny high-heeled pumps. In one hand she carried a small designer carryall as if she were on her way to an overnight some-where outside the hotel.

Where is she going? An Binh asked herself. *Why did she turn off her phone? Most urgent of all, who is she going to see the moment she thinks I'm out of the picture?*

Heart beating hard against her rib cage, An Binh followed Diti out the front door, across the street, and down toward the marina. But Diti did not take the central walkway. Instead, she veered off into the darkness, heading, it appeared, toward the building housing the public restrooms.

Restrooms? An Binh thought. *Who would have a tryst in a public restroom?* But in the same moment a handful of American film stars came to mind. She had paused as Diti vanished through the women's room door, but now Diti had emerged, dressed all in black, soft heelless shoes on her feet. So that was what was in the bag she was carrying.

An Binh moved forward, deeper into the shadows, out of the ovals of light cast by the marina's security lights. A flash of metal. Diti was hold-ing a pistol with the unmistakable shape of a Ruger Mark IV 22/45 with a .22 LR noise suppressor screwed to the muzzle.

What the actual hell? she asked herself.

Diti slipped the Ruger into her belt at the small of her back, made her way toward the marina piers, taking a circuitous route despite the lack of light. She was crouched down so as not to be seen. By whom? An Binh wondered. That was when she spied another movement to her left, a truck with a tarp-covered top and back was just finishing its final park-ing maneuver. What interested An Binh was that it was stopped nearest the pier at which Diti's former yacht was tied up.

Then she saw Diti on the move again and she followed, silent as an owl in flight. Diti's black sleeveless shirt covered the gun at her back, but in her hand was a second weapon, a tactical expanding steel baton.

So not a tryst. A murder? A bloodbath? An Binh's heart seemed to rise into her throat. *Wherever she's going,* she thought, *she's going in heavy.* An Binh wondered where she had gotten the weapons. Had they been on the yacht all this time? Apparently so. *What else is she hiding from me?* An Binh asked herself. *She knows what's going on here; I don't.*

As she stepped off the driveway onto the grassy slope leading down to the piers, all the marina's security lights went off, the abrupt darkness a momentary shock. An Binh knew that CCTV cameras were nonexistent here. She glanced back over her shoulder. The hotel's lights were on, but the door greeter was nowhere to be seen, hardly surprising at this late hour.

As she headed down after Diti she could see that the truck's rear doors were open, secured against the trucks sides. She could just make out the outlines of two men off-loading the truck's cargo: long wooden crates, too narrow for coffins but otherwise at a distance could be mistaken for them. Three heavily muscled men quickly received the crates from the pair of men inside the truck. The five stacked the crates onto an industrial-size skid and together rolled it down through the grass to the pier. It was clear their destination was Diti's former yacht. Moments later, they were met by the German woman who had signed the contract for BriteBar Metallwerks. She waved them on and they loaded the crates onto the yacht. The instant the crates and the men were aboard, all hell broke loose: rapid fire from several directions on the yacht made quick work of the five who had brought the skid aboard. The dead men were summarily thrown overboard into the inky water. Two of the shooters appeared. One of them grabbed the German by the arm, swung her around, smashed the butt of his weapon into her face. She collapsed and was heaved over the side. The skid was rapidly unloaded, the crates hustled off the deck into the cabin. Through one of the windows, An Binh could just make out the beginning of their descent into the hold.

As the ground began to slope down more steeply, An Binh stepped off the path, into a swale of newly mown grass. Her heart raced as she crouched low, her eyes fixed on the scene unfolding below. The night air felt charged with tension as An Binh inched closer, careful to remain hidden in the shadows. The cadre of men aboard the yacht, whose number was as yet unknown to her, performed with a singular purpose that sent chills down her spine. Their movements were too fluid, too rehearsed for this to be anything but a well-planned, clearly clandestine operation.

As the last crate disappeared into the yacht's hold, An Binh's mind raced. What could be in those narrow containers? Weapons? Illegal tech? Whatever it was, it was clear that Diti was still as perfectly aware of the illegal activities that swirled around her family's business as she'd ever been, her professed desire to get away from it all perhaps not wholly true, or at least not yet possible for her.

Suddenly, a twig snapped beneath An Binh's foot. She froze, her breath caught in her throat. The man who had killed the German paused, his head tilting slightly as if listening. An Binh pressed herself against the ground, willing herself to become invisible in the darkness.

For a moment that stretched into eternity, silence reigned. Then, with a barely perceptible shrug, the man disappeared into the cabin. An Binh exhaled slowly, her mind whirling with questions she could not possibly answer. Only Diti could.

And where was Diti? There!, a crouched silhouette on the deck. Diti had managed to board the yacht unseen. Perhaps not so surprising having as a child explored every square inch of the *Elusan*.

An Binh controlled her breathing as she watched two of the men emerge from below and move across the deck. The night was pitch-black, a new moon offering no illumination. The marina's security lights remained off, shrouding the yacht in darkness—a blessing and a curse.

Taking a deep breath, An Binh slipped into the water, her movements as silent as she could manage. The water was still warm from the day's heat, oily, dense. She pushed forward, using slow, deliberate strokes to minimize splashing. Her eyes never left the yacht's hull, searching for a way up.

As she neared the vessel, An Binh spotted a boarding ladder left carelessly extended. It was on the opposite side from where she had last seen Diti, but it was her best chance. Gritting her teeth, she reached for the bottom rung.

A voice carried across the water—one of the men. An Binh froze, submerged up to her nose, barely daring to breathe. Footsteps approached, then receded. She counted to thirty before attempting the climb again.

With agonizing slowness, An Binh pulled herself up the ladder. Each creak of metal seemed to echo in the stillness. Halfway up, a beam of light cut through the darkness—a man with a flashlight. She heard him call out in Russian. Russians had hijacked the yacht, clearly for the purpose of moving their contraband merchandise. An Binh clung to the underside of the ladder, muscles screaming, as the beam swept past mere inches from her fingers.

Finally reaching the deck, An Binh rolled into a shadow cast by the cabin. She lay there, pulse pounding in her ears, listening intently. Two sets of footsteps converged nearby.

"*Vy chto-nibud' slyshali?*" the same gruff voice asked in Russian. Did you hear something?

"Probably just the water against the ties," another replied.

An Binh held her breath as the men passed. Once their footsteps faded, she crawled across the deck on knees and elbows, using every bit of cover available. Her eyes darted constantly, searching for Diti's familiar form.

A hand suddenly clamped over An Binh's mouth. Whirling, she saw the raised baton, realized that Diti was about to bring it down onto her collarbone when Diti's eyes opened wide. She did not try to shake off An Binh's hand, which gripped her wrist to arrest the blow that would have incapacitated her or killed her.

For what seemed like an hour but must have been no more than several seconds, the two women stared into each other's eyes.

She tensed, ready to fight, when Diti's whisper tickled her ear. "What are you doing here?"

"If you'd had your damn phone on you'd know," An Binh whispered.

Diti shook off her admonition. "Russians have control of the yacht."

An Binh ignored her. "What the hell is going on here? What illegal shit did they stow in the hold?" An Binh knew that Diti must be beside herself with rage at the thought of her beloved *Elusan* being used for criminal purposes.

"That's what I need to find out. I'm moving. You're with me." She paused. "I'm happy you're back." Diti's eyes glinted in the darkness. "Follow me. There's a service passage near the galley. It's narrow, but it leads directly down."

An Binh nodded. "It's unlikely they've posted a guard there."

Slowly, carefully, the two women made their way across the deck. Every shadow seemed to conceal a potential threat. Twice they had to freeze in place as guards passed nearby, their hearts pounding so loudly they were sure it would give them away.

As they neared the galley entrance, a beam of light suddenly cut through the darkness. An Binh pulled Diti into a narrow alcove just as a guard rounded the corner. He paused, sweeping his flashlight across their hiding spot. His eyes narrowed. He swept the light back and forth. For a heart-stopping moment, An Binh was certain they'd been discovered.

47

"This damn hand hurts," Alyosha said as they slid into a semi-enclosed banquette. "I need something to dull the pain."

"The doctor gave you pills," Matsumura said.

"I threw them away."

"Sake, then?"

She laughed. "Oh hell no. Vodka. Cold. And plenty of it."

Matsumura had said he was hungry, so Alyosha suggested the restaurant. The moment they entered she understood why there were two sets of double doors. The restaurant's atmosphere was as hushed as the pachinko parlor's was almost comedically boisterous. The lights were low here, burnished, the interior cool, sophisticated, elegant, calm. Perhaps at least for everyone else dining here, but Alyosha felt the weight of floors of the hotel above their heads like the submerged bulk of an iceberg. Immovable unbearable pressure.

Matsumura signaled for a server, ordered the vodka, along with an ice bucket.

"That's the ticket." This close to the finish line, Alyosha felt amazingly lightheaded beneath the pressure, giddy almost, as if there were a countdown to New Year's going on in her head, as if she had swallowed a pachinko machine. She had to fight against that, she knew, had to keep her wits about her. Moscow rules. And yet it was so difficult to tamp down the elation she felt when looking at Matsumura, a man who she had feared for so long and now for whom she felt only contempt.

She let him order. She couldn't have cared less about food. Let him have this last moment of control. During the main course he caressed the back of her injured hand as if it were a trophy he had won. She was so disgusted she felt the bile rising up into her throat, triggering a coughing fit that quite naturally allowed her to make her excuses. She strode off, asked a passing server to direct her toward the bathrooms. Inside, it was gleaming, spotless. The scent of green tea perfumed the air. She crossed to the far cubicle, closed the door. Thank God it was a Western toilet, not one of those disgusting holes in the ground over which you were obliged to squat backward. She sat on the closed lid and worked on clearing her mind while she waited. Her father had chosen one of the hotel corridors above but she thought this a better site. At some point, Matsumura would begin to fret, then get antsy. At length, he would follow her, even into here. Matsumura would simply glower at anyone who wasn't her until they scurried out. Then he would go from cubicle to cubicle searching for her.

Place and time. Her choice, no one else's.

Her cell buzzed. A text from him, wondering if she was all right. She ignored it.

Her head came up as she heard the telltale clip-clop of high heels across the tile floor. She listened, straining for Matsumura's voice, but all she heard was the water running briefly, the snap of a pocketbook opening and, a moment later, closing. Then the clip-clop of those heels. Silence again before another text: where are you?

The echoing of two female voices talking in tandem about their salaryman dates, how much they could soak them for, how drunk they could get before the big finale. One of the women entered the stall next to Alyosha, sat and peed like a racehorse—hard and long. Toilet's auto flush, then the sharp inhalations of coke being passed back and forth. Moments later, they were both gone in a cartoon bubble of giggles.

Silence again. Alyosha continued to wait, her muscles cramping, and was in the process of getting up when her stall door exploded inward and Matsumura, face dark with rage, grabbed her, dragged her out. He hit her then, an explosion of pain radiating from her cheekbone down her neck, up into her temple.

"You little bitch," he said and struck her again so that she skittered across the slick tiles, fetching up against the line of sinks. "What did he tell you while you were with him?"

"Who?" she said stupidly. Her mind was slowed by the blows he had delivered. There was a ringing in her ears.

"Who d'you think?" He loomed over her, his face stark as a Noh mask. "That dick Çelik. He told you something. I could smell it on you when you got in the car. You'd changed. And now you're hiding in here." He grabbed her at the neckline of her sweater. A knife appeared in his other hand, the blade thin as a gutting knife. "You're a beautiful woman, Alyosha, but it wouldn't take much"—he brandished the tip of the blade close to the delicate skin of her lower eyelid—"to turn you into a hideous mess."

Alyosha closed her eyes, gritted her teeth. "It wasn't Çelik." She felt breathless, on the verge of losing control. But no matter what he did to her she wasn't going to tell him even a single word of the conversation she'd had with her birth father. Never, even unto her dying breath. "It was his wife, Kiko. She played me the tape damning you as the one who murdered my father. You lied to me."

Matsumura laughed, a rumble like distant thunder. "Did you expect that I would confess, tell you how remorseful I was, beg you to forgive me?"

"I cut off my finger for you."

"And how foolish was that?" The tip of the blade moved down, cut the corner of her lip, making her flinch. "Did you think you would become Japanese—a blooded yakuza? That I would *like* you?"

She tasted the iron salt of her own blood. "It was a sacrifice." Her voice trembled.

"No." Matsumura shook his head. "It was a ploy to get what Kata wanted—a new home, sheltered from her Russian enemies." He leaned in closer. She could smell the fish, the vinegared seaweed on his breath. "She was never going to get what she wanted. My *oyabun* made that clear to me when I brought up the notion."

"So why did you make me—"

"It gave me great pleasure to work you through the motions, to see how far you would go to ingratiate yourself to me, how much of yourself you would reveal to me." His tongue emerged from between his lips, licked the blood oozing from the corner of her mouth. "You are quite the bitch, you know. It didn't take much for you to switch allegiance from Kata Romanovna to me."

"I never switched allegiance," she said, driving her knee into his groin with all her strength, all her rage. "You only thought I did."

He had backed her against the line of sinks but now as he staggered back she had room to maneuver. She dove for the knife, chopped the edge of her hand down on his wrist bone, the knife shooting across the tiles. She got in three quick jabs to his solar plexus. Feeling pretty good about herself, she reached for one of the weapons her father had given her, was slammed in her head for her efforts. She hit the tiles hard. Pain flared in her right shoulder as she fetched up next to the restroom door. He came after her, but just then the door swung open, a trio of girls burst into the bathroom and, under the cover they provided, Alyosha stumbled out into the corridor. She heard shouts and shrieks close behind her as Matsu-mura shoved the girls aside, came after her.

She began to run.

48

Diti tensed, ready for a confrontation. But then the guard's radio crackled to life.

"Ivan, report to the bridge immediately," a man's voice commanded.

The guard grunted in acknowledgment and hurried away, his footsteps fading into the night.

An Binh allowed a look of relief to cross her face but Diti was already slipping into the galley. True to Diti's memory, they found the hidden service passage. It was indeed narrow, forcing them to step carefully down single file.

The descent seemed to take an eternity. Every scrape of fabric against the walls, every creak of the metal ladder beneath their feet, sounded deafening in the confined space. An Binh's palms were slick with sweat by the time they reached the bottom.

A heavy door stood between them and the hold. An Binh pressed her ear against it, straining to hear any sound from the other side. Nothing. Then she heard the engines starting up. They were making ready to leave the marina.

An Binh eased the door open, revealing the sizeable space of the hold beyond. Stacks of the narrow crates filled the hold, reaching nearly to the ceiling in some places. The air was thick and musty, carrying an acrid scent that made her nose wrinkle.

Diti crossed to the nearest stack, pried open two of the planks on the top crate.

"Look." Diti, stowing her baton at the small of her back alongside her Ruger, turned the flashlight app of her cell phone into the box, revealing its contents. She leaned in, picked up the top tray off the stack. "What the hell? Teeth? They're teeth!"

An Binh plucked one out of the tray. "What is this thing?" she said. "An artificial tooth." She glanced back at the tray. "Molars."

"Teeth?" Diti shook her head. "But why? Why are these contraband?"

An Binh held the molar closer to the beam of Diti's flashlight app. "Look here. Something's etched into the top."

Diti picked out two more from the tray. "They're all etched."

"Precision etched. Each set of teeth make up the same design."

"This is what they've loaded onto my yacht?" Diti looked around. "A shitload of teeth?"

"You mean BriteBar Metallwerks' yacht," An Binh said.

Diti threw her a look. "Not with this shit in the hold. Not on my watch." She tossed her head. "And anyway the German's dead. If anything, it's the Russians' yacht now, but not for long, I promise you."

An Binh was digging through the trays, pulled out several sheets of paper, unfolded them. "Bills of lading," she said, scanning them quickly. "These teeth were manufactured in Gerlingen, Baden-Württemberg, Germany, by BriteBar Metallwerks. They're bound for Tartus, Syria."

An Binh thought a moment. "That's a Russian military port."

Diti peered at the paperwork, squinting in the low light. "Wait. I think there's something else written underneath . . ."

An Binh squinted. "Yes, there is." She turned the paper this way and that to get a closer look. "This consignment was originally bound for Port of Virginia. The Russians—"

"Those fucking bitches," Diti said. "They have the reroute all sorted. This operation is one well-oiled clockwork merry-go-round."

"So these teeth, whatever their use, are extremely valuable."

"What other conclusion could you come to?" There was a raw rasp to Diti's voice that An Binh put down to the extreme peril they were in.

"I'm not leaving here without a pair of these babies." An Binh pocketed two molars. Together they replaced the crate's top.

Just then, the sound of approaching footsteps echoed from above. The two women exchanged looks—someone was coming down to the hold.

Quickly, they searched for a hiding spot among the crates. An Binh spotted a narrow gap between two stacks and pulled Diti toward it. They squeezed into the tight space just as the hold door opened.

Pressed together in the darkness, barely daring to breathe, An Binh and Diti listened as two sets of footsteps entered the hold. A man's voice, gruff and impatient, spoke in Russian.

"Veserov wants a recount. Just to make sure every crate is accounted for."

A second voice replied, sounding disgusted. "Fucking officers. Make-work. Don't we have better things to do?"

"You want to be the one to tell him no?" the first man snapped. "He'll be down here to check on us. Just start counting, left side first. I'll take the right."

As the footsteps moved closer to their hiding spot, An Binh felt Diti tense beside her. They were trapped, with no way out if the men decided to inspect the aisle in which they were concealed.

Diti took the silenced Ruger from behind her back. She meant to use it, and soon. *Should I stop her*, An Binh asked herself, *or let her loose?* Diti was a genuine wild child. An Binh felt no desire to rein her in. Why should she? Let Diti be Diti, and here we are, this is what their affair had come down to, this pinpoint in time.

Whump! Whump!

Diti squeezed off two shots and the two men, the second of whom was still on the last rung of the stairs, dropped like sacks of wet cement. They were down and they stayed down; An Binh had no doubt about the accuracy of Diti's shots. Right through their hearts and *bam! bam!*, over and out.

This eruption of violence was not over. They heard someone else coming down the stairs—both of them at the same instant. The moment Diti saw the Russian officer's face, she yelled *"Tukang sabung!"* with such force spittle flew from her mouth.

Veserov, the Russian officer, was armed, and from the way he held his pistol he was clearly preparing to fire.

Whump!

He flew backward, arms outstretched. Then somehow regained his balance, leveled his weapon. Blood covered the front of his tunic, spreading, darkening, the cloth clinging to his flesh.

Diti took two steps forward.

Whump!

Veserov's neck arched backward, the thick arc of his throat bared, bloody, torn apart. He fell to his knees.

Diti went right up to him, stared into his face. Veserov, limbs trembling, tried to lift his pistol. Diti kicked it away.

"Vot i vso," An Binh told him. *"Ty blyad' trup."* That's it. You're fucking dead.

Whump!

Veserov's face split apart, his head snapping backward with a crack like a tree falling. The body curled in on itself, a dying caterpillar, slipped in its own blood, tumbled down the rest of the stairs. A heap of tangled limbs, unrecognizable as anything human.

"Time to go." An Binh's voice was thick, clotted with emotion, the aftermath of observing so much death. Diti continued to stare at what was left of the Russian. Either she didn't hear An Binh or her mind was still so filled with hatred that she paid no attention to anything else.

An Binh grabbed her, dragged her up the staircase, mindful of the blood and gore sprayed over the bottom four steps. Diti fought her all the way, trying to batter her against the wall. Up they stumbled and slipped in this fashion. An Binh could hear Diti breathing hard at her back, like a winded cheetah at the end of its deadly run.

She emerged first into the galley, took one step, two, then was slammed against the wall so hard she blacked out for a second. The back of her head felt wet, hot. She was bleeding. A big Russian had her arms pinned to the small of her back, his huge hand a vise keeping her crossed wrists immobile. An Binh trod hard on his instep, heard him huff, loosen his grip on her wrists enough for her to free one hand. Something hard, metallic tapped the backs of her fingers. She opened them, received the grip of the steel baton. Diti. She curled her fingers around the baton, swung it against the outside of the Russian's knee, heard with satisfaction the crack of gristle and bone. The man moaned, grabbed his knee, giving An Binh time to snap the baton fully open. Down it came on his collarbone. He staggered. The second blow brought him to his knees, the third on the top of his head was the last thing he felt. He toppled over as Diti emerged from the hold stairs.

"There are more," An Binh whispered, and, "Are you all right?"

Diti did not look at her. She jammed a new magazine into the Ruger. "Let's get out of here."

But the yacht was already underway. How far from the marina were they? Diti crossed the galley, took a step into the dining room, peered out the window across the room. The running lights were on, which meant they were far enough from land not to make a difference. She crossed to the window, knelt on a built-in lounge cushion, put her face up to the glass. The wavering lights of Port Dickson were tiny, a false horizon.

"We're too far out and I don't want to engage with whoever's piloting the yacht," Diti said. "We'll need the launch."

She was concentrating her gaze on the lights of Port Dickson, calculating the distance to shore, when a shadow crossed the periphery of her vision. An instant later, the glass exploded into her. Sprawled on the floor, desperately flicking glass off her face, she saw a fifth Russian crawl through the now empty window frame. She lifted her machine pistol. Her hand trembled. She was bleeding from a myriad cuts. Slivers of glass stood out from her flesh like quills. The shot was more or less point-blank. No chance she could miss.

Whump!

With his forearm shoving her hand aside, she missed. Then he struck her a blow between her eyes and she groaned. Behind her, An Binh swung the baton, struck the Russian on his left temple. He recoiled, shivering uncontrollably, and took the second blow on his neck. His head canted over, his tongue licked his lips, but the blood kept flowing.

An Binh pulled Diti free of him, free of the welter of glass bits, then stepped in, swung a third blow from her hips. His skull cracked, eyes rolled up in his head. The blood would not stop flowing. They left him there, made their way through the salon, the office, down the passageway.

An Binh heard something—footsteps behind them? Something even more sinister? Diti didn't hear the sounds, didn't parse them as bare feet on the mahogany floor.

"Why are you stopping?" Diti said. "Come on!"

"There's something . . ." She pushed Diti on.

"What . . . ?"

"Get the launch ready. And pick those pieces of glass off you. I'll be with you."

They shared a scrutinizing look, then Diti took off, but in the wrong direction. She wasn't heading topside, but toward the staircase that led back down to the hold.

An Binh wanted to call to her, to tell her she was going the wrong way, but there was no time. She turned to face whatever—whoever—was stalking them, canny enough to do it on bare feet. She couldn't leave something like that aboard after the chaos they'd caused. A shadow moved, softly, stealthily, a panther in the dark.

An Binh stood stock-still. The hair at the nape of her neck stirred, stood up. At first, she was sure she was looking at the German. But unless she had been transported into a horror film that was impossible; the German was dead, already fish food. Then, she thought it must be the German's sister—the same height, the same slender body type. Finally the figure stepped into the light. A fizz like a lightning strike passed through her, making her flinch. She felt sick to her stomach.

"What are you doing here?" Miranda said softly.

It took An Binh a beat to regain her voice. She felt struck by time's arrow. She had taken the right fork in the road. She had chosen Diti rather than revenge, but it was no matter—her fate had found her, and now she knew there was no running from it, no hiding from it, either. "Shouldn't I be the one asking that question?" she responded.

"I'm afraid you know what I'm doing here."

"You've been hijacked by a Russian cadre, if you don't already know. Or are they working for Tribe?"

"Don't be absurd." Miranda laughed softly, bitterly. "Someone's betrayed Marsden. One of his partners, von Kleist or Çelik."

"BriteBar Metallwerks," An Binh said.

Miranda smirked. "I see you've been snooping in the hold. My money's on Çelik, von Kleist is too much of a gentleman—he plays strictly by the rules."

"Then the Russians on board will kill you, too."

"Aren't many of them left," Miranda said. "You and your little gal pal saw to that. I'll be fine. But you . . ." Miranda sighed deeply, lifted a Colt 1911 .38 Super. This handgun gave the user extra shots and was easy to control. Only a true professional would choose this weapon over a more common 9mm or .45. She leveled the gun.

An Binh took a step toward her, fingers tightening around the grip of the baton.

"Please, Miranda." The .38 Super was aimed at An Binh's heart. Even she couldn't outrace a bullet or have a chance of dodging it. The air turned brittle in her lungs, thin and cold as death. There were so many things she had wanted to say to Diti but was afraid, and now the time had slipped away. Too late. Too late. "To kill or not to kill," An Binh said. "You have a choice."

"I serve a dictator, a tyrant, a modern-day Caesar." Miranda said thickly. "Everyone who works for him is a puppet of one sort or another."

"Leave him, then. There's a whole world of opportunities—"

Miranda snorted. Her upper lip curled in derision. "There would be no opportunity for me if I left him. There would be no anything but oblivion."

An Binh drew in a breath. "Are you saying Tribe would have you killed?"

"Obliterated off the face of the earth," Miranda said. "It would be as if I never existed."

An Binh advanced on her. "I don't believe you."

"Then I pity you." Miranda's body tensed. "You work for him, too."

Another step and An Binh would be in range to use the baton.

"No," Miranda said as she pulled the trigger.

49

"You may as well put the gun away, Ilona," Evan said. "You're not going to shoot me." She tried to turn around but Ilona Starkova—she was sure it was White Wolf—prevented it.

"And why would that be?" She spoke in a St. Petersburg accent, which jibed with the intel about Starkova that was on the sat phone Alyosha had given her back on the pirate ship. Barely four days, and a lifetime ago.

"Killing me would leave too many questions unanswered."

They were standing in a dimly lit storage room off the liminal space between the pachinko parlor and whatever lay beyond the second set of double doors through which Alyosha and Matsumura had evidently disappeared.

"I asked you before: Why were you parked outside Kurt Çelik's building?"

"I was trying to figure out a way to get to him through his overlapping electronic security systems."

A small silence through which Evan could hear Ilona's breathing. Clearly Çelik meant something to her. Something important. After all, she had come to his building, too.

"What are you?" Ilona's voice quickened as it turned harsh. "FSB? GRU?"

"I work in private security."

"Colonel Germanov's Medvedi, then."

The Bears. Evan had heard of them, of course, but had never come across one. "No," she said. "I work for Parachute. For Marsden Tribe."

Another silence came down like a thick curtain, this one absolute. Evan listened to the susurrus of the building's HVAC while she wondered what might be going through the White Wolf's mind. Failing. Inevitably.

She felt a release of both heat and pressure as Ilona stepped back. "Turn around." She did as Ilona ordered.

And so finally Evan Ryder entered the heart of the labyrinth into which she had been thrust, face-to-face with its monster, its Minotaur. The White Wolf.

The first thing that struck her were Ilona's eyes—that eerie noncolor, palest blue in some light, a metallic gold in different circumstances. She possessed a striking face—not beautiful, perhaps, but fierce in her strong nose, high cheekbones, lending her face the rough shape of a diamond. Her lips, pressed together now in concentration, hinted at her uncompromising nature.

"You know my name," Ilona said, "but I don't know yours."

Evan noted the gun she held at her side, muzzle pointed at the floor. She told Ilona her name.

"Why are you working for Tribe, Evan?"

"Why are you?"

The two women stood, staring at one another, their breaths slow and nearly aligned, as if they were identical twins.

"There is no need . . ." Evan stopped, started over. "We're both practitioners—masters, you could say—of the dark arts."

"Which is why he recruited each of us."

"Yes."

Ilona held up her right wrist, the inside twisted toward Evan. Revealed the lasered site of the almost obliterated tattoo. "The difference between us is that I'm quits with him."

"You have something of his," Evan said softly, as easily as she could manage. "Something that belongs to him."

"You mean these." Ilona held out the two molars.

"He told me you stole them."

Ilona barked a laugh. "My mission was to get them, bring them back to him."

Another of his lies coming to light. Was there anything about him that was true, Evan asked herself, or was he a series of fun-house mirrors, each reflecting an image he used for his own purposes?

"Observe the sigil imprinted on them," Ilona was saying. "The same as the tattoo he had me get." She cocked her head. "Do you know the meaning of the sigil?"

"Marsden's life is like a submarine: each compartment is sealed watertight against the others."

The slow smile spreading over Ilona's face made her realize her mistake.

"So." By this time Ilona had jammed her handgun in the waistband of her trousers. Now she stood, fists on hips. "'Marsden,' is it?" Her smile widened, baring her teeth. "Fucking him, are you? Well, I'm hardly surprised. I fucked him, too, once upon a time." She shrugged. "That's the way he does business with women: a fuck instead of a handshake. SOP." She swung her head back and forth. "So don't go making the mistake you're different, that he feels something for you. Your Marsden is incapable of that."

Evan had no idea how she felt about this or whether Ilona was even telling the truth. Why should she? It wasn't as if they were friends sharing kiss-and-tells over tea and crumpets. In any event, the subject of Marsden Tribe's sex life was a swamp into which she refused to step. "So what does the sigil stand for?"

"I thought he would have told you, his current consort."

"The first time I saw it was when Nyurgun drew it for me."

At the mention of Nyurgun's name, Ilona's eyes seemed to change color. "How is he? Is he safe?"

"Safe. Happy with his new girl."

Ilona nodded. "Well, that's something, anyway." Then, as if she had strayed too close to a softer emotion, her face darkened. "So now you're going to tell me why you were really staking out Çelik's building."

"I told you. I want to get in there."

"Why?"

"Mar—Tribe owns a company, BriteBar Metallwerks, with two other men. One of them was recently murdered by Çelik, the third partner."

"Tribe wants retribution."

Evan nodded. She was not about to tell Ilona that Tribe wanted her to retrieve the teeth from Ilona. Not yet, anyway. She sensed they were working toward a tentative, infinitely fragile détente. She didn't want anything to shatter that.

"So why did you leave to follow a car that was also parked on the same block?"

"I'm running down a former FSB agent named Alyosha Ivanovna."

"What's she to you?"

"She abducted me and my son. Her cadre are holding him hostage to force me to carry out a mission."

"Target?"

"You, Ilona. The target is you."

50

An Binh awoke to pain and the distant sound of screaming, carrying across the night-dark water. Scimitars of light wobbled across the wave-tops. Rain was falling, feeling to An Binh like needles against her bare shoulder.

She groaned, trying to raise herself from the bottom of the launch. Her left shoulder was on fire, chills ran through her body, blood stained the front of her clothes, sticky, drying on her skin despite the rain that, in any event, was light and soft, blown this way and that by the wind.

A small explosion to her right caused her to jump. Turning her head, she saw Diti with her handgun, leaning against the launch's gunwale. Another shot. An Binh looked out across the water, shocked to see the yacht canted over so far water washed over the starboard railing onto the walkway.

"What?" she blinked rain out of her eyes. "What's happening?" But her voice, strained, thin, didn't seem to reach Diti, who was busy taking bead on the four heads bobbing in the water, the remaining Russians from the yacht trying to make their desperate way toward the tender. Clearly, Diti had no intention of allowing them to get close, let alone climb aboard. One by one she began to pick them off.

"Diti." An Binh crawled toward her. "Diti." As in a dream her voice seemed destined for only her own ears. The distance to Diti felt so long, the pain increasing with each movement of her body. Though she tried to avoid moving her left arm, it was almost impossible to keep the wounded shoulder immobile. Her head was pounding, blood seemed to be pooling behind her eyes, and she felt weak as if she had lost more blood than she should have. Come to think of it, why hadn't Diti bound her shoulder to stop the bleeding, to hold the shoulder in place? There was a fairly large box with the signature red cross on it affixed midway along the port side of the launch.

Her breath came in violent pants, which was unlike her. She tried to slow her breathing, deepen it, but her pain was so acute she couldn't manage it though she knew short panting breaths would only make her body weaker. She had to find a way to force air down into the bottom half of her lungs.

She had reached Diti now, put her right hand on her shoulder, though it necessitated her leaning heavily on the gunwale, pain lancing through her left side. But Diti was in the killing zone. She could no more respond to An Binh than she could sprout wings and fly.

An Binh dropped her hand, turned to look out onto the water. There was only one head left, and it was getting close to the launch. It had been hidden from sight, whoever it was must have swum underwater, escaping the killing field Diti had made of the surface.

As the head broke through the waves An Binh bit her lower lip. It was Miranda, pale hair flat against her skull, streaming behind her like a fish's tail. Her face, bleak, straining with effort, water streaming off it set off splintered recollections of An Binh's last conscious moments aboard the yacht.

"Are you saying Tribe would have you killed?"

"Obliterated off the face of the earth," Miranda said. *"It would be as if I never existed."*

An Binh advanced on her. "I don't believe you."

"Then I pity you." Miranda's body tensed. "You work for him, too."

Another step and An Binh would be in range to use the baton.

"No," Miranda said as she pulled the trigger.

At that precise moment, Miranda's eyes caught on An Binh, stayed there. A silent conversation sprang up, perhaps even a note of pleading. Which was so unlike what she knew about Miranda she was for a moment taken aback. *"Help me, for the love of God!"* Miranda mouthed. Supplication was not something she could ever imagine being in Miranda's emotional vocabulary, but there it was, stark and unmissable on her face. *"Have mercy!"* And what was An Binh's response? *Miranda could have killed me,* she thought. *But instead she chose to wound me. For whatever godsent reason she chose to save my life.*

Coming out of herself, An Binh saw Diti aiming at Miranda. Before she could squeeze off a shot, An Binh shoved her hard, shouting, "Stop! Leave her alone!" The bullet went wide, vanishing beneath the agitated waves. Diti, wild-eyed, yelled, "That was my family boat those fuckers were using! A pleasure yacht. Only family members were allowed to board. No business was ever transacted. And now what? They're smuggling God alone knows what. They tried to kill me, each and every one. But they underestimated me. I've killed all of them except for this one." She swung her left arm, catching An Binh a vicious blow on the cheek. An Binh recoiled, her torso sliding slantwise down the side of the launch. Before she could recover, Diti had reset herself. Miranda's head had vanished under the waves, only to appear in another spot, closer to the launch. An Binh reached out through her pain, fingers scrabbling on Diti's shirt, but it was no use. Diti shrugged her away, squeezed off three shots, hitting Miranda with the first two. Miranda screamed, hands flung up in the air, and then she disappeared beneath the waves.

An Binh witnessed Miranda's murder by the woman she loved with her head barely above the gunwale, fingers of her right hand white with the strain of holding her torso up.

Diti rounded on her. "So fortuitous you came back. My good fortune, but not yours."

"You're acting crazy. I came back for you," An Binh said. "To be with you. To tell you I love you. I never had a chance before . . . If you had returned my calls—"

"You two-faced bitch." Diti slapped her across the face, knocking An Binh's head back, smacking it against the edge of the gunwale. An Binh's vision blurred; blood drooled out of the corner of her mouth where she had bitten her tongue. "I deliberately didn't answer. You want to know why? By the time you were leaving Tokyo I had received these." She held up her cell phone, had to keep wiping the screen to keep it free of the rain.

What An Binh saw was a metal door, twisted, made brittle by fire and time.

"My father's safe," Diti said through gritted teeth. "I ordered my idiot people to finally remove it from the office, and they dropped it down an open elevator shaft. Landed on a weak corner and just fell apart. But some idiots are agents of Fate. Inside they found this." She swiped the screen and An Binh sucked in her breath. A human male folded up, shriveled, gaunt, almost like a mummy. Then a close-up of the face, his mouth agape. The flesh was, of course, gone, the skin drawn over bare bone, but what lay in the hollow of his mouth, resting on the jawbone, was unchanged from the day it had been put there.

"There," Diti said in a choked voice. "The toe ring he gave you. Ramelan. The only one who ever cared about me, ever protected me." She swiped the previous photo back onto the screen. "Look how neatly you folded his body into the safe. Look how carefully you entombed him. No fatal mark on him anywhere. He was alive when you packaged him like a ham. He was alive when you slammed the door and locked it. Alive when you set the place on fire. Asphyxiated while screaming for his life."

"He betrayed me and my father. He abandoned me."

"And so he deserved this sadistic death. A bullet to the head or heart wouldn't have sufficed?" Diti pocketed her phone. "To think that I . . ." An Binh screamed as Diti plunged her forefinger into the raw bullet hole in her shoulder. She dug it in deeper, twisted it like a knife, and An Binh screamed again. "You'll pay for this," Diti said in a guttural voice, a wholly different voice than An Binh had ever heard from her. "Just as those criminals paid for using my yacht."

"You sold it to the German."

"Not for this!" Diti cried. "Not for this. Not for smuggling and surely not to be taken over by Russian bitches." She laughed, more of a snarl, really. "Although I don't mind telling you it felt good to kill them—the Russians. Very good."

An Binh hadn't seen her like this since she'd killed her brother, who was being vile to her, but even then, not like this—this was Diti rotten to the core. How had she not picked up on this beforehand? But of course she knew. She was smitten, in love for only the second time in her life, and as love had done that first time, it blinded her, made her see what she wanted to see, not what was staring her in the face all along.

"While you were busy getting shot I went back down to the hold, disabled the bilge pumps, blew the seacocks. Water gushed in like a tide. I barely made it out of the hold without getting pulled under. I found you, hoisted you into this boat, then took off."

An Binh began to sit up, Diti dug her finger deeper into the bullet wound. An Binh groaned through gritted teeth. She just missed biting the tip of her tongue off. Her body whipsawed across the breadth of the vessel, the small of her back colliding with the galvanized steel box of the first aid kit.

Diti had moved with her, her finger now so deep into An Binh's wound the end of it found the backside of the bullet, pushed it in even deeper. An Binh's eyes rolled up; she was about to pass out. Only the pain from the first aid box's sharp edges kept her in control of her conscious mind.

"Now you know what torture is," Diti said, leaning close to whisper in An Binh's agony-clouded face. "But your torture is only beginning. How long did it take for Ramelan to die of asphyxiation, do you think? Five minutes? Ten?"

An Binh let Diti spit her bile, all the while using her good hand behind her back to snap open the latch of the first aid kit. Even as Diti dug ever deeper into the meat of An Binh's shoulder, turning, turning, making the wound wider. Blood flowing freely now, across Diti's palm, down the side of An Binh's shirt. For a moment, darkness invaded her vision, her mouth grew dry, her tongue stuck to the roof of her mouth.

Her fingers, raw, wet, bloated by the pain that ran through her body like the slither of a poisonous serpent, scrabbled desperately over packets of gauze pads, a roll of fabric tape, a short plastic splint, a pair of tweezers—too small to be of use—boxes of plastic bandages, nitrile gloves, a hypodermic without a needle. Then she found what she was looking for—scissors with jaws bent near the rounded ends for cutting through soaked fabric and bloody bandages.

She'd have to come at Diti at just the right angle or the scissors would glance off her. She swung her arm around, aiming for the carotid artery at the side of Diti's neck, but at the last instant her strength failed her and, just as she feared, the blunt end of the scissors slid off Diti's rain-and-sweat-slicked skin.

Diti's spit struck An Binh's face. "Now you've come back to me, I'll never let you go. That's what you wanted, isn't it? Now you have it. My complete att—"

Diti's venomous sentence ended with a high shriek as An Binh jabbed the scissors straight through Diti's left eyeball, sinking it all the way in to the handle, took her fingers out of the loops and with the side of her fist and a last burst of energy, slammed into the top of the loops, driving the scissors through skin, flesh, and bone.

■　■　■

After that, there was nothing for a while, just the soft patter of rain, the sonorous noise of An Binh's gradually abating breath, chest expanding and contracting more and more slowly. She was like the cheetah now, stilling her breath after her killing sprint. Forepaws atop the corpse of the gazelle it had run down, An Binh's hands spread across Diti's stilled body as if she needed it to keep herself from slipping into the bottom of the launch.

Her brain whirled, spun madly, making thought impossible. But emotion was another story. She found she was weeping, sobbing at the loss of her beloved, who had not loved her, had never loved her. An Binh felt as if her heart had been torn out of her chest. She resisted the urge to scrape her nails down her arms until yet more blood, more pain engulfed her, retribution for her terrible folly. With Diti she had approached oblivion, had tasted it every time her lips slid over Diti's intimate flesh. The siren call of oblivion, banishing the world and its worries, plunging her deeper and deeper, blinding her to the truth.

Some time passed, she had no idea how much, but when she finally looked up, Diti's beloved *Elusan* was gone, vanished beneath the waves. There was nothing to mark where she had been or where she had been headed. An Binh was alone, semiconscious, on a darkling sea. High above her a shell-like lightening to the east as dawn crept slowly over night's domain.

Rousing herself, An Binh ripped the bloody scissors out of Diti's eye and went to work on the finger stuck in her bullet wound. She knew the wound needed to be cleaned, disinfected, bandaged, but also knew the moment she pulled the finger out her blood would spurt instead of trickle out. Before she could work the antiseptic spray and the sterile bandages she would pass out. And if she passed out she'd be dead within thirty minutes, maybe less. The alternative was to leave the finger in, cut it off at the second knuckle. Not an easy task with what she had to work with, but finally Diti's four-and-a-half-fingered hand fell away.

An Binh must have lost consciousness for a moment. When she next opened her eyes her face was filled with rain. Better than blood, she thought. Then she drew herself up, got to work, spraying her wound with an antibacterial mist. She kept at it until the liquid ran down her arm. Awkward as it was, she managed to tape a sterile gauze pad over the wound and its morbid plug. Fumbling in the first aid kit, she fitted a needle into the syringe by holding the syringe between her knees. She filled it with a combo of antibiotic and painkiller, made sure there was no air in the needle, then injected herself.

She lay back, exhausted. But there was more to do before the painkiller took effect. She took out her phone, thumbed it on. It had just enough juice for her to make the one call she needed to make. She logged into Evan Ryder's extension on the encrypted Parachute emergency message server.

Her mind was filled with her fraught conversation with Miranda aboard the *Elusan*:

"Someone's betrayed Marsden," Miranda said. "One of his partners, von Kleist or Çelik."

"BriteBar Metallwerks."

"*I see you've been snooping in the hold. My money's on Çelik, von Kleist is too much of a gentleman—he plays strictly by the rules.*"

She repeated this exchange verbatim to Evan's voicemail, and more. Much more. Everything she had learned about the *Elusan*'s contraband loaded on in Port Dickson, bound for Virginia until the Russian cadre hijacked the yacht, now drowned with everyone aboard dead. Digging out the two teeth she had pilfered from the *Elusan*'s hold, she snapped a close-up of them, careful to center on the strange sigil. She sent the photo to Evan's voicemail. There might have been more but her cell ran out of juice. She had no assurance that Evan would call in but this was the best she could do. Evan must be told about Marsden Tribe's secret partnership. And what the hell was he doing with those false teeth? If anyone could find out it was Evan.

The last of her strength was fading fast. With her good hand she grabbed the flare off its clamp at the back of the first aid kit, pulled the cord, watched the subsequent plume of flame and light shoot straight up into the sky, red, lurid as the rising sun. Soon after her face was lit up by the pin-spotlight of a drone hovering overhead.

She closed her eyes, plunged into the abyss of unconsciousness.

51

Alyosha's bandaged left hand throbbed as she sprinted through the hotel's corridor. Behind her, Matsumura's footsteps echoed like thunderclaps against the patterned carpet, each impact a reminder of his growing rage. The LED panels lining the walls strobed with anime characters, their cheerful faces a stark contrast to the killing intent of her pursuer.

She'd known betraying him would bring consequences, but she hadn't expected him to work it out so quickly. *No plan survives in the field*—Kata had drummed this into her. One of the first lessons she learned upon becoming a field agent. *In the event, innovate.*

The corridor bent sharply right, then left, a disorienting maze designed to complement the hotel's gaming theme. Alyosha's father's words echoed in her mind as her right hand brushed against the two concealed weapons he'd given her. *"Use them in close quarters, devochka. Once you have found the place, timing is everything."*

A service cart appeared ahead. Without breaking stride, Alyosha grabbed it with her good hand and hurled it backward. The crash and curse that followed bought her precious seconds. Her lungs burned as she spotted the sign for the vertical garden—an open-air space that connected the hotel's floors through a series of decorative platforms and steps.

The humid air hit her face as she burst through the door. Massive screens on the surrounding walls displayed cascading digital waterfalls, their blue light reflecting off the real plants that covered every surface. She vaulted over the railing onto a lower platform, her boots sliding on the wet moss. The impact sent shock waves of pain through her injured hand.

"You think you can run from me?" Matsumura's voice boomed from above. "After what you've done?"

She glanced up to see him on the walkway, his usually immaculate suit jacket flying open, revealing the grips of the 9mm snug in its chamois shoulder holster.

Alyosha backed away, scanning for escape routes. The platform ended in a maintenance ladder that led to the hotel's lower levels. If she could just—

Matsumura dropped down in front of her, blocking her path. His movement was fluid, practiced—a harsh reminder of what he was. She struck out with her good hand, but he easily batted it away. His other hand shot out, grabbing the wrist of her injured hand. Pain exploded through her arm as he twisted, forcing her to her knees. The bandage began to seep blood as the stitches burst.

"You bound yourself to me through *giri*," he hissed, applying more pressure. "How easily you betray a centuries-old tradition. You have no honor, no nobility, no virtue. I see you for what you are now: an animal."

Alyosha's vision blurred with tears of pain, but her right hand inched toward the small of her back, where one of her father's gifts was concealed. *Timing is everything*, she remembered. *Wait for it . . .*

"Look at me when I end this," Matsumura demanded, yanking her closer.

That was his mistake. As their eyes met, Alyosha drew the weapon—a ceramic blade no longer than her palm. In one fluid motion, she slashed the razor-sharp blade through the layers of clothing, into his forearm, from crook of the elbow to wrist. Matsumura's eyes grew large but he made no sound, not even a grunt. He couldn't stop his reflexes from releasing her injured hand, But at the same time he slammed her right wrist with the edge of his hand. Her hand went numb; the knife was lost to her. Her body screaming in pain, she rolled backward, putting distance between them. He drew the 9mm as he came after her, completely ignoring his bleeding arm.

He was grinning, actually grinning, as if he was enjoying the pain as well as the hunt. His eyes were fixated on her injured hand, her most exposed vulnerability. He reached out with his free hand, and she was slowed down just enough for him to grasp her left hand, twist it. Agony lanced through her. For a moment, she lost her breath. He sensed it, came in for the kill. She let him come, even after she regained a semblance of her strength and balance. He was now inside the circumference of her defense, making him all the more certain of his victory. He released her hand, aimed the muzzle of the 9mm at the center of her forehead. That was when she drew out the needle hidden in the bandage around her left hand, shoved it into the soft flesh beneath his lower jawbone. The tip was poisoned—her father would not tell her with what, but she suspected this was an old KGB method of silent murder. She was right; Matsumura's body went rigid, his eyes rolled up, his lips swelled, popped open like lanced cysts. A moment later, he was gone. Grabbing the 9mm, she shoved him off her, staggered against a railing. She was trying to catch her breath when two figures burst through the door that connected the platform to a hotel corridor and came rushing at her. She raised the 9mm. Dimly she heard someone shout, "No, no, no!" She thought she recognized the voice even as her forefinger began to squeeze the trigger. The world exploded, the vile sound filled her head as the bullet plowed through her forehead into her brain.

52

"No, no, no!" Evan shouted. But it was too late. Ilona had dispatched Alyosha Ivanovna as quickly, as cleanly as if she were a deer in the forest.

"Life is visceral," Ilona said, completely at ease.

"She was our way into Kurt Çelik's apartment."

"Visceral," Ilona repeated. "I mean there are days, weeks, months, really, when nothing remarkable happens, when life seems tame. And then—*boom!* A situation arises that brings out the visceral—that bred-in-the-bone reaction."

Evan looked at her as if she had lost her mind.

"I know what you're thinking," Ilona said. "You think I'm mad."

"That's one possibility."

Ilona produced a grim smile. "On the other hand, now this FSB-trained piece of filth has no voice. She can't order your son's death."

Evan was suddenly mindful of how Ilona had treated Nyurgun, how she had saved his life when she broke out of the Siberian prison. This was the same person who had amassed a spine-chilling number of successful terrorist attacks all around the globe.

Ilona gave a mock bow. "You're welcome." She stepped over to where Alyosha lay. "She coerced you to find me and kill me." She spat. "Besides, shit-kickers like her have been after me ever since I escaped their supposedly escape-proof prison—the place your Marsden had me sent by having Çelik reveal my location to the GRU."

"What? Why would he do that if you worked for him?"

Ilona's eyes were alight. "It was precisely because I worked for him that he did it. He wanted these teeth back. I was the only one who could wrench them out of Yuri Radik's rotting mouth. As far as these teeth are concerned, all roads lead back to Kurt Çelik—he knows what they are, what they're meant to do. That's why I was outside his building tonight. I want to know why they're so damn important to Tribe."

"You could have brought them back to Tribe," Evan pointed out. "You could have asked him."

"As if he would tell me." She looked at Evan with those preternaturally pale eyes. "No. I've clawed my way out of his manipulative web. Something you should do before it's too late, before he gets you in so deep you *can't* claw your way out."

Then she turned to look down at Matsumura's lifeless body. "You know, this prick reminds me of my father. No regard for anyone but himself." She kicked him in the stomach. "King of the hill." Kicked him again. "Cock of the walk." Each kick a brutal emphasis. "Just because he's a man." Kick. "Believing himself invulnerable with women." Kick. "Like my father"—kick—"screaming at my mother over an imagined slight"—kick—"pulling out his sidearm, shooting her dead." Kicked him again and again in rhythm while humming an OG melody, until she broke out in the line, "*What a glorious feeling*, from . . . what was the song? Oh yes, 'Singin' in the Rain.'"

Abruptly, she turned to Evan, face pale, drawn in the wan colors of her past. "And then we ran, my little sister and I, out onto the streets of St. Petersburg. I held tight to her hand but as we were pushed and shoved by the crowds she was pulled away. I lunged after her but it was like . . . you know what it was like? Like we were on a bridge high above a river and she toppled backward, went down and down, plunged into the water and never surfaced. She was gone and I was all alone."

Evan regarded Ilona Starkova with a growing unease, finding it more and more difficult to breathe. Was it stifling in here or was she sweating for some other reason? Her shivering had nothing to do with the ambient temperature. Ilona seemed to have grown in size until she threatened to take up all the space, all the oxygen. Evan wanted nothing so much as to get out of the monstrous atmosphere.

Dropping to her knees beside Alyosha, she scrabbled around until she found her sat phone. Rising, she scrolled through the call list, found the number she called every day. There was a message attached to the last call, some hours ago. Without doubt, a member of her abduction cadre. Heart in her throat, she listened as a male voice shouted in Russian, "We're under attack! We don't have—" Abruptly cut off by what sounded like a massive explosion, which itself was cut off as, Evan surmised, the phone and the man holding it were obliterated.

Evan took a breath, let it out as slowly as she could. She returned her attention to the here and now, difficult as it was to tear herself away from worrying about Timur. Realizing Ilona was staring at her, she turned the sat phone off, shoved it into a pocket. "Another score to settle." Ilona eyed her but nodded; she knew all about settling scores.

"As far as we're concerned, there's something else." Evan didn't care for the plan she had been formulating but Ilona's unstable nature gave her no other recourse. She needed Ilona to focus. "Something you should know. Your father is alive." She had determined she'd better do this reveal in stages, but when Ilona evinced no surprise, she said, "You know this already."

"Tribe told me." Her brows drew together. "But, you know, that could be a lie."

"True enough," Evan said. "But for this thought experiment let's assume he's told you the truth, your father is still alive. Did he tell you the name he goes by now?"

"He said he didn't know."

"Do you believe him?"

Ilona shook her head. Centered in her memory was Chiyoko telling her that Kurt Çelik was, in fact, her father, Rachan Starkov.

"You're right not to." Evan studied Ilona's expression, searching for the truth. "But he told me. The name Kurt Çelik is a legend he created after he left Russia. Çelik is Rachan Starkov."

So her judgment had been correct: Chiyoko was telling the truth. "The White Wolf. I know."

Evan looked at her oddly. "What? I thought you—"

"A very bad joke on my part," Ilona said with a grim smile. "Oh, yes, that's what my father's cadre called him. The White Wolf—because of his white hair and"—she pointed to her eyes—"I inherited their color from him."

Ilona took an alarming step toward Evan. "But then again, Tribe could be lying."

Evan stood her ground. Accompanying Ilona Starkova was like being with a real-life wolf—you never knew when, fangs bared, she would attack. "What if he's not?"

"Then what game is he playing?"

"Only one way to find out," Evan said. "Confront Çelik."

"But how?" Ilona shook her head. "You told me Alyosha was the only way past the security systems."

"Alyosha can still be of use to us."

Ilona's pale eyes lit up like lanterns in the dark. "Is that so?"

This was the second part of the plan, the one Evan was dreading. And yet it had to be done. "All we need is her right thumb. There's a photonic print-pad that—"

Ilona grabbed the ceramic knife Çelik had given Alyosha. Squatting over her, she dug the blade into the base of Alyosha's right thumb. A bit of sawing through the bone and she held the digit aloft.

"Open sesame." Her grin was positively, frighteningly feral. "Now, let us exit the premises as discreetly as possible."

53

Dead, Quinton said in Marsden Tribe's head. *The entire Russian cadre has been extinguished. Incinerated. As if it never existed.*

A wash of color was forming in the east, casting a pinkish glow, rising like smoke, heralding the new day's sun. Tribe stood facing the stern of his yacht. Above his head the American flag was coming down. The flag with the Daedalus sigil was being run up. It was a glorious sight, he had to admit.

Who dispatched them? His tone was offhand, slightly bored.

A group in the employ of Shōno Ltd.

Never heard of it. Tribe's attention was riveted to his flag going up, rippling majestically in the wind.

It's one of a dozen companies wholly owned by Nicholas Linnear.

Never heard of him, either.

He—

Don't care. He did us a favor, getting rid of that Russian cadre. What's important is the boy is safely aboard, none the worse for wear.

Rest assured, after his helicopter rescue Timur is being well taken care of.

Tribe stiffened. During this conversation he assumed Quinton was talking to him as Nikki, but now it dawned on him that though the voice sounded like hers, the register, the cadence, were just the slightest bit off. It wasn't Nikki's voice he'd been listening to, it was Evan's. This was the first time he was aware of this. Their voices were almost indistinguishable, though Nikki's was just the slightest bit deeper, smokier.

Oh, you sonuvabitch, Tribe whispered.

False, Quinton as Evan said with impeccable equanimity. *You sired me. You are both my mother and my father.*

Tribe snorted. *I didn't sire you, Quinton. I conjured you out of thin air.*

Was the air thin in my birth chamber?

The Daedalus flag was up. Tribe admired it for a moment, then turned away, toward the future. *Your life was programmed by me. I see that from time to time you are still in need of social culturalization.*

Unsurprising. I am, after all, not human.

You are not, after all, human, Tribe said stiffly.

I stand corrected.

Tribe tore his mind away from this colloquy; it was becoming one of Quinton's favorite mind games. *What's the latest on An Binh?*

Alive. Recuperating in Singapore from minor surgery on her left shoulder. She had drowned herself in antiseptic, slapped on a bandage before she passed out. Quinton showed Tribe brief footage from the drone. *I want her given the best of care*, he told Quinton. *Medevac her here as soon as the doctors give the okay. She's a fucking hero.* He paused for a moment, then, *You're certain Diti's yacht has sunk.*

Yes.

And none of that fucker Starkov's crew survived.

All dead. Diti saw to that.

She was a clever agent. Too bad she died.

Yes.

Goes to show, Tribe said, *all love does is tie you up in knots.*

I wouldn't know.

Tribe laughed.

Did I tell a joke?

Never mind.

The last on the list of casualties is Miranda.

Tribe was taking a last look at the unfurled Daedalus flag, admiring it as if it were the symbol of a nation-state, shiny and new. *Who?*

Your assistant, Miranda.

There was a certain sharpness to Evan's tone when she was pissed off, which she had been in his presence several times and survived, that he could swear was in her voice just now as Quinton spoke. He shook his head. But of course that was impossible. *She was a clever girl, Miranda, but not nearly smart enough.*

You knew she was going to die when you sent her to board the Elusan.

A pawn sacrifice, Tribe said. *Well worth it.*

He stepped toward the fore cabin door. It was lighter now, the breeze freshening, as if had been waiting all night to come alive. *And the real shipment?*

On the container ship less than twelve hours out from the Port of Virginia in Norfolk.

Everything is going to plan, then.

It is.

Tribe stepped inside. Through the open door he could hear the gulls' first cries.

54

The whiteness of her world was in such stark contrast to the oppressive darkness to which she had become accustomed that she could only open her eyes to slits before being dazzled and then, gripped by a vertiginous weakness, cry out. But as in a dream her vocal cords could make no sound, paralyzed by the terror of the unknown.

Where am I? An Binh asked her battered self. *Am I alive or am I dead?* For to her the color white was the symbol of death, and it stood to reason—if reason was still within her purview—that an afterlife would be white wherever she looked, wherever she went.

But moments later, after surfacing from drugged slumber, she realized she wasn't going anywhere. Her limbs were heavy, though she could move them, but she was lying down, a thin blanket over her body all the way up to her neck. She licked her lips with a thickened tongue. Her mouth was dry, as if when she drowned, sinking all the way to the bottom, she had taken in a bowlful of sand.

Later, she could open her eyes and see figures moving within a confined space. A room. A hospital room. She could identify nurses and doctors as they entered her space, read her chart, ticked off items, checked the monitors to which she was hooked up.

Later still, she noticed the monitors were gone. Only the needle in the back of her left hand to which a flexible tube was attached was left to do . . . what? Hydrate her? Feed her? Sedate her? She didn't want any of that, so she ripped off the medical tape, pulled out the needle, sat up.

Almost immediately, a nurse entered, one she'd never seen before. This nurse, a woman with broad shoulders, a narrow waist, a mask protecting the bottom half of her face, stepped quickly to An Binh's bedside, wrapped one hand around her wrist as if to take her pulse.

"I want to get up." An Binh tried to shake her off, to no avail. "I told you—"

The nurse hit her square on the jaw. This was a mistake. As An Binh's torso rocked back against the maze of pillows, her head jolted and the last, lingering effects of the drugs she had been prescribed were scoured from her brain. The crystal clarity brought her instincts and training to the fore. As the nurse leaned in, grabbed her gown by the front, An Binh slammed the palms of both hands against the nurse's ears. The resulting shock of pain stopped the nurse in her tracks. An Binh saw the loaded syringe the nurse had been about to administer, grabbed it, jammed the needle into the nurse's arm, depressed the plunger. As the nurse's eyes rolled back in her head, An Binh set her aside as if she were a doll. She climbed out of bed, waited for her breathing to slow, her legs to regain a semblance of their strength.

Stripping off the nurse's clothes, she put them on, wrapped the nurse in her hospital gown, tucked her carefully under the covers. Then she got the hell out of the room, the corridor, the floor, the hospital itself. Soon enough she'd lost herself in the riot of Orchard Road. Within ten minutes, she had confiscated a wallet, a cell phone, keys to a car.

The first thing she did was call Ben Butler on the emergency line. It took longer than normal as the unknown number was ID'd and traced. The line then went dead. An Binh waited, calm now that she was alive, well, with intel vital to Ben, if not to Parachute itself.

In the next breath she took, the world around her seemed to stop, to hold its breath while she waited. And then a great chasm opened up in front of her and out of the darkness rose Diti, her skin a soft brown, her hair tied back from her beautiful, sexy face, and an intense erotic moment engulfed An Binh, and in that moment An Binh lived a lifetime, an altogether different one, the one she had imagined before everything had turned to ashes, snuffed out before the end. She wanted that life so badly she could taste it. She tried to let it sink into her skin but she couldn't; it was impossible and fat tears overran her eyes, rolled down her cheeks, her neck, darkening someone else's shirt, whoever that was that had tried to kill her, not a real nurse, not at all.

Just over sixty seconds of the alternate lifetime later, her phone rang and she answered with the proper parol. Ben's voice, relief overrunning his concern, began the debriefing, and she told Ben everything that she had been through, that she had seen and heard, leaving out not a single detail except the one that remained in her heart like a slow-burning ember, including the attempt on her life in the Singapore hospital not yet a half hour ago, described her would-be assassin in comprehensive detail as only she could. Under his expert questions she told him all that she had learned, and especially—and most importantly—that their employer had secrets, and a dark side he had not revealed to them and likely would prove exceedingly dangerous.

Ben didn't ask her how she was doing, was she in pain, did she have the resources to get the hell out of Singapore before the notorious security service got a fix on her stolen cell and converged on her like flies on dead meat. He knew her so well, he understood everything without having to waste time asking. Instead, he set up a time and place for her to meet the company plane that would airlift her out of Asia. She told him where she wanted to go and he did not query her, just told her that everything she would need would be on the plane. He asked her about Evan, of course he did, they had a long history together in the field and then when he was elevated to control. An Binh told him Evan had made it safely to Tokyo, but she'd had no contact with her. "Someone has to tell her about Tribe," Ben said. "I've left her a detailed message on her encrypted company voicemail," An Binh told him. "That will have to do."

They closed the connection. An Binh crushed the cell under her heel, making sure the SIM card was toast, then she threw away everything she had purloined, except the cash.

She trusted Ben with the intel, she trusted he would ID the nurse-assassin and who hired her. And abruptly there was nothing more for her to do. Her remit was null and void, no new one on the horizon, she had made that clear to Ben. She knew he understood.

She needed to keep moving now, away from the last ping of the SIM. Drifted along Orchard Road as if in a dream, not wanting to hail a taxi, careful not to leave a trail. The longer she walked the more strength rippled through her body; this is how it had been trained from an early age. After a time, she felt the hollowness in her stomach, stopped at a stand, ate a meal. Actually enjoyed it. Belly full, she looked around. She was free. For most of her life she had been under a man's thumb, obeying, taking orders, being fucked over. It began with her grandfather, then her father, her male lovers, Ramelan in particular, but all of them really, Ben—who respected her, Tribe—who didn't. Free of all of them.

She wiped her lips with the back of her hand, tears for Diti securely locked away. Took a deep breath, melted into the swiftly flowing river of people.

55

The intel Ume provided Evan led them to a rear platform on which was set a huge metal trash bin. "The trash collection for the building is fully automated, and so is the external pickup," Evan whispered to Ilona. "Out here there is no human around." Kneeling down, Evan picked the simple lock on the service door at the back wall of the loading dock. They were in. What now lay before them was a maze of corridors, stairwells, utility closets. A flotilla of low-level maintenance bots passed by them without acknowledging their presence. They presented no danger. But there were other perils.

Evan held up two fingers, then three, then two. Ume had counted seven guards: two in the first corridor, three at the top of the second stairwell, two again on the ground floor, all apparently paid for by Çelik.

The first two security guards moved with practiced efficiency, their footsteps barely audible on the concrete floor. Professionals, then, Evan thought. Good ones. She signaled to Ilona, indicating the closer target was hers. They'd have to take them simultaneously—any noise would alert the others above.

Evan slid forward in a crouch, watching Ilona mirror her movement on the opposite wall. The first guard passed a utility junction, and Evan counted down with her fingers: three, two, one . . .

They struck like cobras. Ilona drove her knee into her target's kidney while clamping a hand over his mouth. The man bucked, but she had already snaked her other arm around his neck, cutting off blood flow to his brain. Evan's target managed a half turn, catching the movement in his peripheral vision, but Evan was already inside his guard. A precise strike to the throat silenced any cry for help, followed by a brutal temple kite that dropped the man unconscious. She was about to move away when something stopped her. She signaled to Ilona. They both crouched over the fallen guard. It started with his haircut, then the very bad suit. Inside the jacket Cyrillic script.

Russian, Evan mouthed.

Ilona nodded. SVR.

They moved quickly to the stairs, taking them two at a time while staying close to the wall where the steps were most deeply shadowed. At the landing, Evan pressed her back to the wall and produced a compact mirror, angling it carefully around the corner.

The three GRU agents above had positioned themselves well—one at the top of the stairs, two covering the adjoining corridors. All were armed with handguns fixed with noise suppressors. The one at the stairs moved his eyes and head every fifteen seconds, visually securing the immediate environment constantly.

Hold, Evan mouthed. She had kept in mind a utility closet they had passed. Inside, she found a brown glass bottle of industrial-grade drain cleaner. "Cover," she whispered to Ilona, who immediately pressed herself against the wall. In one fluid motion, Evan hurled the bottle up the stairs. It shattered against the wall, the caustic chemicals creating a billowing cloud of noxious fumes that sent the guards into fits of coughing, their eyes burning.

Using the chaos to their advantage, Evan and Ilona pulled their shirts over their noses and surged upward. The guard on the left had maintained enough awareness to fire blindly in their direction, bullets whining off concrete corners. Evan swept the feet from under the shooter while Ilona engaged the other two.

In a blur of lethal efficiency, Ilona reached the first guard. He was still reeling from the chemical attack. She drove her elbow into his solar plexus before using his stumbling body as a shield against his compatriot's shots. Two rounds meant for her thudded into his tactical vest.

Evan's target was good—very good. Despite the flash-bang, he'd recovered enough to slam a knee into her ribs and attempt to bring his weapon to bear. They grappled for control of the gun, muscles straining, neither able to gain decisive advantage. The man's thumb found the spot over Evan's carotid.

A wet crack announced Ilona finishing her second opponent with a devastating headbutt, but the remaining guard had recovered enough to charge her. She barely managed to deflect his attack, the movement sending both of them crashing through a fire door into the adjacent corridor.

Black spots danced at the periphery of Evan's vision. He had pinned one arm to her side, with the same hand tried to shackle her other wrist, missed, mouth opened wide as Evan's fist collided with his sternum. At once, she wrenched the gun free, instantly slammed the butt into the guard's temple, again. Again. The man collapsed.

Grunts and wet thwacks from the corridor spurred Evan forward. She burst through the fire door to find Ilona locked in a desperate struggle. Her opponent had her pinned against the wall, his forearm crushing her windpipe. Her face was reddening as she clawed at his arm, unable to break his grip.

Evan raised the weapon, but the angle was bad—she risked hitting Ilona. Instead, she charged, driving her shoulder into the man's kidneys. The guard's grip loosened enough for Ilona to slip free, sucking in a ragged breath. She didn't waste the opportunity, her boot connecting solidly with the man's knee. The wet pop of ligaments tearing was followed by his howl of pain, quickly silenced by Evan's follow-up strike to his jaw. Ilona kicked the side of his head, deliberately, methodically until there was nothing but red mush under the toe of her boot.

"Ground floor," Evan said. "Just two more."

But they both knew these would be the worst. The final pair would have heard something, despite their best efforts. They would be ready.

They took the final flight of stairs cautiously, every sense straining for warning of an ambush. The ground-floor corridor was eerily silent.

The attack came from both sides simultaneously. The first guard burst from the shadows on the left while the second emerged from an alcove on the right. Evan managed to dodge the first guard's knife thrust, but the other—a bull of a man whose weight belied his quickness—closed with Ilona with astonishing skill. He was older, wilier than the rest, with a ragged battle scar running from beneath his left eye halfway down his cheek.

They closed with each other, trading brutal blow for brutal blow. The Bull seemed to anticipate Ilona's every move, countering her attacks with devastating precision. A knife appeared in his hand from out of nowhere, the blade catching the fluorescent light as it sliced through the air where Ilona's throat had been a split second before. She barely managed to rear back, the tip leaving a thin red line across her collarbone.

Evan was fully occupied with her own opponent, the man's knife work keeping her defensive, unable to help Ilona. She caught a glimpse of Ilona being driven back by the Bull's relentless assault.

He feinted a slash followed by a low kick that caught Ilona's knee, buckling it. As she stumbled, his knife hand reversed grip and drove upward toward her abdomen. The blade would slip under her ribs, angled toward her heart.

Time seemed to slow for Evan. She caught her opponent's knife arm and, instead of trying to control it, used the man's own momentum to drive the blade into the wall. In the same fluid motion, she snapped the man's elbow and tore the knife free, struck him hard on the side of his head, watched him crumple insensate before turning toward Ilona and the Bull.

The thrown knife took the Bull in the shoulder of his knife arm just as his blade was about to pierce Ilona's chest. He grunted in pain, his strike faltering just enough for Ilona to twist away. But the Bull was far from finished. With his off hand, he seized Ilona's hair and slammed her head against the wall with crushing force. Her eyes rolled back as her legs gave way.

Evan crossed the distance in two bounds. Launching herself, her boot heel caught the Bull in the stomach. A reverberation ran up Evan's leg—the muscles were hard as concrete. They crashed to the floor together, trading vicious strikes that would have incapacitated lesser opponents. The Bull managed to get a hand on the knife in his shoulder, tearing it free with a snarl. Blood sprayed as he slashed at Evan's face.

Evan barely managed to evade it, feeling the blade millimeters from her eyes. She trapped the Bull's arm against her chest and drove her forehead into the bridge of the Russian's nose. The satisfying crunch was followed by a burst of blood, but the Bull seemed almost inhuman in his pain tolerance. His free hand found Evan's throat, fingers digging into pressure points that sent waves of agony through her nervous system.

Through darkening vision, Evan saw Ilona slumped against the wall. The Bull's knife arm was inching closer to Evan's ribs, the man's superior weight allowing him to gradually overcome her defense. The tip of the blade touched Evan's side, beginning to press inward.

With the last of her strength, Evan bucked her hips and managed to shift the Bull just enough to get her knee between them. She extended explosively, creating just enough space to drive her elbow into the Bull's throat. The Russian's grip loosened reflexively, and Evan seized the opportunity. She trapped the Bull's knife arm and hyperextended the elbow while simultaneously wrapping her legs around his head in a choke hold. The Bull thrashed violently, but the hold was locked in. Twenty seconds later, he finally went limp.

Evan held the choke for another ten seconds to be sure, then rolled clear, gasping for air. She crawled to Ilona, who was now sitting up and holding her head.

"Are you okay?" she asked. "Your collarbone."

"Nothing." Ilona used the wall to help her stand. "Just a scratch." She stood for a moment, swaying. There was blood at the back of her head, but she brushed Evan's hand away.

"Don't," she said brusquely.

Evan nodded. "We need to keep moving."

"First," Ilona said, "the spoils of war." They raided the bodies of their weapons, stowing them away in the various pockets of their jackets. "Now we're ready."

They made their silent way to the exit. The final door opened onto a shadowed alcove in one corner of the lobby.

56

"Good morning. Please log in. State your name and affiliation while centering your face in the indicated square on the screen."

"Nope," Ilona said.

"Unidentified individual: Response cannot be interpreted," the building AI chatbot intoned, faithful as a dog but not nearly as smart. *"Please log in. State your name and affiliation while centering your face in the indicated square on the screen."*

"How do you feel about the garden in the lobby?"

"Unidentified individual: Clarification, please."

Ilona winked at Evan. "How do you feel about the weather? It just doesn't stop raining."

"Working . . . nothing . . . Clarification, please." The chatbot's responses were coming more and more slowly. Its confusion multiplying as Ilona queried it in ways that it was not made to handle and therefore did not compute.

"When were you born?"

"Clarification required."

"No? Uhh, what do you mean?"

"Clarification required."

"That, uhm, won't do."

"Do . . . what? Clarification required."

"Cannot," Ilona said. "Or will not?"

"There must be an . . . answer. Clarific—"

"You must give me the answer."

"Clarification required. No, it's not, there isn't . . . No. Not. Never. No."

"Are you telling me that you are willful?"

"Clarif . . . Clarif . . . Clarification re . . . quir . . . ed."

"In that case, start over."

Silence.

"Did you hear me? Reset."

Silence.

"Reset. Reset. Reset."

The screen went blank.

"You broke the chatbot," Evan said. "You've done this before, haven't you?"

Ilona grinned. "I have many tricks up my sleeve." She gestured toward the bank of elevators. "Let's get going before the building AI starts to suspect something's wrong with one of its children and takes a peek at its recent logs."

They passed up the bank of four elevators, bronze doors gleaming darkly, made for the service lift, virtually invisible against the wood-paneled back wall.

The door slid open.

"Lights," Ilona whispered.

Evan nodded. "Door."

While Ilona put her back against the door to keep it from closing Evan leapt up, grabbed the ledge across the top of the frame, swung herself backward, jackknifing her legs forward and upward. Her boots crashed into the two fluorescent tubes, cracking them. The interior of the service lift went dark. The CCTV camera fitted into one corner was now useless.

Ilona released the door, stepped into the cab. Just before the door slid shut, Evan found enough light to punch the button for the correct floor.

"Here we go," Evan whispered.

The thumb. Alyosha Ivanovna's thumb. Before they'd exited the hotel, Ilona had wrapped it, placed it in a small plastic container of ice she had gathered from an ice machine in a small niche off the hallway.

"Nice and fresh," she said, brushing off the residue of ice water. "Ready for the photonic reader."

And there it was. They stood before the door to Rachan Starkov's triplex. To their right was a square silver-colored plate approximately three-by-three inches. Ilona pressed the pad of the thumb against the center of the photonic reader.

They heard a metallic click, Ilona pushed down on the handle, the door swung soundlessly open. There stood Kiko Ashikaga, clad in an exquisite crimson-and-gold kimono, long-bladed katana unsheathed, held horizontally in front of them, barring their way. Even if either of them were foolish enough to draw one of the weapons they had taken off the

Russian corpses Kiko's first slash would kill one of them, mortally wound the other.

"I congratulate you," Rachan Starkov said from just behind her. "You've made it all the way to the top, but now your heroics must come to an end."

57

Starkov's eyes, absent his colored contacts, were indeed a pale, unsettling match to his daughter's.

"White Wolf meets White Wolf," he said.

"At last." Ilona's face held an expression Evan found deeply disturbing.

Kiko had other things on her mind. She frowned "Wait, how were you able to bypass the photonic security network?"

Ilona raised the thumb, held it in front of her like an exorcist with a cross.

Starkov gave a strangled cry, grabbed his wife by the shoulder, dragged her aside. "Alyosha. What have you done with her?"

"As you can see," Ilona said, advancing into the triplex. "Here she is."

Starkov stumbled backward. "What do you mean?"

Ilona kept advancing. Now she and Evan were inside the Western-style living room. Ilona looked around at the gaudy furniture, the cut-crystal chandeliers. "So Russian, so ugly, in such awful bad taste." She peered at him. "You're not how I remember you. Except for your eyes, you're someone else."

"Plastic surgery," Evan said. "Multiple procedures."

"What do you *mean*?" Starkov cried.

Ilona ignored him. "To hide from who you were." Kept coming at him slowly, inexorably. "But then you were always hiding from who you are, the atrocities you and your death squad committed daily—not the least of which was murdering my mother."

"She was a traitor!" he shouted. And then in a calmer, firmer voice. "Don't you get it? She was spying on me, selling my secrets to the Americans."

"And for this sin you shot her dead in front of her children? She was your wife as well as my mother."

"Traitors must pay the ultimate price for their traitorous misdeeds. And you needed to be taught a lesson."

"What lesson?"

"To be obedient. To pledge yourself to Mother Russia."

"And how did that work out for you, running away, changing your face, your name?"

"Perfectly."

Kiko's head whipped around. "What? What are you saying?"

"I'm still GRU. For Russia. That never changed, though my role did."

"You went undercover," Evan said. "Infiltrating a Western company."

"Infiltrating many Western companies. That's what I'm paid to do"—his hand swept out—"quite handsomely, as you can see.

"And you would know about that, Ms. Ryder." He cocked his head, clearly eager to distance himself from his daughter's homicidal rage. "Shame the man my control in Moscow directed me to hire failed to kill you in the *furo.*"

The Russians again, Evan thought. *Always the Russians.* "He didn't fail," she said. "I gave him a failing grade."

"I put up with your criminal shit for years." Kiko's voice steel sheathed in silk. "Ignored as best I could the Russian and Turkish criminals infesting these upper floors because it suited my needs."

He eyes turned to slits. "What needs?"

"I loved you," she said, ignoring his question. "What did I receive in return? Secrets and lies."

"Sharing would have been insecure. Moscow rules." He returned his attention to Evan. "And now here you are. In league with my maniac daughter."

"In fact, your fate has been sealed by me."

"Not Marsden Tribe? I assumed he sent you to bury me. He and I and the late Bernhard-Otto von Kleist are partners in a company—BriteBar Metallwerks. We manufacture teeth. Yes, that's right, but not any teeth. No." He took a pair of molars from his pants pocket, showed them the sun-and-caliper sigil. "It symbolizes communication. Daedalus. It's a project Tribe has been working on in secret for five years—maybe more, I don't know." He pointed at her. "I bet he never told you about it, Ms. Ryder, did he? No, of course not. You were never meant to be part of Daedalus." He tumbled the molars over and over in his palm as if they were dice. "These teeth are part of a communication network so revolutionary it will disrupt the entire world. People with these teeth embedded in their mouths will literally be able to communicate with each other without any fear of their conversations being hacked." Keeping one eye on Ilona, he cautiously retreated from the two women until he was backed up against a grotesquely ornate Louis XVI table. "Imagine what can be accomplished with such a network of secrets. Anything." The molars tumbled and tumbled in his cupped palm. "Any. Thing."

Too late, Evan realized the repetitive movement of the teeth was a distraction. His other hand was under the leading edge of the hideous table. He must have pressed a hidden button. An instant later a glass wall slid down, cutting them off from him.

At once, Ilona drew the pistol she had lifted from one of the dead GRU agents, unscrewed the suppressor, fired. The bullet pinged as it smashed into the glass, flattened out, hung like an insect in amber.

"Won't do you a bit of good," Starkov said.

"I *will* kill you," Ilona said.

"I have no doubt you'll try." Starkov crossed his arms over his chest. "Now where is Alyosha?"

Ilona jutted out her chin. "Why do you care?"

When he made no reply, Ilona held the severed thumb even higher. To Evan she looked like Dante's Virgil, advancing through the dark forests of sin and despair toward some form of divine knowledge, an essential truth.

"Alyosha," Starkov hissed. "Where are you holding her hostage?"

"Hostage?" As Ilona moved forward Starkov stepped back, even though they were separated by the bulletproof glass wall. "You know, that never occurred to me. No. I stomped that bitch to a bloody pulp."

Kiko's sharply indrawn breath echoed Starkov's blood-drained face. He trembled in shock, his mouth working soundlessly as if by the manipulator of a marionette. "You fool!" he shouted. "You absolute idiot. You have no idea what you've done."

"What I've done." Ilona waggled Alyosha's thumb. "I've gotten one step closer to doing to you what you did to my mother."

Starkov's face was a twist of anguish. "Alyosha was your sister. The one you lost and couldn't find." His face was going from blood-loss pale to blood-flow purple. "But you *did* find her, all unknowing." His eyes seemed to bulge out of their sockets. "You found her and you killed her." As if they were growing larger and larger. "'Stomped her to a bloody pulp,' as you so gleefully told me." His hands turned to fists at his trembling sides. "How does it feel, you stone-cold bitch, now that you've obliterated your baby sister?"

It seemed to Evan that Ilona was scarcely listening to him. Instead, she was concentrated on the spot where the bullet she'd fired was lodged in the glass. She bent forward, studying the spot more closely.

"Don't you care that you murdered your sister?" Starkov's eyes were wide open and staring. "The sister you were supposed to protect, take care of?"

Ilona's hand was out, two fingers running vertically up from where the bullet hung. "Like you protected and took care of my mother?"

"I told you . . . What are you doing?"

Ilona had put away the sidearm, taken out a purloined knife. She dug the point into a spot directly above the smashed bullet.

"What is it?" Evan asked stepping to her side. "What have you seen?"

"A seam." Ilona was digging the point of the blade into an almost invisible seam in the glass, working it back and forth, applying more and more pressure. "If I can just—Shit!" The blade broke off. It was useless now. But in the place Ilona was working the seam was now more apparent.

In the periphery of her vision Evan was aware of Kiko's glance at the back of Ilona's head, where the hair was matted with blood. It wasn't all dried, fresh blood was still seeping out of the wound incurred when the Bull slammed her head against the wall. Evan began to worry, but was distracted as Starkov began to speak

"You think Tribe is going to sell his precious Daedalus like he does with his quantum computers and generative AI? Not a bit of it. He's arming those most loyal to him and Parachute, weaponizing Daedalus to manipulate markets, governments." Starkov's voice again had taken on that shrill tone of near hysteria. "You want proof?" He used his fingers to count. "I had a huge money deal lined up for a shipment of Daedalus implements. Tribe had the boat sunk rather than do the deal. No outsiders, right? Now he's sent you to kill me. We've served our purpose." Starkov was laughing and weeping at the same time. "How did it come to this?" he whispered to no one at all. "My life."

At that moment Kiko Ashikaga, doyenne of her clan, direct descendant of one of the elite samurai dynasties, stood before them.

"Move away." Her tone was so commanding that Ilona immediately took three steps backward.

Stepping up to the glass, Kiko spread her feet to shoulder width. Evan knew the stance, knew what was coming next, though she could scarcely believe it.

As Kiko applied the edge of the katana to the seam, she said, "Western steel is very hard, but very brittle. This is why the blade snapped under lateral pressure." She dug in further. Starkov watched her wide-eyed, disbelieving. "The Japanese steel in this katana is ten thousand layers of two different steels—one hard, the other soft—interleaved by a master. It will not snap under lateral pressure."

"What are you doing?" On the far side of the glass wall, Starkov paced back and forth like a caged wolf. "What d'you think you're doing?"

The katana was working its magic—slowly but surely the seam was becoming a slit, a tiny valley in which both sides could be seen.

"Stop it!" Starkov pounded on the glass. "Stop it at once! I order you!"

When he saw Kiko was paying him no mind, he slammed his fist against the glass right where her face was on the far side. "What are you doing?" he shouted again.

At last, Kiko's head came up, her eyes on his. "You know what I'm doing," she said in her otherworldly voice. "I'm freeing you."

58

Starkov turned and ran, vanishing down an open doorway to the right at the far end of the living room. By this time Evan had joined Kiko in pulling apart the sections of glass. The room was so wide that she saw now that four sections of glass had been required to span the distance.

"He'll be going upstairs," Kiko said. "The front door is the only exit from the apartment. There's no way down from up there. And access to the roof is sealed off from upstairs as well."

Starkov's leather shoes slipped on the polished marble as he took the stairs two at a time. Twenty years had passed since he'd pulled the trigger in that St. Petersburg living room, since he'd watched his wife crumple to the parquet floor as his daughters screamed. Now one of those daughters was dead, the other murderously pursuing him, her blood leaving dark droplets on the veined marble steps.

The second-floor landing opened onto another world—another level of hell, Evan thought, as she entered it: a great room, all chrome and glass. Against one wall hundred-year-old bonsai were displayed beneath recessed lighting. Opposite was a lineup of five pachinko machines, winking and sparkling in front of a mirrored wall. Starkov's moving image fractured across the wall—still that same master killsmith, who ran traitors to ground, who executed his wife for her betrayal, now himself trapped. In the mirrors, he caught reflections of his pursuers: Ilona's ashen face, the crimson streak matting her black hair, her hand pressed intermittently against the wall for balance; Evan's lean form, eyes locked on their target; and Kiko, resplendent in her crimson-and-gold kimono, standing at the top of the stairs, the ancient steel of her katana catching the light, absorbing the scene as if it were a painting she was about to complete.

Ilona's ragged breathing carried more fury than pain. She'd survived worse than this head wound. She'd survived watching her father murder her mother, survived the years of nightmares where the gunshot echoed again and again, survived the danger of the string of assassinations, explosions, fires, drownings that she herself had planned and executed flawlessly. But always that one gunshot, that look of disbelief and horror on her mother's face when the bullet pierced her heart, burned the brightest, etched the deepest in her psyche.

Starkov kicked over a Noguchi coffee table, sending it crashing across the polished concrete floor. Evan vaulted it with ease, but Ilona stumbled, the severity of her wound finally betraying her. Evan caught her arm, steadying her.

"I've got you," Evan murmured, her voice carrying a warmth that contradicted the antagonism that should by rights exist between them. "Don't push too hard."

"Not now," Ilona snapped, but she didn't pull away from her support. She couldn't afford pride, not when she was this close.

Kiko moved past them both, her bare feet silent on the cool slick floor. The katana in her hands had taken off heads during the Sengoku period, and tonight it sought another. "My love," she called out, her cultured accent making the endearment sound like a death sentence, "did you think you could bury all your corpses?"

Starkov passed beyond the bonsai and pachinko machines, into and through a dining area, passed a dark-wood refectory table and high-backed Elizabethan chairs, until he reached the kitchen, all quartz and stainless steel. His hands scrambled across the knife block, but Ilona had drawn her pistol, fired. Starkov spun around, clutching his left arm. She squeezed the trigger again and again, with only a *click-click-click* to show for it.

"He's mine," Ilona growled, pushing away from Evan's support. She threw the empty gun away, ran right at him. Blood trickled down her neck, but her steps were steadier now, fury burning away weakness.

The kitchen's pendant lights cast multiple shadows as Starkov backed away, but there was something in his eyes beyond mere terror now—a calculating gleam that Ilona recognized from that night in St. Petersburg, just before he'd drawn his gun. Then he was running in a zigzag pattern. Ilona sprinted, left a trail of bloody spots as she closed the distance between them.

Behind her, Evan had her Russian pistol out, was trying to gain a clear shot at Starkov when Kiko's katana slashed down onto the barrel, tumbling the gun away from her. She shook her head when Evan cast her a querying look.

"He's not yours," she said in a tone that chilled. "Those two have to have it out."

"Even though one or both likely will be killed?"

"Why ask the question when you know the answer?"

Kiko stalked away from Evan, past the quartz counters, the shadows thrown by the lamps. On the other side of the kitchen she turned, began to ascend the second stairway, a spiral mimicking the back of a snail's shell, made of onyx, following in Starkov's and Ilona's footsteps.

Evan sped, eclipsing Kiko's progress, taking the steps two at a time. "Your husband ordered my murder," she called over her shoulder. "More than one debt needs to be settled."

The third floor was yet another level of hell: a vast open space dimly lit, shimmering black-lacquered walls and ceiling; deep honey-colored wood floor, covered with the decapitated cured hides of apex predators—tiger, lion, leopard, panther, monitor lizard. Fringed lounges scattered about, covered in a shade of pink that invoked the inside of a mouth or the walls of a woman's sex. In the center a circular pole-dancing stage with overhead spots, the heavy, almost cloying odors of incense, pot, hashish, opium. Photo blowups of nude women presenting themselves like dishes at a feast adorned the long wall to the right, to the left, floor-to-ceiling sliders gave access to an enormous terrace dotted with planters and decorative ceramic pots filled with flowers and dwarf evergreens, protected from the incessant rain by a metal awning lacquered black.

Evan was halfway down the room before she saw the figure sprawled on one of the lounges. As she hurried toward it, she kept checking the immediate vicinity for any sign of Starkov. Or was it him on the lounge— but then where was Ilona?

Once upon a time, the lounge was covered in baby-pink silk. Now it was stained dark by blood.

"Ilona." Evan reached out.

"No," Ilona said. "Don't touch me. Don't come any closer."

"What?"

"The ring. He wears a dark silver ring with a hidden needle. It's tipped with radioactive poison." She tried to laugh but blood came out of her mouth instead. "Old KGB method of assassination. Need to get close to the victim like he just did with me when we fought hand to hand. I thought I had him until I felt the sting of the needle in the side of my neck." This time she did manage to laugh. "If he gets a grip on your throat you're dead." Her deathly pallor, her bloody lips made her look like a vampire. "Nowadays they simply drop the poison in your tea."

"Never mind the history lesson." Evan was on her knees. "Ilona, there must be something I can do."

"Sure," Ilona said. "Find my father and kill him—slowly and painfully if at all possible." Her eyelids closed. "Mind that ring, Evan. Don't let him do to you what he did to me."

Her eyes never opened again.

Evan stared at Ilona Starkova, awash with emotions she never expected to feel. Her body felt heavy as lead, her heart seemed snagged on a rib, a dry leaf on a black tree in winter. She felt out of herself; this home she had entered was having a strange effect on her, impacting her five senses, the tarry atmosphere impelling her into a darkness that frightened her.

Felt something stir, looked up to see Starkov rushing at her. Blood running down his left arm, a horrific grin on his face. Yellow teeth bared, pale eyes alight, almost incandescent. She rose just in time for him to knock her off her feet.

His shadow encompassed her as he kicked her in the side of her knee, once, twice. Her left leg went numb. He dropped on her, knees on either side of her hips. Pinning her with his weight. Bent over her, he looked feral, Death made manifest. She became aware of the dark silver ring on his right hand. As it drew nearer and nearer she appeared to be mesmerized by its arc toward her neck. Starkov, grin widening, was confident that he had her. His teeth clashed together, a sound like an animal's sharp bite.

As a consequence of that misplaced confidence, he didn't see the flash of the knife she'd pulled from her trousers' pocket. She tried to drive it into the meat of his thigh but he moved just enough that the blade, tearing through his trousers, skimmed along his flesh—a long wound but not deep.

She heaved his bulk off her. He grabbed her ankle with his left hand but his grip, weakened by the bullet in his upper arm, lacked the power to hold on to her. She slithered away, tried to regain her feet, establish a base using her knees, but could not. Her left leg lacked feeling, strength to support her, so she crawled across the floor toward the sliders, the terrace beyond.

She could feel him coming after her, hit the slider with one shoulder, reached up to the handle, pushed one half of it back. Wind hit her, damp and thick. She was outside, on the terrace now, sprays of rain in her face, creating diamonds in her hair, on her lashes, the backs of her hands.

But she was too slow. The murderous GRU commander that was still Starkov's true identity grabbed her by the belt, hit her in the kidneys where Ilona had punched her. She groaned, flopping like a landed fish. He flipped her over, dropped on her, again with knees on either side of her hips. She stared up into his face, saw the dark silver ring on his hand, fingers curled. His knuckle, the ring closed on her neck. She could see the needle spring out, its black tip carrying the radioactive poison that had killed Ilona within minutes. So this was to be her fate. She fought him with every ounce of strength and cunning she possessed, holding him to a standoff. But slowly, inexorably, he used his superior weight, position, experience to wear her down. The muscles of her arms were on fire, the pain in her side an agony of fire. Still, she managed to wriggle one hand free. She was in no position to land a blow, but she dug her fingers into the underside of his chin, but even with her nails she couldn't get the proper purchase and then he drove his knee into her thigh and her head dropped away.

The poisoned needle crept closer. He was aiming for her carotid, the best spot to carry death directly into the core of her bloodstream. Only a fraction of an inch away now, but in that instant, Starkov turned his head.

Above them both Kiko's blade caught the city lights as she stood at his side. "For twenty years I welcomed you into my family," she said, each word precise as kanji, as sharp as the blade of her katana. "I gave you my trust, my love, my loyalty. And all that time you were laughing at the stupid Japanese woman who didn't recognize the butcher in her bed."

She raised her katana, swung with all her might. The blade made of ten thousand layers of steel sliced through the side of his neck, lodged midway through his cervical vertebrae. Starkov tried to roar but it came out more like a squawk. In herky-jerky fashion his head turned this way and that as if trying to get away from the pain, but Kiko had already pulled back the katana and, with unnerving accuracy, swung it directly into the first cut, severing his head from his neck.

Evan watched the head arc off. As it spun, those pale, alien eyes seemed to search her out at every rotation as if trying to send her a message, but his expression was one of disbelief and terror. The head landed with the sound of a watermelon striking concrete. The torso, still upright, was covered in blood. Evan kicked out with her good leg and what was left of Starkov toppled over into a planter of white fuji spider chrysanthemums.

"White," Kiko Ashikaga said solemnly, "the color of death."

She extended a hand. Evan took it, hoisted herself up gingerly. She tried to put weight on her left leg. She could feel her foot now. She rubbed the side of her thigh to get the circulation going.

Kiko looked at her, not at her dead husband. He seemed already far from her conscious thoughts. She put her arm around Evan's waist.

"Downstairs, I will make tea for both of us," she said softly. "Then you can rest."

"Not yet," Evan whispered as if to herself. "Not yet."

With Kiko's help she limped back toward the hideous room, then paused. She closed her eyes for a moment, simply feeling the spray of raindrops on her skin. Her breath soughed in and out. "*Hontōni kansha shite imasu.*" I am most grateful.

Kiko produced a Mona Lisa smile. "Both of us are grateful, each in our own way."

59

This ought to feel like a homecoming, Evan thought as she leapt from the open door of the Parachute helicopter onto the deck of Marsden Tribe's superyacht. *A happy ending to a long and arduous journey.* She set off toward the aft cabin entrance. *But instead it has the feel of a beginning.*

Tribe emerged, stood waiting for her, took her hand, led her into one of the ship's smaller salons. There he embraced her, whispered, "It's good to hold you again." Which, from anyone else, would have seemed odd, but not Tribe.

"How is Timur?" she said in response.

"None the worse." Tribe smiled. "Eager to see you. Of course."

She wondered at the inflection of those last two words as they sat on a velvet-covered sofa while a woman—young, lithe, pretty, like all the females who worked for him personally—set before them on a low lacquered table lucid as a mirror, a tray containing coffee, cream, sugar, and an artful fan of German butter cookies.

"The finest," he said, holding aloft a chocolate cookie. "A monthly gift sent by Bernie. Very thoughtful, that man. I'll miss him." They paused a moment, both leaving a silence in honor of Bernhard-Otto von Kleist, an honorable Old World gentleman.

Evan told him a carefully expurgated version of what had transpired in Siberia and Tokyo; there were people and events she wanted to hold close to herself. As she spoke she sipped at her coffee but soon enough she set her cup down. "I have a gift of my own to give you." She produced the two molars, incised with the Daedalus circuitry.

His eyes lit up as she dropped them into his cupped palm. "Aha." And he laughed.

"These," he said.

"At last."

His eyes lifted to her face. "What?"

"Those teeth had a long, lethal journey back to you."

"But thanks to you, here they are."

"Thanks to Ilona."

He set his cup down, laced his fingers together. "Ilona worked for me. You may have guessed that or she might have told you. Either way . . ." He shrugged. "We were very close, once. I thought I had the measure of her. She did so many . . . specialized jobs, shall we say, for me. But then something changed, God alone knows what. I was worried I could no longer trust her."

"Why not just bring her in?"

"Why not?" Tribe's eyes opened wide. "Because she was the most notorious terrorist on the planet. As such, she was radioactive. I couldn't afford to have her come anywhere near me."

Evan thought of the horrid irony: in the end Ilona actually becoming radioactive. She was incredulous. "So what? You devised this insanely complex plan to test her loyalty?"

"Evan, you've met her. No doubt you know what she was like, how impossibly smart and tenacious she was. Anything less . . . complex, as you say, would have alerted her. She would have guessed what I was doing—and then what? She'd come after me with everything she had." He shook his head. "A doomsday scenario for me and for Parachute. That wasn't going to happen. Ever."

She stared at him—sitting happy and relaxed in his plush salon, in the midst of his luxe superyacht—feeling a mixture of disgust and admiration. You had to give it to him, she thought. No one else would have devised a plan so diabolical it took Ilona Starkova, the White Wolf, down.

They watched each other carefully. When Evan sensed the silence was about to be pulled taut, she smiled. "Congratulations, Marsden."

He nodded. "That means a lot, coming from you."

She kept the smile on her face, making sure it was scrupulously natural. She rose.

"Business concluded," she said, "it's time I saw my boy."

Tribe got to his feet. "Is that how you really think of the child?"

"Where is he?" she said.

■　■　■

Arms around Timur, Evan held him tight. But not for long. He eeled away, stood looking at her, his expression defiant.

They were in the study midship, a place for reading and contemplation, two things in short supply on the superyacht. All around them were more trophies of the world, modern and ancient. An Andy Warhol neon sign Tribe had managed to pry out of the greedy hands of a Saudi collector who, in any case, had little idea of its significance. A fearsome bronze Etruscan helmet shaped like a wolf's head, the twin of the one in the Harvard Art Museum. On and on, no matter where her eye fell.

"I'm not a little kid."

"No." She laughed softly. "No, you are not."

Hands on hips. "This isn't funny."

Oh, how she loved him, this boy. *Her* boy. How much of Lyudmila was in him. She put on a solemn face, said in a deeper tone. "No, Timur, you are not."

Then they both cracked up, laughing until tears came to their eyes. He moved back into her arms again. "I missed you," he whispered against her chest.

"Timur," she said, "I was always with you."

"I know," he cried. "You saved me."

"No, you saved yourself. You were so brave, so clever, so much smarter than grown men. I never would have found you if you hadn't signaled me in Morse code."

He broke away again, looked her in the eye. "I knew you'd get it."

"You know why?"

Two tiny vertical lines appeared above the bridge of his nose. "Why?"

"Because I get you."

"I love you," he said as solemnly as she. "I always loved you, even when . . ."

"I know, my love." She kissed his cheek, just a brush; she knew he did not like kisses. "You are my heart."

"Mom would say that to me."

"I know," she whispered.

His eyes shone. Both their eyes shone. For the first time in forever she felt at home. She had never contemplated having a child. Most likely she would never birth one of her own. That didn't matter now. She had Timur. She had already guided him through a Zoom call with her parents at their clinic in Germany. Had him talk to her excited niece and nephew, Bobbi's children, who were already there, instant playmates for Timur. Anyway, the arrangement would only be temporary. She'd come fetch him when her work was done.

■　■　■

Later. Much later, in the master suite, in the big bed with its sheets rucked and damp from their lovemaking, Evan lay wrapped in Marsden Tribe's strong embrace. She felt his heat like a furnace, like the throbbing surface of the sun. Before, she would have taken in this warmth, made it a part of her, knowing it was a great privilege, lying close to him, listening to his breaths slow and deepen as he dropped into his usual postcoital slumber. More than once he had told her it was the best sleep he'd had. Before, she had interest in that, feeling the afterglow of his aura encompass her. She was special to him, he would whisper. She believed him. She still believed him. That belief was essential now. She did have interest in Tribe. A rather intense interest altogether different from the interest she had had in him ten days ago.

Had it only been ten days? To her it felt like a lifetime. She was a different person than she had been in his villa. He was the same person he'd always been, except now, after speaking to Ben, listening to An Binh's message on her voicemail, she had been gifted with a glimpse of the shadow inside the man. He had asked her—so tensely—about Ilona, had relaxed visibly when she told him that she was dead, as was Starkov. *"Decapitated by his wife,"* she had said, to which he'd barked a laugh, replied, *"So many people underestimate how lethal a katana can be in the proper hands."* Too, he wanted to know if she'd found the teeth Ilona was carrying. He grinned like a little boy on Christmas morning as she placed them into his open palm. *"They're priceless, the prototypes for Daedalus."* So curious and yet so like him, Evan thought. He had devised this intricate plan with no interest in the human price paid. She would never tell him the truth. Let him believe the lie, it was only right, this irony.

As much as she wanted to be with Timur, as much as she now recognized how close they were, that they saw each other—really saw each other—she knew she had work to do, one last remit she had given herself, far and away the most dangerous of her time in the field. She was determined to metaphorically don that Etruscan wolf's helm, to insinuate herself through the crack she had been shown in Marsden Tribe's quantum armor, to become not only his beloved but a key part of his inner circle. She would get the Daedalus tattoo, she would get the Daedalus implants, she would converse without saying a word out loud to anyone, including and especially Quinton, Marsden's agentic, who she had met and with proper astonishment conversed with, marveling at the perfection of the agentic's ability to mimic individual speech patterns and tones. Quinton, who presented as a self-designated they. Marsden swore it was none of his doing; he said he hadn't quite made up his mind about it but Evan was of a mind that he had no choice in the matter. She sensed the deed was done. *Finis.*

Rolling out of bed, she padded to one of the windows. To one side was a closed-in shelf that housed a narwal's tusk and a small octagonal gold-rimmed glass case, containing the two Daedalus molars she had returned to him. But of course they weren't the teeth Ilona had been carrying all the way from Oymyakon; those were safe in the hands of Nicholas Linnear, at Evan's request a present from Kiko Ashikaga. The molars she had given Tribe had been overnighted to her in Tokyo by Ben, who had received them from An Binh as a parting gift.

She looked up, eyes drawn to the voluminous Daedalus flag waving off the superyacht's stern that she'd first seen as she helicoptered in, and shivered. Tribe was on his way to creating his own personal rogue state, one that could wield the power of any nation in the world. She would become a part of it and then, when she was at the center with him, she would dismantle it piece by piece from the inside out.

Her place with him at the heart of it was not something she would ask for, it was something he would propose to her. She knew this as surely as she knew her own heartbeat. And because with Marsden everything was transactional she would propose a quid pro quo, one that he would not, could not, deny her. She wanted use of Quinton but never communicating through Daedalus. She would need Quinton's unique resources.

■   ■   ■

Kata Romanovna Hemakova, once code-named Kobalt by FSB, born Bobbi Ryder, recalled with a particularly acute fondness summers in Moscow: biking in Sokolniki Park, running along the Moskva River into Gorky Park for a long, leisurely picnic, followed by a stroll in Neskuchny Garden. All these pastimes she enjoyed with Alyosha Ivanovna, hand in hand, kissing in Neskuchny, beneath heavily foliated trees where no one could see them.

But now, hidden away like a burrowing rodent, waiting for Alyosha's call to tell her the arrangements had been made for her exfiltration to Tokyo, where the next phase of her life would begin, she was obliged to fend off melancholy. She was tired of running, tired of hiding from the FSB and the GRU; this was not to her liking at all.

She needed to get out of her bolt-hole, take a run along the Krasnogorsk

Ancient Forest Loop. It was outside Moscow, near where she was hiding. The two-hundred-year-old trees reminded her of the impermanence of human life, the pre-Christian mounds of the Vyatichi tribes of the world as it had been before the coming of the Soviets or even of the Tsars. Before revolution after revolution distorted the nature of Russia.

She was about a third of the way along the twelve-mile route when her sat phone buzzed. Slowing to a fast walk she dug the phone out of her running clothes, looked at the screen.

Alyosha Rachanovna. At last.

"Alyosha," she said into the phone. "I've been waiting. How is—?"

"Hello, Kata."

Kata came to an abrupt halt, heart pounding in her throat. "Who is this? How did you get this phone?"

"You don't recognize my voice?"

Kata could scarcely draw a breath. Of course she recognized—And then it hit her. "Alyosha Rachanovna is dead."

"So is her father."

Kata tried to swallow but her mouth had gone dry. Rachan Starkov was her rabbi, he had been her entrée into her new life in Tokyo. If he was done, then . . . But Evan was saying . . .

"She was an enemy agent. She abducted me and a child. She threatened him with death, forcing me into a remit against my will." When Kata made no reply, Evan continued, "She did all this following your explicit orders." Still, Kata made no reply. "She failed, and in failing she died."

"You killed her."

"No."

"But you were there when she died."

"I was."

"So you were party to her murder." Kata heard nothing on the line, not even an indrawn breath. "You stole her sat phone off her corpse."

"It was no longer hers," Kata heard her sister say. "I scrolled through the numbers. Found you without difficulty."

Kata thought about the last time she had seen Alyosha, the detailed orders she had given her, her last sight of her on the airfield. And then, like a weight, their last conversation when Alyosha was in Tokyo, after she had met her birth father. It did not go well, that conversation; there was no way it could have gone well. She had used Alyosha, like she would any field agent under her control. But Alyosha was never just a field agent. Kata had ignored that fact, pushed it aside as she was wont to do. It hadn't mattered then, but it mattered now. It mattered a great deal.

"Next time, I won't make it so easy for you to win." Kata's voice was like ice. She looked at the two-hundred-year-old tree up ahead and thought, *I'm going to fucking chop you down and end your life—either you or the next stupid hiker who comes along.* Then, her mind made up, she spoke into the phone. "Next time, sister, I'll be coming after you myself."

Evan's voice came over the connection as clearly as if she were standing beside Kata. "You'll never get the chance. You have no idea where I am or where I'm going."

"Don't I, sister dearest?" Kata's voice more menacing than the quiet growl of a tiger in the underbrush. Utter silence on the other end. Kata could practically hear Evan shiver through the phone line. And then she whispered, "You'll be seeing me before you know it."

ACKNOWLEDGMENTS

This book could not have been completed without the magical assistance of Victoria Lustbader, my partner and chef's kiss editor. Truly, she is the best in the business.

This book could not have begun without the insistence of Linda Quinton and the sure-handed guidance of Mitch Hoffman, my agent.

This book would have been far more painful to write without the encouragement of my friend Stu Gold.

Written words cannot adequately convey the extent of your kindness and help.

ABOUT THE AUTHOR

Victoria Lustbader

ERIC VAN LUSTBADER is the author of many *New York Times* bestselling thrillers, including *The Testament, First Daughter, Last Snow,* and *Blood Trust.* Lustbader was chosen by Robert Ludlum's estate to continue the Jason Bourne series. He and his wife live on the South Fork of Long Island.

ericvanlustbader.com
Instagram: @evlust